O9-BTO-595

TAKEDOWN

Also by Brad Thor

The Lions of Lucerne
Path of the Assassin
State of the Union
Blowback

TAKEDOWN

A Thriller

Brad Thor

ATRIA BOOKS
New York London Toronto Sydney

ATRIA BOOKS
1230 Avenue of the Americas
New York, NY 10020

This book is a work of fiction. Names, characters, places and incidents are products of the author's imagination or are used fictitiously. Any resemblance to actual events or locales or persons living or dead is entirely coincidental.

Library of Congress Cataloging-in-Publication Data

Thor, Brad.
Takedown : a thriller / by Brad Thor.—1st Atria Books hardcover ed.
p. cm
ISBN-13: 978-0-7432-7118-9
ISBN-10: 0-7432-7118-1
I. Title.

PS3620.H75T354 2006
813'.6—dc22

2006040132

First Atria Books hardcover edition May 2006

10 9 8 7 6 5 4 3 2 1

Manufactured in the United States of America

For information regarding special discounts for bulk purchases, please contact Simon & Schuster Special Sales at 1-800-456-6798 or business@simonandschuster.com.

For Robert M. Horrigan—
a beloved patriot who served his country
with courage, honor, and unparalleled dignity

Exitus acta probat

The ends justify the means.

ONE

DJEMMA EL-FNA MARKET
MARRAKECH, MOROCCO
MAY 11

The problem with being in the wrong place at the wrong time is that you never know it until it's too late. That's how it was for Steven Cooke, and the bitter irony was that right up to the very last moment of his life, he thought he had stumbled upon an intelligence jackpot.

The blond-haired, blue-eyed twenty-six-year-old had happened across the meeting completely by accident. In fact, Cooke wasn't even supposed to be in that part of town except that his sister had asked him to bring her a special caftan when he flew home for a long-overdue visit at the end of the week.

Although he had way too much work to do before leaving, Steven had always found it hard to say no to Allison. The two were more than brother and sister. They had been best friends since childhood. In fact, Allison was the only person who really knew what he did for a living. Even their parents had no idea that their son was a CIA field officer.

Steven had been in Morocco just under a year and had gotten to know Marrakech fairly well. The souk at the heart of the small city was a labyrinth of passages and narrow alleyways. Donkey carts laden with merchandise lumbered up and down the hot, dusty thoroughfares, while the ever-present haze hung so thick that neither the city's mud-brick walls nor the high Atlas Mountains off in the distance could be seen from the main square. The heat was absolutely insufferable and as he combed the various covered markets for the perfect caftan for Allison, Cooke was grateful for the shade.

It was when Steven took a shortcut through one of the alleys that he noticed an unremarkable café with a rather remarkable patron—a man who had disappeared two days before the September 11th attacks and for whom the United States had been searching ever since.

If he was correct, his discovery would represent not only a major coup for American intelligence, but it might also place a very distinct feather in his cap and set him apart as one of the more distinguished young field operatives. That would be nice, though Cooke reminded himself that he had joined the CIA to help defend his country, not to rack up *attaboy*'s.

Removing his cell phone, Steven contacted his supervisor and filled him in on everything he had seen, including a mysterious new player who had entered the café and was now sitting at their man's table. With no one close enough to provide support, the best his boss could do was request the retasking of one of their surveillance satellites to help gather additional intelligence. The lion's share of the operation would fall to Steven. There were a staggering number of question marks surrounding the man in that café and the CIA needed Steven to gather as much information about him and what he was up to as possible.

Though adrenaline, fear, and excitement were coursing through his bloodstream, Cooke focused on his training to keep himself under control.

The first thing Steven needed was a record of the meeting. Since there was no way he was going to show his white Anglo-Saxon face in that café and potentially scare away his quarry, he had to get his hands on a fairly decent camera. Moving through the marketplace as fast as he dared, he finally found what he was looking for. The only problem was money—he didn't have enough of it. The souk pickpockets were notorious, and he never carried credit cards and definitely never any more cash than he knew he would need. What he did have, though, was his Kobold Chronograph wristwatch, and the shop owner gladly accepted it in exchange for a Canon digital camera with a fairly decent zoom lens and an extra-high-capacity memory card.

From the edge of a rooftop across the alley, Steven interspersed his picture-taking with pieces of short video he hoped the experts at Langley would be able to decipher. Whatever had drawn the man in the café out of hiding must have been extremely important for him to risk this meeting.

Steven filled the high-capacity memory card and was about to reinsert the low-end factory-included card to see if he could get any pictures of the man's car once he left the café, when he heard a noise behind him.

The garrote wire whistled through the air and then snapped tight around his neck. Steven's hands scrabbled uselessly for it as he felt a knee in his back and the pressure begin to build. When his trachea severed, the camera clattered onto the rooftop, cracking the screen.

The damage made no difference to the assassin as he dragged the lifeless young CIA operative back from the parapet and pocketed the camera as well as the spare memory card. The only thing Abdul Ali cared about was that there never be any record of the meeting in that café.

The Americans would know its outcome soon enough, and by then it would be too late.

TWO

WHITE HOUSE SITUATION ROOM
WASHINGTON, DC
MAY 18

President Jack Rutledge entered the situation room and signaled the men and women around the conference table to take their seats. He was less than five months into his second term and had already been called to this room more times than in the last two years combined.

He had hoped to use his second term to focus on the key domestic policy issues he had campaigned on and which would comprise his legacy. But more than that, the president wanted to leave his successor, Democrat or Republican, a better country than had been left to him. The war on terror, though, had much different plans for Rutledge.

Contrary to what the White House press secretary was spinning to the media, terrorist plots against America and American interests were not on the decline. They were in fact on a very marked upswing, and the United States was running out of fingers and toes with which to plug the dike.

For every attack the United States thwarted, three more popped up in its wake. The operations tempo in the intelligence, military, and law enforcement communities was higher than anyone had ever seen. Despite its phenomenal successes, most of which the average citizen was never aware of, all America seemed able to do was tread water. The country was running well beyond capacity and it was only a matter of time before the overtaxed system collapsed from sheer exhaustion. Something needed to be done, and done soon.

That was the thought on the mind of every person in the room as the president finished skimming the contents of the file folder in front of him and turned the meeting over to General Bart Waddell, director of the Defense Intelligence Agency.

"Thank you, Mr. President," replied Waddell, a tall, dark-haired man in his late forties. As he stood, he pressed a button on a small digital remote, and the plasma monitors at the front of the room, as well as those recessed within the situation-room table, sprang to life with the revolving DIA logo. "The footage I am about to show you was shot this morning. It was developed thanks to two converging pieces of intelligence. The first was a series of satellite surveillance photos ordered up by the Central Intelligence Agency when one of its field officers spotted the subject in North Africa—Morocco, to be exact. The second piece of intelligence was a tip that pinpointed the subject's base of operations more than six thousand kilometers southeast in Somalia."

Waddell advanced to the first slide in his PowerPoint presentation and everyone watched as a dusty Toyota Land Cruiser pulled up in front of the weather-beaten façade of a long single-story structure. "What you are looking at is a Muslim religious boys' school, or madrassa, on the outskirts of Mogadishu. The man getting out of the car on the right is Mohammed bin Mohammed, aka Abu Khabab al-Fari, or as our analysts are fond of calling him, M&M. He is known as al-Qaeda's master bombmaker and head of their weapons of mass destruction committee. Born in Algeria in 1953, he has training in both physics and chemical engineering."

Waddell then advanced through a series of still images as he continued to narrate. "At al-Qaeda's Tora Bora base near Jalalabad, Mohammed not only built and managed a facility for the manufacture of nuclear, chemical, and biological weapons, but he provided hundreds of operatives with training in the use of those weapons. Most of you are familiar with the images that made it into mainstream media showing the scores of dead dogs, cats, donkeys, et cetera scattered outside the complex."

Everyone in the room was indeed familiar with the photos, but it didn't make them any easier to have to see again. Around the table, they nodded their heads in grim unison.

"The photos only heightened some of our worst fears about the ghoulish experiments we suspected M&M was carrying out with anthrax and other biological and chemical poisons.

"When our teams hit the site in 2001, we found hoards of documents authored by Mohammed. They bore little similarity to the other terrorist manuals recovered at al-Qaeda safe houses throughout Afghanistan and Pakistan, which in comparison were extremely crude. Mohammed's manuals contained very innovative designs for explosive devices and represented a huge leap forward in al-Qaeda's technological capabilities.

"On September ninth, two days before the attacks against the World Trade Center and the Pentagon, Mohammed's facility was completely abandoned and he was evacuated to an unknown location somewhere in the Hindu Kush Mountains. Despite numerous leads, we had not been able to assemble any verifiable eyes-on intelligence for him. Until this morning."

"Any idea what he was doing at the madrassa?" asked Secretary of State Jennifer Staley.

Waddell turned to James Vaile, the director of the Central Intelligence Agency, to see if he wanted to field the question.

DCI Vaile looked at Staley and said, "There have been reports that some elements of al-Qaeda are taking advantage of the absence of a strong centralized government in Somalia to reestablish themselves and open up training camps."

Homeland Security Secretary Alan Driehaus shook his head and said, "I suppose the fact that we wouldn't touch Mogadishu or any of that area with a ten-foot pole only adds to its appeal for them."

"How do you know we wouldn't touch it?" asked General Hank Currutt, chairman of the Joint Chiefs of Staff. A patriot who had bled for his country on more than one battlefield, Currutt had never been a big fan of Driehaus's. He felt the secretary's position called for a warrior familiar with combat rather than a career attorney familiar with nothing more than the inside of a courtroom.

For his part, Driehaus resented Currutt's constant implications that he wasn't up to the task and that serving his country for more than two decades in the Department of Justice was somehow less noble than having served it in the armed forces. "Considering the whole Black Hawk Down incident and the fact that our resources are stretched too thin as it is," replied Driehaus, "I just assumed we wouldn't be too hot to jump into another conflict over there. I think we need to start being very sensitive to the perception that we're empire building."

"Empire building?" replied Currutt. "Is that what you think this is?"

"I said that's the *perception,* but you'd have to be blind not to see where it comes from."

"Well, let me tell you something. We've sent a lot of brave young men and women to fight for freedom outside of our borders and the only land we've ever asked for in return is enough to bury those who didn't come home."

The room was completely silent.

Normally, the president embraced healthy differences of opinion among his cabinet members and advisors, but he knew something that Secretary Driehaus didn't. Hank Currutt was at the "Battle of the Black Sea," as that infamous eighteen-hour firefight in the heart of Mogadishu's Bakara Market was known. Eighteen servicemen had been killed and more than seventy wounded.

There were too many pressing issues vying for their attention to allow the animosity between Driehaus and Currutt to become the focus of this meeting. They needed to concentrate on the matter in front of them, and Rutledge was enough of a statesman to know that allowing Currutt to jump across the table and rip Driehaus's throat out was anything but productive.

The president said, "As far as I'm concerned, all options are on the table at this point. Mohammed is one of the most dangerous threats to this country and I have to be honest, up to this point I'd been harboring a secret hope that with all the bombs we dropped on Tora Bora, we had pulverized whatever rock he was hiding under and that's why we hadn't heard anything from him. But now we know differently and I want to discuss what we're going to do about it. General Waddell, it was your folks that gathered the intel. What's your read on this?"

"Well, Mr. President, we know from the documents we've recovered and from our interviews with detainees both at Gitmo and in Afghanistan that Mohammed had been trying to assemble very sophisticated delivery devices for multiple terror attacks inside the United States. We've got eyes on him right now and I think we need to strike while the iron is hot. We're never going to get a chance like this again. I say we take him out."

"Director Vaile?" inquired the president as he turned to the head of the Central Intelligence Agency. "Would you concur?"

"Normally, I would, but we've got a problem in this case."

"What kind of problem?" asked Waddell.

"We know that despite our successes al-Qaeda is reconstituting itself. They have a myriad of attacks at different stages of development here in the United States and abroad, some of which we're on to and many of which we're still trying to smoke out.

"As you are aware, Mr. President, one of the most troubling pieces of intelligence we've uncovered recently is that they're very close to completing a transaction that would allow them to launch an unprecedented nuclear attack on the U.S. Based upon several converging streams of intelligence, including the loss of our field operative and the satellite imagery we pulled from Marrakech, we have a very high degree of certainty the transaction was masterminded and is being controlled by Mohammed bin Mohammed. The CIA's position is that it's vital to national security that he be taken alive for interrogation purposes."

"You mean torture by some friendly government," replied Secretary Driehaus. "The ultimate in American outsourcing."

Vaile fixed the head of the DHS with a very unfriendly stare.

"Where would we send this one? The ex-Soviet facilities in Eastern Europe are pretty much out of the question, especially now that the press has been all over them. Most of the Western Europeans won't allow us to use their international airports as transition points anymore. So, I suppose that leaves us with our old fallbacks. Egypt? Jordan?"

"Which side are you on, Alan?" asked Vaile.

"I side with the rule of law," replied Driehaus.

Everyone in the room knew the secretary was not a fan of the administration's extraordinary rendition policy. It was a strategy that allowed prisoners to be handed over to foreign governments who conducted torture so that the United States could sidestep its own laws strictly forbidding it.

Keeping his eyes locked on Driehaus, the DCI said, "Regardless of where Mohammed might be interrogated, I think the president's policies have served our country, and in particular your department, exceedingly well."

"With all due respect to the president, I think you're wrong," said the DHS secretary. "We're supposed to be a nation that holds the rule of law above all else. We use it to justify every single thing we do, including the invasion of other sovereign nations. If we don't truly place that principle above all else then we can't be any better than the terrorists we're fighting against."

"That's it!" bellowed General Hank Currutt as he rose from his chair and stabbed his thick finger at Driehaus. "I'm not going to listen to any more of this subversive garbage."

"Subversive?" replied Driehaus. "That's a mighty convenient way to label opinions that don't agree with yours."

"Listen, you smug SOB, if you don't like the way things are being done here, then resign your post, pick up a picket sign, and stand on the other side of the fence with the rest of the whackos out on Pennsylvania Avenue."

Once again, things were quickly spinning in the wrong direction. "Let's take our seats and all calm down," said the president. When Currutt didn't comply, the president ordered, "General, I said *sit down.*"

Once the man had retaken his seat, the president looked at Driehaus and said, "You've got a sharp mind, Alan, especially when it comes to homeland security issues and that's why—"

"Mr. President," interjected Driehaus, "our enemies use our extraordinary rendition policy as prime recruiting propaganda. In fact, with all the attention the media has been devoting to it, they don't need to recruit at all. Willing bodies are lined up out their doors and down the block. This policy makes us look like hypocrites."

"No it doesn't," stressed Rutledge, who had been getting progressively more frustrated with his appointee's refusal to be a team player. "The policy makes us look tough. What's more, it gets results. Civilized rules of engagement and jurisprudence mean nothing to a vicious enemy willing to do anything to succeed. If we want to win, we have to adopt the same strategy—success at any cost. I'm sorry, Alan, but if a nation refuses to bend, then that nation is almost certainly doomed to break. In this case we have to suspend the rule of law in part, in order to save it."

That one remark tore at the very few remnants of respect Driehaus had left for the president. "We know Mohammed exchanged information with the Palestinian and Hezbollah bombmakers who helped Richard Reid design the shoe bomb he carried on the Paris-to-Boston flight in 2001. Let's indict him under that. If we put him on trial here, a fair trial, it will go a long way to repairing our image abroad. And it'll send the message that we're tough."

"Ramzi Yousef bombed the World Trade Center in 1993," interjected the attorney general, Laura Finley. "We found him, tried him, and put him in SuperMax out in Colorado, but where'd that get us? His uncle, Khalid Shaikh Mohammed, came back with al-Qaeda and hit the Trade Center again in 2001. Yousef got a fair trial and then he got life in prison. That's pretty tough, if you ask me, but it didn't stop anything. Alan, we've worked together and you know I have a lot of respect for you, but the president's right. We can't bring knives to gunfights anymore."

Driehaus was about to respond, when the secretary of state, Jennifer Staley, piped up and said, "As someone who deals with America's image abroad on an around-the-clock basis, I want to put my two cents in here. Have the press leaks about our interrogations of detainees abroad hurt our image overseas? Yes, they definitely have. But the bottom line is that right or wrong, the United States is safer because of what we're doing."

"So we shouldn't be concerned with what happens to these people once they've been handed over to another government?"

"When we render a suspect, that suspect is often being rendered to his or her country of origin or a country where that individual already has outstanding warrants. Despite how the press warps our involvement, we actually have very little control over what happens from that point forward."

"So there's a slice of absolution in it for us—a washing of the hands, as it were," replied the DHS secretary.

Staley was much too intelligent to walk into that one. Instead she offered, "What I'll say is that even our beloved President Lincoln suspended habeas corpus during the Civil War. I think the intelligence we've gathered through extraordinary rendition speaks for itself."

Driehaus looked around the table. "So I'm the only one? Nobody else has any concern about adding yet another name to the secret prisoner rolls of this policy?"

"Actually," said a voice from the other end of the table, "I do."

Stunned, all heads in the room turned to stare at the FBI director, Martin Sorce. Once he was sure he had everyone's attention, the director continued, "This will be one of the highest-ranking al-Qaeda members we've ever taken down. But because of the wide coverage of extraordinary rendition, some of the more cooperative governments we've been working with have said they won't take any more of our prisoners. We've also had a couple of so-called escapes, which we know al-Qaeda facilitated through bribes, payoffs, or intimidation of some of the people involved with these same governments.

"So, this isn't as easy as throwing a dart at a map and asking the locals to warm up the coffee and jumper cables because we've got a new stepchild. For a prisoner this big and this dangerous, security has to be our number one issue. I want to know that whomever we park this cupcake with, they're not going to lose him."

"That's a good point," said the DCI. "Mohammed bin Mohammed's capture will create a lot of special problems, and security will be the biggest. Al-Qaeda would do anything to get this guy back. If we let the Egyptians or Jordanians host him, there's no guarantee they'll be able to hang on to him. Look at what happened to the USS *Cole* planners in Yemen. On the flip side, if we transport him to Gitmo, our hands are going to be tied in terms of how hard we can press him for details, and we are going to need that WMD transaction intelligence as soon as possible."

"So where's that leave us?" asked Attorney General Finley.

"Between a rock and a public relations hard place," said the secretary of state. "While we can't change the bad press we've already received, Secretary Driehaus does have a valid point. Whatever we do going forward, we'd better not screw it up."

THREE

After twenty more minutes of discussion, the president adjourned the meeting, informing the participants he would take their suggestions under advisement.

Quietly, Rutledge questioned why winning the war on terror and winning the war with the media seemed to be mutually exclusive. How many more September 11ths had to happen before the American people realized what a savage enemy they were facing? It was one of the most trying challenges of his administration, but the president knew that however unpopular his choices might be, he had to put the welfare of the country and its citizens first—even if many of them couldn't stomach what had to be done.

As he was readying to leave the room, Secretary of Defense Robert Hilliman—a graying, heavyset man in his mid-sixties with wire-rimmed glasses and wearing a neatly pressed Brooks Brothers suit—asked, "Mr. President, may we have a moment of your time?" General Waddell stood next to him with a folder in his hand.

Once the rest of the cabinet members had left the situation room, Waddell handed the folder to Hilliman, who opened it and said, "Mr. President, immediately after 9/11 you asked me to task certain agencies within the Defense Department to develop a plan to handle the detention and interrogation of enemy combatants of significant intelligence value."

"Which along with the CIA's efforts is how we came up with extraordinary rendition," replied the president.

"Yes, sir, but we at the Defense Department also foresaw a situation wherein operatives at the very top of al-Qaeda's organizational pyramid, men like Mohammed bin Mohammed, Ayman al-Zawahiri, or even bin Laden himself might pose a special set of challenges incongruent with our rendition policies."

"Are you trying to tell me you've got a different take on how to handle this?"

"Yes, I believe we do."

"Then why didn't you say something during the meeting?" asked Rutledge.

Hilliman answered by pulling an executive summary from the folder and handing it to him.

The president read it through twice and then once more for good measure before saying, "How many people would be in the loop on this?"

"As few as possible, sir," responded Waddell. "It's an extremely unorthodox plan, and we feel the less who know about it the better."

"That's putting it mildly," said Rutledge as he motioned for the rest of the file. As he slowly read through it, he asked, "How confident are you that this can be pulled off? And I don't want a rosy, best-case scenario. I want the real down-and-dirty assessment."

Waddell looked at Hilliman, who replied, "Because of certain elements beyond our control, we put it at about a sixty percent probability of success."

That didn't sit well with the president. "That's not a very good number."

"No, sir, it's not. But considering the situation, we think the benefits far outweigh the liabilities."

"I don't agree with you," said Rutledge. "If this ever became public knowledge, the fallout would be devastating."

"Yes, sir," replied Waddell, "but we have contingencies in place to make sure that doesn't happen."

"With only a sixty percent probability of success," said the president, "you'd better have a boatload of them."

Hilliman and Waddell had been at this game long enough to know when to back off and let an operation sell itself. They also knew that Jack Rutledge would make the right call, no matter how hard a decision it was. He always did.

After a few more minutes of studying the file, the president nodded his head and said, "I want you to keep me up to speed every step of the way on this."

"Of course, Mr. President," responded Hilliman.

General Waddell then picked up one of the secure telephones on the situation-room table, dialed an inside line at the Defense Intelligence Agency, and spoke five words that would have repercussions far beyond what any of them could have imagined: "We're go for Operation Driftwood."

FOUR

Somali Coast
15 Kilometers South of Mogadishu
May 22

Mohammed bin Mohammed tucked a handful of local currency into the front of the boy's pants note by note and then sent him on his way back to the madrassa. The eleven-year-old had been exquisite. Maybe not as exquisite as the European or Arab boys he was accustomed to, but one made do with what one had at hand.

Once Mohammed had finished bathing, he brewed himself another glass of tea and stepped out onto the villa's terrace. It was darker than normal for this time of evening—the clouds of an approaching storm having hidden the stars overhead. A bit fatigued from his illness and his recent trip to Morocco, Mohammed leaned against one of the stone balustrades and listened to the roar of the Indian Ocean crashing against the beach below.

After a few more minutes of salt air against his skin, Mohammed returned inside. There was no telling how much havoc the storm might wreak on satellite communications, and he had a few last elements to put in place. The transaction was nearly complete.

Because of his particular predilections, Mohammed preferred to live at the beachside villa alone, but that didn't mean he was lax when it came to security. Not only did he have his own men posted on the roads in both directions, but he also enjoyed the protection of several local warlords. In addition, the beach had been mined with antipersonnel devices and the entire villa had been constructed with reinforced concrete and steel to protect against any of the remote-controlled Predator Drone attacks the cowardly Americans were so fond of.

With no central government and no outside forces meddling in local affairs, men like Mohammed bin Mohammed were free to do as they wished in Somalia. In just three years, al-Qaeda had opened dozens of covert training camps throughout the country and had significantly added to the organization's numbers, shipping them off to Iraq to gain valuable, real-world combat experience. What's more, after their humiliating defeat at the hands of local militias, the United States wanted nothing to do with this part of the world. It was the perfect base of operations. Everything in Mohammed's world seemed to be improving, even his health.

In one of the villa's small bedrooms, Mohammed carefully unlocked a specially fabricated titanium briefcase and booted up his encrypted Macintosh PowerBook.

As he worked, his mind drifted to the little boy who had left only twenty minutes ago and he started becoming aroused again. With the arousal, though, came something else—a dull throbbing in his back, just below the rib cage, complemented by an overwhelming urge to urinate. *Too much tea and too much sex,* Mohammed thought to himself as he rose to go to the toilet. When he approached the bedroom door, his heart caught in his throat.

"Hands on top of your head," said one of several black-clad figures armed with very nasty-looking assault rifles.

Mohammed was stunned. *How could the house have been breached?*

The man in black told him once more to put his hands on top of his head, this time in Arabic.

Ignoring the order, Mohammed lunged back into the bedroom toward the PowerBook. As he did, a pair of barbed probes from a TASER X26 ripped through his cotton robe and embedded themselves in the flesh of his back. When the electricity raced through his body, his muscles locked up and he fell like a dead tree trunk, face-first onto the stone floor.

His hands and feet were Flexicuffed, and the last thing he saw before being dragged from the room was two of the men going for his laptop.

Had they been paying attention, they might have seen Mohammed smile.

Seconds later an explosion rocked the small bedroom, and the hallway was showered with titanium shrapnel, chunks of plaster, and pieces of charred human flesh.

FIVE

Scottish Highlands
May 29

Eileanaigas House was a twelve-bedroom estate located on the northern end of a private, wooded island in the middle of the River Beauly. In addition to its majestic silver birch, Douglas fir, spruce, and pine trees, the estate also boasted a dramatic gorge, a heated outdoor swimming pool, small formal gardens, an extensive wine cellar, and a security system that rivaled that of any leading head of state. The security was a very necessary precaution, as the man who lived on the island had many powerful enemies—many of whom were his clients.

Known simply as "the Troll," the lord of Eileanaigas House lived by the motto that knowledge didn't equal power, it was the proper application of knowledge that equaled power. And when applied in a very precise manner, knowledge could also equal incredible wealth.

It was in following this mantra that the Troll had made a substantial living for himself dealing in the purchase, sale, and trade of highly classified information. Both his cutthroat business acumen and his gluttonous appetite for the very best of everything stood in sharp contrast to his height. At just under three feet tall, he could barely reach anything in his home without some sort of assistance; normally in the form of miniature stepladders made from ornately carved exotic hardwoods. The house's size was a reflection of how the Troll saw himself and only its most private areas had been retrofitted to accommodate his size.

Another reflection of how the Troll saw himself were the two enormous, snow-white Caucasian Ovcharkas, Argus and Drako, who never left his side. Weighing close to two hundred pounds each and standing over forty-one inches at the shoulder, these giants were the dogs of choice for the Russian military and the former East German border patrol. They were extremely athletic and absolutely vicious when it came to strangers intruding on their territory. They made perfect guardians for the Troll's island domain. And most important for a man who made his livelihood dealing in the art of duplicity and blackmail, the dogs could never be turned against him. In fact, he'd always had an odd premonition that the dogs might one day save his life.

Tonight, Argus and Drako sat warily near the fire as a powerful summer storm raged outside. Despite the warmth and its siren's call to sleep, their eyes were glued to the man who had just arrived at the castle.

"Whisky?" asked the Troll, offering his guest a drink.

"I don't drink," replied the man, his dark, narrow eyes bracketing a once prominent Bedouin nose. "I'm surprised. I thought you would have known more about me."

The Troll smiled as he poured himself two fingers of Germain-Robin Brandy. "Abdul Ali, aka Ahmed Ali, Imad Hasan, and Ibrahim Rahman. Date of birth unknown. Place of birth also unknown, though Western intelligence speculates somewhere in North Africa, most likely Algeria or Morocco, hence the CIA's cognomen of "the Berber."

"Even though no Western intelligence agency has been able to obtain a photo of you, it is speculated that you have undergone multiple plastic surgeries to change your appearance. You speak more than five languages and are at home in at least a dozen countries worldwide, more than half of them in the West. For all intents and purposes, you're a ghost—a man who travels wherever he wants, whenever he wants, with no one ever knowing if he was really there or not.

"It is believed you have both prior special operations and military intelligence training, though with whom no one can, or will, say. You have been suspected in more than thirty-six terrorist attacks on Western targets and have been directly implicated in eleven high-profile assassinations—two of which were MI-6 agents, three Mossad, and four more who were deep-cover operatives for the CIA.

"Your height has been listed as anywhere from five-foot-eight to six-foot-five, you have a spear-shaped birthmark on the back of your left shoulder, and are, in short, one of the highest-priority targets for every organized intelligence agency in the Western world."

Ali was impressed. "That's very good. Everything except for the birthmark. I do not have one."

"You do now," replied the Troll. "I had it inserted in your file and cross-confirmed by three separate sources. It may come in handy someday. Consider it a bonus. Al-Qaeda has given me a considerable amount of business over the years." The Troll then climbed up into his desk chair and said, "Let's talk about why you're here."

"You know why I'm here."

"Of course I do. Your man in Somalia, Mohammed bin Mohammed."

Ali nodded his head.

"Everything I was able to uncover is in the file I forwarded to your superiors. I don't understand your need to see me in person."

"I have learned that even in our delicate line of work, there is no substitute for meeting face-to-face."

"Be that as it may, this is still highly unusual," replied the Troll as he cradled the snifter in his diminutive hands.

"So are the circumstances surrounding Mohammed's disappearance."

"Mr. Ali, the only reason I have agreed to meet with you is because of my long-standing business relationship with your superiors. If you have something to ask me, please do so."

Ali studied the Troll for several moments before responding. "I'd like you to tell me what you uncovered."

"Like I said, it's all in the file. I am very meticulous about my work."

"As am I, but sometimes small details have a way of getting left out."

"I don't leave out details—small or otherwise," said the Troll.

"You never know. Something that may have seemed inconsequential at the time might turn out to be quite important to us now. Please. Humor me."

The Troll took a long sip of brandy. He knew that lying to the man could prove to be a very bad mistake. There was no telling if al-Qaeda had a piece of the puzzle he was not aware of. All he could do was stick to his plan. It was inevitable that they would come to interrogate him. He was one of the few people who knew where Mohammed bin Mohammed had been hiding. "Your man in Somalia was targeted by an American covert action team."

"American," repeated Ali, "not Israeli? You're sure of that?"

"As the file I sent your superiors clearly states, he was taken by a private vessel to waters off the eastern seaboard of the United States and then flown by helicopter to somewhere in New York City."

"And he is still alive?"

"From what I understand, but he wasn't in very good health to begin with. Apparently he has a serious—"

"Kidney problem," interjected Ali, finishing the Troll's sentence for him. "We know."

"To his credit, it seems to be making his interrogation quite difficult for his captors."

"This is where I get confused. If it was the Americans, why would they bring him to America straightaway? Why not take him to a cooperative country for interrogation first?"

"I don't interpret intelligence, Mr. Ali. I simply facilitate its transfer. Now, if there's nothing else?"

"Actually, there is," said the assassin. As his hand moved toward the inside of his sport coat, the Ovcharkas began to growl.

The Troll placed his finger on the tiny trigger of a special customized weapon recessed beneath his desk and with his other hand signaled the dogs to be silent.

Well aware that there was a weapon trained on his stomach, Ali slowly removed a piece of paper from his jacket, leaned forward, and slid it across the desk.

The Troll took his time in reading it. Now, the al-Qaeda operative's real reason for wanting to meet face-to-face was out in the open. "Your organization doesn't pay me for advice, but I'm going to give you some anyway. No charge. Cut your losses and move on. Even if I could pinpoint his exact location, what you are suggesting is suicide. It can't be done."

"That's not your concern. All we want to know is if you can put a team and equipment in place by the specified date." said Ali.

"With enough money anything is possible, but—"

"Twenty million dollars, on top of which you'll be paid twice your normal fee and a bonus of five million once the operation has been successfully completed."

"Meaning once you have recovered your colleague."

Ali nodded his head. "Think of it as an added incentive."

The Troll was silent for several moments as he pretended to reflect upon the offer. They had played right into his hands. With this kind of money he would have enough to buy what he needed from his contact at the NSA, but his mole at the Department of Defense would be much more expensive. Nevertheless, he was confident he could get the information he needed with plenty of money left to spare. Finally, he said, "The biggest problem I see you facing, Mr. Ali, is time. If you can allow for more, it might help increase your probability of success."

"No, there is no more time. Mohammed is scheduled to complete a very sensitive transaction for us in the very near future."

"Then I would suggest you get somebody else to do it."

"There is nobody else. The man Mohammed has been negotiating with will only deal with him. If Mohammed fails to appear, we forfeit our place in line and the man will simply contact the next prospective buyer. If that happens, we will end up losing much more than just a highly valued member of our organization."

"What is it you are buying, if you don't mind my asking?"

"It is none of your concern," responded Ali.

The Troll smiled. He knew exactly what they were buying. There were very few things al-Qaeda would be willing to pay so much to get their lead negotiator back for. "If you're successful, the Americans will throw open the gates of hell itself to find you—all of you."

Abdul Ali wasn't quite sure if the dwarf was referring to their rescue of Mohammed bin Mohammed, or what they intended to do once Mohammed's transaction was complete. Either way, it didn't matter. "You have our offer. Take it or leave it."

Considering that the Troll had dreamed about this exact opportunity for years, how could he do anything other than accept?

As Abdul Ali left the manor house, he couldn't help smiling. That the Troll would accept the assignment and help them in their task was a foregone conclusion. What amused the assassin more was that the little man had no idea that al-Qaeda knew that it was he who had betrayed

Mohammed bin Mohammed to the Americans. Their network of contacts might not have been as vast, but it could be incredibly efficient.

Soon, the Troll's usefulness would run its course, and when it did, Abdul Ali would take particular pleasure in bringing the man's parasitic existence to an extremely painful end.

SIX

MONTREAL, CANADA
JULY 3

When Sayed Jamal entered the bedroom of his government-subsidized apartment, Scot Harvath slammed the butt of his H&K right into the bridge of his nose, knocking the terrorist to the floor and causing him to bleed profusely.

"Don't you know that Allah prefers playing to a full house?" said Harvath as he Flexicuffed the man's wrists behind his back. "He doesn't like it when you skip out of morning prayers early. And neither do I."

As Harvath stood up, he gave Jamal a sharp kick to his ribs to emphasize his unhappiness with the man's premature return to the apartment.

Like Ahmed Ressam—the Algerian-born terrorist who had been caught at the Canadian–U.S. border with over 120 pounds of explosives and a plan to blow up Los Angeles International Airport on New Year's Eve 1999—Sayed Jamal was yet another Algerian national who had taken advantage of Canada's liberal asylum policy to hide out just north of the border and plan attacks against the United States.

With its quaint cobblestone streets and European architecture, Montreal was a city that made many people forget they were only twenty-nine miles from New York State. Scot Harvath, though, was no longer one of those people.

Finding a Canadian penny mixed in with his U.S. change once or twice a year, Harvath used to joke that Canada was the most patient invading force in the world—one penny at a time, one pop singer at a time, one actor at a time. . . . It might take them ten thousand years to conquer the United States, but they were on the move, and the American people needed to wake up. But when Canada started to become an operational staging ground for Middle Eastern terrorists bent on destroying the United States, the joke was no longer funny.

Upon reaching Canada or its territorial waters, all that these "asylum-seekers" had to do was claim status as political refugees, and they would be granted Canadian protection under the UN Convention. That was it. The screening process was so poorly managed that nearly one hundred percent of them were granted a formal hearing complete with free legal advice, money, and a place to stay while they often waited more than two years to appear in front of a Canadian magistrate—if they even bothered showing up at all for their hearing.

With laughable screening procedures and nonexistent enforcement, significant numbers of these fake asylum-seekers found their way to Montreal where they joined Muslim terrorist organizations with strong ties to al-Qaeda. One such organization was known as the Algerian Armed Islamic Group, or GIA, and it was the GIA that had brought Agent Scot Harvath to Canada.

The United States had been trying unsuccessfully to convince the Canadian Government to extradite Sayed Jamal to stand trial in the United States. Jamal was a former chemistry professor who somewhere along the line found religion—radical Islam, to be specific—joined the GIA, and followed several of his GIA counterparts to Iraq, where he took up arms against the Western imperial crusaders, aka the American military.

Interestingly enough, of all the foreign fighters in Iraq, the majority—over twenty percent—came from Algeria. And while several Syrian terrorist groups were known for producing exceptional snipers, it was the Algerians—the GIA in particular—who were known for being the best bombmakers in the business. In fact, the most horrific roadside bombs—the ones that scared the hell out of even the most experienced EOD, or Explosive Ordnance Disposal techs, were the ones produced by the GIA's most proficient bombmaker in Iraq, Sayed Jamal.

With over two hundred American servicemen and women killed and wounded as a result of Jamal's specialty IEDs known as EFPs, or explosively formed projectiles, which could penetrate up to four inches of armor from over 300 feet away, the United States had pulled out all the stops to track him down. When the heat got too intense in Iraq, he fled to Canada. There, he spun an elaborate cover story and was granted full refugee status. But while you can take the jihadi out of the jihad, you can never really take the jihad out of the jihadi. NSA intercepts revealed a dramatic increase in terrorist chatter suggesting that Jamal was coordinating future attacks within the United States.

Once the United States had pinpointed the terrorist's location, they began extradition requests. Despite a mountain of evidence in favor of the extradition, the Canadians refused. The liberal prime minister wasn't convinced that Jamal was who the Americans said he was. Even so, the PM made it clear he wouldn't even begin considering extradition unless the United States promised to waive the death penalty in the case. As far as the United States was concerned, there was no way in hell that was ever going to happen.

Soon after talks broke down, a copy of Jamal's Canadian Intelligence dossier magically appeared on the president's desk. Jack Rutledge didn't need to ask where it came from. He knew how back channels worked, and he also knew that there were several high-ranking members of the Canadian Security Intelligence Service who were sick of seeing their country's benevolence exploited by Muslim extremists. Considering the sensitivity of the assignment, he knew there was only one person he could call.

With Jamal now zip-tied and under control, Harvath turned his attention back to the most dangerous part of the assignment—securing Jamal's laptop.

He'd been briefed that the United States had recently lost two very experienced operators when they attempted to retrieve a high-ranking al-Qaeda member's PowerBook. Harvath didn't know what spooked him more—the fact that the United States had taken down an al-Qaeda operative so high-ranking that even with his above-top-secret *Polo Step* clearance he couldn't find out who it was, or that as the two members of the assault team had gone for the terrorist's laptop, it had detonated, killing them instantly.

All Harvath knew was that Jamal's computer was believed to contain a veritable treasure trove of information and that because of some association with the aforementioned high-ranking al-Qaeda member, his laptop most likely had been rigged with similar explosives and a mercury tilt switch.

It was at times like this that Harvath would have given a year's pay to have had a good EOD tech along for the ride. But he didn't have a good EOD tech; he didn't even have a bad one. All he had were two empty aerosol cans and a Styrofoam cooler packed with dry ice.

The idea had been to render the mercury in the tilt switch useless with a product used for flash-freezing biological specimens known as Quick-Freeze. After the tilt switch was immobilized, it would create a window of several seconds during which he could pick up the laptop and place it in the cooler. It then could be transported back across the border where a team was waiting to defuse it. At the time, the plan made sense. What nobody had counted on was Jamal coming home early. Because of it, Harvath's attention had been diverted and now he didn't have enough Quick-Freeze left to attempt refreezing the tilt switch.

He had to think of something else. Returning empty-handed, or worse, *no-handed* were not options he was willing to consider.

Though Harvath was just two careers removed from his days as a United States Navy SEAL, the lessons he had learned with the Secret Service at the White House and now as a covert counterterrorism operative for the Department of Homeland Security only served to reinforce his Special Operations training—there was an answer to every problem, you just had to look hard enough to find it.

Glancing at the special Suunto X9Mi watch he'd been issued for the trip into Canada, Harvath saw that he was very close to falling behind schedule. He had a rendezvous to keep and if he missed it, it was going to be hell getting out of the country and back across the U.S. border.

As he cycled through various options in his mind, something suddenly bubbled to the surface. Sayed Jamal was a bombmaker and unfortunately a pretty good one. From the intelligence reports Harvath had read, he knew that the man was meticulous. And if he was meticulous, he was probably also very safety conscious. The question was would he have what Harvath was looking for and if so where did he keep it?

Dragging Jamal up by the hair, Harvath put his gun under the man's chin and said, "You've got a lot of soldering equipment in here, Sayed.

If a fire broke out it could be pretty expensive—not to mention the undesirable attention it would draw. That was Ramzi Yousef's mistake with that little chemical fire in the Philippines. If I recall correctly, his pal got busted going back later for their laptop, didn't he? But you're smarter than that. I can tell. So tell me, where's your fire extinguisher?"

Jamal spit in Harvath's face and cursed him in Arabic.

"Ebn el Metanaka!" Harvath responded as he jammed the silenced barrel of his weapon into the painfully soft tissue beneath Jamal's chin. "We can do this in Arabic or English. I don't really care. I just want to know where it is."

The bombmaker tried to spit at him again, but Harvath cut him short with a knee to the groin. He'd had a feeling he wasn't going to get much help, but it was always polite to ask—and Scot Harvath was nothing if not polite.

He dragged the terrorist to the kitchen, where he found what he was looking for under the sink. "Good choice, Sayed," he remarked as he pulled it out. "Powder extinguishers leave such a nasty residue. CO_2 is much cleaner and a lot colder."

Looking around, Harvath then asked, "Now then, where do you keep your falafel mitts, asshole?"

SEVEN

Forty-five minutes later, Harvath pulled his car over to the side of the road, yanked Jamal out of the trunk, and shoved half a tampon up each of his nostrils to stem his nosebleed. After putting a Windbreaker over the terrorist's shoulders and zipping it up the front to hide his stained shirt, Harvath slid him into the front passenger seat, fastened his seat belt, and warned him what would happen if he tried to make any more trouble.

Once again, Jamal tried to spit, but Harvath was ready for him. He nailed him with a blow to his solar plexus, doubling him over and knocking the wind out of him.

Reaching back into the bag of goodies he had bought at the convenience store just outside Montreal, Harvath withdrew a PowerBar and a bottle of spring water. At thirty-six, his carefree days of unlimited cheeseburgers and beers were now behind him. At five feet ten and a muscular 175 pounds, Harvath was in better shape than most men half his age, but he found it took more and more work just to maintain his level of physical fitness. If an assignment in a Muslim country required that he grow a beard, after a couple of days he soon saw traces of gray mingled with the light brown that matched the hair on his head. His father, a Navy SEAL instructor who had died in a training accident when Harvath was in his early twenties, had gone completely gray by forty.

Despite the small lines starting to form at the corners of his bright blue eyes, it wasn't anything Harvath couldn't live with. Everybody had to get older sooner or later. What the signs of aging did make him wonder about was how much longer he wanted to put up with the stress of working for the government. The fact that he couldn't get any good information that might have helped him on this assignment about the high-ranking al-Qaeda terrorist the United States had recently bagged was just another in a ongoing string of frustrations he was grudgingly putting up with.

While he respected his president and loved his country, the mounting bureaucratic bullshit was really beginning to piss him off. Having been both a SEAL and a Secret Service agent at the White House, Harvath understood the value of rules, regs, and a proper chain of command. But when the president had created a special international branch of Homeland Security dubbed the Office of International Investigative Assistance and had offered Harvath one of its plum assignments, Scot had thought things were going to be different.

Known as the Apex Project, Harvath's covert unit was supposed to represent the collective intelligence capability and full muscle of the United States government to help neutralize and prevent terrorist actions against America and American interests on a global level.

Though it "technically" didn't exist and Harvath was nothing more than a benignly titled "special agent," just last year a self-aggrandizing senator with her sights set on the White House had been able to discover enough about him and his involvement with the Apex Project to force his resignation. Though it was only temporary, not knowing what his next move would be or what his life might be like with his cover blown was not a very pleasant experience.

He knew that his was a quiet, thankless profession that could only be lived in the shadows, but he was growing very tired of being at the mercy of partisan hacks and career politicians who sought advancement by stomping on the backs of true patriots guilty of nothing more than a deep love for their country.

He was so fed up with all the crap that he'd recently presented his boss, Gary Lawlor, with a .50-caliber bullet wrapped in red tape. The bullet was designed to take out targets at extremely long distances and Lawlor understood that it represented Harvath, who was constantly being sent on missions overseas to take out terrorists. The red tape was self-explanatory.

The job might have been a bit more palatable if it afforded him time to pursue any semblance of a personal life. Most of his buddies, even his former teammates from the SEALs, were pretty much married off and starting families. Though he didn't necessarily want to start one of his own tomorrow, it would be nice to see a point in his not-too-distant future where his career would allow him to. Of course, that presupposed finding a woman who would want to start one with him as well. Most, he found, were unable to put up with the demands of his job, which regularly sounded the death knell in his burgeoning relationships. There'd only been one woman he'd ever been able to see himself actually making a full go of it with. She was even prepared to uproot her life and move to DC to be with him, but in the end, the demands of his job had made it impossible.

The bright side of everything, if you wanted to call it that, was that if he decided to go through with leaving government service, he was not at a loss for job offers from the private sector. In fact there was one job in particular Harvath was thinking very seriously about taking—an instructor position with a world-renowned tactical training center in Colorado called Valhalla. What haunted him, though, was the fear that once he entered the private sector he would no longer be able to look in the mirror and still consider himself a patriot.

That said, it was still a decision he had to make and he knew that it would undoubtedly weigh heavily on his mind over the upcoming holiday weekend.

Rounding a bend in the otherwise deserted country lane, Harvath's attention was drawn to more pressing matters as his vehicle was met by a police roadblock.

A smile began to metastasize across Sayed Jamal's face. The terrorist clearly saw his salvation at hand. No matter who Scot Harvath was and what American agency he worked for, he could not legally take him from Canada against his will. This was about to end up very badly for the United States. The American had been a fool to ever remove him from the trunk. Had he left him there, the man very likely could have driven straight across the border without ever being searched. Sayed knew that it was only a matter of moments now before he would be free and then he would tell every reporter he could find about his terrible ordeal at the hands of the imperialist Americans.

Slowly approaching the roadblock, Harvath kept his cool.

"Can I see your license and registration, please?" asked a machine gun–toting officer in a Royal Canadian Mounted Police uniform when Harvath rolled down his window.

Harvath made a show of patting his pockets and replied, "I was so excited about coming to Canada I must have forgotten to bring them."

The officer looked around the vehicle and then said, "We get that a lot. Who is your passenger?"

"Help me!" screamed Jamal, sensing this was the only chance he was going to get at freedom. "I have been taken against my—" he continued, but was cut off when Harvath slammed his elbow into the man's mouth.

"Don't mind him," said Harvath, well aware that the Royal Mounted Police not only didn't carry machine guns, but also didn't patrol Canada's borders. "He's just a little moody. It's his time of the month."

"Yeah," replied the officer. "I can see the tampons."

"I think he's just nervous about crossing into the States."

"I would be too," said the CSIS agent posing as a Mountie. He then waved for the roadblock vehicles to clear the road and added, "Especially if I'd been responsible for killing and wounding all those American military personnel."

Jamal's bloodied face went pale. *The Canadians were in on it.*

"We just wanted to make sure you got your man," said the agent. "Anything else about the operation we should know?"

"You'll want a team to sweep his apartment. He's got a lot of bombmaking materials in there, but other than that, it was pretty smooth."

"Okay, then," said the man as he tapped the roof of Harvath's car. "Thank you for visiting Canada. Have a safe trip home."

"We will," said Harvath, smiling and giving a little wave as he drove away.

Two kilometers later they came to a small clearing, and Harvath exited the car. Checking their GPS coordinates on his Suunto, he activated the preplanned-route feature, grabbed the Styrofoam cooler from the backseat, and pulled Jamal out of the vehicle, shoving him toward the woods.

Less than half a klick in, they heard a branch snap and Harvath knew they weren't alone. As he looked over his left shoulder, he saw a small team of heavily armed men decked out in digital camouflage materialize from among the trees.

"Welcome to the United States," said one of the men. "Do you have anything to declare?"

"Yes I do," replied Harvath as he offered up Jamal and the cooler with the frozen laptop. "Canada's a fabulous country. Great beer, great people, and they have just started a wonderful terrorist lending program."

The team drove Harvath and Jamal out of the woods to the small town of Rouses Point, New York, where the operation had kicked off and where Harvath's car was waiting.

EIGHT

After a short debrief, a man named Mike Jaffe, who was the lead Joint Terrorism Task Force agent, asked, "So where to now? You going back to DC for the Fourth of July weekend?"

Harvath shook his head. "I'm stopping in New York City to see an old friend who just got back from Afghanistan."

The man smiled and asked, "Where are you going to watch the fireworks from?"

"Probably a bar stool."

"You gotta be kidding me," said Jaffe, the pronounced New York accent unmistakable in his voice. "Let me tell you something. The best place to watch them is in Brooklyn on Furman Avenue between Atlantic and Cadman Plaza."

"I'll keep that in mind."

"And if you're hungry afterwards, go to Lundy Brothers on Emmons Avenue for a real bowl of New York red. Don't miss their egg cream either. They throw in a pretzel for a swizzle stick."

Harvath laughed and shook his head. He had no idea what a bowl of New York red was, much less why it was important that he search out a "real" one. And he'd never had an egg cream in his life. But that was New Yorkers for you. The sun rose and set by their city. Anyplace else in the world was only second best.

"You getting all this?" asked the intense, silver-haired Jaffe, sensing Harvath's mind was wandering. "Or do you want me to write it down for you?"

"I think I got it," replied Harvath. "What about you guys? A weekend in the Catskills before running our pal down to sunny Guantánamo Bay?"

Jaffe laughed. "Actually, we were thinking about stapling all of his indictments to him and stringing him up outside Fort Drum. We figured we could sell tickets at a buck a whack and tell the soldiers he was a Muslim piñata."

Harvath liked the JTTF agent's sense of humor. "You'd probably make a fortune," he responded, knowing that New York's Fort Drum was the home of the 10th Mountain Division Light Infantry and that they'd lost more than their fair share of people in Iraq, especially to IEDs.

"But unfortunately, we don't have time for that," replied Jaffe. "The Bureau wants him down at 26 Federal Plaza in Manhattan today for his initial processing. After that, though, he'll be somebody else's problem."

Harvath didn't envy the people who would have to spend the holiday weekend away from their families and friends while they interrogated Sayed Jamal, but that was how the business worked and Harvath knew it all too well. America couldn't afford to take a day off from its fight on terrorism, not even on the anniversary of its independence. The bad guys were always working; always probing for another soft spot they could exploit, and America had to remain one step ahead.

As Harvath watched Jaffe walk away to join his men, he lamented the immutable fact that no matter how hard it tried, the United States would never be able to be on top of everything. This time, just like so many times before, they'd gotten lucky. That was it. Though they'd pulled a rather big player off the field, there were innumerable second-stringers standing in the shadows ready to take his place.

For all of the setbacks the enemy had supposedly suffered, their roster of fresh bodies seemed to roll on without end.

And the one unspoken truth that every American involved in the war on terror knew was that it wasn't a matter of *if* the terrorists would hit us again, it was only a matter of *when*.

Harvath prayed that he would never see that day, because he knew that when it came, it would make 9/11 look like choir practice.

NINE

New York City

The drive from Rouses Point to Manhattan normally took five and a half hours, but with the help of a thermos full of coffee, a heavy foot, and George Clinton and Parliament, Harvath made it in four.

With the sunroof open, the windows rolled down, and "Tear the Roof Off the Sucker" pumping from the speakers of his black Chevy TrailBlazer, Harvath rumbled across the George Washington Bridge toward Manhattan a little after 2:00 PM. As he took in the skyline and watched the tidal wave of fleeing holiday traffic, the weather couldn't have been better—low eighties, bright sunshine, and only a trace of humidity. It was going to be a perfect weekend.

An hour outside the city, Harvath had phoned his pal, recently retired Delta Force operative Robert Herrington—better known to his friends as "Bullet Bob"—and established a rendezvous point for their meeting.

Because Bob was still wrapping things up at the Manhattan VA, they decided to meet at one of Harvath's favorite pubs near Times Square called the Pig & Whistle, where they'd begin the first leg of their bar-hopping Alcoholics Unanimous meeting.

After driving around the neighborhood for twenty minutes, Harvath settled on the cheapest garage he had seen, agreed to hand over his first born, three pints of blood, and a vital organ to be named at a later date as payment, and then walked four blocks over to the Pig.

Inside, the staff and the customers were glued to TV sets. Harvath grabbed a seat at the bar, ordered a pint of Bare Knuckle Stout, and tried to piece together what was happening.

The stations were covering a hostage standoff at a grade school in the Bronx. *What a way to start the Fourth of July weekend,* thought Harvath as he ordered a late lunch and tried to forget about the world and its problems for a while.

His mind drifted to the first time he and Bob Herrington had met. They'd been assigned to a unique Joint Special Operations program training the special forces of an allied South American country. The soldiers' final task at the end of the training was to show off their new skills in a series of high-end exercises culminating with them assembling on a mountain plateau where the country's president, its top generals, and other assorted VIPs were sitting in a reviewing stand. The catch was that it had to be done in a very tight time frame.

Though the soldiers were performing better than any of their American instructors thought they would, once they hit the run up the steep mountain face, it was obvious they weren't going to make it up to the parade ground by the specified time. So what did Bob do? Once they arrived at the base of the mountain and were out of sight of the reviewing stand, he gathered up all the soldiers' rifles, strapped them to his pack, and ran ahead of them.

For his part, Harvath couldn't understand what Herrington was doing. Just below the plateau, he stopped and then handed a rifle to each one of the soldiers as they passed. Up on the parade ground, there were several moments of confusion as the soldiers traded rifles back and forth until each was with its rightful owner. As Harvath walked to the edge of the parade ground, he saw Bob smiling, and it was at that moment that he learned his greatest lesson about leadership—the only thing that matters is that your team achieve its objective together. How that happens is immaterial as long as you all cross the finish line together.

Bob could have taken credit for the soldiers' success, but that wasn't his style. He was happy just to see them succeed. Harvath had liked Bob from the minute he met him, but on that dusty parade ground in South

America, he had developed a real respect for him and that respect had turned into a friendship that transcended the years and more than a few assignments together. In fact, Harvath often joked that Bob had become the older brother he never wanted.

Forty-five minutes later, Harvath was about to order another beer, when Bullet Bob materialized out of thin air and slapped a Joint Special Operations Task Force coin down on the bar. The rule was that if you and a colleague had both been given the same coin for an operation or a team you'd been on and you didn't have your coin with you, you were responsible for buying the round. If you did have it, then the man who issued the challenge had to pick up that round. Harvath was way ahead of his old friend. Reaching down, he lifted his cocktail napkin and revealed his coin.

After asking if there was any Louis XIII Cognac in the house, Harvath shook his buddy's hand. "Nice try, my friend," he said, careful of Bob's injured shoulder.

"You win some, you lose some," replied Herrington, who was at least three inches taller than Harvath and a bit broader in the chest. His similarly colored brown hair was cut neat, but he still sported his *go native* Afghanistan beard. His narrow green eyes took in everybody and everything in the room. Turning to the bartender, Herrington said, "Bring us another round of whatever he's drinking and make mine a double."

"He's having a pint of stout, love," the Irish barkeep said flirtatiously.

Bob smiled his most charming smile and replied, "Then bring me two of them. I don't like the fact that this guy's got a head start on me."

The woman rolled her eyes as she went in search of three new glasses.

"I think she likes you," said Harvath once the woman was out of earshot.

"Hearts and minds. It's what I'm all about."

Harvath laughed. It was nice to see Bob in reasonably good spirits. Under the smile and devil-may-care attitude, though, he knew the man was not taking his forced retirement well. That was a big part of why Harvath was spending the Fourth of July weekend in New York City.

The other part was because at present, he didn't have a solid relationship with anyone worth spending the weekend with. The only woman Harvath could have seen himself with was otherwise engaged, quite literally, and on her way to marrying someone else.

As if he could read minds, Bob wasted no time in asking, "So, how's Meg?"

Harvath knew the subject was bound to come up. Both he and Bob had been part of a hostage rescue team that had freed Meg Cassidy from a hijacked airliner just a few years prior. Because Meg had been the only one to see the key hijacker's face, she had been recruited to help track and ID him for termination. A good part of her training for the assignment had taken place *behind the fence,* as it was known, with Bob and several of his colleagues at the Delta Force compound at Fort Bragg. "This time next year, you and I'll probably be attending her wedding," said Harvath.

"You've gotta be one of the dumbest people I've ever met, you know that?"

"Good to see you too, Robert," replied Harvath as the bartender returned with their beers and set one in front of Harvath and two in front of Bob.

After she walked away to take care of another customer, Bob said, "Meg Cassidy is hands down the best woman I've ever seen you with and you let her slip right through your fingers."

"It's complicated."

"She's a woman," said Bob as he took a sip of his stout and let his response hang in the air between them. "They're always complicated."

It was a subject Harvath really had no desire to get into. "It's over, okay?"

"It's okay with me if it's okay with you."

"It's okay with me," said Harvath centering his beer on its coaster.

"So who are you dating now?" asked Bob.

"Nobody."

Herrington smiled, "So then you're not *really* okay and its not *really* over, is it?"

"Give me a break, would you?"

"At least tell me you're gay. SEAL or no SEAL, you were in the Navy, after all. Being gay comes with the territory for you squids. What do they say? *When you're under way, gay is okay?"*

"Fuck you," replied Harvath, who then added, "You know if at any point you want to pull that excessively large nose of yours out of my personal life, I'd be more than happy to discuss what happened in Afghanistan."

This time, it was Bob's turn to be silent. Though he hadn't meant to, Harvath had dragged a piece of sandpaper over a very raw nerve.

When Herrington finally spoke he said, "How many men did you lose when the president was kidnapped?"

"Too many."

"Yeah," said Bob, nodding his head knowingly. "It sucks. But you know what can be worse?"

Harvath shook his head.

"Having men under your command seriously maimed and in constant pain. That's worse than seeing them die. At least when they're dead, they're not in anguish anymore."

Harvath signaled the bartender to bring him another round and said, "What happened in Afghanistan?"

Bob waited until Harvath had his beer and after a little more prodding responded, "We were tasked with taking down a target near Herat. Somehow, they must have known we were coming, because they hit us first and hit us hard—real hard."

"We had a guy attached to our unit who'd messed up his ankle and I was helping hump his load. I should have seen that ambush coming, but I couldn't. I wasn't on point. I was the third guy in the column, making my way back up to the lead when it happened. The two guys in front got it real bad. I got off easy compared to them, but it doesn't matter. Because of me, all three of us were handed medical retirements."

"You think this is all because you weren't on point?"

"A team leader leads, period."

"That's bullshit, Bob, and you know it," said Harvath. "Nobody can be on point all the time, not even you. That's why the position gets rotated."

"But it was my turn to be up front."

"Yet you were humping the pack of an injured man. You can't do both."

"Not anymore, apparently."

"Shit happens, Bob."

"Not to me it doesn't and not to *my* team. We hadn't even had so much as a hangnail in almost two years and then *bang,* three of us are out. One of my guys will never walk again, will never be able to make love to his wife, and the other one's blind. He'll never be able to watch his kids grow up. All of this because I wasn't up front when I should have been."

Harvath knew Bob pretty well and he knew his reputation firsthand. In fact, most people in the Special Operations community knew it. Bob could carry an entire battalion on his back. He was an incredible athlete, and that athleticism made one of the best soldiers the United States had ever created. Since the day he'd joined the Army right out of high school, through his time as a Ranger and into 7th Group and then Delta, Bob had always led the way. It wasn't an ego thing, it was just Bob—you couldn't hold him back.

The fact that he was taking the injuries of his teammates so personally was not surprising to Harvath. That was also the kind of guy Bob was. It was the way most American soldiers were. Truth, freedom, and the American way played well for the cameras, but the fact of the matter was that in the frenzied heat of combat, you weren't fighting for your country, you were fighting for the guy right next to you.

Looking his friend in the eyes, Harvath tried to assuage some of the man's guilt by repeating, "Bob, shit happens."

"Yeah, maybe. But, it's not the way I wanted to go out," replied Herrington as he paused and took a long swallow of beer. "I wanted to go out on top. I would've liked just one more chance to prove not only to my team, but to myself that I could still do it—that what happened had nothing to do with me getting old, too slow."

Harvath was not going to let this become the tone for the entire weekend. Bob needed to snap the hell out of it. "You and your team competed in how many triathlons when you were home last year?"

"Two."

"And the worst showing you had?"

"Fifth place."

Harvath pretended to think about it for a moment and then responded, "You know, I think it probably was a good idea for the Army to cut you loose after all. I mean, only two top-ten international finishes? You're obviously on a downhill slide."

Bob wasn't looking at him, but Harvath could see the faint traces of a smile form on his face and he decided to push the humor a little further. "Jesus Christ, Bob, you're forty years old. Someone oughtta be fitting you for false teeth and a new hip, not giving you a gun and sending you out on this nation's most dangerous assignments. That's what us young guys are for."

Herrington's smile now spread from ear to ear. "First of all, you're only four years younger than I am, and second, SEAL or no SEAL, I could whip your ass in a New York minute, so don't get cocky. You'd have a hell of a time meeting women this weekend if I end up dotting both of your eyes for you."

Harvath was about to suggest Bob abandon the commando motto of silent, swift, and deadly in favor of senile, slow, and deaf, when Herrington looked up at the television and said, "That's not good."

Harvath looked up and noticed that several NYPD Emergency Services Unit trucks had gathered at the site of the Bronx school standoff.

"The ESU normally turns out in smaller trucks. Two per squad," continued Herrington. "Those big rigs are their rolling armories. They don't move those in unless the situation is really bad. I count at least four up there. That means four squads responding. This is no run-of-the-mill hostage situation."

Harvath knew that outside the military, the NYPD's ESU was not only the largest full-time SWAT response group in the country, but also one of its absolute best. And while they were all brothers in arms, each squad preferred to work alone and only called in backup when it was absolutely necessary. Scenes of the Beslan school massacre in Russia began to race through Harvath's mind. A school was a perfect terrorist target and an attack on one would have an unbelievable impact here in the States. Harvath often wondered why a terrorist group hadn't tried it yet. The media coverage, as well as the communal American heartache would be off the charts.

He was about to mention this to Bob, when one of the TV anchors cut in with two additional breaking news stories—a fire at New York City mayor David Brown's Emergency Operations Command Center in Brooklyn and a sniper targeting aircraft out at LaGuardia in Queens.

After listening to the reports, Herrington shook his head. "If I didn't know better, I'd think that somebody was skimming the cream. That school standoff in the Bronx has got to be one hell of an assault to get that many ESU squads there."

"Just like Beslan," said Harvath.

"For all we know," Bob continued, "more squads are already en route. Then there's the airport. They've got that place so gridded out they know every rooftop, draw, and grassy knoll within a two-mile radius that could accommodate a shooter. Anyone able to get inside that perimeter and stir up this kind of trouble has got to be a pro."

"Or this all might be just one really shitty day in New York."

"I don't know."

"C'mon, Bob. Why would somebody want to tie up all those tactical teams?"

At that moment, the TV station cut back to footage of the raging fire at the mayor's Emergency Operations Command Center beneath the Brooklyn Bridge, and Herrington replied, "Maybe for the same reason somebody would want to take out the city's backup command-and-control facility."

"You don't seriously think this is part of some larger attack, do you?" asked Harvath.

"Who knows? But if you don't mind, I'd rather not be sitting in a bar in the middle of Times Square if it happens."

TEN

Despite both the air-conditioning and the antiperspirant his handler had insisted he wear, Nassir Hamal's purple Polo shirt clung to his sweat-covered body. All of the martyrs had been offered drugs—Valium, to be specific—in order to help them remain calm when the time came. The mullah from the mosque in New Jersey who had counseled them had assured them that taking the drugs would in no way jeopardize their entry into paradise. Though several of the others accepted the offer and tested the pills in advance to gauge their effects, Nassir had refused. He was confident that when the time came, he would meet his end with a heart made strong by his love of Islam. But now, as Nassir sat in the interminable traffic along 64th Street with nothing but his thoughts and a broken FM radio to keep him company, he wasn't so sure.

Looking at the cell phone on the seat beside him, he considered calling his handler, but then decided against it. They had stayed up all night together praying, reading verses from the Koran and talking about paradise as the others slept. His handler had become almost like an older brother to him, confiding in the younger man that the Prophet Mohammed himself, may peace be upon Him, had visited the handler in his sleep and had instructed him that Nassir be given one of the most important and most difficult of the assignments. It was an honor that Nassir accepted with the utmost sincerity and obligation to duty.

Though he had not been allowed to say a proper good-bye to his mother and sister, both of whom had immigrated to the United States with him ten years prior, he hoped they would understand. He also hoped they would appreciate the annuity his handler had said each of the families of the martyrs would be receiving. Islam took care of its own—an attribute Nassir saw sorely lacking in the culture of the West.

Regardless of how his family felt, in his heart Nassir knew he was doing the right thing. When he had been approached in his mosque on the north side of Chicago and asked if he wanted to study with a very wise and learned Imam visiting the city, Nassir had jumped at the chance. Disenchanted with a failed business, a failed marriage, and what he saw as his downtrodden American existence, he had looked everywhere until he found the one thing that filled the emptiness inside him—Islam.

In time, he had thrown out his record collection, had stopped smoking, and was chastising his younger sister on a daily basis about the evils of dancing, the type of friends she associated herself with, and the revealing American clothes she wore. One day, she finally worked up the nerve to suggest that if he didn't like America and its ways, then maybe he should go back to their home country. Nassir had seriously considered it, had even saved for a plane ticket and made arrangements to stay with extended family once he got back, but then the Imam had come into his life. After they had gotten to know each other he had suggested another idea—one that would require him to place the greater glory of Allah above his own self-pity and self-serving desires.

As the traffic started moving again, Nassir swung the counterfeit FedEx van onto Third Avenue and headed south. A few blocks later, he saw his target. Without even thinking, he began reciting the special verses from the Koran that all of his fellow martyrs had been given to provide strength and courage for the moments ahead—the last moments any of them would ever know.

ELEVEN

It was 4:30 now and out on the street, most people were oblivious to anything but getting started with their holiday weekend. As he and Herrington walked away from Times Square, Harvath tried to make sense of what they were doing. A healthy bit of paranoia was a prerequisite in their business, but at what point did it become too much? The rational side of Harvath's brain said leaving a perfectly well-stocked bar and an above-average looking bartender was that point, but his gut said Bob might be right on the money.

"Where are we going?" he asked.

Pointing south down Broadway, Bob said, "Times Square has gotta be pretty high on the terrorist hit parade. I know a good restaurant not far from the VA. Let's go there."

"The VA? You've spent enough time there as it is. Don't you get sick of being anywhere near there?"

"You'd be surprised. It's not your grandfather's VA anymore, Scot. They've come a long way."

"Sterilize the instruments and everything now, do they?"

"Even better, if they amputate a limb, you get two bullets instead of one to bite on."

At least Bob hadn't lost his sense of humor. "What about my truck?" asked Harvath.

Seeing a cab that had just dropped off its fare, Herrington made a beeline for it and said, "Leave it. We'll come back and pick it up later."

As they drove, Harvath looked out the window at the hordes of people crowding the sidewalks, and his mind wandered back to the news reports they'd been watching in the Pig & Whistle. Taken as isolated incidents, the events unfolding just outside Manhattan were indeed serious, though nothing to panic about. But when you lumped them together as a whole, they were just too coincidental—and coincidences were something neither Scot Harvath nor Bob Herrington believed in. In fact, no one in their line of work did. They had been taught to always try to connect the dots and look for a bigger picture.

Even though he was supposed to be on vacation relaxing, Harvath couldn't stop thinking about what Bob had said and so repeated his earlier question. "Let's say you're right about what's going on across the river. Why do you think someone would want to tie up all of those tactical teams?"

"I can think of about a million answers," replied Bob as he eyeballed a graffiti-covered truck idling outside a nearby bank, "and none of them have a happy ending."

"But if you break this down into its simplest parts, the reason you'd want to tie up tactical teams is to prevent them from interfering with your objective or your egress, right?"

As their cab sped up, Bob's eyes moved to a group of taxi drivers who had double-parked near a falafel stand and were chatting animatedly to one another. "So?"

"So if you were a suicide bomber or were going to fly a plane into a building, you wouldn't care about tactical teams. By the time they knew what you were doing, theoretically it would be too late."

"It depends on what you were doing. What if you weren't a suicide bomber or planning on flying a plane into a building? What if you had other plans?"

Harvath looked back out his window and asked, "Like what?"

"I don't know," replied Herrington. "I just saw all that stuff happening on TV and it gave one of those *uh-oh* feelings."

"Old habits are hard to break."

Bob smiled.

"That's better," said Harvath as he decided to change the subject.

They were both a little too on edge. "Now, am I going to be able to get that shot of Louis XIII you owe me at this place we're going?"

"Probably not. For that we'll need to find you some high-end gay bar. But maybe there'll be some cute Navy guys there you can hook up with."

Harvath gave his friend the finger and Bob laughed.

Below 34th Street the traffic began to back up and Herrington started giving the driver directions.

Fifteen minutes later, as they crawled down 28th, the cab's radio erupted with terrified voices shouting in a language neither Harvath nor Herrington understood.

When Scot asked what was happening, the driver stammered, "The Queensboro Bridge!"

"What about it?"

"It just exploded!"

TWELVE

Long Island Expressway

Tim and Marcy didn't mind driving the girls into the city. In fact, they actually preferred it. This way, the girls could have a few drinks and not have to worry about who was driving home.

As they drove, they could see that the five-o'clock traffic coming out of Manhattan was bumper-to-bumper as people fled to places like Fire Island, the Hamptons, and Montauk Point. Tim looked over at Marcy, and she could immediately read his mind. "Thank God we won't have to be sitting in that," she said.

The girls had given them the entire rundown on what they planned to do. First they were going to hit SoHo for shopping and then meet up later with some of their friends for dinner at a trendy new restaurant in Chelsea. After that, there was a hot new club in Midtown they wanted to hit, but they didn't want to be there too early. Heaven forbid they be the first ones there. So, it had been decided that if upon the initial drive-by there wasn't already a line in front, they'd kill time at a spot they all liked on 56th called Town. They'd have a glass or two of wine and then try the club again later.

Though Marcy had been cool about letting the girls listen to whatever they liked in the car, she facetiously begged five minutes of forgiveness as she changed the radio over to WCBS to get a local read on traffic. She wasn't a worrier by nature, but with what was going on in the Bronx, Brooklyn, and Queens, Marcy wanted to make extra sure they were steering well clear of any potential tie-ups.

According to WCBS, it looked like smooth sailing down to the Williamsburg Bridge and across into lower Manhattan, so Marcy switched the radio back to Power 105 and focused on the drive.

The girls laughed, gossiped, and lamented their last summer of real freedom before graduating from Yale—all the while acting as if the two adults sitting up front weren't even there. That was okay with Tim and Marcy. They were more than used to being ignored.

When they hit the Williamsburg Bridge, traffic began to tighten up. Marcy put up with it for as long as she could, but it was maddening. Once she had enough space to slide over into the left lane, she signaled and made her move. About six car lengths later she could see why traffic was moving so slowly. An ugly, paper-bag brown utility truck labeled *Birchman Landscaping* was going at least fifteen miles an hour below the speed limit while everyone else was trying to do at least twenty over.

Marcy rolled her eyes at Tim and he responded, "Don't even say it."

"Just watch," replied Marcy as she pulled alongside the truck.

Sitting inside were two dark-skinned males. *Probably Mexicans.*

"I told you," she said.

"Give it a rest, Marcy. It takes all kinds to make up the world."

"I know it does. The Germans are the fast drivers. The Italians the crazy ones, and the Mexicans are the slow ones."

"I resent that," replied Tim. "I'm Italian."

"And that's why I'm driving. I rest my case."

Tim smiled. Marcy would never change. "I'll tell you what," he said. "That truck's got to be the ugliest color I've ever seen."

"You'd think landscapers would be a little more creative, wouldn't you?"

"Paint some flowers on that thing, or something."

Now it was Marcy's turn to smile. Sometimes she thought Tim had missed his calling in life. He really was pretty artistic. Although she figured that must come with being Italian. Caravaggio, da Vinci, Michelangelo . . . all Italians.

"Oh, check this out," Tim added. "You work for Birchman and you not only get an ugly truck and matching uniforms, but they give you matching watches as well."

Marcy looked out the passenger-side window and saw the men looking at their watches. "They must be late for their next appointment. That's why they're in such a hurry."

Tim stifled a chuckle. He couldn't help it. Though Marcy was often a little too off-color for his taste, she could be pretty funny. It used to bother him, but they'd been together for so long now that he'd come to accept it as part of who she was.

Marcy pressed down on the accelerator and as she passed the landscaping truck said, "How do you like that?"

Tim leaned forward, trying to see what she was looking at out her window. "What?"

"There's another one of those landscaping trucks stuck in traffic the other way."

"Where?"

"We just passed it."

"Boy, would I like to have a piece of that action. Their trucks are everywhere."

"And at this time of year they must be making a killing."

Moments later, an enormous explosion detonated behind them. The girls screamed as the windows shattered and Marcy lost control of the SUV. There was the horrible, wrenching sound of metal on metal, followed by a deafening crash as everything went black.

THIRTEEN

Lake Geneva, Wisconsin

Jack Rutledge had always been of the mind that pilots and presidents shouldn't be seen drinking; at least not in the afternoon. There was something too unnerving about it. So even though he would have enjoyed a nice vodka and tonic right about now, and despite the fact that he was technically on vacation, he stuck to his Arnold Palmers.

As he sipped his half lemonade, half iced tea, he reflected that there were few places in the United States he enjoyed as much as Lake Geneva. He couldn't understand why he hadn't discovered it sooner. His old college roommate, Rodger Cummings, a successful real estate developer from Chicago, had bought a home here three years ago and already the president had been to visit six times. It had been his retreat during the rigorous campaign—the place he came for a day or two of rest to get away from it all, and continued to be his preferred getaway; more so than even Camp David.

The area was referred to as the Hamptons of the Midwest and though it was an extremely beautiful place to visit in the summer, the president found that there really was no bad time to visit.

His love of Lake Geneva was a bit ironic as just across the lake from where he now stood was the home of the deceased industrialist, Donald Fawcett, who had orchestrated his kidnap several years ago. It was also the home in which two United States senators who had conspired with Fawcett had met a very grisly end.

Watching the sailboats and assorted pleasure craft crisscrossing the lake, the president was glad he'd taken his old roommate up on his most recent invitation. There was something instantly soothing about arriving here. The lake seemed to have a profound effect on him and allowed him to put the cares and concerns of being the leader of the free world on hold as he focused simply on being Jack Rutledge the man.

He had brought along a stack of novels that he couldn't wait to dive into. Unfortunately, he wouldn't be able to do that until tomorrow, after the daily presidential briefing that happened every morning, no matter where in the world he was. Right now, though, he had to "sing" for his supper, as his old friend had put it. It was just a small gathering. Only about fifty people, many of whom, thanks to Cummings's fundraising prowess, had been major contributors to his recent presidential campaign. Cocktails and light hors d'oeuvres and then he was off the hook. Then he could really relax for the next three days.

The only thing that would have made the holiday weekend perfect was if his daughter Amanda had been there with him, but it was summertime, she was growing up, and she had friends of her own.

Knowing the president would be tired, Rodger had been kind enough to start the party early. The brilliant white pier in front of the large house, which had once belonged to an Illinois railroad tycoon, jutted out into the warm, spring-fed waters of the lake. It had been tastefully decorated by Mrs. Cummings with fresh flowers, potted palms, and small wicker lanterns. The guests stood talking on the end of the pier near a group of bright blue Adirondack chairs as well as on the expansive aft deck of the estate's magnificent sixty-foot 1915 steamship, the *Jolly Rodger.*

Rutledge made it a point to invite Meg Cassidy, who was also a Chicago resident and Lake Geneva homeowner, to the estate whenever he came to town. Meg had done a particularly significant service to her country when, as a civilian, she had agreed to help track down one of the world's most dangerous terrorists. Without her ability to ID the faceless terrorist, the United States might never have stopped him.

Meg brought along her new fiancé, and while he seemed a decent enough man, he definitely didn't have the charisma of Scot Harvath.

The president had always been sorry that the two of them hadn't been able to work things out. They still seemed perfectly suited for each other, but with the demands of both of their careers, he also saw that their breakup just might have been inevitable.

The trio was enjoying a pleasant conversation when the head of the president's security detail, Carolyn Leonard, discreetly approached. She apologized for the interruption and then whispered into the president's ear. Immediately, Rutledge's entire body stiffened.

"I'm sorry," he said, shaking first Meg's hand and then her fiancé's. "A situation has come up and I have to leave."

"I hope it's not serious," said Meg, but the president had already been joined by several more agents from his Secret Service detail and was being escorted off the *Jolly Rodger.*

"What's going on, Carolyn?" asked Rutledge as he looked over and saw the wet-suited SEAL Team that augmented his maritime activities surface with their weapons at the ready.

"New York has been hit," replied Leonard.

"What do you mean, *hit*?"

"I have very few details at this point, Mr. President. I think it would be better if your own people briefed you on that once we're in the air."

Rutledge didn't want to wait until they were in the air. He wanted answers now, especially considering the fact that his daughter was spending the holiday weekend with friends on Long Island. But as he turned to put the question of Amanda's well-being to his chief Secret Service agent, the rotors of his rapidly approaching helicopter quickly made talking impossible.

FOURTEEN

New York City

With traffic at an absolute standstill, Harvath threw twenty bucks onto the front seat of the cab, and he and Bob jumped out.

According to Herrington, they were only about six blocks away from the VA, and so they decided to make that their destination.

In every bar and restaurant they ran past, people were glued to the televisions and scenes of the devastating explosion on the Queensboro Bridge.

When they arrived at the VA, the lobby was in chaos. Everyone, including the VA police, was huddled around the television sets. Bob led Harvath through the crowd and upstairs to the office of Dr. Sam Hardy. Hardy was in his late forties, tall and fit. He was balding and had a look in his eyes that suggested he'd been around the block more than a few times.

Hardy looked up from the TV set on his desk when Harvath and Herrington entered and said to Bob, "It looks like multiple attacks."

"Multiple?" asked Harvath as Bob introduced him to Dr. Hardy. "We just heard about the Queensboro Bridge. There have been more?"

Hardy nodded his head. "The reports are just starting to come in, but it looks like all of the bridges and all of the tunnels into and out of Manhattan have been hit."

Harvath was at a loss for words. He stood there with his mouth agape as they watched the television on Hardy's desk. Finally, he stated, "I guess now maybe we know why they wanted to draw off the tactical teams."

"And why they wanted to take out the Emergency Operations Center," added Bob as he turned to Hardy and asked, "Have you heard from anybody else?"

"No," replied Hardy, "but I think they'll start showing up here real soon."

"Who are you talking about?" Harvath asked.

Herrington ignored him and said to Hardy, "Can I borrow your keycard?"

"What for?"

"I want to take Scot up to the roof and get a look at what's going on."

"I'll go with you," said the doctor. "I want to get a look too. Let me just leave a note in case anyone comes by while we're up there."

Up on the roof, they could see enormous clouds of smoke coming from the direction of the Queensboro as well as several other points around the city. Down on the street, people were in a panic, many of them sprinting down 23rd Street toward the East River, presumably so that they could get a better view of what had happened to the Queensboro and Williamsburg bridges.

For what seemed like an eternity, no one on the roof spoke. They were dumbfounded as they stood there taking in the horror and devastation.

"Bridges and tunnels," Harvath finally said, "and at the beginning of one of our busiest holiday weekends. How many dead are we going to be looking at? Thousands? Tens of thousands?"

"At least," replied Dr. Hardy, shaking his head. "At least."

As they stood taking it in, not one of them needed to draw the parallel to that warm September morning in 2001 when a handful of hijackers brought the Twin Towers crashing to the ground. They were all feeling the same thing—the fear, the confusion, and finally the bitter anger that the enemies of America had once again been able to rain such death and destruction down on so many innocent people.

"Al-Qaeda," Bob said, almost beneath his breath.

Harvath knew he was right. The attacks had al-Qaeda's fingerprints all over them. Distract and then flank with multiple coordinated attacks. It was ripped right from their playbook. Harvath's thoughts of leaving government service and going into the private sector suddenly seemed much less pressing. What he wanted at this point more than anything else was justice—a shot to get even, and he knew that Bob Herrington felt exactly the same way.

As they stood watching plumes of gray-black smoke twist into the late afternoon sky, the roof door slammed open and three figures emerged. They were just as Bob had described them in his e-mails and Harvath had no problem recognizing them.

"Are you all okay?" asked Hardy as the newcomers approached.

"They hit everything!" exclaimed Paul Morgan, a dark-haired, twenty-four-year-old who stood about five feet eleven. His preppy outfit of neatly pressed khakis and a crisp linen shirt stood in sharp contrast to the heavy Bronx accent he had grown up with. When Morgan said the word *everything,* it came out *ever-ree-ting.* "Every bridge and every tunnel, doc. They nailed them all."

"We don't know exactly what they've hit, Paul. Let's just calm down here," replied Hardy.

"Morgan's right, Doc," said Tracy Hastings, a twenty-six-year-old woman whose blond hair was braided into two pigtails. It was a look Harvath had always liked. Pigtails were for little girls, but when big girls wore them there was something sexy as hell about it. And just as Bob had said, Hastings was in incredible shape. She was obsessed with working out and she had sculpted her five-foot-seven-inch frame into a work of art. Normally, Harvath was not drawn to women who were as buff or maybe even more so than he was, but there was something very attractive about her that he just couldn't put his finger on. Tracy must have noticed Harvath looking her over because she turned her face away as she continued, "It's all over the TV. They hit every bridge and every tunnel—some of them more than once."

"Redundancy," added Rick Cates, the third and final member of their party. He stood at least six feet three inches tall, with dark eyes, a shaved head and a T-shirt that read *Guns don't kill people. I kill people.* "This is the exact attack we've all been talking about," he added with a look on his face that mirrored the mix of rage and frustration that they were all feeling.

Hardy tried to calm them down. "We don't know what's going on, so let's just take a deep breath, okay?"

"Every bridge into and out of Manhattan has been blown," insisted Hastings, "and you want us to just calm down?"

"Yes," replied Hardy. "Everybody just stop a second."

Harvath didn't understand what the doctor's connection with them was, but they all seemed to listen to him, including Herrington. After the moment of forced silence, Hardy formally introduced Corporal Paul Morgan, United States Marine Corps; Lieutenant Tracy Hastings, United States Navy; and Sergeant Rick Cates, United States Army.

As Harvath finished shaking hands, a blue-and-white NYPD Bell 412 EP helicopter roared right past the rooftop. It was so close that through the open cabin door they could see an NYPD sniper armed with one of the department's high-end .50-caliber rifles, which was capable of taking out targets over a mile away.

"Hoo-rah!" bellowed Morgan as he pumped his fist in the air. "Go get those fuckers!"

Like spectators in a one-way tennis match, all their heads swung northward to watch the chopper as it raced up the East River toward the smoldering Queensboro Bridge. Whether there'd be anybody left worth getting once they got there was anybody's guess, but as soldiers, they all appreciated the sight of fellow warriors going into battle, especially ones with an immediate opportunity to avenge an egregious wrong so in need of righting.

The helicopter was out over the middle of the East River, rapidly closing the distance to the bridge, when a white contrail of smoke suddenly appeared in the sky. Cates was the first one to process what they were seeing and as if the pilot of the chopper had any chance of hearing him he yelled, "RPG!"

FIFTEEN

Abdul Ali didn't need to hear the explosion to know that it had happened. He had almost a sixth sense for these things, especially when working with such highly trained soldiers. The Chechens were exceptional and had been an inspired choice. With their hair cut short and their faces clean-shaven, they drew much less attention than Arabs would have. Though they were the most expensive element of the operation, their Russian Spetsnaz special forces training was worth every penny. So far, the Troll had proven to know exactly what he was doing.

While Ali had been concerned with using only two specific subterfuges to detonate the bridges and tunnels, the Troll's plan to use fake landscaping trucks as well as vans disguised as Federal Express vehicles had worked. Even if one of them had been selected for a random police inspection, bags of fertilizer would not seem out of place for a landscaping business and no NYPD or Port Authority officer would have had the audacity to open any of the FedEx packages—unless they suspected one of the drivers, but Ali had selected only his best operatives for this most important of martyrdom operations. They had spent their last evening on earth shaving the hair from their bodies, reading the Koran, and ritually cleansing themselves for their entrance into paradise. Even the handful he had worried about losing their nerve had carried out their assignments perfectly. His martyrs had served both him and Allah well.

Based on what they were hearing over the radio, their efforts to make all of the bridges and tunnels, including those used for the subway and PATH trains, impassable had exceeded even Ali's best expectations. Random sniper and rocket-propelled-grenade fire would now bring all helicopter, airplane, boat, and ferry traffic above and around Manhattan to a standstill. All law enforcement and emergency services personnel would now be totally engaged, and it would be some time before they could be reinforced, which was exactly what the terrorists wanted. Allah had blessed their entire undertaking.

Their two black SUVs with tinted windows and visor-mounted police strobe lights purchased over the Internet now roared up onto the sidewalk in front of a brownstone on West 84th Street. A brass plaque in front read *Transcon Enterprises.* With enviable military precision, the heavily armed and armored occupants of the two Tahoes poured out and took up defensive firing positions. From their boots to their balaclavas, they were clad completely in black, except for the large patches they wore on their uniforms falsely identifying them as members of the FBI's Hostage Rescue Team, or HRT for short.

As half of the team raced to secure the side entrance, the rest dashed up the front steps, disabled the video surveillance cameras and affixed a large plastic explosive shape charge to the front door. Yelling a warning to the others, the men in front took cover and detonated the plastique. Their colleagues at the side entrance did the same, and with an assortment of fully automatic weapons up and at the ready, they all poured into the building.

Though the gray-haired, chain-smoking receptionist inside immediately went for her Beretta subcompact, she wasn't fast enough. Bullets tore through her body as half of the tactical team made a sweep through the lobby and the others fanned out over the rest of the three-story building.

They eliminated every Transcon employee they saw—both the men and women, many of whom poured out of offices and cubicles brandishing pistols and even a couple of short-barreled machine guns.

Less than four minutes after the killing began, the team's weapons fell silent. A fog of cordite hung in the air. Ali removed his balaclava and radioed his men. As their situation reports came in, none contained the response he wanted to hear. There was no sign of Mohammed bin Mohammed anywhere in the building. As one of the men placed the electronic devices the Troll had explained would make the Americans believe each facility was still functioning, Ali quietly cursed and looked at his watch. Reloading his weapon, he tried to compute how long it would take to make it to Midtown.

SIXTEEN

Rooftop
309 East 48th Street

"What do you mean, you *can't* get a helicopter in here?" demanded Mike Jaffe as he gripped his encrypted satellite phone so tight it threatened to crack. "That's bullshit. I'm telling you right now, if you don't find a way, then our angel's feet are going to end up touching the ground."

Jaffe listened for several moments to the yelling on the other end of his phone and replied, "Negative. They can come in black after nightfall and lift us out. If not, I'm going to make other arrangements. Do we understand each other?" With that, Jaffe hung up and tossed the sat phone to his number two in command, a tall, ruggedly built, twenty-five-year-old Marine sergeant named Brad Harper.

"No go on the evac?" asked Harper as he tucked the sat phone into the back pocket of his jeans.

"Apparently, they're not yet one hundred percent convinced that the attacks are connected to our pal downstairs."

"You've got to be kidding me. They're the ones who informed us about the intercept in the first place. Al-Qaeda knows he's here."

"They know he's in New York, we don't know that they know he's in this building."

"So what are we supposed to do?"

"For the time being we stay put. An NYPD helicopter was just brought down by sniper fire, so now the air space above Manhattan is officially frozen until further notice."

"Let's go out by water."

Jaffe shook his head. "NYPD, Port Authority, and Coast Guard craft have all come under heavy-caliber sniper fire as well on both the East River and the Hudson. They've also been ordered to pull back until further notice."

"Then we're not going to get any reinforcements."

"It doesn't look like it."

"So what's the plan?"

"We run this just the way we rehearsed it," replied Jaffe. "Full battle dress and weld the doors shut on our floor."

"And then?"

Jaffe looked at Harper and said, "And then we turn up the heat on our prisoner and get the information we need out of him before it's too late."

SEVENTEEN

When Harvath's BlackBerry rang, he was still in a state of shock. Though nearly every civilian in New York City would find it impossible to use their cell phone at this moment because of the overloaded system, Harvath's worked because it was tied to a special government program that granted priority access in times of crisis or emergency. Excusing himself, he walked to the other side of the roof. "Harvath," he said raising the device to his ear.

"Scot, thank God," replied his boss, Gary Lawlor. "Where are you?"

"In Manhattan. Twenty-third and First, on the roof of the VA Medical Center."

"What can you tell me about what's going on there?"

"We're under attack. That's what's going on here. I just saw an NYPD helicopter blown out of the sky by an RPG. And from what I've heard, all the bridges and tunnels into and out of Manhattan have also been destroyed."

"That's exactly what we're hearing here at DHS. All available local, state, and federal assets have been dispatched—marine units, aviation, you name it. They're revving into full-blown search-and-rescue mode right now."

"If you want me to suit up," responded Harvath, "just tell me where I need to be."

Lawlor pulled a paper from his desk and said, "There have been explosions at Air Traffic Control radar stations in New York and New Jersey, which have knocked the ATC system off-line in your area. Based on the intel I'm seeing, I'm worried that whoever did this may have a secondary agenda."

"You think they're trying to pull another 9/11?"

"We have no idea. When the sniper situation broke out at LaGuardia, the FAA started diverting flights, but anything is possible. Since you're there, we need you to figure out what's going on."

"How am I supposed to do that?"

"I don't know. From what I hear, it's already anarchy in New York. They've got a lot of good people on the job, but their coordination is falling apart, just like on 9/11. Everyone's rushing to the nearest attack site to try to help pull out survivors. The overwhelming number of sites is breaking down response capabilities. I won't be able to get you any support. At least not right now."

Considering the magnitude of the attacks, Harvath wasn't surprised, but he needed more information to go on. "Gary, there are eight million people in New York City. Who am I looking for and what is the target?"

"A communication was intercepted earlier today. In it was a reference to 'Allah's bombmaker,' who had been brought 'against his will and in violation of international law' to New York City."

"That's impossible," said Harvath. "No one could have put something like this together that fast. We grabbed Sayed Jamal this morning. How would anyone know we have him, much less where we have him?"

"That's what you need to find out," responded Lawlor, "I want you to question Jamal yourself. If this turns out to be an al-Qaeda operation, there's a good chance he had a hand in planning or training the people involved. Either way, he may know the end game."

"He's in JTTF custody now. Why don't we let their interrogators handle it?"

"Because somebody had to have leaked the fact that we grabbed him and have him in New York, that's why. Until we can identify and plug that leak, I can't trust anyone else but you on this. Is that clear?"

"Have you tried reaching the president?" replied Harvath, who could tell by the tone of his voice that Gary Lawlor was just as angry as he was.

"Of course I've tried, but DC's just as chaotic as New York right now. Apparently, he was someplace in Wisconsin, but now they're rushing him to *Air Force One*. Listen, we both know that he's going to be locked down so tight only his closest people will have access to him for the next several hours. We're on our own and I'm giving you a direct order. Lean on Jamal as hard as you have to. I don't want any more people to die. We'll worry about the consequences of the interrogation later."

That was all Harvath needed to hear. But convincing the JTTF to allow him to conduct the kind of interrogation on their prisoner that he wanted to conduct, even after today's events, was something that Harvath thought was going to be a lot easier said than done.

EIGHTEEN

AIR FORCE ONE

A president needed to be able to separate his personal life from his professional, but right now Jack Rutledge couldn't do it.

He had never made any excuses about being a father first and a president second. Since he had lost his wife to breast cancer several years ago, his daughter, Amanda, was all he had left, and right now he didn't even know if he had that.

"Anything?" asked the president the minute Carolyn Leonard entered his private suite at the front of the custom Boeing 747.

"Still nothing yet, sir. I'm sorry," she replied.

"How's that possible? They were in two cars, correct?"

"Yes, sir."

"And you haven't been able to reach either of them?"

"No, sir, but Amanda and her friends were riding with Marcy Delacorte and Tim Fiore. I picked them myself as the lead agents for your daughter's detail. They're the best. I'm sure we'll hear something soon."

The president wanted to ask her *how soon,* but it would have been inappropriate to burden her with his fears. He needed to remain strong. Besides, he knew Carolyn was already doing everything she could. In the end, though, there was only so much that could be done. For the time being, they were both helpless. "Anything from the local authorities?"

"They've got the route into Manhattan that the detail was traveling, as well as the last GPS coordinates for their vehicles. We'll find her, Mr. President. I promise you."

"Thank you, Carolyn," replied Rutledge. "Let me know the minute you hear anything."

"I will, sir," replied Agent Leonard as she backed out of the suite so she could buckle up for takeoff.

Because this was supposed to be a vacation, the president had left his staff back in DC so they could be with their families over the holiday weekend. That meant that as he tried to focus his attention on New York City, he was going to have to tackle everything via secure video links from his airborne office.

He'd learned early on that the first hurdle in a situation of this magnitude was separating fact from fiction. Much like the hours following the September 11th attacks, rumors were running rampant across the country and emergency action plans were being put into effect left and right. All anyone knew for sure was that America was under attack, *again*.

After being briefed over the video link by his chief of staff, Charles Anderson, during the plane's taxi and takeoff, the president replied, "That's it? That's all we know?"

"We're still trying to gather information, sir."

"How the hell is that possible, Chuck?"

"The flow is pretty slow coming out of New York."

"I thought after September eleventh we put procedures in place to change all that."

"We did," replied Anderson, "but with any occurrence like this there is a certain amount of event resonance."

"Meaning?"

"Meaning no matter how good our procedures are for transmitting data, human beings have to snap out of their shock, assess the situation, and pass it up the chain of command. It just takes time."

The president didn't like that answer, especially when thousands of lives were hanging in the balance, including his daughter's. "That's not good enough. We've got people injured and dying. They're trapped on bridges, they're trapped down in tunnels choked with smoke and fire, and they're trying to stay afloat in the Hudson and East rivers. If we don't start communicating properly, those people won't have a chance, and I can't have that. The American people won't stand for it. Not after 9/11.

"I don't care how many asses you have to kick, put your boots on and start kicking, damn it. We put those response systems in place for a reason. We were supposed to have learned from our mistakes, so let's start acting like it. Understood?"

"Yes, Mr. President," replied Anderson.

"Good," said Rutledge. "Now, when can I talk to the mayor?"

"It could be some time. His emergency command center was targeted in a run-up to the attacks and we're having trouble locating him."

The president threw up his hands in disgust. "I don't believe it. What about the governor?"

"He's en route from Albany right now, but he knows even less than we do. Do you want me to get him on the line and patch him through?"

"No, I want to talk to Mayor Brown first. I want to hear from him how his people are doing and what they need. I don't want things being filtered through the governor. That was a big part of the problem with New Orleans."

"There is a chain of command, sir."

"Not with something like this. I want you to track down the mayor and put him through to me as soon as possible. Now, so far we have no intelligence that any other cities have been targeted, correct?"

"Yes, sir. That is correct."

"I guess we can thank God for that," said Rutledge as he laid his briefing folder onto the table in front of him and massaged his face with both hands. "What about an appearance?"

"I think right now that would be a little premature," said Anderson.

"Premature? Chuck, people are panicked," said a voice from next to the chief of staff. The camera pulled back to show Geoff Mitchell, the president's press secretary. "They *need* the president to reassure them and it needs to be done sooner rather than later."

"Reassure them of what? We have no idea what's going on in New York, we can't control it, and we have absolutely no idea who's behind it. I hardly think any of that's reassuring."

"You can't keep the president walled off, Chuck. It doesn't matter that he doesn't have all the answers yet. People need to see him. That's all. They need to hear him say everything is going to be all right. Hell, if we play this right, it might even be okay for him to admit he doesn't have all the answers yet, but that he's working very hard to get to the bottom of what's happened. And then of course he needs to state unequivocally that America's response to this barbarism will be swift, sure, and severe."

"We can talk about releasing a videotaped statement once we decide where the president is headed after Mountain Home Air Force Base," stated the chief of staff.

"We're not going to Idaho," replied Rutledge. "We're on our way back to DC."

"Mr. President," began Anderson, "I don't think that—"

"Chuck, you said it yourself. No other cities have been targeted. My place is in the White House. America needs leadership right now. I've already okayed putting the continuity of government plan into action, but other than that, nothing else changes. Do we understand each other?"

"Yes, sir."

The president then addressed his press secretary. "Geoff, I want you to start drafting some remarks. Keep them short. Chuck is right. At this point we don't know a lot, and the less we say the better. Let the networks know that I'll be making a live statement as soon as I get back to the White House. I think that about does it. Let's get to work."

"Mr. President," said Robert Hilliman, the president's secretary of defense, from his secure link at the DOD, "if I could have a moment of your time in private please, sir?"

"Go ahead, Bob," replied the president once he had gone into private conference mode. "What is it?"

"Well, there are some concerns about an intelligence intercept we had this morning."

"What about it?"

"Apparently, reference was made to the United States abducting a foreign national and bringing him here against his will in direct violation of international law."

"This is nothing new, Bob. We hear this stuff all the time, especially since all of the press on our extraordinary rendition policy broke."

"I know, Mr. President, but this is different."

"Different how? They could be talking about any one of thousands of people we've detained."

"This conversation made clear that the person in question was a bombmaker who had been brought to New York."

"Which means . . ." said the president, trailing off.

"It could only be one of two people."

"Both of whom we've got at the same location."

"With no effective way to protect or evacuate."

NINETEEN

26 Federal Plaza
Joint Terrorist Task Force

Harvath looked at the JTTF duty officer and exclaimed, "What do you mean, *you don't have him*?"

"We don't have him," the young man blasted back. Like many others, he was not dealing well with the stress of the terrorist attacks.

"Maybe he's already been processed," offered Herrington, trying to prevent the situation from escalating into an all-out, interagency pissing match. "Did you check with the Federal House of Detention on West Street?"

"What am I, new?" replied the duty officer. "Of course I checked. They haven't heard of him either."

Harvath was about to come unglued. They had covered the entire two-and-a-half-mile distance to the JTTF headquarters at the FBI field office in lower Manhattan on foot, and now some rookie was telling him that not only did they not have Sayed Jamal, but that nobody had ever heard of him. "I want you to find Mike Jaffe right now."

"Who?" said the duty officer.

"What do you have, sand in your ears? *Mike Jaffe.* I transferred the prisoner in question to him and a team of agents from this office this morning."

The young man was tired of having his valuable time wasted by some DHS knuckle-dragger. "You've got your agencies screwed up, Agent Harvath. None of our guys were involved in a prisoner transfer this morning, and we don't have anyone in this office—JTTF, FBI, or otherwise—named Mike Jaffe."

It was like banging his head against a brick wall. Harvath's blood was beginning to boil and he was getting very near his breaking point. He needed to go over this kid's head and was about to do so, when Bob thanked the duty officer for his help, grabbed Harvath's arm, and steered him out of the JTTF and into the stairwell.

"What's the matter with you?" demanded Harvath.

"Shut up," replied Herrington.

"The hell I will. I've got to find Sayed Jamal, and your getting in my way like that isn't going to—"

"They don't have him."

"Or so says the dumb ass at the front desk. Sometimes you've gotta go higher up the food chain to get answers."

"Well, you are going higher up the food chain, all right, because Mike Jaffe doesn't work for the Joint Terrorism Task Force," Herrington replied. "He's with DIA."

"The Defense Intelligence Agency?"

Bob nodded his head. "I met him in Afghanistan back in 2001. My unit was assigned to a very high-speed task force going after the top of the al-Qaeda leadership."

"And Mike Jaffe was a part of that task force?" asked Harvath.

"He was in charge of it."

"So why the hell would he pose as a JTTF agent?"

"We had a saying that both the Lord and the DIA work in mysterious ways. Obviously, he had a very personal interest in your prisoner."

"A little too personal," said Harvath as he began walking down the stairs.

"Where are you going?"

"To make a phone call. Then I'm going to find Mike Jaffe if I have to turn this entire city inside out."

TWENTY

It was the tapping at his window that caused Tim Fiore to snap back into consciousness. His reflexes kicked in, and in a flash he had his SIG Sauer drawn and pointed dead-on at the threat.

"Mister, the bridge is going to collapse. You've gotta get the hell out of here," a stranger yelled from the other side of the glass.

Fiore's head hurt like hell. It felt like someone had smacked him with a lead pipe. For a moment he didn't know where he was. Then slowly it started coming back to him. "On the ground!" he yelled at the man. "On the fucking ground—now!"

Terrified, the Good Samaritan fled for his life.

Though he was a seasoned Secret Service agent, nothing could have prepared Fiore for what he saw when he turned and looked over his shoulder.

The entire back half of the armored vehicle they'd been traveling in was gone; *evaporated.* It had taken the sliding gun drawers beneath the cargo area, along with the third row of seats, where Agents Grossi and Swartley had been sitting.

An enormous piece of twisted metal that looked like a pitchfork had pierced the second row of seats, impaling both of Amanda Rutledge's friends. Amanda was unconscious, but Tim didn't see any wounds. He reached for her and felt for a pulse; it was weak, but at least she was alive. For how much longer, though, he couldn't tell.

Fiore looked over at his partner, whose chin was slumped against her chest.

"Marcy?" he said as he felt for her pulse. "Marcy, can you hear me?"

There was no response.

Twisting out of his seatbelt, Fiore kicked his door open and began yelling into his radio. "This is Echo One. We've been hit. I repeat, *Echo One has been hit.* All units respond. Over."

Hopping out of the SUV, Fiore scanned for threats as he came around to the rear passenger door. *Where the hell was the other Secret Service vehicle?* It should have been right behind them. It was then that he began noticing the screams. Screams of terror. Screams of agony. All around, cars were overturned and huge sections of the bridge were missing. Their van had been slammed perpendicularly into the guard rail and, judging from the marks on the roof and hood, had flipped at least three or four times. It was only out of sheer luck they had landed upright and had managed to stay on the bridge at all. This wasn't the work of just one bomb, there had to have been at least two, probably more. The injured were everywhere, and those who weren't wounded sat frozen in their cars, wandered aimlessly in shock, or ran for their lives.

Fiore tried to open Amanda's door, but it wouldn't budge. With the extensive damage their SUV had sustained, going through the shrapnel-ridden cargo area was also out of the question. He was going to have to go around the other side and pull the president's daughter over the bodies of her two dead friends.

As he came around the rear of the vehicle, Fiore noticed that along with everything else that had evaporated, so had their medical trauma bag. All that was left was a collapsible litter, and being careful not to gash himself, he climbed inside and grabbed it.

He continued to try to raise the other agents as he raced around to the driver's side of the SUV. Because they'd been trained on what to do in case of just such an assassination attempt, Fiore was able to react almost without even thinking about it.

Yanking the rear driver's-side door open, Fiore crawled in as far as he could go. Gently, he unbuckled the first daughter, supported her neck as best he could, and backed out of the SUV, guiding her around the jagged edges of the steel pitchfork that had eviscerated her friends until he could lay her down on the litter.

With two enormous holes behind them and being nearer to the Manhattan side of the bridge, Tim scanned the nearby buildings for a safe haven. His training dictated that he get Amanda to high ground as soon as possible, where he could better control their situation and hold out until their helicopter could arrive. Trying the Secret Service Command Post, he said, "Skybox, this is Echo One. Do you copy? Over."

"Roger that, Echo One," came the response from the command post. "What is your status?"

"We've been hit. At least two vehicle-borne explosives timed to coincide with our route. Echo Two is gone, we've got two agents missing from our vehicle, a third unconscious, and the package has been damaged. Request you initiate Operation Upswing immediately. Over."

"Negative, Echo One. No can do," said the command center control agent. "All bridges and tunnels into and out of Manhattan have been hit. We've got a report of an NYPD helicopter down, possibly due to hostile fire. Until further notice, NYC airspace is too hot and has been shut down. Is your vehicle operable? Over."

All the bridges and tunnels? How the hell could that be possible? As incomprehensible as it was, there was no time to even try to make sense of it now. "Negative," replied Fiore. "Our vehicle has been totaled. Over."

"Echo One. Stand by. Over," said the voice.

Stand by? Was this guy nuts? They were completely vulnerable out in the open like this, and Fiore wasn't convinced that they just happened to be in the wrong place at the wrong time. What if there was a secondary attempt on Amanda's life in progress right at this moment?

While watching the pandemonium around them, he bent down and checked her pulse again. Though each protective detail had a medical agent as part of the team, they all had gone through extensive medical training. Fiore suspected that if Amanda didn't get help soon, she wasn't going to make it.

"Skybox, we need to evac *now!* Over."

"Stand by, Echo One. Over," repeated the controller.

Fiore was about to tell the controller what he could do with his *stand by*'s, when he heard someone coming around the front of the vehicle.

Instantly, he moved his body to shield Amanda Rutledge while raising his pistol and applying pressure to the trigger.

The next thing he saw was a gun as it swung around the front bumper. He knew it—a secondary attack.

He was about to pull the trigger the rest of the way, when he heard, "Jesus, Tim. Don't shoot! It's me. Marcy."

TWENTY-ONE

"You scared the hell out of me," Fiore said as he lowered his pistol. "Why'd you come around the front of the vehicle?"

"Because my door was jammed and yours was open," replied Marcy, a little unsteady on her feet. "What happened?"

"Terrorists with multiple vehicle bombs. Apparently, all the bridges and tunnels in and out of Manhattan have been hit. Echo Two is unresponsive, and Grossi and Swartley are gone."

"Gone?"

"Our vehicle took a pretty bad hit."

Marcy looked down at the president's daughter and referred to her by her codename. "How's Goldilocks?"

"She's alive, which is more than we can say for her girlfriends."

Delacorte peered into the backseat and felt like she was about to retch. It was a gruesome sight. As she regained her composure she began to ask about their plan of action, but Fiore stopped her. He had a transmission coming over his earpiece and signaled for her to listen in.

"Echo One, this is Skybox. Do you copy? Over."

"Roger that, Skybox. We copy. Over."

"Echo One, we want you to evacuate the package to the west end of the bridge immediately. When you get there find a secure location and dig in. We're mobilizing our tactical team and will get them to you ASAP. Over."

Marcy, who had now bent down to examine Amanda, responded, "Negative, Skybox. The package needs immediate medical. There's no time to wait for the tac team. Over."

"Echo One, ambulances have been dispatched to multiple attack sites, including your location. Can you get the package to the west end of the bridge and seek medical attention there? Over."

"Will do. Echo One out," replied Delacorte, who then looked up at Tim and said, "How do you want to play this?"

"Let me get us some muscle so we can walk shotgun. I'll be right back."

Removing his credentials, Fiore ran up to two large men who had just helped extricate a woman from her badly damaged car and said, "U.S. Secret Service. I have a priority injury I need your help with over here."

The men followed Tim back to where Amanda Rutledge lay on the litter next to the sheared SUV. "She don't look so good," one of them commented. "Are you sure you want to be moving her?"

"We don't have a choice," replied Marcy. "If we don't get her to help soon, she's going to die."

"You're the boss," said the other man as he waved his buddy to the rear of the litter while he grabbed the handles near Amanda's head.

"Gently now, fellas," said Fiore. "On three. Ready? One. Two. Three."

The men delicately lifted the litter as Tim and Marcy took up security positions on either side.

Looking down again at the young woman who lay unconscious on the litter, one of the men remarked, "Hey, is this who I think it is?"

Marcy was about to respond, when there came the sound of groaning metal followed by cries of terror. The group turned to see the number seven subway train on the upper deck behind them teetering on the edge of an enormous blast hole that revealed the river below and sky above.

A moment later, there was the horrible sound of metal scraping on metal as subway cars tumbled one after the other through the hole on the upper deck, straight down through the hole on the vehicle level and then plunged toward the East River below. It was one of the most horrific sights any of them had ever seen.

As if that wasn't bad enough, suddenly, the bridge beneath their feet began to shake violently. Large pieces of metal buckled and yawed as the structure prepared to meet its watery death.

Not a man to mince words, Tim Fiore looked at his group and yelled, "Run!"

TWENTY-TWO

WASHINGTON, DC

"This is a real bad time to be asking me for favors," Stan Caldwell, the exhausted forty-two-year-old deputy director of the FBI, said into the phone.

"Who's asking for favors?" replied Gary Lawlor, who had been both Caldwell's mentor and his predecessor before moving over to DHS and the Office of International Investigative Assistance to head its covert counterterrorism initiative known as the Apex Project. "I'm asking you to do your job."

"I *am* doing my job, and I'm up to my eyebrows in shit right now. Do you have any idea what the preliminary death toll is coming out of New York City?"

"It's not good. I know. I've been getting the same reports you have."

"You're goddamn right it's not good."

"Stan, I'm not trying to make more work for you," he said from his office across town, "but there are a couple of things here that don't make sense, and I need you or somebody in your office to get to the bottom of it for me right now."

"There's nothing to get to the bottom of. Whoever your guy talked to at the JTTF office in New York is wrong. That's all there is to it."

"Don't bullshit me, Stan. We've got too much history together. I want to know what the DIA's role is in all of this. Why were they posing as JTTF agents for Sayed Jamal's handoff?"

"Gary, I'm going to tell you one more time, and then I've gotta get back to my desk in the SIOC. The men your agent worked with in upstate New York are JTTF, plain and simple. Whoever pegged them as DIA is wrong. Tell your man that if he wants to help out in Manhattan, I suggest he grab a hard hat, attach himself to a search-and-rescue team, and start digging." With that, Caldwell hung up the phone.

"Did he buy it?" asked FBI Director Martin Sorce.

"I don't think so. Especially since he had to leave four messages over here before I called him back."

Sorce turned to the other man in the room and said, "What should we do now?"

From behind his frameless glasses, the Defense Intelligence Agency's chief of staff, Timothy Bedford, fixed the two FBI men with a steady gaze and replied, "Nothing. We'll handle it from here."

As Bedford stood up to leave he added, "And, gentlemen, please remember the national security implications of this issue. As far as anyone is concerned, our meeting never took place."

Once Bedford had left the director's conference room and the door had shut behind him, Sorce remarked, "I never did like that guy. It's no wonder Waddell uses him to do his dirty work. What does he mean, *this meeting never took place?* At least two dozen people saw him come in here. What an asshole."

Caldwell smiled. "The fact that his tie is knotted a bit too tight notwithstanding, what are we going to do about this?"

"What can we do?" asked Sorce as he stood up from his chair. "You saw the letter he was carrying from the president. We've been told in no uncertain terms to stay out of their operation."

"And in the process lie to people we should be working with—in particular, Lawlor, who's a former deputy director of the Bureau?"

"I don't like it either, Stan, but that's the way it is. Listen, we've got too much on our plates now anyway."

"And it could skyrocket if Gary is right about a secondary attack," said Caldwell as his attention was drawn to an urgent message coming in on his pager.

Sorce opened the door of the conference room and nodded to his staff that he was ready to return to the floor of the Strategic Information and Operations Center, or SIOC, for a quick morale booster. But before he left, he turned and said, "The next several hours are going to be absolutely critical, so let's make sure we're focused on doing our job."

"Which is, using anything and anyone at our disposal to stop any further terrorist attacks, correct?" queried Caldwell as he looked up from the message on his pager.

The director's ability to read people was the sine qua non of his successful leadership of the FBI. He knew what his deputy was driving at. "As long as you operate within the framework of the law and remain faithful to your oath of duty, you'll have my full support."

"Even if it means potentially pissing off the president?"

Sorce looked Caldwell in the eye and said, "For the record, I left the room after I told you to operate within the framework of the law—"

"And remain faithful to my oath of duty," added Caldwell. "I got it."

TWENTY-THREE

NEW YORK CITY

Scot Harvath slid his BlackBerry back into the plastic holder at his waist and said, "The official word from the FBI is that the JTTF duty officer has no idea what he's talking about."

Herrington looked at him and replied, "He seemed pretty sure of himself to me."

"Even so, they suggest we find a search-and-rescue team and focus our efforts in that direction."

"I think I'd rather focus my efforts on catching terrorists."

"Me too," said Harvath.

"So where are we?"

"Apparently on the corner of Ignorance and Bliss without a goddamn clue."

"Why would the FBI cover up the DIA's involvement in all of this?" asked Herrington.

"Who knows? I can't figure any of these people out anymore. Subterfuge on top of subterfuge, all wrapped up with prime government red tape. It's getting harder and harder to believe we're all on the same side."

"Agent Harvath," yelled a voice from behind them. "Agent Harvath!"

They turned to see the JTTF duty officer running out of the revolving door of 26 Federal Plaza.

"I think I might have something for you," he said.

"Like what?" asked Herrington.

"NYPD picked up a guy at the temporary PATH station at the World Trade Center just off Church Street. They think he was supposed to be one of the bombers."

"What makes them think that?" asked Harvath.

"They found him with a backpack full of explosives that failed to go off. There's nobody from our office who can get over there right away, so I've been authorized to give you first crack at him, if you want it."

"Authorized by whom?"

"Stan Caldwell, deputy director of the FBI."

As Scot and Bob walked toward the NYPD's 1st Precinct on Ericsson Place, the street scenes were surreal. On some there were absolutely no signs of life. On others, entire avenues were taken over by throngs of people still pouring out of lower Manhattan, making their way north. As part of the city's emergency plan, the subways had been shut down and many streets were restricted to emergency vehicles only. The drivers who were still out, searching for a way off the island, faced an absolute traffic nightmare, with most of their routes blocked by people who had abandoned their vehicles and had fled on foot.

To make matters worse, the sky was obliterated by a smoky haze, while a powdery gray ash, as if it were the cremated remains of the victims themselves, had begun falling across the city.

Harvath, though, tried to force the macabre scene from his mind by focusing on the matter at hand. "For some reason, Stan decided to throw us a bone" was all Gary had said when Harvath called him to relay the update.

Turning to Herrington, Harvath wondered aloud, "First Caldwell says the JTTF duty officer doesn't know what he's talking about, and then he sends him chasing after us with an interrogation on a silver platter. It doesn't make sense."

"There's a little too much fruit in this salad, but what do I know?" replied Herrington. "As far as I'm concerned, we shouldn't look the gift whore in the mouth."

While chatting with the arresting officers, Harvath was handed the evidence bag that contained the few items the man was carrying when he was picked up. His backpack was with the bomb squad and held nothing of interest other than the explosives that failed to go off.

Scot and Bob were shown into the brightly lit interrogation room. Cuffed to a chipped Formica table in the center was a Middle Eastern man in his early-to-mid-twenties. His face and arms were covered with cuts and bruises. Whether the injuries came from having been in the PATH tunnel when one of his colleagues' devices went off or if he had "slipped" getting into the squad car, Harvath didn't really care. What he wanted was information, and he hoped this bomb jockey had something that they could use.

"Masaa al-Khair," said Harvath as he pulled the metal chair out from the other side of the table and sat down. *"Kayf Haalak?"*

The man looked up at Harvath and spit at his face.

Why were they all spitters?

Herrington, who had been trying to up the intimidation factor by leaning against the wall behind the prisoner, sprung forward, grabbed a handful of his hair and jerked his neck back so that he could stare into the man's face. "My friend asked you how you were doing. It would be polite to respond."

"Elif air ab tizak!" groaned the Middle Easterner.

Bob, who could also speak Arabic, was familiar with the insult involving the placement of an unfathomable number of male private parts into a certain orifice of his body and responded now with an even less tasteful insult of his own, *"Elif air ab dinich."*

The prisoner was enraged with the reference to his religion and struggled to free his head from Herrington's grasp. "Bastard fuck you. Bastard fuck you," he yelled over and over again.

Harvath signaled for Bob to let go of him and step back. Upending the evidence bag, Harvath poured its contents onto the table and said, "Any more spitting and I'm going to leave you and my friend in here alone for some etiquette lessons. Understand?"

"Lawyer. Give me lawyer," the man replied in his broken English.

That really pissed Harvath off—just as much as the fact that there were Americans who would fight to the death to see that this piece of shit got a fair and just trial. Where was the justice for the thousands, if not tens of thousands, of Americans who had just been killed by this asshole and his pals? "You don't get anything unless you cooperate. No lawyer, no judge, nothing until you give us some answers. Let's start with your name."

"I no hear you. I talk lawyer."

Harvath signaled Herrington, who came off the wall and slammed the man's head right into the table.

"Can you hear me now?" asked Harvath as blood gushed from the man's broken nose.

When he didn't respond, Herrington cuffed him with an open-handed slap to the left side of his head and added, "How about now?"

Waving Herrington back, Harvath stated, "Let's talk about this brand-new Casio watch of yours. They make pretty good detonators, don't they? Your colleague Ramzi Yousef used one of these to detonate a little saline solution bottle filled with nitroglycerin on a plane bound for Tokyo a while back. He called it his microbomb, but it didn't bring the plane down like he hoped. We caught him before he could improve upon the formula, Allah be praised."

"Waj ab zibik!" yelled the man, wishing Harvath an infection in a very private place for invoking the name of his god.

Harvath ignored him and continued, "This watch wasn't meant as a detonator, though, was it? I'd be willing to bet that all of you got the same new watch for synchronization. Am I right?"

The man said nothing. He just sat there as blood rolled down from his nose, along his chin, and dripped onto his shirt.

"How about the phone?" pressed Harvath. "Motorola iDEN. Pretty nice, but a bit out of your league, don't you think? I mean, digital wireless phones like this are meant for *business*people. Two-way digital radio, alphanumeric messaging, fax capabilities, high-end Internet access. That's a lot of features just so you and your buddies can set up blow-job parties at the local mosque, Allah be praised."

"Nikomak," the man growled.

Harvath ignored the suggestion of what he should do to his mother and toyed with the phone as he continued posing questions. "Since at least one other bomb went off in the PATH tunnel, we're assuming you were either a primary or a contingency operative, or was the plan to wreak as much damage as possible?"

The man remained silent.

"How were you recruited for this job? Who contacted you?"

Nothing.

"When were you first contacted?"

Still nothing.

"What else do your colleagues have planned? More bombs? Something with an airplane? Other cities? What is it?"

At this, the prisoner smiled.

Bob was about to reach out and strike him again, when Harvath stood up and stated, "I'm going to post a flyer over at the World Trade Center site to see if there are any lawyers willing to represent you." Turning to Herrington he said, "Let's go."

Once outside the interrogation room, Bob stopped Harvath and said, "We were just getting started in there. The fear was absolutely wafting off that guy. You could smell it."

"I was definitely smelling something, though I don't know if it was fear. Listen, we're both fans of the art of not-so-subtle persuasion, but we don't have the time to work this guy over the way we'd like to. Even the NYPD is going to have a limit as to what they'll let us do to a terrorist suspect in their custody."

"So let's remove him from their custody," said Herrington. "We'll take him back to 26 Federal Plaza, or to a quiet hotel room, an abandoned building, wherever. It doesn't matter. He knows something. You could see it in his face."

"What he knows is that we're desperate. If we put the testicle clamps on him maybe he'll tell us something of value, maybe not. We'd need to have psychological leverage—have his family in custody or something like that. But at this point, we don't even know his name."

"Give me five minutes with him and you'll have it."

"This guy could turn out to have been nothing more than cannon fodder for al-Qaeda—a means to get a bomb into the PATH train tunnel. I don't want to waste any more time on him. Besides, he may have already helped us out without even knowing it."

"How?" asked Herrington.

Harvath held up the cell phone and said, "With this."

"Are you going to tell me this moron was dumb enough not to erase his call log?"

"Nope. In fact I don't think his phone was used for calls at all."

"So what's it for, then? Text messaging?"

"Let me ask you a question. You've been in Iraq as well as

Afghanistan. How many people does it take to detonate a suicide bomb?"

Most people would have thought it was a trick question, but Herrington knew better. "One, plus a handler nearby with a remote detonator in case the bomber chickens out. You think that is what this is all about? Backup detonation?"

"Not necessarily. There were too many bombers to have had handlers physically following each one of them. I think this is a coordination issue. These phones work on a combination of cell phone towers and GPS. I've got a very similar setup on my BlackBerry. If all of the bombers had these phones, they'd have access to maps of New York City that would allow them to always know where they were. A good feature if you'd just been brought in from out of town."

"And provide their handler a way to keep track of them at all times," added Herrington.

"Exactly. If one of them got pulled over driving into a tunnel, the handler would be able to see that they were stopped and either call or text the operative to see what the holdup was, or automatically warn the other bombers and put a contingency plan into effect. It's a pretty clever way to coordinate multiple attacks on a large scale."

"Do you think you can backtrack the signal?"

"That kind of stuff is way beyond my ability," replied Harvath. "But I think I might know somebody who can."

TWENTY-FOUR

"I'll put it next on my list—right after finding the cure for cancer. Are you nuts?" asked Kevin McCauliff from the other end of Harvath's cell-phone call. The two were members of an informal group of federal employees who trained together every year for the annual Washington, DC, Marine Corps Marathon. In addition to being a fellow runner, McCauliff also held a position within an important government agency that Harvath had turned to once before for help—the National Geospatial-Intelligence Agency.

Formerly known as the National Imagery and Mapping Agency, the NGA was a major intelligence and combat support subsidiary of the Department of Defense. And in this situation, that was potentially one of its biggest drawbacks.

"So what you're saying is you can't do it," replied Harvath.

"No," returned McCauliff, "What I'm saying is that I don't *want* to do it. Not if you're asking me to hide it from my superiors."

"That's exactly what I'm asking you to do."

"I could get fired, Scot. What would I do then?"

"If you get fired, I'll make sure you get work over at Homeland Security."

Even though he was all the way down in Bethesda, Maryland, Mc-

Cauliff laughed so loud, it sounded like he was standing on the street right next to them. "Thanks, but no thanks. I'd rather collect unemployment."

"For Christ's sake, Kevin, this is serious. Have you seen what's happened up here?"

"Of course I have. It's all over the place. Worse than 9/11, they're saying."

"And it could get worse still if you don't help."

"Scot, you're going to have to tell me what I'm doing this for."

"For me, Kevin."

"We're close friends and all, but that's not good enough."

"I'll take your sister to dinner again, okay? How about that?" said Harvath. He knew the analyst's sister had a thing for him. After the last time McCauliff had helped him out on a hush-hush case, that had been the payment he'd asked for in return.

"We weren't in the middle of a national crisis that time. We're not supposed to be diverting any resources right now. If I get caught, I'm going to need a cover story."

"And I don't have one for you," said Harvath. "You're going to have to come up with one on your own. Please, Kevin. We think the people behind the attacks today may have something else planned. I need you to do this for me so we can stop them."

"And the reason you're not doing it out of your department?"

"Is because nobody in my department can do this stuff as well as you."

McCauliff remained silent so long, Harvath felt he had no choice but to let the other shoe drop, "*And* because this morning, before the bridges and tunnels blew, I was involved in a covert operation with what I thought was the Manhattan Joint Terrorism Task Force. It turns out they were actually DIA agents posing as JTTF. Whatever they're up to, word somehow leaked. Terrorist chatter intercepted today shows that they already know all about the op."

"That doesn't make any sense. We're all on the same side. Why wouldn't these guys work with you and tell you they were DIA?"

"That's what I hope to find out, but none of it matters unless I can figure out what the terrorists are planning to do next. Are you going to help me or not?"

McCauliff thought about it for a moment and then said, "A lot's going to depend on the cell phone data. If it's transmitted in a clear format, we can grab it. If it's over a secure channel like SSL, I'm going to need some time to work on decoding it."

"We may not have time."

"You said these phones were on Nextel network?"

"Correct."

"I know a guy over there who might let me peek behind the curtain. I'll work that angle as well as the GPS tracking company's servers. I'll call you back in a half hour."

Harvath gave McCauliff some additional information from the phone he had "forgotten" to put back in the NYPD evidence bag and then hung up.

"What do we do now?" asked Herrington.

"McCauliff's the best guy on something like this. If anybody can turn this to our advantage, it's him."

"And then what? If we pick up a trail on the terrorists, there are still only two of us."

"To tell you the truth, I hadn't thought that far ahead yet," said Harvath.

"*I* have," replied Bob. "Let's get back to the VA and see if we can't improve our odds."

TWENTY-FIVE

With their two litter bearers, Tim Fiore and Marcy Delacorte pounded down the bridge as fast as their feet would carry them.

When they reached the end of the bridge, three ambulances were already pulling away—packed with injured.

Tim yelled to an NYPD officer about twenty feet ahead, "Stop that ambulance!" but the officer knew there wasn't room in any of them for even one more person.

"There's more ambulances on the way," he shouted back.

"We can't wait," replied Marcy as she flashed her credentials. "U.S. Secret Service. We have a priority injury here."

"The ambulances are gone, ma'am. There's nothing I can do."

Fiore tilted his head in the direction of the officer's squad car, and Delacorte knew exactly what he was thinking.

"We need your patrol car."

"I can't do that," said the officer.

"And I'm not asking," replied Marcy as she raised her weapon.

The cop put up both his hands. "Okay, okay. It's yours."

"Let's get her into the car," Tim said to the two men who were helping them.

They rushed to the patrol car, and as the officer watched them place Amanda on the backseat, he asked, "Is that—?"

Fiore nodded his head. "Where's the nearest hospital?"

"Beth Israel," replied the cop. "Fifteenth and First. The NYU hospital downtown is going to be overloaded."

"You can't drive," stated Marcy as she got in the back with Amanda. "You don't know your way around."

Tim looked around and then spotted something on the dash of a car idling in the gridlock not far from where they were. Running toward it, Fiore removed his credentials and held them up when he reached in the window and grabbed the device. "U.S. Secret Service" was all he said.

Sprinting back to the squad car, Tim propped the Garmin iQue GPS handheld on the dash, fired up the vehicle, and hit the lights and siren. Motorists tried to get out of their way, but the effort was useless. There was nowhere for them to go. The traffic was absolutely locked down.

Aiming for the sidewalk between two parked cars, Fiore yelled, "Hold on," and hit the gas.

TWENTY-SIX

As Ali knew from the information provided by the Troll, there was no telling which location Mohammed bin Mohammed was being held at. All they knew was that until they found the right one, each location was going to be very difficult to penetrate and each would pose its own special set of challenges.

The rather benign store on 47th Street between Fifth and Sixth, in the heart of New York's diamond district, looked like any other, but Ali and his men knew it was only a front. The windows and doors were mounted with bulletproof Lexan glass reinforced with high-tensile steel frames. There was an airlock-style double entrance that required patrons to be buzzed in the first door and have it close completely behind them before the next would be allowed open. Discreet vents near the floor were capable of pumping in an incapacitating nerve agent in the event the high-voltage-electrode woven "shock" mats were not enough to fell any would-be intruders. Even among the extremely security conscious merchants of the diamond district, this store was in a league of its own.

It was the Chechens who had decided to avoid the airlock all together. As far as they were concerned, there was no reason the balance of their force couldn't go right in through the windows—provided, of course, someone was kind enough to "open" them up first.

Dressed like the ubiquitous Hasidic Jews who did business up and down the street, two of the Chechen operatives were buzzed into the store with nondescript briefcases in hand. Moments later, as the store staff was distracted by the blacked-out Chevy Tahoes that crashed up onto the sidewalk outside their windows with their lights blazing, the Chechens carried out their plan.

Both briefcases were detonated with deafening pressure concussions and blinding flashes of white light. Before any of the staff could react, they were gunned down by one of the operatives while the other slapped shape charges to the inside of the largest window. By the time the charge blew, both of the men were already at the vaultlike door leading to the heart of the store's true operation.

Three U.S. marines, dressed in civilian clothes and body armor, were able to take down the first terrorist with fire from their short-barreled M16 Viper assault rifles, but as skilled as they were, they could not escape the high-velocity shrapnel from the grenade the man's partner lobbed into their security room.

With the marine contingent down and the rest of the team in the store, the terrorists made their way into the bowels of the building, shooting anyone and anything that moved.

Three-and-a-half minutes later, the rooms had all been cleared. Two of the men body-bagged their comrade while the others reloaded their weapons. As Abdul Ali reached into his vest for another magazine, he noticed he was still carrying his cell phone—an unforgivable oversight, especially as it was no longer necessary. If the Troll or anyone else needed to reach him, they knew how to do it.

Removing the battery, Ali smashed the phone with the butt of his weapon and gathered up the pieces. As he exited the store, he threw the remains into the nearest storm drain.

"Are we done here?" Ali asked an enormous bear of a man named Sacha.

The Chechen leader unslung his bag of electronics, threw it into the lead Tahoe, and nodded his head.

As the SUVs pulled off the curb, Ali looked at his watch and tried to compute how long it would take to maneuver through the streets to their next destination. He also wondered if it would be where they would finally find Mohammed bin Mohammed.

• • •

Half a world away, the Troll was lying on a long leather sofa as his Caucasian Ovcharkas, Argus and Drako, dozed on the floor next to him. He was enjoying an exquisite snifter of Calvados and an original copy of the Friedrich Dürrenmatt play *The Visit,* when a tiny chime sounded from the direction of his desk.

Setting the slim volume on the table next to him, the Troll swung his legs over the edge of the couch and hopped down onto the floor. Immediately, the dogs snapped to attention and followed their master to the manor house's enormous dining hall. There, any traces of the hall's original function had been erased by the rows upon rows of high-end computer servers and satellite equipment that filled the room.

A raised platform with a sleek, yet child-sized glass-and-chrome table sat accompanied by a tiny leather desk chair at the far end of the hall. Suspended above the table were three flat-screen monitors. Sitting down in the chair, the Troll punched a series of keys on a Lucite keyboard recessed within the table's surface and the monitors sprang to life. It was amazing how far the Troll had come in his little life.

Moments later, a series of multicolor status bars began charting the enormous chunks of encrypted data that had already begun downloading to his servers. Thanks to his bag of sophisticated electronic tricks, Sacha had fulfilled the first part of his assignment perfectly.

Removing the Treo device from the pocket of his sport coat, the Troll ignored the desire to contemplate the course of his life and authorized Sacha's first bonus. So far, so very, very good.

TWENTY-SEVEN

Back at the VA, Harvath waited in Dr. Hardy's office while Bob went up to the roof in search of his three friends. The images of death and destruction Scot saw on the small television on Hardy's desk were worse than anything he'd ever seen in any combat zone. The macabre horror of it all made it difficult to tear his eyes away, but he had to. He needed to think beyond the devastation and try to put the pieces of what he knew into some kind of coherent picture in his mind.

To do that, Harvath focused on one of the framed diplomas hanging on the wall. Because of Bob's injured shoulder he had automatically assumed that Samuel Hardy was an M.D., but as he read, Harvath realized the man was actually a PhD. *How the hell could a PhD be in charge of Bob's physical therapy,* he wondered. *Unless—*

Harvath's train of thought was interrupted as Dr. Samuel Hardy, PhD, entered the office. "Anything new?" he asked as he threw a stack of folders on his desk and gestured toward the television.

"The body count projections have been raised twice in the last twenty minutes," Scot replied.

"God help us all."

Harvath nodded his head and said, "Can I ask you a question?"

"Of course."

"What kind of therapy are you doing with Bob Herrington?"

Hardy looked at Harvath a moment and then crossed over to his desk. "With all due respect, that's really none of your business."

Harvath begged to differ with the doc and politely replied, "I'm assuming it's not physical rehabilitation."

"No," said Hardy, careful with his choice of words. "Physical rehabilitation is not my specialty."

"And the others I met on the roof—Cates, Morgan, and Hastings? What about them? Bob told me they were pals from his *rehab.* I figured that meant physical therapy—kind of like workout buddies."

"That's not too far from the truth, but again, I'm not at liberty to—"

"Discuss your patients," said Harvath, finishing Hardy's sentence for him. "I understand."

"Actually, I don't think you do."

"Then why don't you help me?"

"I'm a psychologist."

"That's it? Just plain old psychologist?"

"There's nothing that plain about psychology. Old, maybe, but nothing is ever plain in my work."

Harvath wasn't a big fan of circumlocution. He got his fill of it on a daily basis working in Washington. "Let me cut to the chase," he said. "Up until five minutes ago, I thought Bob Herrington was putting together a team of ex-service people that I could rely on. Now I'm not so sure, so forgive me for being blunt, but what exactly do you do here?"

The doctor reached into his lower desk drawer and pulled out a black-and-white photograph of four soldiers. They were standing along a riverbank wearing vintage Vietnam-era tiger-stripe camouflage. "That's a much younger me there on the left," he said. "That picture was taken at Nha Trang when I was with the 5th Special Forces Group."

"You were a Green Beret?" asked Harvath.

"Yup."

"How'd you end up a psychologist?"

"When I got out of the Army, I was dealing with a lot of issues." Hardy paused a moment and then said, "Bob told me you were a SEAL, is that right?"

"Technically, I still am," replied Harvath. "I've just been on loan to a couple of different government agencies."

"Well, then you may be able to appreciate some of the problems I was facing. I burned through a lot of doctors when I got home from Vietnam—both psychologists and psychiatrists alike. They all had one fundamental thing in common that made it impossible for them to truly help me—none of them had ever been in combat. Their code as human beings was based upon the Judeo-Christian ethic, while mine was based upon the warrior ethic. They couldn't even begin to understand the things I had been asked to do, and which I had done so willingly for my country. That's why I decided to go into psychology."

"So you specialize in helping treat people who have been in combat?"

"Not just anybody," replied Hardy. "Only the best of the best. My area of expertise is with Special Operations personnel."

"Like Bob," remarked Harvath, whose brain then took the next step, "and Rick Cates, Paul Morgan, and Tracy Hastings."

Hardy allowed his silence to serve as his answer.

"What are we talking about here? High-end PTSD?" asked Harvath.

"Post Traumatic Stress Disorder is a relatively common issue for combat veterans, but less so for our elite warriors. What we see in them, especially when they've been forced to leave active duty prematurely, because of an injury or whatever, is an inability to reconcile the 'real' world—a place not often governed by loyalty and honor, with the world they have just left behind—a brotherhood that prides itself on character and integrity."

Harvath was intrigued, but he was still having trouble deciphering what exactly the doctor's role was. "So your job is to help them adjust to life outside the Spec Ops community?"

"More or less," replied Hardy. "Every combat vet has issues—no matter who they are. But people in the Special Operations community often share several in common and that's why group therapy in some cases can be so helpful in making a smooth and productive transition back into the civilian world."

Harvath let the idea tumble around in his brain for a few moments and wondered if there were any issues he might be keeping at bay, which he had never really taken a good look at. Bob's words from the Pig & Whistle about letting Meg Cassidy get away rang in his ears, but he tried to ignore them. Dr. Hardy was talking about deep psychological issues, not his decision to place his career over a healthy interpersonal relationship with a member of the opposite sex.

Pushing that thought from his mind, Harvath asked the one question that was most pressing at the moment. "Without violating doctor-patient confidentiality, is there anything going on with any of them that I should be concerned about?"

"That depends. How well do you know them?"

"Bob has told me about each of them in his e-mails, but this is the first time I've ever met any of them in person."

"Without knowing the details of what you're asking them to do," replied Hardy, "it's very hard for me to answer your question."

That was a fair enough response. "I may not be asking them to do anything," said Harvath. "In fact I hope that turns out to be true. But the flipside is that I may be asking them to step up to the plate in a way they haven't been asked to in a little while."

"The terrorists aren't done yet, are they?" asked Hardy.

Harvath shook his head. "We don't think so."

"Well, each person reacts to the stress of combat in different ways. What I can say is that Bob Herrington is an exceptional leader. If Rick, Tracy, and Paul are the people he wants on your team, then I'd take that as a serious endorsement."

"But what if things get ugly?"

"There's no way to predict. Unfortunately, you won't know until something happens."

"At which point it could be too late."

Hardy nodded. "Many symptoms exhibited by soldiers outside the realm of combat have more to do with adjusting to the *real* world than anything else. Put them back into the stresses of battle and nine out of ten times their symptoms disappear."

"And that tenth time?" asked Harvath. "How do I deal with that?"

"You can't. Only that soldier can. It comes down to facing his or her personal demons, and that's a battle that requires more courage than anything you might ever face on the other end of a gun."

It was an answer that Harvath not only understood, but could appreciate. The only problem was that the possibility that one of the people on his team could very well freeze up when they were needed most scared the hell out of him.

TWENTY-EIGHT

"Tell me what's going on in New York," said the DHS secretary, Alan Driehaus, as he walked in to Gary Lawlor's office unannounced and pulled the door shut behind him.

Lawlor had never cared much for the man in either his U.S. Attorney role or the position he now occupied at DHS. As diplomatic as he was, it was becoming harder and harder for Gary to hide his dislike. "Apparently there's been some sort of terrorist attack in New York. It's all over the news."

"Don't give me your condescending bullshit. What's your involvement in this?"

"Me? I swore off terrorism years ago. It was a prerequisite for getting this job."

The continual lack of respect he was shown throughout the department galled Driehaus to no end. "Shortly before all of this happened, one of your people grabbed a Muslim immigrant whom the Canadians had granted political asylum to and dragged him back across our border. True or false?"

"Who the hell told you that?" replied Lawlor, stunned that somebody was leaking classified information, and to of all people the pinhead secretary of the DHS.

"I've got my sources."

"Well they're wrong."

"Like hell they are," replied Driehaus. "None of you people get it, do you? We can't hold ourselves out as a country that cherishes the rule of law only when it suits our purposes. We play right into our enemies' hands when we do that. It's hypocritical."

"What would you have us do, Alan? Wait for the bad guys to make their move and then throw them in jail?"

"No. I have no qualms with preemption, but there have to be limits. We have to obey the rules."

"Really? Tell that to the families of the people who died today and see if they give a rat's ass about limits or the rule of law. PC or not, we're smack-dab in the middle of a crusade, and the only way Western civilization is going to survive is if we meet radical Islam's force with overwhelming force of our own."

"But Western civilization isn't *about* brute force. It's about the power of ideas—one of the greatest of which is the rule of law and that as all men are created equal, they are equally bound under those laws."

"Wake up, Alan. The sword is the midwife of civilization and everything that has happened since civilization's birth has happened at the tip of that sword. I don't care how many Starbucks are in my neighborhood, how many digital pictures my secretary can cram onto a single memory card, or how realistic the imagery is on my nephew's new PlayStation, we still live in a world where might makes right. The moment we lose sight of that *rule* and start shrinking from our duties as a nation, is when we'll all need to begin trading in our minivans and baseball mitts for prayer rugs and Arabic lessons."

Even as a product of the 1960s, Driehaus had never seen the nation so ideologically divided. *Why did so many have such a hard time seeing the damage that the current policies were doing to America?* "So we just toss the rule of law out the window?"

"No," replied Lawlor. "What I'm suggesting is that we stop believing that Western principles apply to our enemies. We can't win the war on terror playing by a set of rules our opponents refuse to recognize."

"And that's where you come in? You and your collection of former soldiers and ex-intelligence agents hidden away in the bowels of DHS operating from budgets I've never even heard about?"

"Careful, Alan. You're wiping your feet on the threshold of a very dangerous house. One, I should point out, into which you haven't been invited."

"I don't care. I want to know right now what people you have in New York. These are people who are operating under the umbrella of this agency, of which *I* am in charge."

Lawlor's patience was quickly coming to an end. "Don't let your philosophical judgments cloud your ability to execute your job. You know how this works. My division may be *in* DHS, but it's not *of* DHS."

"So all animals are created equal, but some are more equal than others, is that it?"

"I prefer to see it as we all make our own unique contributions to the welfare of our nation."

"That's an interesting way to characterize blackmail, kidnapping, and assassination."

Lawlor sat with his best poker face waiting for the secretary to actually make a point or get the hell out of his office.

"What happened today is a real wake-up call for our country, Gary. The war on terror is not working. The pace at which attacks are being plotted against the United States is beyond exhausting. We can't win with this strategy. Don't you see? Just because we perceive ourselves as having the right to do something doesn't mean we *should* do it. We can either lead by our example or be reviled for it."

Lawlor turned to a stack of paperwork on his desk and barely masking the disgust in his voice said, "I suggest you get back to the war room. I guarantee you'll be much more appreciated there."

Driehaus was pretty sure he'd gotten the information he wanted from the OIIA chief and opened the door.

As he was about to step into the hallway, Lawlor said, "By the way, Mr. Secretary?"

"Yes," said Driehaus as he turned around.

"Just for the record, it wasn't Western civilization that made all men equal. It was Samuel Colt."

TWENTY-NINE

The White House

President Rutledge traded drafts for his television appearance with his press secretary all the way back to Andrews Air Force Base in Maryland. The only break he took was when Carolyn Leonard brought him an update on his daughter. Knowing that Amanda's friends had been killed—as well as presumably all but two of her protective detail—and that they were trying to get her to a hospital for treatment of her unspecified injuries, made it very difficult for Jack Rutledge to concentrate on the task at hand. Carolyn promised to brief him every twenty minutes, whether she had any new information or not.

With confirmation that Amanda's friends had not survived the attack on the Williamsburg Bridge, Rutledge contacted their parents from *Air Force One* and delivered the heartbreaking news personally.

When the president arrived at the White House, he read through the final draft of his speech and nodded his head. No one had heard him utter a word since entering the building. The man's face was resolute, and it was clearly evident that he was both enraged and distraught beyond communication.

Waving off the makeup artist, Rutledge stared into the camera and waited to be given the signal that he was on the air. When it came, he began speaking.

"Good afternoon. Today, our great nation has come under attack. With the despicable terrorist acts of September eleventh, 2001, still fresh in our minds, the forces of evil lashed out at our very way of life by once again targeting New York City.

"Americans in the thousands have died as a result of these deliberate and cowardly acts. The victims come from all walks of life. They were businessmen and women, doctors, teachers, students, children, moms, dads, sisters, and brothers—all of whom were preparing to celebrate the nation's birthday. Many more were injured, including my own daughter, Amanda, who along with two of her friends, now deceased, were making their way into New York when the attacks occurred. As a father, as president of this great nation, and as an American I feel the pain of the people of New York.

"The images of burning bridges and smoldering tunnels have filled us all with shock, sadness, and a determined, unrelenting anger.

"The goal of these attacks was to extinguish the greatest beacon of hope and freedom in the world, but America's light will not be dimmed. We shall emerge from this trial and we shall do so with our beacon of hope shining brighter than ever before.

"While the terrorists may be able to shake the foundations of bridges and tunnels, they cannot shake the foundations of our great country.

"We have once again been forced to stare into the face of evil, but I know that as Americans we will not let that evil divide us. I urge everyone to remain calm. The full resources of the American government are being brought to bear to identify and locate those responsible for committing these despicable acts. As we have said continually, those who harbor terrorists are just as guilty as the terrorists themselves and we shall make no distinction between the two.

"I want to thank the members of Congress who stand with me in so strongly condemning these attacks. And on behalf of the American people, I also want to thank the many world leaders who have already contacted me to express their condolences and to offer assistance. Most of all, I want to thank the rescue workers, police, fire, and EMS, as well as the millions of Americans across the country who are lining up to give blood and are already putting in place the charitable mechanisms that will be so needed in the days, weeks, and months ahead to help heal one of the greatest cities on this earth.

"To the people of New York I say you have suffered an unfathomable loss, but you are not alone. Each and every American stands shoulder-to-shoulder with you right now and you are in both our thoughts as well as our prayers. Our hearts are heavy with sadness at your loss, a loss borne by all freedom- and peace-loving people across America and around the world."

Geoff Mitchell watched from just off camera as the president prepared to wrap it up. The remarks were pitch-perfect, and Rutledge had delivered them flawlessly. After showing a quick excerpt from the Declaration of Independence about America pledging its sacred honor to help the victims and their families, the cameras would fade to the presidential seal and that would be it.

Though the circumstances were horrible, the press secretary had always hoped he'd be given a chance to write a speech that would be remembered for eternity. He felt pretty confident this was going to be one of those speeches. What he didn't know was that why it would be so well remembered was still yet to come.

As the president came to the end of his remarks, he abandoned his script.

"And to the terrorists responsible for this revolting act of cowardice, I say this. America will never stop until we have hunted every last one of you down. We will go to the far corners of the earth, draining every swamp and turning over every rock along the way. And when we find you—and we *will* find you—we shall use every means at our disposal to visit upon you a death one thousand times more hideous than that which you have delivered to our doorstep today.

"America has defeated the greatest evils of the modern world and it *will* defeat the scourge of radical Islamic fanaticism as well.

"Thank you and God bless America."

The red light atop the main camera switched off, but no one spoke. Not even the floor director, whose job it was to inform the president that they were safely off the air.

"Am I clear?" asked Rutledge.

The irony was not lost upon the director, who replied, "I'd say you were crystal clear, sir."

Knowing it would take several minutes for the technical people to pack up their equipment from the Oval Office, Chuck Anderson asked, "Mr. President, may I have a word, please, in my office?" Pointing at the press secretary, he added, "You too, Geoff."

Once they had gone through the adjoining door and it had closed firmly behind them, the chief of staff said, "Do you have any idea what you've just done?"

"We're not going to hide behind politically correct labels anymore, Chuck."

"I'd say you made that abundantly clear. Along with the fact that the Christian West is now officially at war with Islam."

"I didn't say we were at war with *Islam.* I said radical Islamic fanaticism," replied the president.

The chief of staff looked at the press secretary. "Am I wrong, Geoff, or are we now officially at war with the Islamic religion?"

"I think you're taking the president's remarks slightly out of context," said Mitchell.

"And you don't think that's what's being done right now by every two-bit imam and petty despot in every Muslim nation around the world?"

"I don't think it's beyond repair. He was angry and with very good reason. We can smooth it over."

"Just hold it," ordered the president. "We're not retracting, repairing, or smoothing anything over. I'm tired of dancing around. This country is going to stand by those remarks."

"All the same, sir, I wish you would have run them by me first," said the press secretary. "Going off-the-cuff like that can be very damaging, no matter how well intentioned."

The chief of staff, a longtime friend of the president's, shrugged and said, "The president doesn't do anything off-the-cuff, Geoff. He knew very well what he was saying."

"I don't understand," responded Mitchell.

Rutledge took a deep breath. "Am I angry? You're damn right I am. Our country has been attacked, and I have no idea if because of those attacks my daughter is going to live or die. I said what every single American and every single Western world leader wanted to say and needed to say—radical Islam must be stamped out. Everyone tiptoes around the elephant in the middle of the room while the elephant continues to eat and grows bigger and bigger right before our eyes."

"What about our Muslim allies?"

"What about them?" scoffed the president. "Radical Islam is an even bigger threat to them, and yet they sit idly by and do nothing at all about it."

"What about the regular Muslims who might see this as a slight against them and their religion?"

"To hell with them. Mainstream Islam has done absolutely nothing to stop this cancer metastasizing within their midst. They haven't even wholeheartedly condemned it. As far as I'm concerned, they don't get a pass anymore. No more sitting on the fence, waiting to see which way this all goes. Either they're part of the solution or they're part of the problem. Period."

The chief of staff as well as the usually verbose press secretary were both at a loss for words.

Finally, Geoff Mitchell said, "Then I guess we really are at war."

THIRTY

For security reasons, they had agreed that real names would not be used. From an operational standpoint, it was much better that way for all of them. To tell them apart, Jaffe and his team had assigned nicknames to the two foreign intelligence agents working with them. The lanky, dark-complexioned man in his mid-thirties with the Brillo-pad hair and breath that reeked of garlic was called Rashid, while the older, more experienced operative with the pockmarked face, jet black eyes, and Turkish mustache was referred to as Hassan.

Outside the interrogation room, Jaffe banged one of the monitors on the AV cart, hoping to improve the quality of the satellite downlink. "C'mon, damn it," he mumbled as he tried to tweak the signal.

"I think we're really crossing the line with this one," said Brad Harper as he stood and watched the ghostlike images fading in and out of focus from halfway around the world. "Mohammed's only been in U.S. custody for six weeks. We can break him. We just need to give it more time."

"We might not have any more time."

"But now we're talking about noncombatants. *Kids,* for Christ's sake."

"Really?" said Jaffe. "What about all the kids killed on the bridges and in the tunnels today? Do you think these people gave a damn about them?"

"Obviously not, but—"

"How about all the other kids who will be killed if that sick son of a bitch in there gets away with launching multiple nuclear attacks on our soil?"

"That still doesn't make it right, and I want to go on the record as being completely against this."

"Duly noted," replied Jaffe as the signal finally improved enough for them to proceed. "I don't know how long we'll be able to hold the downlink, so get in there and make sure we're ready to go. And by the way," he added as Harper began walking away, "I want you to remember that I didn't get to where I am by being stupid or soft."

Harper had considered the man neither stupid nor soft. In fact, he might have even been too hard for his own good. Nevertheless, there was nothing for Harper to say. All he was left with was a sick feeling in the pit of his stomach. Marines were honorable, and they sure as hell didn't torture children.

Even though it was going to happen on the other side of the globe, Harper felt as responsible for what was coming as if he were standing in North Africa carrying out the orders himself. He could only hope that God would have mercy on their souls for what they were about to do.

Moments later, the door to the interrogation room opened and Mike Jaffe rolled the AV cart inside with its multiple cables snaking behind into the hallway. Before turning the monitors back on, he addressed the prisoners, who were Flexicuffed to two very uncomfortable wooden chairs. Both of the men spoke English well enough, so there was no need for a translator.

"It took us quite a while to make the connection between you two. In fact, we almost missed it. We'd spent so much time looking for any of bin Laden's or Zawahiri's children who might have gone into the family business, that we foolishly never considered your lineage, Mohammed. You must be very proud of your nephew here. He seems to have really taken to the profession.

"I've been trying to figure out what the bin Mohammed-Jamal family crest might look like. Maybe two lions holding a roadside bomb, or would it be more subtle? Maybe a chain of blasting caps over a nice banner that read *Women and children first?*

"Anyway, we decided to do a little more genealogy, and guess what we found?" Jaffe nodded his head and Harper activated both of the monitors. "Ra'na is quite a lovely village."

As the monitors glowed to life, one showed the battered, mud-brick exterior of a large village house, while the other showed a family of women and children huddled in one of the rooms inside. Several men in black fatigues with dark balaclavas covering their faces held them at gunpoint.

Sayed Jamal instantly stiffened in his chair. It was exactly the reaction Jaffe had been hoping for. "I guess I don't need to ask whose house we're looking at."

Mohammed knew that he was looking at his nephew's home and family, but he remained completely impassive.

"Take a good look at them," said Jaffe, as he held up his cell phone. "The men in that house work for me. They obey my orders, and unless you start cooperating, things are going to get very unpleasant for your nephew's family. Now tell me about the nuclear material."

Jaffe counted quietly to three and asked the question in a different way. "We already know where the material was stolen from a top secret European facility. We also have a pretty good handle on when it was stolen. What we don't know is who's planning on selling it to you and how you planned to use it. Tell me what I want to know, and I'll have my men leave that house right now."

When Mohammed refused to answer, Jaffe raised the cell phone to his ear and said, "Start with the oldest daughter."

Immediately, there was a frenzy of activity on the monitor as the order was relayed and one of the gunmen pulled a screaming young woman away from her family and dragged her out of the room. The family members wailed and the image shook as the camera was removed from its tripod and rushed down the hallway. It caught up with the gunman in what appeared to be a bathroom. A large copper tub was filled with water and the gunman was holding the woman's head underneath.

Sayed Jamal cursed his captors in Arabic as tears began to stream down his face. Jaffe, though, paid no attention to him. His eyes were locked on Mohammed bin Mohammed.

Jamal quickly realized what was going on and turned to his uncle, begging him to tell the Americans whatever they wanted to know. Mohammed yelled at him to shut up.

Brad Harper didn't give a damn if it was insubordination or not—he couldn't allow this to go on any longer. Approaching Jaffe, the powerfully built marine said, "That's it. We're not doing this. You're going to have to find another way."

Without taking his eyes off Mohammed, Jaffe drew his pistol and pointed it at Harper's head, stopping the marine in his tracks. "Every member of this family will die, slowly and painfully, unless you tell me what I want to know," said Jaffe, his eyes boring into Mohammed's. "Who is selling the nuclear material?"

When the man still refused to answer, Jaffe spoke into his cell phone again. "Kill her."

The command was relayed to the gunman on the monitor, who drew his sidearm, placed it over the edge of the tub, and fired two shots.

Jamal was hysterical with rage and screamed first at the Americans and then at his uncle for having killed his daughter.

Mohammed looked at him and told him to shut up.

Jaffe didn't bother asking about the nuclear material now. Instead he spoke into his cell phone, and once the camera had returned to the room where the family was corralled, he said to Mohammed, "Why don't you pick the next one?"

THIRTY-ONE

Harvath had just hung up with Kevin McCauliff when Herrington walked into Dr. Hardy's office with his crew and said, "Everyone's in."

Harvath looked Morgan, Cates, and Hastings over—sizing them up, as it were, trying to divine whether they'd be up to what he might call on them to do.

Bits and pieces of the things Bob had told him about them in his e-mails floated to the forefront of Harvath's mind. Cates, who had relocated to New York from Oklahoma, was the son of evangelical parents. Though he himself was not particularly religious, he saw the war on terror exactly as his enemy did, as an out-and-out crusade. The physical stresses of the job had bought him a ticket out of active duty when both his knees blew on an assignment in the south of Afghanistan.

Morgan, the youngest team member, had been raised by a single mother. He'd been in big trouble with drugs and street gangs and had joined the Marine Corps as his ticket out and a way to see the world beyond New York. Though a head wound left him unfit for duty, many doctors, including Hardy, questioned if he wasn't already just a bit off—a bit too reckless with his own life long before that fateful day in Iraq.

Finally there was Tracy Hastings—the Naval EOD tech. She was the daughter of a wealthy New York family; her parents had seriously disagreed with her decision to join the armed forces, but the attack on the *USS Cole* had helped her make up her mind, and the headstrong young woman wouldn't be dissuaded. She hadn't joined the Navy in spite of her affluent upbringing, she had joined *because* of it. She thought that if anyone had an obligation to serve their country, it was people who had profited so handsomely by it.

Tracy used a little makeup to cover the facial scars left by an IED disposal gone bad, but the damage was still visible. From what Herrington had told Harvath, her injuries had been quite severe, but the surgeons had done a remarkable job—right down to matching the particularly pale blue color for her artificial eye.

Harvath could tell by looking at each of the people standing there that they were a tightly knit group. That was good. The question was, could they function both as individuals and as a cohesive unit under the stress of combat? And just as important, would they accept him, an outsider, as both one of their own and as their leader?

As Hardy went to check on some of his other patients, they had the office to themselves. Harvath asked Herrington to close the door. Once it was shut, he said, "I am going to be completely honest with all of you. You're not my first choice for something like this, and you're not even my last choice. But the situation being what it is, you are my *only* choice."

"Fuck you too," said Morgan.

Herrington held up his hand and said, "Let him finish."

Harvath waited a beat and then said, "State, local, and federal resources are completely, and I mean *completely,* tied up with search-and-rescue efforts. Air traffic over and maritime traffic around Manhattan has been suspended due to sniper and RPG fire. What helicopter and boat traffic there is, is working off the opposite sides of both the Hudson and East rivers. Somebody doesn't want any reinforcements making it to Manhattan. That means that we will have no support for this assignment whatsoever. Your participation will be in an unofficial, unrecognized, and most definitely unsanctioned capacity."

"Meaning what?" asked Cates.

"It means you're not federal employees and you are not being recognized as active duty soldiers—in essence, your disabled status hasn't changed."

"I guess it's lucky for you then that even though they took our jobs, we all got to keep our training," replied Cates.

Harvath liked that answer. Continuing, he said, "We're dealing with an extremely well organized enemy of indeterminate size and resources who is presumably still operating somewhere in Manhattan."

"You mean they're not done yet?" responded Paul Morgan.

Harvath shook his head. "I don't know. That's why I wanted to be completely straight with you. In short, we have very little idea of what we're up against. This could turn out to be nothing, but I've got a feeling it might be an extremely dangerous assignment. Anybody have any other questions?"

"Yeah," joked Cates, "so what's the bad news?"

A wave of tense laughter rolled through the room.

Tracy Hastings raised her hand halfway and asked, "If we don't know who these people are and what their objective is, how are we supposed to find them?"

"I just got off the phone with someone who's working on it," replied Harvath. "We might have something very soon, so we need to be ready to move. In the meantime, we've got a bigger problem. All I have is a pistol, and it's in my truck back up in Midtown. We're going to have to figure out what we're going to do for weapons."

Another wave of laughter rolled through the room, but this time it was anything but tense.

Twenty minutes later Paul Morgan removed a piece of false drywall from the back of a closet in his small Gramercy Park apartment and said, "Go ahead and take your pick."

It was a veritable arsenal. In the pistol department Morgan had two Unertl MEU SOC 1911's, a Glock 19, and a four-inch-barreled .357 Smith & Wesson 620. Hanging next to them were a Mossberg 590 12-gauge shotgun, a Remington 40-X .308 sniper rifle, and a fully automatic Troy Industries CQB-SPC A4 assault rifle that Morgan had chanced a big official ass-whupping for smuggling out of Iraq.

"So much for our weapons problem," said Harvath as he gazed at the display. "I'm going to ask another stupid question, but how are you set for ammo?"

Once again, the group laughed. Morgan crossed into the kitchen, which was covered with travel posters for places he hoped some day to see—Paris, Rome, Hong Kong—and removed a set of keys from his pocket. The refrigerator was a mosaic of snapshots showing Morgan as a marine in a number of other exotic locations around the world that were normally much more humid or dusty than Paris, Rome, or Hong Kong.

He unlocked a small padlock on the side of the freezer door and swung it open. Inside, boxes of shrink-wrapped ammunition stood in a neat series of rows.

"Where do you keep your grenade launcher?" asked Herrington.

"Dr. Hardy told me that grenade launchers are for paranoids, so I sold it to a buddy of mine a while back."

Morgan let them stand there wondering for a second longer and then smiled and said, "Kidding. Only kidding. I never had a grenade launcher. Besides, with what the surface-to-air missile battery I've got up on the roof cost me, who could afford a grenade launcher?"

Everyone laughed, but secretly none of them would have been surprised to find that Morgan did have a crate of SAMs stashed somewhere upstairs.

Clearing off the kitchen table, Morgan hoisted a KIVA technical backpack stuffed to the gills with gear and set it onto one of the chairs.

"Is that your bug-out bag?" asked Hastings.

The marine nodded his head and began unloading his pack. "A week's worth of the very best survival equipment money can buy."

As Morgan pulled out MREs, chemlights, water purification tablets, parachute cord, and other items, Cates said, "A week's worth? Whatever happened to seventy-two hours?"

"Hurricane Katrina, that's what." The marine looked at Harvath. "Even DHS is now telling people they need to have at least a week's worth of supplies on hand in case of trouble, right?"

Harvath nodded his head knowing that they were talking about having people raise it to a month or even two. Not only did he have a bug-out bag ready to go at a moment's notice in case of a terrorist attack or some other sort of disaster, but so did most of the military, law enforcement, and intelligence people he worked worth. Even civilians had them. The way Harvath saw it, it was pretty stupid for anyone, government employee or otherwise, not to be ready in case of an emergency. That said, his bug-out bag was sitting in the back of his TraillBlazer in a garage uptown. It weighed at least fifty pounds, and it would have been quite uncomfortable to carry everywhere with him. Even so, there were several items in it he would have liked to have with him right now.

As Morgan continued to remove items from his seemingly bottomless bag, Hastings asked, "Where'd you get all the money for this stuff?"

"Let's just say that in my old life I was a good saver."

"A real good saver," added Cates as he checked the labels in a couple of the sport coats hanging in Morgan's closet.

The marine laid out an assortment of extremely high-quality knives from Chris Reeve as well as a brand-new Gerber LMF II-Infantry, which could be used to carve one's way out of a helicopter fuselage, and respectfully offered Harvath first pick.

Though they were all exceptional, Harvath already had his never-leave-home-without-it Benchmade auto in his pocket, and if they made it back to his TrailBlazer he'd have access to a superb fixed-blade knife from LaRue Tactical.

"I don't suppose you've got some flashbangs in there?" said Harvath as he watched Paul Morgan continue to pull gear out of his bag.

"No, but I do have this," replied the marine as he withdrew a Blackhawk medical pack.

Harvath was about to say that he hoped they wouldn't need that when his cell phone rang. It was Kevin McCauliff.

After chatting with him for only a few seconds, two things became apparent. Kevin had some pretty good news. He also had some pretty bad news.

THIRTY-TWO

Harvath listened as McCauliff gave him the good news first. The NGA analyst had been able to hack the server containing the tracking data for the terrorist's cell phone that Harvath had "borrowed" from the NYPD's evidence bag. It was one of over forty-seven different phones operating off the same account. It and one other had continued to broadcast a signal after the bridges and tunnels had been blown. That "other" phone was recognized by the server as the lead wireless reception device. McCauliff explained that all of the units had been programmed to text message positioning data to the lead phone at regular intervals. Now it was time for the bad news.

Wherever that lead phone was, it was now no longer transmitting a signal. McCauliff had no way to tell Harvath its current location, only where it had been—an address on the Upper West Side and another in the diamond district on West 47th Street.

Even though the lead phone appeared to have been disabled, McCauliff strongly suggested that Harvath make sure that the positioning software on the one he was now carrying was turned off. Harvath told him he'd already done so back at the police station and, as he grabbed a pen and paper, asked McCauliff to repeat the addresses the lead phone had been at one more time.

When Harvath asked if there was any satellite imagery available for those locations, McCauliff told him that was also part of the bad news and that Harvath would understand what he meant once he saw it. All Kevin needed was an e-mail address. Harvath saw the cable modem next to the PC on Paul Morgan's desk, crossed his fingers he'd be able to get online, and gave McCauliff one of the Hotmail accounts he used when he didn't want to run things through the DHS servers.

Five minutes later, Harvath downloaded the first in a series of e-mails and saw exactly what McCauliff meant about the satellite imagery also being part of the "bad" news. The smoke from all of the fires made it very difficult to make anything out. Three e-mails later, he waved Herrington over and said, "Do you see what I see here?"

Bob stared at the screen and slowly scrolled through the images from the building on West 84th Street. When he was finished, he backed up and did it again, then repeated the process several more times. He wanted to be as sure as possible before rendering any kind of opinion. Finally he said, "The image quality absolutely sucks, but if I had to make a guess, I'd say that those are pictures of two vehicles carrying two breaching teams of anywhere from four to seven men each."

"That's what I think too," replied Harvath as he clicked on the imagery of the diamond district address. "How about here?"

"These pictures are even worse than the others," said Bob. "Those could be our two vehicles, or they could be completely different ones. With all the haze and interference from the smoke, you can't tell for sure."

"Well, there's only one way to find out."

"Hoo-ah," shouted Cates, mocking Morgan, but doing it with the Army yell. "Let's go get those fuckers."

Hastings paid no attention to Cates. Looking at all the gear, she said, "Don't you think we're going to draw a lot of attention running around Manhattan with all of this stuff?"

"Good point," replied Herrington as he looked at Morgan.

The marine crossed the room and pulled several backpacks from his hall closet. "A buddy of mine is a rep for CamelBak. These are their new scabbard bags. You can throw a rifle or a shotgun into the scabbard in the center and then pack the rest of your gear in the compartments around it."

Harvath studied the cleverly designed bags and remarked, "It's still going to look like we're packing some serious firepower."

Morgan pulled three rain covers from behind his snowshoes. "We'll use these for the Remington, the Troy CQB, and the Mossberg. Nobody will have any idea what we're carrying."

For someone who had his hair parted seriously enough by a bullet to be medically discharged from the Marines, so far he seemed to have his act together. This guy didn't miss a trick. "Okay," remarked Scot. "I guess now all we have to do is figure out how the hell we're going to get where we're going."

Looking out one of the windows and down the street of the lower-floor apartment, Rick Cates replied, "I've got an idea, but I've also got a feeling nobody's going to like it."

THIRTY-THREE

Eyeing the collection of dirt bikes outside Cox Cycle Shop, Harvath cautioned Cates not to let things devolve into a *That's my chopper Charlie, this is my gun Clyde* kind of situation.

As they stood on the sidewalk watching the Army Civil Affairs specialist spin his story to the cross-armed, heavily tattooed staff of the motorcycle custom shop, Harvath, Herrington, Hastings, and Morgan tried to come up with a Plan B.

They agreed that the fastest way to the diamond district from Gramercy Park was to try to go straight up Fifth Avenue, but it was reserved for emergency vehicles only, and most of the cops they'd been seeing weren't particularly helpful. Unless you were driving an official vehicle, they weren't letting anyone through, not even a car full of surgeons they'd seen who needed to get to an uptown hospital as quickly as possible. Harvath was wondering if maybe they would be better off heading north on foot, retrieving his vehicle and using its lights-and-siren package to try to barrel through the rest of the distance, when Cates was shoved backward onto the pavement by one of the tattooed bikers.

Immediately, Harvath and the rest of his group stepped forward, but Cates held up his hand and waved them back. Showing extreme patience and control, he got up off the ground, dusted himself off, and reengaged the man who had just shoved him.

Harvath and the others watched as Cates went toe-to-toe with the 250-pound biker and their exchange got progressively more heated.

Moments later, the biker grabbed Cates by the throat and swung his other arm around in an attempt to hit him in the side of the head. Cates parried the blow and brought his free hand crashing into the man's jaw. Before the tattooed giant could respond, Cates whipped his head forward and shattered the cartilage in the man's nose with a vicious head butt.

The bike store manager rammed his knee into Cates's abdomen, but the Special Forces reservist quickly returned the assault by kicking the big man in the groin, causing his knees to buckle and for him to fall to the pavement in pain.

"If you guys would like to help," yelled Cates over his shoulder as the rest of the biker staff in the shop began grabbing wrenches, pipes, and assorted bludgeons, "now would probably be a good time."

Harvath and company drew their weapons and rushed forward. Upon seeing the display of firepower, the biker shop staff laid down their arms and retreated into the back of the garage.

Cates kicked his assailant in the gut and walked inside, located the keys for the motorcycles they wanted, and then hit the button to lower the garage-style door. Once it was down, he jammed a screwdriver into the holes where the padlock normally went, pulled two sets of Flexicuffs from Paul Morgan's pack, and secured the front door.

"What did I tell you about not turning this situation into a confrontation?" demanded Harvath as they climbed onto the motorcycles.

"I couldn't help it," replied Cates as he fired his up. "Did you see that guy's tats?"

"He's got a million of them—so what?"

"You obviously missed the one on his left arm," said Cates as he pulled forward onto the sidewalk. "He had a picture of Uncle Sam with a black eye and underneath it the letters F-T-A."

"Fuck The Army?" yelled Morgan over the whine of his Suzuki. "Fuck that asshole. Hoorah, Cates."

Herrington and Hastings both flashed Rick the thumbs-up, and Harvath had no choice but to flash his as well. To be kicked out of the service for what was known as the Big Chicken Dinner, or more correctly a *bad conduct discharge* meant that the bike shop manager was one screwed-up individual and had committed the equivalent of a serious felony.

To proudly boast that fact underneath a disfigured tattoo of Uncle Sam was unforgivable. He deserved everything Cates had dished out to him and more.

"What do you say, boss?" yelled Morgan as he revved his motorcycle.

Harvath noticed that the team was looking to Bullet Bob for guidance, and as Herrington shot a questioning look in Harvath's direction, Harvath nodded his head for him to take control. These people respected Bob's experience and looked to him as their leader.

"Forty-seventh and Fifth," yelled Herrington, "as fast as we can get there."

Lowering his head and rocketing his bike out into traffic, Harvath decided he could worry about chain-of-command issues later. Right now, they had a very strange puzzle to start putting together. The only question was, were the few pieces they had going to be enough to make any sort of progress?

THIRTY-FOUR

Gary Lawlor tried to discern a connection between the two addresses Harvath had given him. The terrorists were obviously looking for something, but what? What could they possibly want in a brownstone on the Upper West Side and a location in the diamond district in Midtown? Neither seemed typical terrorist targets.

Compounding the problem was that someone at the DIA was playing some sort of role in all of this, but until he had a better handle on who and what it was, there was no way Lawlor was going to tip his hand to them. They were a collection of superspooks bound by completely different rules of engagement than the rest of the intelligence community. Theirs were the rules of war, and there wasn't much they couldn't do—including locking him up indefinitely without charge for even sniffing around the edges of one of their operations. Call it interagency mistrust or a strong instinct for self-preservation, but until Lawlor got a much better feel for the lay of the land, he was going to stay as far away from the DOD and its Defense Intelligence Agency as possible.

In the meantime, as the director of the Apex Project, he had a host of other resources at his disposal. Logging on to his computer, he accessed the shared intelligence database network and entered the two addresses that Kevin McCauliff had provided Harvath with. When the search results came back, they were more than disappointing—they were downright impossible. According to the database, there was no information available for either address—no utility records, no mortgage or business license information, nothing. Both locations appeared to be operating in a vacuum—a big *black* one.

Someone had scrubbed both addresses so completely clean that neither offered a single trail leading anywhere. That kind of sterilization normally happened only in covert government operations so deep they were referred to as happening at "crush depth"—a status reserved for issues of vital national security. For one reason or another, these issues were sometimes better handled in the civilian arena, rather than on military bases or at established intelligence agencies, but even so, the crush depth locations Lawlor had known during his career were like mini-fortresses.

Gary still wasn't any closer to understanding what was going on in New York, though. If the imagery from Kevin McCauliff did indeed show two crush depth locations being hit, what was the reason? Better yet, how in the world could the terrorists have known about them? The operational intelligence would have been Polo Step at the very least. The fact that they had hit not one but two suggested a security compromise so devastating that its repercussions could very well be felt for years, if not for decades, to come.

Lawlor jumped over to the DHS server, pulled up the most current FEMA damage map for New York City and filtered out as much "noise" as possible. He wasn't interested in casualty estimates or the positioning of emergency equipment. All he wanted to know was where the terrorists had specifically struck. Once that information was isolated, he added secondary problem spots such as reported sniper and RPG locations, apartment building and property fires, as well as any other major events that demanded a large police, fire, or EMS response. With those in place, he added the last layer—the secret Upper West Side and Midtown locations the terrorists had just struck.

He tried to make sense of it, but the harder he stared at the screen the more the questions piled up in his brain. If these were crush depth locations, what agency or group was running them and what was their purpose? With all the chaos in New York, was whoever oversaw those locations even aware that they'd been hit? That was one of Lawlor's biggest questions.

The only obvious thing in the whole muddled mix was that if the terrorists were pinpointing and hitting actual crush depth locations, then the United States was in even bigger trouble than it thought.

Lawlor realized that he was going to have to go against his better judgment and talk to people outside his immediate circle. Whatever the fallout might be, as long as he could stop the terrorists before they struck again, it would be worth it.

THIRTY-FIVE

NATIONAL SECURITY AGENCY
FORT MEADE, MARYLAND

Mark Schreiber poked his head into his supervisor's fluorescent-lit office and said, "I think we've got another problem in Manhattan."

"No kidding," replied Joseph Stanton, jerking his thumb over his shoulder toward the flat-panel televisions on the wall behind him. "Some idiot blogger started a rumor that a bio agent was part of the attack and no matter what Mayor Brown says, nobody is listening to him."

"That's not what I'm talking about," replied Schreiber as he stepped the rest of the way inside and closed the door behind him. "Transcon and Geneva Diamond are unresponsive."

Stanton stopped what he was doing and laid down his purple highlighter. His bespectacled face was bloated from a diet too rich in sodium, along with too many Hennessy-and-Cokes after hours. His hair was unkempt and his entire wardrobe seemed to be permanently wrinkled. He wore a seersucker suit that should have been retired years ago and a striped regimental tie decorated with coffee stains. "Unresponsive how?"

"Nobody's answering e-mail."

"Did you try calling them?"

Schreiber nodded his head. "The phones don't seem to be working."

"How about pinging the servers?"

"I did that and it comes back A-Okay. Still processing."

"So what's the problem?" asked Stanton.

"If we can ping the servers via satellite and get a response, then why isn't their e-mail working? It piggybacks off the same system."

"New York's in chaos right now. We don't know what the damage is or what services have been interrupted. Let's not worry about it."

"You don't find it a bit odd that we can't connect with two of our substations?"

"Considering everything that's going on up there, not really. The servers are still churning, right? You said so yourself. So, someone has got to be processing data."

"Yeah, but I just have a bad feeling about it," replied Schreiber.

"We're under attack, so having bad feelings is understandable. Give it a little while longer. I'm sure we'll hear something."

"And if we don't?"

Stanton didn't have time for this. "Then we'll have a friendly neighborhood beat cop stroll by and give us a report."

"You're joking, right?" said the young man.

Of course he was joking, and if this kid spent a little more time interacting with real live people and a little less time at his computer, he might know it. Picking up his highlighter and turning his attention back to the stack of paperwork on his desk, Stanton replied, "It's going to be a very long night, Mark. Why don't you take a few minutes, relax, and then see what kind of sourcing help they're going to need upstairs."

"Fine, but if we still don't hear anything from New York?"

"Then we'll dig a little deeper. But for now, I want you focused on helping the people here who need it the most. I've been to Transcon and Geneva Diamond. Believe me, those folks know how to handle themselves."

THIRTY-SIX

NEW YORK CITY

Navigating through the traffic as best he could, Fiore kept the Secret Service Command Center apprised of their status, while Marcy fed him updates from the backseat. The bottom line was that their progress was horrible and their patient was getting worse.

With the FDR completely impassable, Tim was forced onto side streets, most of which were jammed.

At 7th Street near Tompkins Square, Marcy yelled, "Tim, she's crashing! We're losing her!"

Rapidly scrolling through the iQue's options, Tim found what he was looking for. "I'm going to cut through this park. Hold on . . ."

Jumping the curb at Avenue B, Fiore raced through Tompkins Square and came out again at 10th Street and Avenue A. He barreled through a police barricade at First Avenue and, after hanging a tire-screaming right turn, pinned the accelerator and raced for Beth Israel Hospital. His only hope was that they'd be able to make it there in time.

THIRTY-SEVEN

The lone NYPD officer standing guard outside the battered Geneva Diamond and Jewelry Exchange storefront was relieved when Harvath appeared and flashed his DHS credentials. The fact that he had pulled up on a dirt bike along with four other rather hard-looking individuals didn't faze him a bit, not with everything else that had already happened that afternoon.

The officer had been waiting for backup since stumbling onto the scene forty-five minutes earlier while en route to another location. With every pair of professionally trained hands in the city needed to help search for survivors in the rubble of the bridge and tunnel bombings, random lootings weren't on the patrolman's priority list. But when a group of 47th Street merchants flagged him down and told him what had happened, the officer immediately changed his mind.

After moving onlookers away from the front of the store, he ventured a few feet inside. What he saw had caused him to remain there until help arrived. He was just about to reluctantly abandon the post, when Harvath showed. Now, he was more than happy to turn things over to someone with more authority and greater jurisdiction. In all his years on the job, nothing had prepared the patrolman for the carnage he'd seen inside.

Now it was Harvath's turn. With Bob Herrington and the rest of the team in tow, they picked their way around the dead bodies and brass shell casings at the front of the store and headed toward the vault-style door at the back.

The door was half open and as they approached it, Tracy Hastings ordered the team to stop.

"What's up?" said Harvath.

Hastings pointed to the pockmarks on the walls and ceiling around the frame and replied, "Shrapnel. We can't touch that door until we're sure it's not rigged."

Harvath thought she was being a little too cautious, until Herrington said, "Trust her. She knows what she's doing."

"All right," he responded, stepping aside to let her get a better look at it. "But make it quick."

Once Hastings was convinced it was safe, she waved the rest of the team forward.

Inside, they found a high-tech security control room that had been blown apart by what Hastings claimed was probably one or more fragmentation grenades. Lying on the floor were the badly mangled bodies of three men in tactical vests with modified M16s lying nearby.

"These guys are jarheads," remarked Morgan as he rolled one of the bodies over.

"Plenty of guys in the security industry cut their hair too short," said Cates. "That doesn't make them marines."

Morgan ignored the remark and pointed at the men's feet. "The Marines only use the best gear, and these guys are all wearing Quantico Desert Boots."

While Harvath preferred Original S.W.A.T. boots, Paul Morgan did have a point. Many of the marines he'd known were particularly fond of Quantico Boots, but even with the M16s, there still wasn't enough evidence to qualify the bodies as being marines.

As if reading his mind, Morgan slid a plate out of one of their tactical vests, wrapped on it with his knuckles and said, "U.S. military–issue Interceptor body armor. Harder than Kevlar and can stop anything up to a 7.62-millimeter round."

Cates whistled and said, "These guys certainly were prepared."

"But for what?" replied Harvath, more for his own benefit than anyone else's. "Whoever took these marines out must have been very good. Let's finish clearing these rooms."

Bob and the rest of the team relieved the marines of their SIG Sauer P228 pistols, as well as their machine guns and as many loaded magazines as they could carry, before sweeping the balance of the Geneva Diamond and Jewelry Exchange. As they did, Harvath tried to figure out what the hell the operation's real function was. In the heart of New York City, no jewelry store—no matter how busy or how well connected its owners—was going to be granted the protection of three machine-gun-toting U.S. marines.

As they went from room to room, it became apparent that the operation was completely paperless. Whatever secret it held had either been taken to the grave when its personnel had been raked with gunfire, had been stolen by the terrorists, or was locked up in its workstations and racks and racks of servers.

Exercising the only other option left available to him, Harvath collected whatever photo identification he could from each of the fifteen corpses, including the three U.S. servicemen whose IDs listed them in fact as active-duty marines.

He hoped Gary would be able to make some sense out of it, because at this moment, Harvath had absolutely no idea what or who they were dealing with.

THIRTY-EIGHT

Less than halfway through their list of locations, Abdul Ali considered himself lucky that they'd only lost one of the Chechen soldiers. It was a treacherous but necessary path they'd been forced to follow. The Troll had explained that each location would be more difficult to assault than the last, and that was why Ali and his team were taking them in ascending order of difficulty. There was no sense starting with the most difficult location and working their way backward only to find that Mohammed bin Mohammed was being held at one of the less fortified sites. It seemed reasonable and there was a consolation, however small, that with each location they scratched off their list, Abdul Ali was one step closer to recovering Mohammed.

Whether the man was waiting inside this location or the next made no difference to the Chechens. Unbeknownst to Ali, the Troll was paying them on a per-assault basis, and so it was in their financial interest that the attacks continue until the very bloody end.

What Ali did know was that the Troll had been one hundred percent correct about the American government's penchant for secrecy—especially when it came to the deep-cover operations on their list. Both the left and the right hands purposefully strove to keep each other in the dark and thereby created a considerably uncommunicative culture.

It would take days to sort out what had happened to the various New York undercover operations, and by then, Allah willing, Abdul Ali and Mohammed bin Mohammed would be long gone.

As the team approached its next objective, Ali was supremely confident that its occupants had no idea they were coming. He girded himself with the hope that this might be the last assault they would have to conduct.

The vents for the Lincoln Tunnel vent shaft were located at the West Midtown Ferry Terminal, also known as Pier 79, on Manhattan's West Side. As Abdul Ali and his Chechen mercenaries arrived, the vent shaft towers were still belching plumes of acrid black smoke high into the air from the hundreds upon hundreds of vehicles burning in the tunnel beneath the Hudson River.

Emergency personnel were everywhere as they tried to use the ventilation shafts to evacuate survivors. With over forty million vehicles passing through the tunnel each year, it was one of the busiest in the world and a perfect target. Ali quietly marveled at the chaos. Allah had indeed blessed their undertaking.

Attached to the north ventilation tower was a New York Waterway bus garage, and Ali instructed Sacha to park just past it alongside two large dumpsters. The men readied their weapons and then donned their gas masks and black tactical helmets. In practiced unison, they exited the vehicles and raced into the nearly empty garage accompanied by a very special Trojan horse.

Most of the bus staff had raced next door to try to help extricate survivors from the tunnel and only a handful remained behind. They were quickly dispatched by three of the Chechens who then dragged their bodies to the rear of the garage, where they could be hidden away out of sight.

The secondary stairwell secreted within the north ventilation tower had been constructed to be very difficult, if not impossible, to find without proper help. Once it was located, the team readied its secret weapon and sent "Ivan" hobbling down the stairs.

Via a fiber-optic camera mounted inside the animal's collar, Ali and his Chechen handler watched as the small yet sturdy border collie with its brightly colored search-and-rescue vest, limped forward toward a large steel door. Three feet away, the handler depressed a button on his remote, which caused the dog's collar to beep twice in quick succession. Immediately, the dog began whimpering and laid itself down.

For a moment, it appeared that their tactic was not going to work. Then the groan of metal on metal resounded through the corridor and up the stairwell as the steel door began to slowly open. Two men outfitted similarly to the marines at the Geneva Diamond and Jewelry Exchange appeared, and seeing no one else in the corridor, shouldered their weapons and cautiously approached the injured dog, wondering how it had made its way down there. They assumed it must have been part of the search-and-rescue efforts in the tunnel and had somehow lost its way.

What the marines should have been asking themselves was where the animal's handler was.

Once the marines were close enough, Ivan received another cue, got up and limped inside the facility.

Having seen enough from Ivan's collar-mounted camera, Ali nodded to the handler, who then signaled the rest of the team to get ready. The dog was then sent its final cue.

Ivan bit down on a tab at his right shoulder and pulled it forward, causing the heavy vest packed with plastique and ball bearings to activate and fall to the ground. The speedy dog was halfway to the stairs before anyone inside knew what had happened.

With the deafening roar of the explosion still ringing in the ears of those not instantly killed by the detonation, Abdul Ali and his men rushed inside with their weapons blazing. They plowed a bloody trail through the odd submarine-like structure as they searched for the man al-Qaeda was willing to risk anything to recover.

But once again, it was all in vain. Not only was Mohammed bin Mohammed nowhere to be found, there was no sign he had ever been there to begin with.

When they were safely inside the Tahoes and back out into the maddening traffic, Abdul Ali quietly went over the plan for taking down their next target. From everything he had read, this one was going to be their most difficult yet, and for the first time since they had started, he questioned his team's chances for success.

THIRTY-NINE

Scottish Highlands

The Troll had gone through only a fraction of the information from the Geneva Diamond and Jewelry Exchange when the Lincoln Tunnel data began to stream in. It was time for another payment to Sacha's account. The Chechen was easily worth his enormous weight in gold—especially when it was someone else's. The fact that Abdul Ali had no idea what his al-Qaeda money was really buying made the transaction even more delicious for the Troll.

It could conceivably take a lifetime to sift through all of the information now gorging his servers. Each piece on its own had a certain amount of value, but the skill—the art, if you will—was in knowing how to join together just the right tidbits to create a true masterpiece. That was where the Troll excelled in his profession. It was quite amazing, especially for someone whose prospects in life had been seen as so negligible that even his parents had given up on him early in life.

When it became obvious the Troll was not going to grow any further, his godless Georgian parents made no attempt to find a suitable loving home for their son, nor did they try to find even a half-decent orphanage. Instead, they abandoned the boy, selling him as if he were chattel to a thriving brothel on the outskirts of the Black Sea resort of

Sochi. There, the boy was starved, beaten, and made to perform unutterable sex acts that would have shamed even the Marquis de Sade himself.

It was there that the Troll learned the true value of information. The loose-lipped pillow talk of the powerful clients proved a goldmine once he had learned what to listen for and how to turn it to his advantage.

The whores, most of them life's castoffs as well, felt a kinship with the dwarf and treated him well. In fact, they became the only family he ever knew, and he repaid that kindness by one day buying their freedom. Those who had been unkind to him were evicted to fend for themselves, a fate made even more unbearable when the Troll had the madam and her husband tortured and then killed for the inhuman cruelty he had spent years suffering at their hands.

He had indeed come a long way, and once his servers were full from this transaction, the world could go to hell, as far as he was concerned. The data he was now hoarding was the ultimate annuity. With the money he stood to make, he could do and buy anything he wanted.

As the Troll scanned the data coming in, he enjoyed a bouchée of escargots and morel mushrooms followed by a magret of Duck Martiniquaise with caramelized leg confit, all complemented by an exquisite bottle of Château Quercy St. Emilion Bordeaux from his cellar. Though many, many dots would need to be connected, if the data flow stopped right at this moment, the Troll couldn't have been happier. The information being stored on his servers represented thousands upon thousands of man-hours, which he would never have to expend, but more importantly would never have to pay for.

Riding the heady wave of windfall, the Troll decided a little semi-retirement party was in order. There would be Kobe beef for Argus and Drako, and for himself, three of the most exquisite girls a certain *mariscala* he knew in Madrid would be more than happy to provide.

After e-mailing a request for the woman's most recent catalog, the Troll placed an order for hampers full of the most outrageous delicacies London's Fortnum & Mason had to offer—caviar, aged cheeses, foie gras, charcuterie, pies, chocolate, and chutneys. It was going to be the party to end all parties. The Georgian castoff had hit the ultimate jackpot.

FORTY

Except for the IDs Harvath had recovered from Geneva Diamond and Jewelry Exchange, the scene had been a complete bust. In fact it had raised more questions than it had answered, which left them with only one remaining lead—the Upper West Side location.

Since they were not that far from where Harvath had parked, they swung by to grab his bug-out bag. As only soldiers could, Cates, Hastings, and Morgan marveled at Harvath's custom-designed, high-end Tactical Electronics pack, as well as the wide variety of goodies it held.

Dumping it out in the rear cargo area, Harvath began repacking it with just the essentials he thought he might need, only to have Bob say several times, "You won't need that. Nope, that either."

Finally, with Bob's seal of approval the bag was packed and Harvath changed out of his jeans and polo shirt into a pair of 5.11 Tactical TDU trousers, an Under Armour shirt, a Blackhawk tactical vest, and his Original S.W.A.T. desert boots. He was now ready for anything, or so he hoped.

The team jumped back on their motorbikes, raced out of the garage, and headed north toward 84th Street.

Inside the Transcon building, the carnage was almost identical to

Geneva Diamond. The assailants had apparently entered via two breaching points—a front and side door. The men and women who worked inside were dressed in business attire and possessed a fair amount of weaponry. The weapons, though, had done them little good. Their dead bodies were sprawled across the floors or slumped over desks that were slick with blood, while the walls were strike-pointed with multiple-caliber bullet holes.

"Jesus Christ," exclaimed Cates as he surveyed the damage. "Who the hell is doing this?"

"More importantly, why are they doing this?" asked Hastings.

Paul Morgan looked at Harvath and asked, "What's the connection between these two places?"

Harvath was asking himself the same question, but so far he wasn't coming up with any answers. "Let's split up and take a look around. If you find anything out of the ordinary, let me know."

"Out of the ordinary?" replied Cates as he looked around. "What's ordinary at this point? Space aliens?"

"You know what he's talking about," said Herrington. "We're all equally in the dark here."

Cates didn't buy it. He had a feeling Harvath knew more than he was letting on, but he snapped Herrington a half-assed salute and walked down the hallway.

"What do you think?" asked Bob, once the rest of the team had dispersed.

Harvath took a slow glance around the room, the smell of blood and cordite tap-dancing a little too heavily on his already uneasy stomach. "I don't know what to think," he responded. "Obviously, these places were fronts for something, but what? And why are the terrorists so interested in them? After a successful series of attacks on major New York targets, why hang around to do this?" Harvath swept his arm in a wide arc, taking in the devastation around them. "It doesn't make sense. It's small-time, compared to what they've already accomplished."

Herrington studied the scene for several moments and then said, "Maybe this has to do with why they were trying to draw off the cream."

Harvath wasn't following him.

"The hostage crisis in the Bronx, the fire at the Emergency Command Center in Brooklyn, the sniper targeting aircraft at LaGuardia?

All of it served to tie up high-end tactical assets in those boroughs and potentially draw more away from Manhattan. Then the bridges and tunnels go, and every available local, state, or federal law enforcement officer rushes to the scene of the nearest attack, rolls up his or her sleeves, and starts helping pull people out. They're heroes—don't get me wrong—but one of the things you rarely hear talked about when people discuss what went wrong on September eleventh is that too many people wanted to be a hero that day.

"It wasn't like New Orleans after the hurricane hit and the levees broke and cops abandoned their posts. In New York, *all* of the police, fire, paramedics, and everyone at 26 Federal Plaza rushed to the World Trade Center on 9/11 to help. They saw it as their duty, and right or wrong, they ignored their commanders and ran down there as fast as they could. What if somebody was counting on that happening again?"

Harvath looked at his friend. "Are you telling me you think the attacks on the bridges and tunnels were diversions?"

Bob shrugged his shoulders. "I don't know. You tell me. Why shut down the air traffic control system? Why have snipers target boats and helicopters around Manhattan?"

That had been troubling Harvath as well, and there was only one answer he could come up with: "To prevent it from being reinforced."

"And why wouldn't you want the island reinforced?"

"Because having to engage reinforcements would either hinder your escape or—"

"Prevent you from accomplishing your primary objective."

Harvath shook his head. "That's where this thing loses me. We've been saying for years that another attack is not a question of if, but when, and now it's happened. The death toll from the bridge and tunnel attacks is easily going to exceed 9/11, so how can that not have been their primary objective?"

"That's the problem with the way we look at these ass-hats," replied Herrington. "Too often we give them credit for being a lot smarter than they actually are. It makes us feel better that way when they beat us. But I'll tell you something, taking out those bridges and tunnels isn't really an issue of *smarts,* it's an issue of *manpower.* You throw enough manpower at any problem and you can solve it, especially when your manpower is willing to die to achieve your goal for you."

"But we're talking about a lot of manpower here," replied Harvath. "The shitbag we interrogated at the First Precinct proves they had some sort of redundancies in place."

"Two backups, three backups, so what? Look at the London bombings. Look at Madrid. They just took Manhattan and threw more manpower at it, that's all. Even if we never know exactly how they did it, they *did* it, and that's all that matters at this point."

"Okay," said Harvath, playing devil's advocate for a moment. "Suppose everything you're saying is correct and the bridges and tunnels, the snipers, RPGs, and ATC site bombings are all intended to isolate Manhattan and prevent reinforcements from interfering with the terrorists' primary objective. From what we can tell, they hit this location and then moved to Midtown to hit the other in the diamond district. What are they after?"

"That's the hundred-thousand-dollar question," replied Herrington. "If we can figure that out, we might have a shot at stopping them. If you want my opinion, I vote we go back and convince the NYPD to turn over your pal with the overactive salivary glands so we can take him somewhere and interrogate him properly this time."

Herrington had a point. The surviving terrorist was the only concrete lead they had.

As a plan began to form in Harvath's mind he suddenly wondered if maybe dead men *could* tell tales.

FORTY-ONE

"Three," replied Kevin McCauliff as Harvath readied his pen to take down the information. "Each from a different phone in the group, but all to the same number."

Harvath had chastised himself for not thinking of this earlier. If they knew which phones the suicide bombers had been using, it made sense to check on their call records. It was McCauliff's mention of a contact at Nextel that had planted the seed in the back of Harvath's mind.

"And what were you able to find out about the number?" asked Harvath.

McCauliff drew in a deep breath and said, "You're not going to like this."

"Unless you're going to tell me that these guys were dialing the front desk at the Defense Intelligence Agency, I think I can handle it."

"The calls went to an alphanumeric pager purchased two weeks ago which was paid for in cash along with upfront local service."

"One-way or two-way pager?"

"One-way," answered McCauliff. "VHF frequency with really no way to trace it."

"You're right," replied Harvath. "I don't like it. The guy could be anywhere."

"I'm sorry."

"It's not your fault. Thanks for checking into it for me."

"That's what friends are for, right? Listen, if you need anything else call me back, but if I'm away from my desk, do me a favor and don't leave a message, call me on my cell or send me a benign text. Okay? I'm still pretty keen on keeping my job here, and I never know when Big Brother is looking at my communications."

With those words, a series of tumblers clicked in Harvath's head. Excited by the idea that had just flashed across his mind, he gripped his cell phone tighter and said, "If I asked you to, could you send a text message to that alphanumeric pager and make it look like it came from the cell phone I liberated from the NYPD?"

"Sure," replied McCauliff, "but why?"

"Because I think maybe we can make Mohammed come to the mountain."

FORTY-TWO

The White House

Jack Rutledge looked up as Carolyn Leonard entered his office. "What's going on?"

"We just got an update from Amanda's detail agents in New York," said the Secret Service agent.

"Is she all right?"

"She's at Beth Israel Hospital now. We've got agents en route from the Manhattan field office as we speak."

"That's not what I asked, Carolyn. I asked if Amanda's all right."

"We don't know, sir. Apparently she stopped breathing on the way there and Agent Delacorte had to give her mouth-to-mouth."

"Oh, my God."

"They're prepping her for surgery, and we hope to have more information soon."

"Inform the hospital that I'll want to talk with the doctors myself as soon as they know something. In fact, Dr. Vennett is somewhere in the building. I want her to be in on the call as well."

"Yes, sir. I'll have someone find the Surgeon General right away."

"Thank you, Carolyn."

Once she had left the room, the chief of staff said, "Amanda's a strong woman. She'll pull through. Don't worry."

Rutledge laughed. *Don't worry?* How could he not worry? This was his twenty-one-year-old daughter they were talking about, for God's sake.

Bringing the conversation back to what they'd been discussing when Carolyn Leonard had come in with her update, Charles Anderson asked, "What about Secretary Driehaus?"

"Let him wait. Maybe he'll get bored and go back to his office."

"He's the Secretary of Homeland Security, Mr. President. You can't *not* see him."

"He shouldn't be here, Chuck, and you know it. Not now. He should be back at DHS running his part of the operation."

"I agree with you one hundred percent, but the fact is he's here, and more importantly, the press knows he's here. If you snub him, it's going to make people question how well this administration is handling this crisis."

"Damn it, I don't have time for this. His visit has nothing to do with this crisis."

The chief of staff softened his tone and said, "We know that, but as far as he's concerned it has everything to do with it. Give him three minutes and then I'll have Rachel buzz with a call from one of our allies. This way he gets to say his piece and won't be able to claim that you wouldn't see him."

"Fine," said Rutledge. "I'll do it. But I want you to know that I think this is a mistake."

"I know you do."

"Let's get it over with. Show him in."

Anderson buzzed the president's secretary in the outer office and told her they were ready. Ten seconds later, the door to the Oval Office opened and Alan Driehaus walked in.

"Thank you for seeing me, Mr. President," said Driehaus as he shook the president's hand.

"Of course, Alan. Please take a seat," replied Rutledge as he sat back down. "I've only got a couple of minutes, so why don't you tell me what it is you couldn't address over the phone?"

"I thought I explained myself to Chuck—"

"And I have to be honest with you, Alan. I told Chuck I didn't think now was the time to be discussing this. Not with everything else happening."

"I can understand that, Mr. President, but I have several pieces of intelligence which I find quite disturbing."

"Such as?"

"First of all, I have it on good authority that less than twenty-four hours ago, an agent or agents of the United States government crossed illegally into the sovereign nation of Canada, and then assaulted and kidnapped a guest of that country who had been granted political asylum."

Rutledge shot his chief of staff a look conveying how angry he was to be having this meeting and then turned back to Driehaus and asked, "Why don't you tell me who this good authority is that you're basing this rather serious accusation on?"

"I'd rather not, Mr. President. I'd rather you tell me if it is true or not."

Rutledge's rope was very short today, and he was quickly coming to the end of it. Raising his voice, he replied, "How dare you come into this office and make demands of me? In case you've forgotten, Alan, I'm the president of the United States, and you work for *me*."

The president's reaction was answer enough. There was only one more question Driehaus had. "I understand we intercepted terrorist chatter indicating they not only knew we had violated another country's sovereignty, abducted a foreign national, and brought him to America against his will, but in particular the chatter stated that we had brought the person in question to New York City, of all places. Is this true?"

Rutledge leaned back in his chair and said, "You and I have nothing further to discuss. This meeting is over."

"You're right, Mr. President," said Driehaus as he rose from his chair and removed an envelope from his breast pocket. Placing it on the edge of the president's desk he said, "I can no longer support the policies of this administration. I will remain at my post for as long as you and my country need me to help get through this crisis, but then I'm gone. I've left my resignation undated. Fill it in whenever you see fit."

As Driehaus headed for the door, the president said, "That isn't necessary, Alan."

The secretary turned, a pulse of hope coursing through his body. *Maybe the president could be made to see things the right way.*

But the man's hopes were dashed as the president picked up a pen and said, "I'll fill today's date in right now."

FORTY-THREE

New York City

In an ambush, the enemy sets the time, but the attacker gets to set the place, and that was exactly what Harvath and the rest of the team had done. The trick was to select a good location that was also within a reasonable distance of the Geneva Diamond and Jewelry Exchange. Kevin McCauliff felt relatively confident that he was going to be able to spoof what they all hoped was the lead terrorist's pager.

The idea was to make it look like it was receiving positioning updates from the cell phone of the captured Middle Eastern man whose backpack had failed to explode and who was currently cooling his heels in an NYPD jail cell.

While it might be very odd for the lead terrorist's pager to be getting updates, it might just be odd enough to pique his interest and cause him to look into why the failed bomber was apparently trying to reconnect.

"And if the lead man tries to call or message our guy's cell phone?" asked Herrington.

"It doesn't matter. No cell phones except for first responders and law enforcement are working now anyway. Kevin's pal at Nextel says he'll make sure all anyone gets when they dial the number is a fast busy signal and any text messages will fail to go through. All we have to do is keep the updates coming sporadically enough to keep their interest," said Harvath.

It sounded like a reasonable enough plan, though it potentially had two fatal flaws. The team was divided over whether or not the terrorists would have had a contingency plan—a *what to do if you can't hit your target or your bomb fails to go off.* If they did and one of the bombers diverged from that contingency plan—like returning to a predetermined location and contacting an outside player—it might set off alarm bells and instead of drawing the remaining terrorists in, actually push them away. The second potential pitfall was whether or not the suicide bombers would have been privy to the rest of the operation. It was another sticking point that could just as easily work against them as it could in their favor.

There was a third problem that they all agreed on—they had no idea who or what they were going to be looking for. They could set up the world's best ambush, but if they couldn't identify their quarry, how would they know when it was time to spring the trap? In the end, they decided they would just have to jump off that bridge when they came to it.

The south end of Central Park fit the ambush bill better than anything else they could think of. It provided ample cover and concealment and multiple vantage points, and with all of the mayhem across the city, the people who had decided to congregate there away from tall buildings or other potential terrorist targets were by and large in the open expanse of the Sheep Meadow. That was a big plus, as the last thing they wanted was unnecessary collateral damage or a ready supply of potential hostages if the ambush went sideways, which at this point none of them were prepared to rule out.

Their goal was to draw the terrorists into the narrow area just north of the underpass that ran beneath the 65th Street Transverse known as the Denesmouth Arch. From there, Bullet Bob, the team's most skilled long-gun shooter, would have an unobstructed field of fire from both directions. Though he couldn't argue with Harvath's rationale, Herrington would have much rather preferred being with the rest of the team. The idea of not being in on the actual ambush didn't sit well with him at all.

With the light fading, Harvath took Tracy Hastings aside and handed her the night-vision device from his bug-out bag.

"So you've got no problem giving the girl with one eye a monocular?"

"Do I look like I have a problem with it?" he replied as he pulled a pair of Motorolas out of the pack.

"Then how come every time I turn around, you're staring at my face?"

Without even thinking about it, Harvath looked away from her. "You remind me of somebody, that's all."

"I'll bet I do," she replied, not taking him seriously.

"Listen, being an EOD tech, you've been trained to pay attention to the smallest details, and that's what we need right now. As long as you pull your weight, I don't give a damn that you're a woman. And as far as having only one eye, I don't care about that either. You got a night-vision monocular because that's all I have with me."

Hastings was surprised by his honesty. "That's it?"

"That's it," replied Harvath as he turned and walked away to assign Cates and Morgan their positions.

FORTY-FOUR

Abdul Ali was beyond angry. Either Hussein Nassir had lost his nerve or his bomb had failed to detonate. Regardless, the Jordanian peasant would undoubtedly choose the latter as his excuse. The man's involvement had been a mistake, Ali could see that now, but a beggar could seldom choose from whom he received his alms. The operation had necessitated the activation of almost every sleeper al-Qaeda had within the United States and even then additional men had to be smuggled in from both Canada and Mexico.

Martyring oneself, at least in an operation of this nature, did not call for a superior intellect, not even superior courage, but rather a blinding faith that one's reward would be delivered in paradise.

That said, Nassir was a fool who was putting the rest of the operation in jeopardy by trying to track the team down. How he knew where they were was beyond Ali. All he knew was that keeping the details of an operation of this size quiet was very difficult. Someone must have told Nassir more than he needed to know. The positioning messages didn't lie. The man had gone to both the Transcon office and the Geneva Diamond Exchange, and now for some reason had situated himself in Central Park. The idiot was going to get himself captured and would compromise everything. Ali had no choice but to go after Nassir and secure him until the rest of their work was done. Then he would find out how he had learned about the rest of the operation.

Though it was going to have a significant and detrimental impact upon their schedule, Ali instructed Sacha to turn around and head for Central Park. He just hoped he could get there before Nassir made any more stupid mistakes and gave them all away.

FORTY-FIVE

When Gary Lawlor fed the names Harvath had collected at the two crush depth locations into the shared intelligence database, he once again came up empty-handed. They were ghosts, every one of them—figuratively and, unfortunately now, literally. But while sterilizing civilian backgrounds was one thing, Gary had a feeling that erasing a marine's life might be a little bit different—especially if his only role had been to provide security.

Picking up the phone, he dialed the number for USMC Lieutenant Colonel Sean Olson. The ropy, five-foot-six Olson was a graduate of the FBI's law enforcement leadership program known as the National Academy. Conducted on the Bureau's Quantico, Virginia, campus, the program included courses in law, behavioral science, forensic science, leadership development, communication, and health and fitness. Its expressed mission was "to promote the personal and professional development of law enforcement leaders," but many argued that the most valuable thing that was formed at the National Academy were the incredible relationships and vast network of contacts among its graduates.

Lieutenant Colonel Olson was head of the Law Enforcement Security & Corrections Branch for the entire Marine Corps. If anyone could get Lawlor the information he needed on the mystery marines, it was his fellow National Academy graduate, Sean Olson.

"I'm neck-deep in shit right now, Gary," said the lieutenant colonel when his assistant put the call through, "so I'm going to save us both a lot of time. What do you need?"

Lawlor appreciated his colleague getting right to the point and he returned the favor. "Sean, we've got reason to believe that the bridges and tunnels in New York weren't the only targets."

"Jesus Christ," replied Olson as his attitude shifted from impatience to genuine concern. "You think there's going to be more?"

"We believe there already have been."

The man was shocked. "Where? How come we haven't heard of it here?"

If by *here* Olson meant the Marine Corps Security Division, it was easily explainable, but if by *here* he really meant the Pentagon, then Lawlor wasn't so sure the deep crush attacks *hadn't* been heard about. "This is a very delicate situation. The attacks I'm referring to were not civilian targets."

"What were they? Military? Government?"

"That's just it. We don't know. We've got two locations in Manhattan that appear to have been involved in some sort of covert operations—there's nothing about them or their employees that we can pull from any of our databases. The only connections we can find between them are that everyone was well armed and all the work they were doing was via paperless workstations."

"And how were these locations attacked?" asked Olson as he shifted the phone to his other ear.

"From what we can tell, two assaulter teams hit each location and gunned down everyone inside."

"What for?"

"We don't know," replied Lawlor.

"Gary, I appreciate the update," offered the lieutenant colonel, "but why are you telling me all of this?"

"Because three of those killed were U.S. marines. I need to find out who they were and what they were doing there."

Olson was already running on an unstable fuel of adrenaline and pure hatred of Islamic terrorists, but to now hear that on top of everything else today the terrorists had purposely taken out three marines sent him around the bend. It took all he had to keep his anger under control and craft a professional, un-obscenity-laden response. "Believe me, I would like to help you, but this is way above my purview. You need to get in touch with DOD directly."

"That's just it," replied Lawlor. "I can't."

"Why the hell can't you? You've got three marines dead, not to mention a bunch of their civilian colleagues. I'm pretty confident they'll make this a priority."

"Just give me five minutes, Sean, to explain. If after that you still don't think you can help me, I'll find somebody else."

Olson reluctantly agreed.

Three-and-a-half minutes later the lieutenant colonel had heard enough. He hung up with Lawlor, called his assistant into his office, and began giving orders. Getting to the bottom of what had happened to those marines was now one of his top priorities.

FORTY-SIX

The Chechens had never met Hussein Nassir. In fact they hadn't met any of Ali's bombers, so asking them to find him and bring him in was out of the question. Besides, it was Ali's mess. It was he who should clean it up.

Changing into street clothes, Ali secreted a nine-millimeter Spanish Firestar pistol inside a copy of the *New York Post,* tucked it beneath his arm, and had the team drop him on Central Park South.

Though Ali had studied his map well, the park was still unfamiliar territory and made him nervous. He had decided on his way over that this was not going to be a rescue. He was going to put a bullet in Hussein Nassir's head and hide his body so that by the time it was found it would be too late to make any difference.

From what Ali could tell, the last three messages to his pager placed Nassir somewhere near the Central Park Zoo. At least the fool hadn't forgotten all of his training. The area was normally well frequented by tourists, many of them foreigners, and if he remained calm, there was no reason he would draw any undue attention to himself. The more disturbing offshoot of that logic was what would a Middle Eastern man, or anyone else, for that matter, be doing at the zoo when New York had just suffered the worst terrorist attack in history? Anyone with any sense, especially a Middle Eastern man, would not be wandering the city but would be off the streets enjoying the safety and concealment of his home or hotel room. Nassir was an even bigger idiot than Ali gave him credit for.

Ali bore no concern over his own appearance. His surgeries had softened his Middle Eastern features, and he was often told he looked more Sicilian than anything else. If put to the test, his Italian was exceptional, and even a native speaker would be hard-pressed to question his pedigree.

Approaching from the southwest, Ali decided to avoid the more direct thoroughfare into the zoo for as long as possible. Though he had precious little time at his disposal, he tried not to rush. Something was beginning to trouble him about the situation. Coming alone might have been a mistake. He radioed the Chechens to ascertain their positions, but it did little to calm his unease. They needed to keep moving. Staying in one spot too long risked discovery. Though they spoke English, it was heavily accented. Only Ali could have passed for an American, and without him in the lead vehicle, they were asking for trouble by just sitting in one spot, waiting for him. A very nervous part of him hoped that ordering them to keep moving was the right decision.

Emerging from beneath the somewhat hidden and rarely used Inscope Arch, Ali's senses were on fire. He climbed the short flight of stairs at the end of the underpass and found himself on the pathway known as the Wien Walk. Making his way toward the zoo, Ali scanned the area for any sign that he was walking into a trap.

He passed a group of people—three women and a man—who were obviously distraught over the bombings and felt nothing but contempt for them. What they had experienced today was only the beginning for America. It had proven it would never learn its lesson, and therefore it would drink from the same bitter cup it had forced on the Muslim world for decades.

Arriving at the zoo, Ali was eager to finish his business and be on his way. He soon discovered that everything was closed—including the café where he had expected to find Nassir. He would have to comb the area.

As he did, he lost even more time. With every minute he wasted, he vowed to make Nassir's death as painful as possible.

Nearing the building known as the Armory, Ali noticed a figure up ahead. Even though it was from the back, he could tell it was a man about the same height and build as Hussein Nassir. He was sitting alone, wrapped in a Mylar space blanket, the kind given to runners after a marathon or to victims needing to stave off shock after a major calamity such as a terrorist attack. Abdul Ali was confident that he had found his man.

Reaching inside his *New York Post,* he wrapped his hand around the butt of the Firestar and quickened his pace. It would all be over in just a matter of moments now.

FORTY-SEVEN

Tracy Hastings spoke into the microphone hidden beneath her collar and said, "Contact. Probable target thirty yards and closing. Mid-forties, dark hair, wearing dark trousers and a black button-down shirt."

"Is this our guy, Tracy?" asked Harvath from his position on the other side of the Denesmouth Arch.

"He doesn't look very Middle Eastern—maybe Spanish or Italian, but I can't say for sure."

"Is he carrying anything?"

"Just a newspaper."

"How's he carrying it?" said Harvath.

"Under his left arm."

"Can you see his hands?"

"Negative. They're folded across his chest. One looks like it might be actually inside the paper."

That was enough for Harvath. He signaled Herrington and said into the radio, "I need you to tag him for Bob and then see if he's got any trailers. You know what to do. Be careful."

"Roger that," replied Hastings. Getting up from the bench she had been sitting on, Tracy headed south on the Wien Walk toward the suspect. With a concerned look on her face, she removed her cell phone from her pocket and began sweeping it through the air as if she were trying to get a signal.

As she neared the man in the dark shirt and trousers, she stopped and did a complete three-sixty, holding the phone high in the air. Though she pretended to be too wrapped up in finding cell service to notice, she could feel the man's eyes all over her. It wasn't the same feeling she got when people stared at the scars on her face. This was something completely different. It gave her chills, but she had tagged him, and right now Herrington would be tracking him with his rifle.

She kept walking, and once she was convinced no one was following the man, she cradled the cell phone against her shoulder and spoke into her collar, "He's alone."

Hastings waited for a confirmation that Harvath had received her message and when none came, she repeated it again. Still, there was nothing. "Scot, can you read me?" she asked. When there was still no response, she knew something very bad had happened.

"Drop your weapons and keep your hands where I can see them," said a voice from behind.

Both Harvath and Cates did as they were told.

"The man on the bench," the voice said. "Your buddy in the space blanket. Tell him to come over here."

"Take it easy," replied Harvath. "We're legit."

"Do it," commanded the voice.

Harvath heard the unmistakable click of a pistol hammer being cocked and so he signaled Paul Morgan to get up and join them.

When Morgan approached, their captor ordered him to drop his weapons and get his hands up. Harvath nodded his head and Morgan reluctantly complied, dropping his machine pistol.

There was a crashing through the brush ten yards away and they all turned to see Bob Herrington forced onto the path by a second NYPD mounted patrol officer who had found him on the arch.

The cops had ruined their ambush. Their target had picked up on the commotion and was now walking away in the other direction. Harvath had to do something. "I'm with the Department of Homeland Security. We've got a potential terrorist subject nearby—"

"On the ground—now," replied the cop.

The man was very jumpy. Stumbling upon a bunch of heavily armed, plain-clothed people hiding in Central Park right after a string of devastating terrorist attacks was extremely serious. Harvath needed to tread very carefully.

"I've got my badge in my pocket," he said. "Nobody wants any trouble here, okay? I'm just going to reach for my wallet."

"You're not reaching for anything. This is the last time I'm going to say it," commanded the officer as his partner radioed for backup. "Everybody on the ground—*now.*"

"You're interfering with a highly sensitive counterterrorism operation."

"I don't know what the hell we've stumbled onto here and until I do, you're going to do as I say."

Harvath had no choice but to comply. "Listen," he said as he lay down on the ground. "There's a man retreating along the pathway—dark hair, mid-forties, with dark pants and shirt. He looks Spanish or Italian. That's who we were waiting for. He may be connected to today's bombings. We need to apprehend him for questioning. Please."

The officer looked down at Harvath and then over at his partner. "Frank, you wanna take a look?"

"Sure," replied the partner. "Why not?"

Before Harvath could object, the officer's horse crunched through the brush and clattered out onto the paved walkway, its hoofbeats echoing like machine-gun fire off the stone walls of the Denesmouth Arch.

"You see anything?" yelled the first officer.

"Nope," replied the partner, who then said, "Wait a second, yeah I think I do. Wait here. I'll be right back."

Spurring his horse into a trot, the partner rode along the pathway and disappeared beneath the arch.

"You're making a mistake," said Harvath.

"First you want us to apprehend the guy, and now we're making a mistake?" said the cop in his thick New York accent. "What's wrong with you? You retarded or something?"

"He didn't want *you* to go, dumb-ass," replied Herrington. "He wanted *us* to."

"Watch your mouth, smart guy."

"Your partner's going to scare him off," said Morgan.

"Or worse," added Cates.

"Okay, everybody shut up," demanded the mounted patrolman. "You. Homeland Security," he said as he pointed his pistol at Harvath. "I want you to very slowly use your left hand to remove your creds from your pocket. Remember, very slowly."

Suddenly, there was a burst of activity over the officer's radio as his partner yelled, "The suspect is fleeing. West towards Fifth Avenue and the Sixty-fourth Street exit. One-Baker-Eleven in pur—"

The transmission was cut short by the unmistakable crack of gunfire.

The officer who had remained behind to watch Harvath and the other three men radioed *shots fired* to his dispatcher and then said, "One-Baker-Eleven, come in. Frank, talk to me. What the hell is going on?"

"Here," said Harvath as he flipped open his wallet and revealed his ID. "*We're* legit. Let us up."

The cop was torn. On one hand his partner could be in grave danger, and on the other all he could think about was how Timothy McVeigh had been captured by an alert highway patrolman shortly after the Oklahoma City bombing. While everyone had been looking for Arabs, that officer had been smart enough to realize that McVeigh and the circumstances under which he was stopped warranted a closer look. It was just as true here. The cop couldn't let these people go, ID or no ID. "No dice. Everybody stay where you are."

Harvath couldn't believe it. "Our suspect's getting away and your partner could be dying or dead, for all you know."

"One-Baker-Eleven, this is One-Baker-Twelve. Talk to me, Frank, God damn it. Talk to me."

Harvath was about to appeal to the officer again, when a voice came over the earpiece attached to his Motorola. He listened to it for several seconds and then said to the patrolman, "I've shown you my ID and I'm going to stand up now. If you want to shoot a fellow law enforcement officer, that's up to you, but I'm not going to lose that suspect."

"I swear to God," said the cop, "if you move I *will* shoot you."

"I don't think so," replied Harvath as he slid his hands off his back and placed them palms-down like he was about to do push-ups.

"This is your last warning!" barked the patrolman as he steadied his weapon and took aim.

Suddenly, the well-trained police horse reared up on its hind legs. The officer was taken completely by surprise as Tracy Hastings's deftly wielded tree limb connected with his chest and knocked him from his mount. To the man's credit, he managed to hold on to his weapon, but it made little difference.

Cates got to the patrolman before he could find his feet and quickly stripped him of his gun.

"Cuff him," said Harvath as he approached the startled horse, grabbed the reins, and swung up into the saddle.

"What the hell are you doing?"

"I'm going after our suspect."

FORTY-EIGHT

It had been a long time since Harvath had ridden a horse, and he quickly discovered that riding one on pavement was nothing at all like riding on grass or sand. Racing out from under the Delacorte Clock, the horse slipped and Harvath thought for sure they were going down, but the animal righted itself and then lunged forward.

On the north side of the Armory, Harvath saw the other horse and just beyond it the second patrolman—both had been shot, both were on the ground, and neither was moving. Harvath radioed the information back to Tracy Hastings and kept riding toward the park's 64th Street exit.

Once he emerged onto the sidewalk at Fifth Avenue he looked in every direction but couldn't see the suspect. Then he noticed two black SUVs identical to the ones from the satellite imagery turn down 65th Street and head east. *It had to be them.*

With their flashing red and blue strobes, the blacked-out Tahoes looked one hundred percent authentic. It was incredibly brazen, but in a city where both residents and law enforcement were used to getting out of the way of such vehicles, the ploy made perfect sense.

After almost getting killed crossing Fifth Avenue, Harvath galloped up 64th Street and tried to close in on the SUVs. Had the street been wide open, there was no way Harvath could have ever caught them, but with the traffic impeding the SUVs' getaway, he actually had half a chance of catching up.

As soon as there were only four car lengths separating him from the nearest Tahoe, Harvath drew his .40-caliber H&K USP Compact and tried to synchronize himself with the rhythm of the horse. They were on the sidewalk, and the last thing Harvath wanted was for one of his shots to go wide and for some innocent bystander to get caught in his line of fire.

Squeezing off at least three rounds, Harvath blew out the rear window and drilled two holes through the Tahoe's rear tailgate doors. If he didn't have the terrorists' attention before, he definitely had it now. In fact, he had everyone's attention. The drivers of the cars behind the Tahoe panicked at the gunshots and slammed on their brakes, causing a dangerous chain-reaction collision.

From the backseat of the SUV, two men in black balaclavas raised submachine guns and opened fire. Harvath pulled up on the horse's reins and as he did so the animal caught a round to the neck. The beast slipped and once again lost its footing. This time, though, it didn't recover. Harvath followed it headfirst, straight down into the pavement.

FORTY-NINE

When Harvath came to, the first thing he saw was Bob Herrington. "So much for operating as a team."

Harvath didn't want to hear it and ignored his friend as he tried to move.

"Take it easy," said Bob. "Don't try to get up too fast. Are you okay? Anything broken?"

Harvath slowed down and tried moving his fingers. Next he moved his toes and then worked his way through the rest of his body. "I think I'm okay. What about the horse?"

Herrington looked over his shoulder, then back at Harvath, and shook his head. "Nope."

"How about the cop by the Armory?" asked Harvath.

"Two rounds to the chest. Morgan had one of those QuickClot sponges in his bag and got it on him right away. Probably saved his life. I think he's going to make it."

Harvath pushed himself into a sitting position and leaned back against a parked car. He rubbed his brow along his shoulder to get some of the sweat out of his eyes and then saw that it wasn't sweat, but blood.

"Don't worry," said Morgan, the team's self-appointed medic, as he pulled some supplies out of his pack, including a tube of medical Krazy

Glue known as Dermabond. "You've got one hell of a road rash on the left side of your face, but as long as we can get those cuts closed up, I don't think it's going to be too serious."

"So much for me being the only pretty face in this group," said Hastings.

Harvath's smile quickly turned into a wince as Morgan swabbed his wounds with antiseptic.

"We heard the shots from the park," said Cates. "Were you able to hit any of them?"

"I don't think so."

"What about faces, or something distinct about the vehicle?" asked Herrington.

"At least four faces," said Harvath, "all covered. And as for the vehicle, it's a late-model black Tahoe which now bears the distinction of having lost its rear window while gaining a bullet hole in each of its rear tailgate doors."

"That's a start," said Herrington, trying to remain upbeat and bolster his buddy's spirits. "Not a very good one, but a start nonetheless."

"So what you're telling us is that you got an NYPD horse killed and yourself beat to shit for nothing?" asked Cates.

As Morgan began applying the Dermabond to close his wounds, Harvath surrendered to the inevitable. They had just blown their last and only lead. Holstering his weapon, which Hastings had found and now handed back to him, Harvath said, "Yeah, I guess it was all for nothing."

FIFTY

Washington, DC

"Please tell me you're calling because you've got something good to report," said Gary Lawlor.

From his office at the Pentagon, Lieutenant Colonel Sean Olson replied, "I'll let you judge for yourself how good this is."

Lawlor grabbed a pen. After finding a clean sheet of paper on his desk he said, "Go ahead."

"The men your agent identified in New York City are definitely active-duty marines. At least they were as of their last fitness reports."

"Which was when?"

"Eighteen months ago."

"Eighteen months ago?" replied Lawlor. "Don't the Marines conduct fit reps every twelve?"

"Yeah," said Olson, "but for some reason the paper trail on these marines stops exactly eighteen months ago."

"Any idea why?"

"Based on what you've told me, I think that's when someone took them off book."

"That would make sense," said Lawlor. "Were you able to find out anything else?"

"They were all Marine Security Guard School graduates and had been doing embassy security."

"Where?"

"Pretty much all over the place, but one thing they had in common was that they each had requested high-risk postings."

"What do you mean by *high-risk*?"

"They wanted to serve embassies that were operating under very high threat levels, like Bogotá, Athens, Kabul, Baghdad . . . you name it, and these guys were not only willing, but wanted to go."

"Can you place them together at MSG school or in one of the embassy postings? There must be a bigger connection."

"That was one of the first things I looked for, but they all graduated from different classes and never served at the same embassy at the same time either."

"So what's that leave us with?" asked Lawlor.

"Those avenues in particular don't leave us with anything, but I dug a little deeper and found something that may be helpful."

"I'm all ears."

Olson pulled a file up on his computer and said, "While they're deployed, the Marines are under the operational control of the State Department, but their coordination, logistics, and training is still handled by the Marine Security Battalion out of Quantico, and here's where it gets interesting. The battalion maintains a low-key group of force readiness officers responsible for assessing the strengths and weaknesses of Marine Security Guard details in over one hundred and thirty embassies and consulates worldwide.

"The same force readiness officer filed very complimentary reports for the three marines whose names you gave me, as well as at least fifteen more, all of whom had their trails wiped clean as of eighteen months ago."

"You think this guy recruited these marines into whatever off-book operation we're looking at in New York?"

"All I can say is that I think it's worth checking into."

FIFTY-ONE

Captain Bill Forrester's small English Tudor was on a quiet street, in an equally quiet neighborhood in North Arlington, Virginia. Everything about it suggested it was inhabited by a normal, unassuming citizen—right down to the green-gray Subaru Outback parked in the driveway. What gave him away as something more were the Marine Corps and POW flags hanging from a pole above the front door.

Parking his car in the street and walking up the flagstone pathway, Gary Lawlor hoped the Subaru meant that somebody was home. He rang the doorbell and waited.

Moments later a solidly built man in his mid-fifties with salt-and-pepper hair cut high and tight, answered the door and said, "Can I help you?"

Gary raised his ID and said, "Captain Forrester?"

"Yes?" replied the marine.

"I'm Agent Lawlor from the Department of Homeland Security. I'm investigating the terrorist attacks of this afternoon and I need to ask you a few questions."

"Why would you want to talk to me?"

"May I come inside, please?"

Forrester opened the screen door and showed Lawlor inside to a bland kitchen with cheap cabinets and yellow wallpaper. He pointed to a table with a view of the backyard and told his visitor to have a seat. "Can I get you something to drink?" he asked.

"I'll take a beer if you've got it," replied Gary. "It's been a long day."

Forrester didn't know what to make of a Federal agent having a beer on company time, but something told him this DHS operative was not all he seemed to be. "You want a glass?" he asked as he withdrew two beers from the fridge.

"Please."

Forrester poured the beers, handed one to Lawlor, and said, "What can I do for the Department of Homeland Security?"

Gary slid the printouts of three service photos Olson had e-mailed him across the table. "Do you recognize these men?"

The captain studied the photographs for a moment, slid them back across the table, and said, "No, I don't."

"If you need a little more time, that's okay."

"I'm pretty good with faces, Agent Lawlor. If I say I don't recognize someone, I don't recognize them."

"From your glowing assessments, I would have thought these marines unforgettable."

The man was toying with him, and Forrester didn't like it. "What do you want?"

Removing the rest of the photos and sliding them across the table, Lawlor replied, "I want to talk about the recruiting operation you've been running out of the Marine Security Battalion."

"I don't know what you're talking about."

"I've read assessment reports for each of the marines in those pictures and they were all written by you."

Forrester took a long swallow of beer, using the time to carefully craft his response. As he set the glass down on the table he looked at Lawlor and said, "I assess hundreds of marines every year. So what?"

"Not like these. These marines were exceptional, and eighteen months ago the ones you gave the highest marks to dropped off the grid."

The captain rolled the base of his glass on the tabletop and fixed his guest with a steady gaze. "You're talking to the wrong guy."

"Why? Because you *really* don't know what I'm talking about or you were just following orders? Captain Forrester, I don't have a lot of time, so I'm going to cut to the chase. Of those marines, the first three I showed you are dead. They were killed today, we think by the same group responsible for blowing up the bridges and tunnels in New York, and something tells me that more marines are going to die very soon if you don't help me out."

FIFTY-TWO

309 EAST 48TH STREET
NEW YORK CITY

"Satisfied?" asked Mike Jaffe as he turned off the monitor.

Brad Harper was stunned. "So those were female DIA operatives dressed to look like his kids?"

"Why do you think the camera never made it into the bathroom until their heads were already bent over the edge of the tub?"

"Why didn't you just tell me?"

"Because you wouldn't have given it the same reaction," replied Jaffe. "It was perfect. Worthy of an Academy Award."

"But I wasn't acting."

"I know. That's why it was so perfect. Mohammed would have smelled the good cop/bad cop routine a mile away. Right now he thinks you're terrified of my methods. If he thinks you believe I'm unstable and will stop at nothing, then he's going to start believing it too."

Harper didn't like being used.

"So are we good here?" asked Jaffe in response to the marine's silence.

Harper wasn't quite sure how to respond to that.

"Are we good?" repeated Jaffe, slowly and deliberately.

The subtext was obvious. Jaffe wanted to know if Harper was going to continue to play ball, or if he had some sort of a problem that needed to be addressed. Harper had some serious doubts as to how Jaffe might handle any dissension. After all, the man had pointed a loaded pistol at his head, point-blank.

As long as the kids were out of the picture and no longer potential casualties, he figured he could go along with almost anything else Jaffe had up his sleeve. Harper nodded his head and said, "Yeah, we're good."

"Excellent. I've got three large rolls of Visqueen in the office at the end of the hall. I want you to go get them. It's going to get pretty bloody in there."

"Excuse me?" replied the young marine.

"Visqueen," repeated Jaffe. "Rolls of plastic sheeting."

"I know what Visqueen is. What are we going to need it for?"

"I just told you. Right after you told me we were good. Did I misunderstand something?"

"No," said Harper.

"No, sir," corrected Jaffe.

Harper wanted to deck this deranged piece of shit, but he choked the impulse back and responded, "No, *sir.*"

"Good, because I'd hate to think you were going soft on me, Harper. I asked for marines on this assignment because marines are tough. Marines have got guts! And we're gonna need all the guts we have to face down these two shitbags in the other room."

"I understand," said Harper, "but plastic sheeting? Are we really going to need it?"

"It's not for us. It's for the two foreign intelligence agents who are assisting us. They requested it."

"Rashid and Hassan? What are they going to do with it?"

"They're probably going to use it to keep blood off the walls and off the carpeting."

Harper had figured things were going to really get ugly at some point, but the ugly he had anticipated was from psychological stress applied to their captives. They were in New York City, for Christ's sake, not some third-world torture chamber.

Jaffe could read the young marine's mind just by looking at him. "What'd you think this was going to be, son? We call them a few names, withhold everything but high-sugar foods, keep them up for days on end until they eventually crack, tell us what we want to know and then we go home to sleep in our warm beds with crystal clear consciences?

Is that how you saw it going down? Because if you did, you're not the man—wait, scratch that—you're not the marine I thought you were."

"Sir, I respect your command, but I'm going to ask you not to impugn my integrity as a United States marine."

"Fuck that," said Jaffe, getting into the taller man's face. "Duty, honor, courage. Fuck all of that. That's why guys like Humpty and Dumpty in the other room are beating us in the war on terror."

The man was nuts. Harper was sure of it. And because he was nuts, Harper also knew that he couldn't be reasoned with.

"You don't believe me?" said Jaffe.

"No, sir. I believe whatever you say," replied Harper.

"Bullshit, marine. It's written all over your face. You think I'm a few cans shy of a six-pack, don't you?"

"No, sir I didn't say—"

"Quit lying to me, son. I can smell it from a mile away. You think I'm nuts? That's fine by me. I probably am to have taken this job and stayed with it as long as I have, but I'll tell you one thing. If we don't start executing this war on terror in the *correct* fashion, we're going to be overrun.

"We're fighting for our civilization's very survival here. They might not talk about it that way in the newspapers or on the evening news, but that is exactly what's happening. Your country is depending on you. It's depending on *us.* You and me. And that's why what we're doing here matters. It matters big-time. Because if we don't stop these guys from going nuclear, thousands if not hundreds of thousands—maybe millions of innocent people are going to die. So keep that in mind the next time you want to question how I'm running this interrogation. Are we clear?"

"Yes, sir," replied Harper flatly.

"Good. Now go get the Visqueen."

FIFTY-THREE

THE WHITE HOUSE

"I know you're distraught over Amanda's surgery, but you can't be serious. Tell me you're not serious," pleaded Charles Anderson.

"I couldn't be more so, Chuck," replied the president.

The chief of staff threw his hands up in defeat. "Of course you are! You've declared war on Islam, and then you fired the Secretary of Homeland Security. A trip to New York with the terrorists still at large would be the icing on the cake. It'll be a public relations trifecta. Should I get Geoff in here to draft a release?"

"First of all, I didn't declare war on Islam. We've already been through that. Secondly, I didn't fire Driehaus; he resigned."

"No, you didn't fire him, but you didn't prevent him from resigning either."

"Semantics. What difference does it make?"

"It makes a lot of difference to you, to this presidency. I'd also make the case that to have him step down in the middle of all this erodes public confidence in our government."

"That certainly wasn't the case when the FEMA director bowed out in the aftermath of Katrina."

"The key word there, Mr. President, is *aftermath*. Besides, the FEMA chief was inept and everyone knew it. I think letting Driehaus go in the middle of a horrific national crisis is a very bad idea."

"The hell it is, Chuck. DHS isn't working, and we all know it. I'm not going to let Alan Driehaus bully this office. He calls himself a patriot? Well, let me tell you something. A patriot doesn't pull petty political gamesmanship in the middle of a crisis. You put your personal problems aside and you put the welfare of your country above all else. He couldn't do that, so he's out."

Anderson thought about it. "Maybe there is a way we can use his resignation to our advantage. Anyone with half a brain will read between the lines and believe he resigned because he mishandled the terrorist threat. That could work for us."

"No way," said Rutledge. "We're not going to throw Driehaus to the wolves just to divert attention away from what happened."

"Why not? You think the American people wanted accountability after 9/11? They're going to be packing the streets demanding a lot more than accountability this time. They're going to want blood, and plenty of it."

"And why shouldn't they? Their government has failed to protect them, again."

"So why shouldn't Driehaus be the first one to the guillotine? With each one we throw them, the bloodlust will ebb."

"Or it'll surge. Blood is a funny thing, Chuck—especially in politics. Once people get a taste of it, they often want more and more and more. So we're not throwing anyone under the bus yet. I'm going to personally call for full and open hearings when the dust has settled. I want total transparency. The American people are going to agree to nothing less. It's the only thing that is going to help restore the sacred trust because I'll tell you what, today that trust has been utterly shattered. Now let's get working on my visit to New York. I want us to be under way ASAP."

"With all due respect, sir—"

"She's my daughter, for Christ's sake, Chuck. This is what fathers do."

"Fathers maybe, but not presidents, sir."

Rutledge wasn't going to be swayed. "ASAP."

"Fine," said Anderson, the resignation in his voice thick with sarcasm. "Should we use *Air Force One* or do you want me to see if the tooth fairy is flying up that way? I think we may actually have her cell phone number."

"Watch it, Chuck. Not only does my daughter need me, the American people need to see their president in New York City."

"I'm sorry, sir. I agree with you, but all of this should and will be put together in due time. Right now we can't even get the National Guard into Manhattan. The terrorists have the entire island locked down, including the air space. How are we supposed to accomplish what even our military can't do at this point?"

"That's not my problem. It's yours. Talk to the Secret Service."

"I don't need to talk to the Secret Service. I already know what they'll say. In fact, wait a second." Opening the door, Anderson stuck his head into the hall and said, "Carolyn, can you come here a moment, please?"

"Yes, sir, Mr. Anderson. What do you need?" replied the head of Jack Rutledge's protective detail as she stepped into the doorway.

"The president wants to go to New York City," stated the chief of staff. "Manhattan, to be precise."

"Of course. We're already starting to plan the logistics."

"I don't think you understand. The president wants to go now. Tonight."

Looking up, Secret Service Agent Carolyn Leonard saw the president's face and realized he was serious. "I'm sorry, sir, but that's not possible. Not just yet at least."

"Why not?" demanded Rutledge.

"It's a war zone. The fact that the terrorists have snipers with high-powered rifles *and* RPGs makes it an absolute no-go."

"What do you want me to do, Carolyn? Sign a release absolving the Secret Service of any and all responsibility should something happen to me?"

"Of course not, sir. I just want you to understand that there's no way we can guarantee your safety at this point. You'd make too attractive a target, and not only to the terrorists."

"Are you suggesting there are Americans who would want to harm me?"

"I can't say for sure, sir. All I know is that the situation on the ground is starting to heat up a bit."

"Heat up how?" asked the president.

"There are reports that scattered looting and mob violence against immigrants and Arab-Americans has begun."

Rutledge looked at his chief of staff.

"It's in the next briefing. I didn't think you'd want me bring you updates every three minutes. We want to nail down whether these are isolated incidents or if we're seeing some sort of groundswell," said Anderson.

Rutledge was not happy with that answer. "All the more reason I should make a direct appeal to the people of New York from New York."

"Sir," said Leonard as she tried to suggest a compromise, "we could arrange for you to be someplace, maybe upstate—maybe in the capital—and then take you in to Manhattan once things cool down."

"Once things *cool down?* When's that? A week from now? A month?"

Leonard understood the president's anger. Everyone was angry right now. The hard thing was directing that anger in the appropriate direction. She knew the president didn't mean to take it out on her, and she was enough of a professional to let it roll off her back. What she needed to do was to persuade him against making the trip—at least for the time being. "Sir, my job is to advise you of the risks and what course of action the Secret Service feels is best to assure your safety and well-being."

"And if it were up to you, I'd be locked in a bunker someplace right now."

"Yes, sir."

"But it's not up to you. It's up to me."

"That's correct, sir."

"Carolyn, my daughter is there."

"I know, sir, but how do you think it would look to the people of New York if the president could get in to see his daughter when even the National Guard hadn't been able to make it in yet to help assure order? It might not look like you were truly there for the people of New York City."

She had a point, and Rutledge knew it. Frustrated, he quietly pounded his fist on top of his desk and then nodded his head. "You're right."

"Thank you, Carolyn," said the chief of staff as he showed her back into the hallway.

Closing the door, Anderson looked at the president and said, "If you want another opinion, I'll get General Currutt in here and let him give you the Joint Chiefs' take on trying to get into New York at this point."

The president sat down, exhausted, and replied, "That won't be necessary. I'll stay put. For now. But, Chuck?"

"Yes?" replied the chief of staff as he stopped, his hand on the doorknob.

"I want results, and I want them soon, or I am going to New York, even if I have to pilot my own plane to get there."

FIFTY-FOUR

NATIONAL SECURITY AGENCY
FORT MEADE, MARYLAND

Mark Schreiber dropped the printout onto Joseph Stanton's already overcrowded desk and said, "That makes three now: Transcon, Geneva Diamond, *and* the Strong Box beneath the Lincoln Tunnel. Are you still going to sit there and tell me we don't have a problem on our hands?"

"Take it easy," replied Stanton as he looked over the printout. "Even if we wanted to, there's nobody we can call for help now anyway."

"There's got to be somebody."

"There isn't."

"Are you serious? We don't have a contingency for this?"

"For what, Mark? We still don't know what we're dealing with."

Schreiber looked at his boss like he was nuts. "We've got three substations that are unresponsive."

"Unresponsive, but still processing as far as we can tell," clarified Stanton. "New York has been overwhelmed. Give it a little more time."

"That's what you said the last time I came in here."

"And as the director of this program that's going to be my answer no matter how many times you come in here and ask."

"What if the sites have been compromised?" ventured Schreiber.

"Then we wouldn't be seeing any processing at all. You know how the systems work, Mark. You also know what the communication protocols are. Listen, we're all angry with what's happened today and we're all concerned about the people we know and work with in New York, but I'm only going to tell you this one more time. Stay focused on your job."

"But what if we—" began Schreiber, but he was cut off by the ringing of Stanton's phone.

"It's from upstairs," he said as he pointed toward the ceiling and reached for the receiver. "I need to take this in private."

Once Schreiber had left the room and closed the door behind him, Stanton said, "Why the hell are you contacting me on this line?"

"Because you haven't exactly been answering your cell phone," said the caller.

"If you turned on your television set once in a while, you'd see we've got our hands pretty full today."

"Fuller than you think."

"What are you talking about?" replied Stanton.

"Not over the phone. We need to meet."

"That's impossible. Not today."

"Yes, today," said the caller. "And I want you there in a half hour."

"That's insane," said Stanton. "Do you know what the traffic is like between here and there?"

"Use one of the company helos."

"We've got a major national crisis going on. Helicopters are for emergency use only at this point."

"This *is* an emergency. Somebody knows about Athena."

FIFTY-FIVE

NORTHERN VIRGINIA

The Bell JetRanger helicopter touched down in the parking lot of a large warehouse, and out stepped Joseph Stanton. With his heavy-rimmed glasses, seersucker suit, and suede bucks, he looked nothing like Gary Lawlor had pictured. Superspooks came in all shapes and sizes, but this was the first time he'd ever seen one who was a dead ringer for a sloppy Warren Buffett.

Once they were sure Stanton had come alone, Gary and Bill Forrester got out of the car and met him halfway across the parking lot. The Marine captain made the introductions and as Lawlor began to speak Stanton said, "Not here. Wait till we're inside."

Inside turned out to be a well-appointed office suite at the back of the structure that Stanton and Forrester used for their meetings. Sitting down on a leather couch, Stanton smoothed out his trouser legs, picked a few pieces of lint from inside one of the cuffs, and then said, "Okay, what the fuck is going on?"

Ever the marine, nobody bullied Bill Forrester, especially not some Ivy Leaguer in a seersucker suit. "Why don't you tell us, Joe? It's your op."

"What do you mean, tell *us?* As far as I'm concerned captain, the only *us* that should be in this room is you and me."

"Well, suck it up," said Forrester, "because Agent Lawlor here might just be the only one able to save your bacon."

"Who says my bacon needs saving to begin with?"

"Listen, Joe, I didn't come out here to get jerked around."

"Neither did I."

"Good. So let's save the 'my dick's bigger than your dick, but I can't show it to you because we don't work for the same agency' crap for the time being."

"If you're suggesting, captain, that we bring Agent Lawlor into the know regarding Athena, that's not going to happen."

Forrester had a very short fuse and burned real quick. "Three of my marines are dead, so yeah, it is going to happen."

"Wait a second," said Stanton. "I haven't heard anything about any marines being killed."

"That doesn't surprise me. They never were a priority, in your opinion. Now, I want some goddamn answers."

"Had you given me a little more insight into why you called this impromptu meeting, maybe I would have been able to prepare some for you."

It was pretty apparent these two were not going to get very far if left to verbally slug it out, so Lawlor decided to step in. "Mr. Stanton, what is the Athena Program?"

"I'm sorry, Agent Lawlor, but I am not allowed to discuss NSA business without proper authorization."

Forrester was disgusted with his arrogance. "I wanted you to hear it from him, but if he won't tell you, I will."

"No, you won't."

"If it means preventing any more of my marines from dying, then just watch me." Turning to Gary, the captain said, "The program is named after the Greek goddess of wisdom, as apparently the Greeks didn't have a goddess of blackmail. It's a deep-black-data-mining operation. Using both the Echelon and Carnivore systems, the NSA has been gathering otherwise overlooked intelligence that can be used as leverage against various foreign concerns."

"Like al-Qaeda?" asked Lawlor, not completely understanding what Forrester was getting at.

"No. More like governments, heads of state, and influential foreign businesspeople. Basically, the Athena Program collects and sorts extremely dirty laundry. Once they have their teeth into something particularly juicy, like the Princess Diana crash, TWA 800, or Yasir Arafat's death, they assign teams of operatives to flush out the big picture and uncover as much supporting evidence as possible. That way, when it comes time to use it, they have the victim pinned against the wall so tightly, there's absolutely no room for him or her to wiggle free.

"And if they uncover a conspiracy involving several powerful foreign figures, it's like hitting the jackpot."

"You're going to jail for a very, very long time, Forrester," said Stanton as he solemnly shook his head.

Lawlor ignored him and asked the captain, "Tell me about the locations in Manhattan."

"You already know about Transcon and Geneva Diamond. They were the first two tiers. Most of the field agents worked out of Transcon. Because a limited amount of sensitive data was handled there and because all of the employees were field rated and came to work armed, it was decided by Mr. Stanton here that they didn't need extra security—a position I had always been against. Subsequently, none of my marines were stationed there.

"Geneva Diamond was the next step up. That's where most of the data coming in is sifted."

"Sifted how?" asked Lawlor.

"Don't say anything more, Bill," cautioned Stanton. "I'm warning you. You're already in way over your head."

Forrester disregarded the admonition and plowed ahead, "Whatever intelligence is deemed political in nature goes to a facility hidden beneath the Lincoln Tunnel known as the Strong Box. The location had been conceived during the Cold War as a means to evacuate high-ranking allied-nation UN personnel from the city via submarine in the case of a nuclear attack, but the project was eventually deemed unfeasible and abandoned. The NSA quietly took over the space and used it as a signals intercept and deciphering station. A stairwell is hidden in the south airshaft and allows access to the facility via a bogus storeroom at the New York Waterway bus garage. Like Geneva Diamond, with the high value of the work that goes on there and the fact that the employees are predominantly analysts, my marines provide round-the-clock security.

"As for the personal intelligence side of things, which is often significantly more damning, it goes to a rather ingenious location very near—"

"I warned you," said Stanton as he drew an extremely compact .45-caliber Para-Ordnance P-104 pistol from his suit pocket, pointed it at Forrester's head, and pulled the trigger.

FIFTY-SIX

Gary Lawlor didn't wait for Stanton to point the pistol at him. Instead, he bolted for the door.

Stanton fired, just missing Lawlor's head and splintering the doorframe. The man was insane. First he killed an officer of the United States Marine Corps, and now he was trying to take out a Homeland Security agent. Gary didn't have to think about what to do next. His reaction was instinctual. It was either him or Stanton.

Belying his age yet again, Lawlor dove for cover behind a long, wooden credenza in the outer office and drew his Beretta Px4 Storm. There was a wheeled desk chair next to the credenza, and he sent it spinning into the center of the room to draw Stanton's fire. As tufts of batting wafted up into the air, Lawlor came around the credenza on one knee and sent a wave of .40-caliber lead right where the NSA man had just been firing from. The problem, though, was that Stanton knew what he was doing and quickly moved to a new location. He wasn't going to be easy to kill.

"Mr. Stanton," yelled Lawlor after he had ducked back behind the safety of the credenza. "I'm only going to give you one chance. I want you to throw your gun and then come out with your hands above your head. Do you understand me?"

"The security of those installations was Forrester's responsibility," replied Stanton.

It was a very out-of-place response, considering the situation. "Mr. Stanton," said Lawlor. "Throw out your weapon, come out with your hands up, and we'll talk about it."

From the other room, Stanton laughed. "Sure we will."

"These terms at not negotiable, Mr. Stanton."

"He shouldn't have been talking. I don't care what good he thought he was doing his marines. He knew better than that."

"Mr. Stanton, I am ordering you to come out of that room with your hands up, right now," replied Lawlor.

"One of the most beneficial intelligence-gathering programs this country has ever developed and that idiot is ready to let it all out of the bag to save his precious marines. Marines die. That's their job."

As Stanton continued ranting, Lawlor crept from around the credenza and tried to maneuver himself for a better line of fire.

"Forrester put *his* needs and the needs of his marines above the people of this country," yelled Stanton. "Do you have any idea how many lives have been spared because of this program? It might not be the prettiest way to do business but it's goddamn effective."

Lawlor now had a clean line of sight into the inner office. By the sound of Stanton's voice, he was somewhere over to the right. If he had to, Lawlor was fairly confident he could take him out by firing through the drywall, but now that the playing field was a little more level, he wanted to take the man alive, if at all possible. "Your time's up, Mr. Stanton. No more talking. I want you to slide your weapon out the door and then follow with your hands clasped on top of your head."

Once again Stanton laughed. "That's not going to happen, Agent Lawlor, and you know it. Only one of us is going to walk out of this building today. The question is, which one?"

Gary didn't bother responding. Like he had said, they were done talking. If Mr. Stanton thought only one of them was leaving the building alive, he was in for a very big surprise.

A company called Guardian Protective Devices of New Jersey had approached the Department of Homeland Security a while back with a very interesting pepper spray device. Very intelligently, DHS had snapped up as many as they could get their hands on, as did many other branches of the military, intelligence, and law enforcement communities. As Lawlor removed the small three-ounce can from the tiny holster on his belt, he was grateful for the ingenious "set it and forget it" feature it contained.

Unlike most pepper sprays that required a button to be continually depressed or a trigger to be pulled to dispense its contents, the Guardian device had a mechanism that allowed the canister to be primed and thrown into a room where seconds later a fog of pepper spray would pour out, making the space completely uninhabitable.

Lawlor triggered the device, pitched it inside the inner office, and with his Beretta up and at the ready, waited for the NSA operative to stumble out hacking and choking.

When he did, Stanton came out with his gun blazing, shooting in all directions, and Gary had no other choice but to return fire.

FIFTY-SEVEN

New York City

"You couldn't have just winged him?" asked Harvath.

"I had no time. His bullets were way too close for comfort," replied Lawlor from his cell phone back in DC. "Whatever was going on, he and Forrester took it to their graves together. Everyone at the NSA is being incredibly tight-lipped, including my contacts, and despite the urgency of this situation, all they've said is that they'll get back to me. They're not even prepared to admit that Stanton was one of theirs."

This was exactly the kind of bureaucratic bullshit that was encouraging Harvath to seriously consider resigning his position. "So they don't care if their next location gets hit?" he asked.

"They won't even admit there is a fourth location, much less a first, a second, or a third."

"What are we supposed to do?"

"You've got all the information I was able to get before Stanton killed Forrester. I think you should make your way to the third location as quickly as possible and see if you can find out anything there."

"And if we don't?" asked Harvath.

Listen," replied Lawlor. "This has been a hard day for everybody. Just see what you can do. I'll keep working things from this side."

"Fine, but Gary?"

"What?"

"If Stanton thought this program was worth killing to protect, and his people know you've uncovered it, you'd better watch your back."

"I will. Don't worry," replied Lawlor. "Just get to that Strong Box location and let me know what you find."

When they found the bodies of the slain employees in the back of the New York Waterway bus garage, Harvath knew they were already too late. Nevertheless, Bob Herrington led the way down the hidden stairwell—the more senseless destruction he saw, the more the demons from his last mission in Afghanistan seemed to haunt him. He insisted on being on point, and out of all the members on the team, he was starting to concern Harvath the most.

After making their way down the metal stairs, the first thing the team noticed was the enormous door that had been blown off its hinges. As they carefully entered the facility, they saw that shrapnel had pitted both the walls and the ceiling. Whatever kind of bomb had gone off in here had done incredible damage. Blood was everywhere and several bodies had been sawed completely in half.

As Harvath tried to pinpoint how long ago the attack had occurred, the one thing he was confident of was that it had happened before their botched ambush in Central Park. They couldn't have made it here in time even if they had wanted to.

"What the hell hit this place?" said Rick Cates as he stepped around the bodies of what looked like three more dead marines. "This was no fragmentation grenade."

"This was more like the type of bomb suicide bombers use," replied Tracy Hastings, who had witnessed the aftermath of suicide bombers more times than she cared to remember.

"Are you saying somebody walked in here and blew him or herself up?" asked Harvath.

Tracy looked around some more and then replied, "Maybe. All I can say is that I think we're looking at a tight and very powerful package of plastique packed with ball bearings as the projectile."

"Any idea how it got in here?"

Tracy shook her head.

"Maybe the pizza guy brought it," said Cates as he bumped the edge of a personal pan-pizza box still sitting on someone's desk.

The team spread out and combed the facility. Like the others before it, it was all computerized. Now, though, they knew the reason why. Morgan found a functioning workstation, but without a password, he couldn't gain access to the system. Not only that, but as Harvath studied the shiny dials built into the frames of the computer displays, he realized they weren't cameras, as several on the team had suspected, but actually retinal scanners. The Athena Program took the handling of its data very seriously.

It was hard to tell if anything had been stolen. From what Harvath and the rest of the team could tell, everything seemed to be there; it was just shot to hell—including the employees. The only thing that had avoided the carnage was the server room, just like in the previous two locations.

But why risk so much just to take out the employees? What the hell was al-Qaeda's game? Was it some sort of payback? And what did any of this have to do with Sayed Jamal and Mike Jaffe? None of it made any sense.

That said, Harvath had a bad feeling in the pit of his stomach that once he did uncover the answers he was looking for, he wasn't going to like them.

As they left the server room, everyone was helping collect identification from the dead, when Herrington swung his weapon into the firing position and yelled, "Nobody fucking move."

Harvath and the rest of the team had no idea what the hell he was talking about until they noticed two strangers at the far end of the room pointing a pair of very nasty-looking short-barreled M16 Viper machine guns at them. The strangers ordered Bob and the rest of the team to drop their weapons and remain absolutely still. It was a Mexican standoff—although this time they wouldn't be able to count on Tracy Hastings sneaking up behind their adversaries with a big leafy tree branch.

"Everybody stay cool," cautioned Harvath. "What do you guys want?"

"What do we want?" demanded one of the strangers. "Why don't we start with who the hell are you?"

"My name's Scot Harvath and I'm with the Department of Homeland Security."

"Who are the rest of these people?" the man asked, indicating the rest of the team with the barrel of his weapon.

"They're with me. Who you are?"

"Homeland Security? Bullshit. DHS doesn't have anything to do with this facility."

"We do since Captain William Forrester was shot and killed less than an hour ago," replied Harvath.

"Captain Forrester is dead?"

"As a doornail," said Morgan as he shouldered his weapon and pulled a half-liter of water from his pack.

Tracy saw the men tense and begin applying pressure to their triggers. "Paul, are you nuts?" she responded. "Quit screwing around. You're going to get us all killed."

"No, I'm not," said Morgan. "And you know why? Because marines don't kill other marines."

FIFTY-EIGHT

Once the two strangers had lowered their weapons and downed the water Morgan had given them, Harvath asked, "What are you guys doing here?"

"It's our shift," said the lead man, who identified himself as Staff Sergeant Steve Gonzalez, United States Marine Corps.

"With all the shit going on in the Lincoln Tunnel, why didn't you come earlier?" asked Herrington.

"Orders. Believe me, Tommy and I wanted to come down here as soon as we heard, but it was against the protocol."

"Whose *protocol*?" replied Harvath.

"Captain Forrester's," said Lance Corporal Thomas Tecklin. "He ran us through every contingency he could think of. The last thing he wanted was for any of the security personnel to be caught in a secondary blast meant to target newcomers rushing to the scene."

"Wait a second," interjected Gonzalez, the bodies of his Marine Corps colleagues—and the people they were charged with protecting—littering the floor. "Let's start by talking about what the hell happened here."

"That's what we're trying to find out," said Harvath. "Captain Forrester gave us this location."

Gonzalez didn't believe Harvath. "He wouldn't have done that. This place is above top secret."

"He didn't have a choice," replied Herrington, who appreciated the man's loyalty to his mission and his commanding officer. "He didn't want to see any more of his marines die."

"More?" repeated Morgan. "What do you mean, he didn't want to see *more* marines die? What marines?"

"Two other sites were hit," said Harvath. He chose the words very carefully, as he wanted to see how much the marines knew.

Gonzalez was very concerned. "Which sites?"

"Transcon Enterprises and Geneva Diamond and Jewelry Exchange."

"Jesus Christ," said Tecklin. "How bad?"

"Equally as bad as this. No survivors."

"Who was it?"

"We believe it was al-Qaeda."

"Al-Qaeda? Why?"

"We don't know why," answered Harvath. "We were hoping that was something you could help us with. Is there anything in particular about the information being processed here that could be beneficial to them?"

"Officially," replied Gonzalez, "we didn't know anything about the information that flows through here. Our job is to guard this site."

"And unofficially?"

"Unofficially? People talk, you know? You couldn't help but overhear things here. It was all political stuff. Some of it run-of-the-mill dirty dealing and some of it extremely volatile. Like well-placed spies in foreign governments, murder cover-ups, assassination plots, coup attempts—it goes on and on. There is stuff even hotter than that, if you can believe it, but the hotter it is the quieter everyone here is—*was*—about it. At the end of the day, we actually overheard very little. And none of it directly valuable as far as al-Qaeda is concerned—at least nothing I can think of that would justify all of this," said the lead marine as he took in the devastated facility.

Three locations and zero leads. It was driving Harvath nuts. The more they uncovered, the less sense it all made. No matter how many steps they took forward, they still couldn't seem to catch up with whoever was behind these attacks. "What about the fourth site?" he asked.

"What fourth site?" said Gonzalez.

"Sergeant, we know there is a fourth and final site. Captain Forrester mentioned it before he was killed. If we're correct, that's exactly where the terrorists are headed next."

Gonzalez didn't respond.

"He's right," replied Tecklin. "We need to warn them."

"Quiet," ordered Gonzalez.

"Why? These guys know about the fourth site, and they're right that the terrorists probably do too."

"We don't know that."

"Sarge, they've hit three out of four. I'd say the chances are pretty good al-Qaeda knows about the last location. We can't just sit here and let our guys get killed. We've got to warn them."

Gonzalez was torn. On one hand there were the lives of fellow marines at stake and on the other were a set of orders that didn't seem to make much sense at this point. Nevertheless, orders were orders.

"Will you at least call the fourth location and warn them?" asked Harvath.

"It doesn't matter. I already tried from one of the pay phones outside before we came in here."

"No answer?"

"All I got was a fast busy signal and a 'circuits are overloaded' response."

"Did you try calling Transcon and Geneva Diamond?"

Gonzalez again nodded his head. "Same thing."

"You've got to tell us where that fourth location is."

"I'm sorry, but I can't discuss any other location or locations."

Bob Herrington had had enough. "For fuck's sake, Sergeant. Those people are going to die over there if you don't help us out. Make a goddamn command decision."

"I can't."

"The hell you can't. Your CO has been shot by the NSA program manager, and at this point you are the most senior marine on site. You think they're going to court martial you for trying to save that other location?"

"The NSA program manager?" remarked Tecklin.

Gonzalez didn't want to know anything further. He'd made up his mind. "I'm sorry, I have my orders."

"Well, you and your orders can kiss my fucking ass," said Herrington. "I thought marines were smarter than this. I guess I was wrong."

As Bob walked away in disgust, Harvath pulled Gonzalez aside and said, "Steve, I've got a lot of respect for your orders, but at least take Morgan and get over there. You guys might be able to help even the odds. The terrorists have enough players on their team to fill at least two Tahoes."

The sergeant shook his head. "No can do. We've got to secure this site and make sure no one else gets in or out until help arrives."

"You know that could be quite a while."

"It doesn't matter. This information needs to be protected."

"Even if that means other marines might die?"

Gonzalez looked at Harvath and slowly nodded his head. Come hell or high water, he was going to stand his post. In the process, though, several of his comrades were most likely going to lose their lives.

For a fleeting moment, Harvath wondered if they could muscle the marine and get him to crack, but he decided against it. As wrong as he believed the man's decision to be, Harvath wasn't going to torture a fellow serviceman faithfully executing his duty.

He was about to make one more impassioned plea, soldier to soldier, when Paul Morgan caught his attention and signaled that he needed to talk to him.

"What's up?" said Harvath as he crossed over to where Morgan was standing.

"I know where the fourth site is."

Harvath couldn't believe it. "How?"

"Tecklin gave it to me. We both went through basic at Camp Pendleton. It turns out we had the same D.I."

"So because of a drill instructor he just gave the information to you?"

"No," replied Morgan. "His brother is part of the security detail at the fourth location. When they joined the Marines together, they promised their old man they'd do everything they could to make sure nothing bad ever happened to the other. He respects Gonzalez, but the way he sees it, the Marines not only taught him how to follow orders, but also to react when old orders didn't make sense anymore and lives were on the line.

"That's why he wanted us to have the location. But wait till you hear where it is. At first I thought he was pulling my leg, but he swears it's for real."

"Where is it? Where's the fourth location?"

Morgan held up a diagram made by Lance Corporal Tecklin, and it made such perfect sense that Harvath almost couldn't believe it.

FIFTY-NINE

Abdul Ali watched as Sacha drew his Para-Ordnance 1911 pistol, affixed its silencer, and finished off his wounded comrade. They had done all they could to save him, but it was clear to everyone that Khasan wasn't going to make it. He was slowing them down, and that made him a liability. As cold as the decision was, they had no choice. Their own survival necessitated the act. Just like the man who had been killed during the assault on Geneva Diamond, Khasan's payment would be made to his family, including the bonus at the end of the job. Sacha would see to it personally.

Ali knew that the lead Chechen, as well as the rest of his men, held him responsible for this most recent death. Ali had almost walked into an ambush in Central Park and had brought whoever had orchestrated it out after them. The man on horseback had fired his first shot through the rear window of one of their Tahoes, hitting Khasan at the base of the throat. The man's next shot had gone straight through the tailgate, killing the Chechens' dog, Ivan, while the third shot had punched through the other side of the tailgate and missed by a matter of millimeters one of their men gunning from the backseat. As far as Ali was concerned, the first shot was all that mattered. The team was down two men now and still had two more locations to go.

With the rear window shattered and the back row of seats covered in Khasan's blood, Ali decided they not only needed to get rid of both the bodies they were carrying, they needed to get rid of the damaged Tahoe as well. First, though, they needed to find a suitable vehicle as a replacement.

Nearby in the tony Lenox Hill neighborhood, Sacha saw what they were looking for. The all-black GMC Yukon Denali was as close to perfect as they were going to get. Three blocks later, they dumped the damaged Tahoe, the bodies of their two dead comrades, and the body of the woman from whom they'd just carjacked the Denali.

They drove south toward Midtown east and their next assault. With multiple breaching points some distance apart at this location, timing was going to be everything. Though Ali would have preferred to have been on one of the street-level breaching teams, he had no choice but to go with the team that would be coming up from underneath. Theirs was the most perilous trek, and it was also the most likely to encounter resistance from inquisitive police officers. If push came to shove, only Ali and his grasp of American English could help the subterranean team pull it off.

The Denali sped toward 50th while the intact Tahoe pulled up onto the sidewalk of 49th Street, and Ali's team unloaded its equipment. Startled onlookers backed away as men in balaclavas and black tactical gear set up a utility company–style screen, sparked a Gentec portable acetylene torch, and began to cut through the sidewalk grating. Once the grating was pulled free, a high tinsel tripod complete with enormous rubber feet and a pulley and winch system was suspended above the opening, a rope was fed through, and Abdul Ali prepared to be the first one down.

The goal was to fast-rope in as quickly as possible. That all changed when only halfway down an MTA officer spotted Ali and reached for the radio mic clipped to his shoulder. With the laser sight of his MP5, Ali painted a red dot on the man's chest and pulled the trigger, quieting any premature announcement of their arrival.

When Ali hit the ground, it took him several moments to pull the officer's body from the platform and hide it beneath one of the nearby trains. Once he was done, he radioed for the rest of the men to hurry up.

Though rappelling in made much more sense than trying to gain access to the tracks by walking through the middle of Grand Central

Terminal, Ali wasn't going to feel safe until they had left this location far behind them. His sixth sense was speaking to him again, and he didn't like what it was saying.

Once the rest of the team had joined him, Ali led the way across the tracks toward 50th Street and the Waldorf-Astoria's secret railway platform. Built in the early 1930s, the platform provided VIP guests with their own private railway cars—a covert alternative to Penn Station or Grand Central Terminal. The platform had been used to gain access to the hotel by such notables as Generals Douglas MacArthur and John Pershing as well as President Franklin D. Roosevelt, who appreciated yet another feature of what became known among the cognoscenti as the Waldorf's secret station.

In the middle of the platform was an enormous six-foot-wide freight elevator capable of transporting Roosevelt's 6,000-pound, armor-plated Pierce Arrow from the Waldorf station up to a highly secure and cleverly hidden section of the hotel's garage, which had its own private exit.

In addition to being the official residence of the United States Ambassador to the United Nations, Abdul Ali prayed to his God that the Waldorf-Astoria was housing one other noteworthy guest—Mohammed bin Mohammed.

Approaching the freight elevator, Ali looked at his Casio and paused to catch his breath. Three minutes later, he entered the code given to him by the Troll and listened to the hum of the elevator as it made its way down to the platform. When it arrived, the team worked quickly to get themselves into place. Once they were all situated, Ali depressed the button for the elevator's one and only other stop, and the team began its ascent.

When the man sitting in the emergency hatch gave the command, Ali halted the elevator. The torch was quickly lifted up, and the man set to work on the grate covering the old airshaft tunnel. Once it had been removed, the rest of the team crawled inside.

SIXTY

The marines guarding the entrance to the Grail site, so code-named because its analysts handled the most valuable of the Athena Program intelligence, had no idea what hit them when Ali and his team burst from a wall-mounted air duct with their guns blazing. Two additional teams simultaneously appeared from a hallway and a nearby stairwell.

Dropping to the floor of their bulletproof cubicle, the marines scrambled for their assault rifles. Ali's men, though, didn't let up for even a fraction of a second. In a perfectly choreographed ballet of deadly fire, the Chechens assaulted the security hut in wave after wave, never giving the marines a chance to return fire. So engaged, neither Ali nor his mercenaries noticed when a heavy metal plate was slid open in the upper corner of the wall behind the marines, and a large-caliber machine gun opened fire.

Two of the Chechens were mowed right down, their bodies torn to shreds by the heavy lead rounds. Falling back, the teams retreated to their breaching points as Sacha yelled orders to his men.

As the Chechens directed all their fire toward the marines in the security booth and the opening in the wall where the machine gun had appeared, Sacha loaded a fast-arming M381 high-explosive round into the 40mm grenade launcher mounted beneath his assault rifle and let the golf ball–sized projectile rip.

When it connected, the explosion was deafening, and it not only succeeded in knocking out the machine gun, but it tore a huge hole in the upper corner of the wall. One of the Chechens raced toward the security booth armed with his 9mm pistol and a good-sized shape charge, but neither did him any good. The two marines inside had opened a narrow slot in the bulletproof glass and began to return fire, killing the man before he could reach their position.

By focusing fire on the slot, the Chechens were able to push the marines back and keep them pinned down while another one of their teammates rushed forward and attached the shape charge to the side of the booth. Even if they had tried to escape, the marines never would have had a chance. The charge leveled the structure, killing both of its occupants instantly.

While the team kept watch for any more peepholes or slide boxes through which weapons could be fired, another shape charge was affixed to the facility's main door. Retreating a safe distance away, the team donned their gasmasks, blew the charge, and immediately launched a series of tear gas canisters into the series of rooms on the other side.

When the first of the Chechens ran inside, two marines fully outfitted with gas masks of their own were waiting for him and blew the man apart. Stunned at their mounting losses, the Chechens came to a momentary standstill, but Sacha and Ali drove them forward. They hadn't come this far to give up now.

By the sheer force of the resistance they were encountering, Ali felt in the depths of his soul that they had finally found where Mohammed bin Mohammed was being held captive. All they needed to do now was put down the last of the resistance. Loading another fast-arming M381 into his launcher and pointing it at the marines, Sacha looked ready to do just that.

The round exploded with an overwhelming concussion wave that knocked almost all of the Chechens to the ground, but when the Americans eventually arrived to claim their dead, they'd have to scrape what was left of their precious marines off the walls and the ceiling if they intended to have any sort of a burial for them.

Regaining their feet, the remaining Chechens quickly and methodically made their way through the facility. Ali was filled with anticipation with each door he kicked open, positive he would stumble upon Mohammed at any moment, but as the team swept into the last of the rooms, the man again was nowhere to be found.

Ali slammed a fresh magazine into his weapon, beside himself with both rage and frustration. *How could they have hit four sites and not found him?* Ali was about to share this thought with Sacha, when the red-haired giant took his small bag of electronic devices and headed toward the facility's servers. At that moment, Ali's sixth sense began speaking to him again. He probably should have pushed the outrageous thoughts from his mind, but he let them stay. Something told him that what he was thinking might not be so far off the mark. Ali was developing more than a sneaking suspicion that he had been used.

As Abdul Ali seethed, downstairs near the platform, fatally wounded MTA officer Patrick O'Donnell had finally summoned enough strength to radio for help.

SIXTY-ONE

The debate, if it could have been called that, was over before it began. Tracy Hastings was right. There was only one way they could cover that kind of distance in enough time to have a chance to catch the terrorists on the other end.

While the team had been able to somewhat weave in and out of traffic and even ride down the sidewalk when necessary, it was still perilous and too often very slow going. That was where Tracy's idea came in.

When they got to Times Square, they weren't surprised to find that just like all the other subway stations in New York this one was closed too. A heavy iron gate at the bottom of the stairs had been locked tight. Harvath looked at Morgan as he dismounted from his bike and drew the Mossberg 590 12-gauge shotgun from his scabbard pack.

Morgan ejected his shells, replaced them with breaching rounds, and headed down the stairs. The subway system of the city that never sleeps had not intended its locks to ever be subjected to any real assault, so Morgan had the gate open with one deafening blast from his Mossberg. Less than a minute later, he had blown through a second lock on the handicap access gate near the turnstiles, and returned to the bottom of the stairs to wave the rest of the team on down.

Their motorbikes came clattering down the stairs and zipped past him. Once Morgan had retrieved his bike and had closed the gate behind them, the team rushed out onto the platform and zoomed down the access stairs into the tunnel.

Harvath had smelled worse, but this was still no garden walk. Rats and rotting garbage mingled with pools of urine and human feces. Even the relatively cool air, a break from the oppressive heat on the streets above, brought little comfort.

They chose the number 7 Flushing local line because it provided the straightest shot to Grand Central Station. They weren't in the tunnel for more than three minutes when they heard a rumbling noise over their engines and saw a light appear up ahead. They all knew it wasn't the proverbial light at the end of the tunnel, so, coming to a stop, they all hugged the tunnel wall.

Soon, a slow-moving, bloodred subway train passed, carrying a mixture of survivors and exhausted emergency personnel from the number 7's tunnel that passed beneath the East River on its way to Queens.

It was surreal. Men and women inside were covered from head to toe in gray ash. Their eyes, no matter what color, looked like dark, hollowed-out sockets, giving their heads the appearance of being nothing more than skulls. They looked like the undead, and as they stared out the train windows, they gave no indication of seeing anything other than their own morbid reflections. They could have just as easily been recently departed spirits being ferried across the River Styx toward the hereafter. It was a chilling sight.

When the train had passed, the team continued on their way.

At the Grand Central stop, they emerged onto a single island–style platform. The rounded ceiling above reminded Harvath of the London Underground or Paris Métro and he remarked again at how little he really knew of New York.

At the center of the platform, they took one last moment to go over their plan. They had no idea what to expect when they hit Grand Central Terminal itself. All they knew was that they were not going to stop for anybody or anything—that included any police or military.

Nodding his head, Harvath revved his bike and took off. Herrington, Cates, Morgan, and Hastings followed right behind.

According to Tecklin's diagram, the secret Waldorf station was located between tracks 61 and 63. It took them several minutes to find the right platform and twice they had to double back. The entire station was easily deserted. Once they were sure they were in the correct spot, they leapt their motorbikes down to track level and headed north.

Harvath had never been this deep inside an underground train depot before, much less one the size of Grand Central. The amount of tracks, equipment, and machinery that filled the cavernous underground space was beyond incredible. It seemed to stretch for miles.

The Waldorf platform was more than six blocks away from where they had started. As they neared, Harvath had the sinking feeling that they were already too late. Two MTA officers were tending to a colleague whose chest was covered with blood. As Harvath pulled up alongside, he displayed his credentials and asked, "What happened?"

"He's been shot, and we can't get any medical personnel to respond down here. They're all tied up at other locations," replied one of the officers.

Harvath didn't need to say anything. In a flash, Paul Morgan was off his bike and had broken out his medical kit.

As Morgan tended the wounded man, Harvath tried to get more information out of the other two officers, but all they knew was that some sort of assault team had rappelled down from one of the sidewalk grates, shot their colleague, and had made their way upstairs via the Waldorf platform freight elevator.

After Morgan explained to the MTA officers what to do until help arrived, the team headed for the elevator. Harvath punched in the code Tecklin had given them, but nothing happened. Either the code was incorrect or the elevator had been locked down.

"What now, boss?" asked Cates.

It was a strange way for any of them to be addressing him, but apparently the mantle of leadership had been passed. Harvath looked up and down the platform. According to the diagram, there were two sets of stairs to the Grail facility, but they were locked behind heavy, exit-only iron doors at the 49th and 50th street sides of the hotel. There was also the hidden private garage exit, but Tecklin had made only brief mention of it to Morgan, and it wasn't specifically indicated on the diagram. The marine had anticipated the team going in the way the rest of the Grail facility employees entered, via the Waldorf platform. Harvath had a decision to make.

Turning back toward the MTA officers, Harvath asked for the quickest way up to the street level. One of the officers pointed to a doorway at the other end of the platform and told him the stairs led to a service corridor just off the hotel lobby. Leaving their motorbikes behind, the team ran for the door and bounded up the stairs. When they hit the service corridor, they raced toward the lobby door, and that's when they heard the telltale sounds of gunfire.

SIXTY-TWO

Abdul Ali ejected his newly spent magazine and slapped in a fresh one. *They must have found the body on the train tracks.* It was the only reason he could think of for the police having found them. But at the same time, such a disproportionate response could only mean that the officer he'd shot wasn't dead. The man must have radioed in the details, because what had just showed up was no ordinary police unit.

The heavily armed ESU team laid down waves of suppression fire. They were incredibly accurate and extremely disciplined. Through the fog of the firefight, there was something else that was clearly evident. These men were angry. Their city had been attacked. Fellow policemen and citizens had been killed and now they were prepared to fight to the death if they had to. It made Ali extremely nervous. He knew that a motivated, determined enemy was the most fearsome foe of all.

The ESU team threw so much lead in their direction that even the five battle-hardened Chechen Spetsnaz soldiers were showing signs of concern. While an eventuality like this had been considered, it hadn't been deemed very probable. Their plan from the beginning had been to tie up as many tactical units as possible and then never to stay in any one location long enough for any to catch up with them. The ESU team that had found them must have been attached to a nearby high-probability attack site, maybe Grand Central itself. Whatever the case, Ali had no choice but to order his men back into the 49th Street stairwell.

Once everyone was inside, Sacha slammed the door shut. As he followed his soldiers up the stairs, he removed the last two fragmentation grenades from his tactical vest. Halfway up, he rigged a crude booby trap. Though it wouldn't hold their attackers back indefinitely, it would at least slow them down and hopefully thin their ranks by two or three men.

Bursting into the Grail facility's entry corridor, Sacha began barking orders at his four remaining men. In the event that they couldn't find another way out, they were going to have to make a stand right where they were. Both Sacha and Ali knew that the longer they stayed there, the greater the chances that the Americans would be able to summon backup. If that happened, not only would Abdul Ali's mission be in jeopardy but so would the lives of all the men on his team.

The escape route that seemed to make the most sense for them was the one they immediately dismissed. If it *was* the MTA officer who had drawn the ESU team to the scene, then it was very likely there were police on the train platform downstairs outside the freight elevator. Going back the way Ali had come was definitely out of the question. That left them with either the 50th Street stairwell or the private exit from the garage.

Staring at the carnage that had been created during the assault on the Grail facility, Ali began to formulate a plan.

SIXTY-THREE

By the time Harvath and his team stormed through the Waldorf's Lexington Avenue entrance, the sound of gunfire had already stopped. They couldn't help but suppose the worst.

Running toward 49th Street, the team pulled up short just before the corner of the building. Peering around the side, Harvath saw a very well equipped NYPD Emergency Services Unit preparing to breach what appeared to be a Grail facility stairwell door.

Raising his ID above his head, Harvath whistled to get the men's attention and began walking toward them. Seeing the weapon tucked into his waistband, several of the officers spun and squared up on Harvath ready to fire. He didn't have to see the red dots painted on his chest to know that their laser sights were lighting him up like a Christmas tree. He moved purposefully, but without making any sudden moves that could be misinterpreted.

"Department of Homeland Security," said Harvath as he came within earshot of the team commander.

The commander waved him off, yelling, "We've got active shooters on site. Get the hell out of here, now!"

"Negative," said Harvath as he continued approaching. "My team and I have been on their trail most of the evening. Trust me, you're going to need our help."

Though reluctant to waste any more time, or accept assistance from a Federal agent he knew nothing about, the commander was smart enough to realize that Harvath might very well have intelligence that could prove helpful. Leaving a contingent of men to watch the door in case the shooters reemerged, he moved behind the safety of a blacked-out Tahoe parked on the sidewalk to speak with Harvath. "Okay," he said, "you've got about thirty seconds to tell me what's going on here."

Harvath really didn't care about maintaining the secrecy of the NSA and its covert operation, but nevertheless he remained circumspect. "The men inside that stairwell have hit three other government installations this afternoon."

"Three *others*?" replied the man whose name tab on his vest identified him as McGahan. "This is a hotel, not a government installation. The closest thing we've got to government inside this building is the residence of the U.S. Ambassador to the UN."

"There's a special freight elevator from the train platform beneath the hotel," said Harvath. "It goes to a secret facility within the hotel that is being used by one of our intelligence agencies."

McGahan looked at him like he was nuts. "Are you for real?"

Harvath gave the commander the broad brushstrokes of what they had witnessed up to that point and then let the man make up his own mind.

It didn't take McGahan long. "And you're sure about the diagram that marine gave you?"

"One hundred percent," said Harvath.

McGahan walked over to one of his men, relieved him of his radio, and brought it over to Harvath. "I wish I had more, but that's all I can spare. Our truck is two blocks over and I don't think either of us want to waste any more time."

"You mean, *this* isn't your truck?" asked Harvath as he took a step back from the Tahoe.

"This belongs to whoever the shooters are."

Harvath should have known they wouldn't leave their escape vehicle too far away. With its lights left flashing, who would have suspected it was anything other than a very official vehicle on very official business? It really was a clever idea. "Did your people look through it?"

"We were just wrapping up a quick cursory when the shooters came out of the stairwell and began firing at us."

"Did your men find anything?"

"No. It's pretty clean."

Harvath nodded his head. A more thorough search of the truck would have to wait. Hopefully, though, it wouldn't be necessary. Pulling the LaRue tactical knife from the sheath on his vest, Harvath punctured both passenger-side tires. One could never be too careful.

"Okay, then," said the commander. "Get your team over here. I want to brief them and be inside that building in less than three minutes."

Harvath signaled Herrington, who brought the rest of the team from around the corner and up 49th Street to where he and the commander were standing.

Compared to the special response unit, Harvath's team was woefully underequipped, but there was nothing they could do about it. Even if the NYPD officers had wanted to help out, it wasn't as if they drove around with duffels full of extra helmets, kneepads, and body armor. What they did have, though, were explosives.

After synchronizing their watches, the Emergency Services Unit breacher tapped Harvath on the shoulder, handed him a small canvas bag with det cord and everything else necessary to blow a heavy metal door off its hinges, and said, "Just in case."

SIXTY-FOUR

THE WHITE HOUSE

Pulling the secretary of defense to the side of the situation room, the president demanded, "Where's General Waddell?"

"He's still tied up at DIA and asked me to give you his regrets."

"Regrets? What the hell does he think this is, a tea party?"

"Of course not, sir, but—"

The president cut him off. "Don't defend him, Bob. This situation has gotten way out of control. It's worse than I could have imagined. How the hell did al-Qaeda figure out we have Mohammed bin Mohammed in New York in the first place?"

"Again, sir, we don't know that the intercept specifically referred to Mohammed. It could have been referring to Sayed Jamal."

"Like hell it was," replied Rutledge. "It only happened this morning, and you and I both know that Scot Harvath conducted a perfectly clean grab. He dragged the man back through the woods to get him across the border, for crying out loud. Nobody was following them. This attack on New York is in retaliation for Mohammed."

"Either way, someplace there's a leak, and we're working overtime on identifying it."

"What about the operation itself? Whether al-Qaeda knows about

Jamal or Mohammed doesn't matter. They know we have one of their people in New York. How do we know they're not mounting some kind of rescue operation?"

Hilliman chuckled and said, "I think that's highly unlikely, sir."

The president didn't find any of this amusing. "What should have been highly unlikely is anyone finding out that we had either one of those men in New York in the first place, but it still happened, didn't it?"

The smile fell from the secretary's face. "Yes, sir, it did."

"So what's being done to help reinforce the men running this operation?"

"Nothing," replied Hilliman.

"Nothing? What are you talking about?"

"Sir, in all fairness, the intercept didn't specify a location. All it referred to was our taking a subject to New York City."

"What about the man who's running the operation for us—what does he think?"

"Mike Jaffe? From what I was told, he wanted immediate evacuation."

"So why wasn't it granted?"

"Sir, the only way we can preserve Mohammed's legal status is to make sure he doesn't touch U.S. soil until we're ready to close out the interrogation phase and move him to trial. If we evac him, we'd have to position an appropriate vessel outside our territorial waters and airlift Mohammed back out to sea. When that NYPD helicopter was shot down, a bubble was placed over Manhattan. No air traffic in or out."

"But that was hours ago."

"And in that time, Jaffe and his team have reported no problems whatsoever," said Hilliman as a bit of a cocky smile crept back across his face.

"What are you saying?" asked Rutledge.

"I'm saying that if al-Qaeda knew where we were holding Mohammed, they would have tried something by now. They're not coming, Mr. President. These horrible attacks on New York were just that—horrible attacks. Al-Qaeda was doing the only thing they could do in retaliation for our grabbing Mohammed. It shows you how devastated they are by his capture." The secretary waited a moment for that to sink in and then said, "I know it's an incredibly high price to pay and

I know it doesn't look like it now, but we beat them, Mr. President. The nuclear attacks Mohammed was spearheading would have been a significant turning point in the war on terror, and it would have turned the war in their favor, but we cut them off at the knees. What we saw today was their death knell. We've clamped the lid down and as soon as we break Mohammed, we'll begin nailing that lid to the top of their coffin."

The president wanted desperately for his secretary of defense to be right. He wanted to be able to tell himself that as horrific as today's attacks were, the Americans who had perished hadn't died in vain—that their deaths meant something and that they marked a long-awaited turning point in the war on terror.

But as much as the president wanted to believe Bob Hilliman, a man who in over five years had never steered him wrong on matters of national security, he had learned early on in his presidency that things were never exactly as they seemed, especially when it came to terrorism.

SIXTY-FIVE

While a two-man contingent of McGahan's officers used the gear from the back of the Tahoe to rope down through the sidewalk grate and cover the Waldorf platform, Harvath and his team ran back up Lexington toward the 50th Street stairwell.

When they arrived, they found not another Tahoe but a black Yukon Denali double-parked on the sidewalk. It had the same dashboard-mounted lights that flashed bright halogen strobes of blue and red. As Harvath carefully peered inside, he saw crushed CD jewel cases, South Beach Diet bar wrappers, and a stack of textbooks littering the floor. Two or three hair scrunchies were wrapped around the gearshift, and a pink snowflake air freshener dangled from the front passenger door handle.

The terrorists had been driving two identical Tahoes, but not anymore. Harvath must have caused more damage than he thought to force them to steal a new vehicle. Judging by the thin mist of blood that had been spattered on the driver's-side headliner, the owner of this vehicle had not met with a very pleasant end. Removing his knife once more, he plunged it to the hilt in two of the tires, just in case the terrorists were able to slip by them.

The bad guys had blown the lock out of this door just like the one on 49th Street. When Hastings realized the door was open, she replaced the det cord and slung the demo bag over her shoulder. Backing away, she signaled everyone to take their places. Harvath radioed McGahan and told him that his team was ready.

"Roger that," came the commander's voice. "Teams one and two in place."

Listening to McGahan's countdown over his headset, Harvath counted backward on his fingers from five. When he closed his fist and pulled it down like a trucker blowing an air horn, Hastings pulled the door open.

With Harvath in the lead this time, they all poured into the stairwell and took the stairs as quickly and as quietly as they could.

Simultaneously, McGahan's breaching team hit the door on 49th Street and bounded up the stairs.

By the time the lead man noticed the booby trap, it was too late. Shrapnel ripped through the tightly packed stairwell, killing two officers and wounding three more. It was complete pandemonium.

Despite barely being able to hear as a result of the explosion or breathe because of the smoke, McGahan radioed his team's situation to help warn the others. After hearing the details, one of the special-response officers below on the platform responded that he was leaving to get the medical kit from their truck. Harvath told the man to remain at his post, but the NYPD officer ignored him. He didn't take his orders from DHS. He had injured colleagues who needed immediate medical attention, and that's what he was focused on.

With the 49th Street assault team out of commission and the team on the platform down to only one tactical officer and two MTA patrolmen, the brunt of the assault had just fallen squarely on the shoulders of Scot Harvath and company.

Harvath held up a closed fist to stop his team so that he could relay the information. It was then that a man in a black balaclava appeared at the top of the stairs with a grenade and all hell suddenly broke loose.

SIXTY-SIX

With their vehicle on the 49th Street side compromised by the presence of the police, exiting by the 50th Street side made the most sense, but somehow something just didn't feel right about it for Abdul Ali. If the police knew about the railroad platform and the 49th Street entrance, then they very likely knew about the 50th Street stairwell too. Ali could be running right into another trap, and so he made sure to choose their method of egress very carefully.

Because the Grail facility's private garage entrance let out onto the 49th Street side of the building, it was immediately ruled out. That seemed to leave them with no alternatives until Ali realized that the hotel had at least two more perfectly acceptable exit points—the main doors at the rear of the hotel on Lexington Avenue as well as those at the very front of the Waldorf on Park Avenue. The only question was how they were going to get there.

As the secret garage exit opened only from the inside of the facility, Ali was fairly confident that they would not find a swarm of police officers waiting for them on the other side. Once in the garage, they could locate a service entrance to the hotel and from there make their way to either the Park or Lexington Avenue exits. Considering that everything was happening at the east end of the hotel, near Lexington, Ali leaned heavily toward making an escape via Park Avenue. They could decide what to do next, once they were safely out of harm's way.

As Ali put the finishing touches on one of the little surprises they planned on leaving behind, Sacha dispatched men to check the status on each of the stairwells. Osman was the first to report. From what he could tell, the booby trap in the 49th Street stairwell had been triggered and the police had been forced to retreat. Yusha reported not seeing any signs of pursuit via the 50th Street stairwell, but then he suddenly broke off. When Sacha asked him what was going on, the man quietly spoke into his microphone to say that he thought he heard people approaching. Sacha told him to fall back and wait, that they were coming to support him, but the overconfident warrior told his commander not to bother. He had the high ground and could handle it himself. It was the very last Sacha heard from him.

SIXTY-SEVEN

With the man at the top of the stairs lined up right in the center of his sights, Harvath yelled "Grenade!" and lunged backward, knocking his team down the stairs. As he fell with them, Harvath repeatedly squeezed the trigger of his weapon until its magazine was empty.

The team hit the landing in a pile of twisted limbs and then scrambled to descend farther to safety. When the grenade detonated, they were pressed against the opposite wall a story and a half down. Harvath had quite literally saved their lives.

As the stars began to clear from their heads, Harvath inserted a fresh mag and they remounted the stairs twice as fast, knowing that the terrorists' colleagues couldn't be far behind.

When they reached the uppermost landing and stepped over what was left of the man's corpse, they could see he was probably dead before the grenade even detonated. Most of Harvath's shots had found their marks—in both the man's head and chest area. Falling to the ground, the grenade must have rolled backward into the corridor where, a few feet later, it detonated and tore huge chunks away from the concrete walls and ceiling.

As the team stared at the dead body, they all noticed that it appeared too pale to be Arab. "He almost looks Caucasian," said Hastings, not realizing that in the truest sense of the word she was absolutely right.

"Who the hell are these people?" asked Herrington as he removed the man's balaclava so they could get a good look at his face. "Are we sure we're dealing with al-Qaeda?"

Harvath went through the man's pockets but found nothing helpful. He was just as in the dark as his team was. All he knew was that they were less than a step behind the terrorists now and he didn't want to lose any ground.

The group fell into a stack formation, pushed on into the corridor, and got ready for the fight they all knew was waiting for them just up ahead.

When they hit the Grail's entry chamber, it looked like a scene straight out of Iraq or Afghanistan. The charred walls were riddled with bullet holes. The floor was covered with spent shell casings, blood, and body parts. Off to the side, three more Caucasian corpses, their balaclavas removed, were lying facing the Lexington Avenue wall. *Or had they been positioned that way—facing east toward Mecca?* Harvath filed that part of the scene away, and once they had gone through the dead men's empty pockets, he led the team deeper into the facility.

The carnage inside was just as bad, if not worse than what they had seen at the three previous sites. The marine guards were all dead, as was each and every facility employee. And for what? *What were these people after? Why risk so much just to attack these sites?* No matter how hard Harvath tried, he just couldn't wrap his head around it.

The other thing he couldn't understand was where the rest of the terrorists were. Including the man he had gunned down in the stairwell, there were five corpses in the Grail facility, all dressed in the same black Nomex fatigues with patches identifying them as members of the FBI's Hostage Rescue Team—*yet another ingenious ploy.* With everything going on today, the cops were even less likely to question federal officers than their own Emergency Service personnel. What's more, the NYPD for the most part knew very little about the makeup of HRT. The chances of the terrorists being uncovered as frauds, at least in the short run, seemed pretty minimal.

As Harvath and his team continued to clear the facility, they readied themselves for the inevitable. *There had to be more men somewhere*—the satellite photos had shown at least two teams of four to seven men.

Would the four dead men have needed to come here in two separate vehicles? There had to be others and they *had* to be close. Harvath could feel it.

Walking back into the center of the main room, Harvath took another look at its raised floor platform. It was about thirty by thirty and similar to those he'd seen in brokerage houses, as well as in the FBI and DHS crisis management centers. Framed within the polished aluminum railings that defined the platform's edges were the facility's computer workstations. On the first pass, Harvath had thought he'd heard something strange, and now as he stood still, he could almost make out what it was—a strange beeping coming from one of the computers.

As he hopped up onto the platform, he radioed the special response officer downstairs on the train siding. Since no one had come out the 50th Street stairwell and he knew that even the wounded McGahan and his remaining officers had their eyes on the 49th Street stairwell and the adjacent garage, the only remaining egress the terrorists had was via the elevator.

The officer reported back that not only had they not seen anything, they hadn't heard anything either. Wherever the elevator was, it hadn't moved—he was certain of it.

Harvath was pretty sure of it too. Just as he was sure they hadn't finished off the last of the terrorists. *But if they hadn't taken the elevator, where the hell were they?*

The question was still banging on the front door of Harvath's mind as he approached the beeping computer. Suddenly Tracy Hastings yelled, "Stop!"

As Harvath looked at her she added, "Whatever you do, don't move."

SIXTY-EIGHT

The beeping of the computer had been joined by something else—something barely audible just below the surface of the first noise. Harvath hadn't been able to hear it until he neared the work station. It sounded like the high-pitched whine a professional photographer's flash makes as it charges back up. The funny thing was, Tracy Hastings had heard it too and she wasn't even standing on the platform. That could mean only one thing—the whining noise hadn't actually begun until Harvath neared the computer.

"Stay put," cautioned Tracy. "Don't even shift your weight. Do you understand me?"

"What's going on, Tracy?"

"I think you tripped a pressure switch."

"A pressure switch?" repeated Harvath. "Are you sure?"

"EOD's all about attention to detail, right? You said so yourself."

As Tracy tried to find an access panel to get under the floor and see what they were dealing with, the rest of the team stood there, not knowing what to do. Harvath looked at Herrington and said, "If you want to watch me wet my pants, we can do it later once I down that bottle of Louis XIII you owe me. In the meantime, why don't you guys figure out how our terrorists got out of here. If this ends badly, I'd rather face Allah by myself. Speaking of which—"

"Those three outside?" replied Herrington. "Yeah, I noticed. They were all left facing east towards Mecca."

"What do you think?"

"If they're Caucasian Muslims allied with al-Qaeda, then they've gotta be Chechens."

"I was thinking the same thing," said Harvath.

Bob was just staring at him wordlessly, so Harvath said something for him. "Get the hell out of here. Can't you see Tracy and I want to be alone for a while?"

Herrington forced a smile and replied, "See you soon."

Harvath nodded and watched as Cates and Morgan followed him out of the room. Once they were gone Harvath asked, "How are we doing down there?"

Several moments went by without a response so Harvath tried again. "Talk to me, Tracy. What are we looking at?"

Still nothing.

"Hey, Tracy. How about a situation report already?"

The waiting was interminable, especially when it was his ass on the line and he could do absolutely nothing about it. He was about to call out again, when Hastings popped her head up over the edge of the platform. Harvath was going to ask her if it was actually a bomb and if she could handle it, but he didn't have to. The look on her face said it all.

"It's a bomb. A big one."

"Great," replied Harvath as he began to shift his weight to his other foot and then caught himself just in time. "So what's the bad news?"

"I don't think I can defuse it."

"Oh yes you can."

Hastings turned her scarred face away.

"Tracy, you can do this stuff in your sleep," said Harvath. "Let's just take it one step at a time."

"I can't, Scot."

"Did I ever tell you what a good dancer I am?"

She looked back over at him, unable to keep the smile from her face. "What does that have to do with any of this?"

"It has everything to do with this," he replied. "I was going to wait for a more romantic opportunity to ask, but I was hoping I could take you out when we're all finished with this."

"You want to take me out? Dancing?"

"That depends. If you don't defuse this bomb, I think our budding friendship is going to be a little bit strained."

Hastings smiled again.

That was what Harvath needed to see. "You can do this, Tracy. Get back down there and tell me what you see."

"I can tell you right now," she replied, the smile disappearing from her face. "It's almost identical to the last bomb I handled."

"Then it should be a piece of—" said Harvath who suddenly realized what she was saying.

The last bomb Tracy Hastings had attempted to defuse had detonated, taking her left eye, half her face, and life as she'd known it along with it.

SIXTY-NINE

"Walk me through what you did on the last bomb," said Harvath, trying to help Tracy hold it together.

"It was pretty unsophisticated," she replied.

"Unsophisticated, how?"

"Everything. The plastique, the initiator, everything."

"Okay, if it was so unsophisticated textbook, what went wrong?"

"I don't know. I never knew. I did everything right, but it didn't make a difference."

Harvath had to work on keeping his cool. He was no good to himself or Tracy if he lost control. For both of their sakes, he had to remain calm. "Let's just focus on this device. Can you go back under the platform and pop up one of the adjacent panels so I can see what you're doing or at least talk to you a little more easily?"

Hastings nodded her head and disappeared back below. A few seconds later a floor panel next to Harvath popped up, and Tracy slid it out of the way.

"Perfect," he said. "Now we can talk. Is there any way we can immobilize the pressure plate?"

"I already checked that," said Hastings. "We can't."

"Then we're going to do everything from scratch, okay? Do it for me. Just check it one more time."

Hastings did as he asked, but her response was the same. "The pressure plate is a dead end."

"Excellent choice of words, Tracy."

"Sorry."

"What about the main charge? Can you separate it?"

She looked at the device and then back up at Harvath, slowly shaking her head.

"Do you see any place to insert a safety pin of any sort?"

Hastings scoured the device, but came back with the same answer, "None at all."

Harvath was running out of options. "What about minimizing the damage then? What can you tell about the projectiles?"

She took several moments before responding. "It looks like a lot of it has been cobbled together on the spot. They're using broken glass and bits of Lexan for the projectiles."

"Is it a directional device?"

"No. The projectiles are set to radiate out in all directions. Effective range about two hundred meters, I'd say. Apparently they didn't want anybody getting out of here."

The same thought had gone through Harvath's mind. The fact that the bomb appeared to be cobbled together with materials found on the scene was also running through Harvath's mind. There was something else, but he couldn't put his finger on it. The rational part of his brain kept avoiding it, blaming the stalemate on Hastings, a trained EOD technician who *should* know what to do. Because he couldn't stand the silence, he posed a very stupid and very obvious question: "Is there a way to interrupt the detonator?"

"C'mon, Scot. Like Rick said back at the VA, I might have lost my job, but I didn't lose my training. That was one of the first things I looked for."

He didn't know what it was, but something about what Hastings had just said raised a heavy curtain in his mind a fraction of inch, teasing him with the answer he was looking for. *Damn it.* It had been so long since he had worked with explosives. The majority of his explosives training as a SEAL had been in the detonation, not the diffusing department. The joke in the Teams had been the only explosives equation a SEAL needed to remember was *P* for *plenty.* Even in the Secret Service, there were dogs and specialty technicians to handle the bombs.

And yet, something kept knocking at the back of his brain. *What the hell was it?*

Harvath looked down at Hastings and said, "You're sure the device looks rudimentary?"

"Totally."

"Why is that? What we've seen of these guys so far is anything but simple. They seem pretty sophisticated and definitely know what they're doing, correct?"

"Yeah. So?"

"So why are you not seeing the same level of tactical sophistication in that device down there?"

"Who knows," replied Hastings. "There could be a million reasons. They were probably in a pretty damn good hurry. People often resort to the basics when they're pressed for time."

Harvath shook his head. "I don't think so. Not these guys. I think they want you to believe that bomb is paint-by-numbers."

"What for?"

"So that you'll miss something. Something you wouldn't have missed if you were being extracareful."

Just then, something clicked, but it wasn't for Harvath, it was for Hastings. "Jesus, you're right," she said.

"What is it?"

"Hold on" was the last thing she said before disappearing once again beneath the floor.

Standing on top of a pressure plate, even a few minutes could seem like a lifetime. Harvath had not heard anything from Hastings and he was beginning to wonder if maybe she had lost her nerve and was lying beneath the platform completely paralyzed with fear. Not that he could blame her. After having a bomb go off in her face, he couldn't even begin to image what it was like tackling one again, much less a device almost identical to the one that took her eye and scarred her appearance for life.

When Hastings did reappear, it wasn't beneath the open floor panel just to his right. She rolled out from beneath the platform and stood a wary distance away. She seemed stunned. Her expression was hard to read. Was it anger? Fear? Suddenly Harvath wondered if maybe it was *regret*.

"What's going on?" he asked, but Hastings didn't answer.

As she turned away from him, she ran out of the room muttering, "There are only two rules. Rule number two, see rule number one."

Immediately, Harvath was transported back to the conversation he'd had with Samuel Hardy, PhD: *Each person reacts to the stresses of war in different ways.*

But what if things get ugly?

There's no way to predict. You won't know until something happens.

At which point it could be too late.

Hardy had nodded and said, *Many symptoms exhibited by soldiers outside the realm of combat have more to do with adjusting to the real world than anything else. Put them back into the stresses of combat, and nine out of ten times their symptoms disappear.*

And that tenth time? Harvath had specifically asked him. *How do you deal with that?*

You can't. Only that soldier can. It comes down to facing his or her personal demons, and that's a battle that requires more courage than anything you might ever face on the other end of a gun.

Or on the other end of an IED, thought Harvath as Hastings disappeared out the door, and he realized that she had just left him alone . . . to die.

SEVENTY

Harvath had begun gauging the weight of objects within an arm's reach, wondering if he could fool the pressure plate into making it think he was still standing on top of it. He knew it was useless. But he also knew that this was not how he wanted to die. His mind flashed to the descriptions of Bob Herrington's wounded men and he remembered his friend saying that sometimes being wounded in combat was worse than dying. Harvath had seen men shredded by land mines and different explosive devices, and at this moment he found it hard to envision living the rest of his life without the use of his arms or legs. To a certain degree, he'd rather the bomb kill him than maim him.

By the same token, Harvath had been trained to recognize this counterproductive, defeatist self-talk, and he slammed an iron door down on the inner conversation. The only thoughts he could afford to entertain were how to get out of the situation and do so without being killed *or* injured.

Wiggling the thin metal cubicle-style partition next to him, Harvath was seriously considering using it as poor-man's body armor, when he heard a voice at the other end of the room.

"I told you not to move."

He looked up to see Tracy Hastings marching right toward him. She was armed with a small toolbox and a look of pissed-off determination.

"What?" she said seeing the look on *his* face. "Did you think I wasn't coming back?"

"The thought had occurred to me. I wouldn't have blamed you if you didn't."

"What? And miss an evening of dinner, dancing, and sparkling conversation?"

"I don't know about *sparkling* conversation."

"Neither do I, but it doesn't matter. I never leave a soldier behind. Especially another anchor clanker."

"Hooyah," replied Harvath with as much confidence as he could muster as Tracy disappeared back beneath the platform.

Once she was situated, she said, "Those fuckers are pretty clever. You were right. It is *too* simple, but I couldn't see it."

"Couldn't see what?"

"This is exactly how they got me in Iraq. I can see that now. Two of the most important rules we learned in handling IEDs were never to assume there was only one device and rule number two—"

"See rule number one," said Harvath, finishing her sentence for her. Finally the curtain had lifted from his mind, but he had to give Hastings the credit for it.

"No matter how positive you are that there isn't another device, you *always, always, always* assume the presence of at least one more. I blew that in Iraq, and I almost blew it here. If I'd touched the one you're standing on right now, we'd both have been wall covering. The magic lies in the second device."

"Which you've found?"

"Yeah, I found it. Goddamn, these guys are good."

"How good?" asked Harvath, the tentativeness evident in his voice.

"Not as good as me. You and I are going dancing. And trust me, the conversation is going to be sparkling. Now, be a good boy and zip it so I can do my job."

"You sure that thing's not going to detonate?"

"No, and that's why I need absolute quiet. Discovering the second device is only half the battle. The hard part is making sure neither of these things go off."

SEVENTY-ONE

Strategic Information and Operations Center
FBI Headquarters
Washington, DC

Director Sorce summed up his command in two words as he left his secure SIOC conference room, "Do it."

His deputy director, Stan Caldwell, wasted no time. First he ordered a chopper, then he called Gary Lawlor and told him to be ready.

As the pair flew toward Fort Meade, Caldwell gave Lawlor the *Highlights for Children* version of what the FBI had learned. The NSA's director, Lieutenant General Richard Maxwell, had called the FBI director personally for interrogation assistance. He explained that the NSA had been running a highly classified intelligence gathering operation out of New York City and that three of its four facilities there had been taken out and all the personnel killed.

Of course, none of this was news to Lawlor. He was the one who'd informed the NSA of the situation, including how he'd shot and killed Joseph Stanton after the man had killed Captain William Forrester and was in the process of trying to kill *him*. What was news was that the NSA had already identified the person who had leaked the locations of the crush depth facilities. They had a strong suspicion that the attacks on their facilities and the attacks on New York were connected, which made them doubly angry and desirous for justice.

The final piece of information, which Lawlor could have seen coming a mile away, was that the fourth NSA crush depth location was now unresponsive. Since his was the only qualified tactical team with relatively current top secret clearances, Lawlor was the obvious choice to bring along. What still wasn't making sense to Gary was what the DIA's role in all of this was.

He couldn't help but wonder if his pending visit to the NSA might reveal more than just who had leaked the classified locations of the New York facilities. Now that he was face-to-face with Stan Caldwell, he had one question in particular he was very anxious to ask, but he was smart enough to know that he should save it until after the interrogation.

SEVENTY-TWO

Lieutenant General Maxwell's assistant met Gary Lawlor and Stan Caldwell at the helipad and steered them inside to the director's office. It had been said that the letters *NSA* actually stood for *No Such Agency,* or if you were an employee, *Never Say Anything.* So far, the National Security Agency's well-known penchant for obfuscation was holding up quite well. What would be interesting to see was how candid Dick Maxwell was actually prepared to be.

They were shown into a modestly furnished office hung with photos of Maxwell in a variety of desolate, far-flung locations around the world. It was the first time Lawlor had met the man, and when the lieutenant general stood up and walked around his desk to welcome his guests, Lawlor was immediately struck by how much he resembled George Patton—his facial features, his bearing, almost everything about him. The only things missing were the ivory-handled Colt .45s and a bull terrier trotting alongside. If he wasn't sure that it had been remarked upon a thousand times already, Lawlor might have said something, but it wouldn't have been professional, and it had nothing to do with why they were here. Lawlor was here for answers, not to become buddy-buddy with the enigmatic head of the Puzzle Palace.

"Thank you for coming, gentlemen," Maxwell said as he showed Caldwell and Lawlor to a seating area at the far end of his office. "Can I get anybody anything? Coffee? Tea? Something a bit stronger, maybe?"

"No thanks, Dick," replied the FBI's deputy director.

"Nothing for me either," said Lawlor.

"Okay, then, let's get right to it. Based on information we have received, we now believe that all four of our program facilities in New York City have been hit."

"What sort of information?" asked Gary.

"The facilities are not responding correctly to specific computer-generated requests from this end. Someone apparently wanted it to appear as if it was business as usual, but we've been able to figure out that it's not."

Now they were getting to the heart of what Gary wanted to know. "And what exactly is *business as usual* for this program?"

"That's classified," replied Maxwell.

"You mean it *was* classified."

"No," said the NSA director. "Even though the operation has apparently been compromised, it's still classified."

"As is the reason one of your senior operatives believed it was worth killing for?"

Maxwell shook his head. "Unfortunately, there's not much I can tell you there either, but not because I don't want to. Joe Stanton went off the deep end."

Be that as it may, Lawlor needed more information, and he knew Maxwell had it. "Exactly what type of information was being processed at the New York facilities?"

"I'm sorry, but as I said, that's classified."

"Then why are we here?"

"Deputy Director Caldwell is here to conduct an interrogation. I agreed to allow you to be present out of professional courtesy."

Not only was Lawlor a fairly good judge of people, he was also better than average at reading between the lines. But Maxwell was very difficult to figure out. In fact, so was Stan Caldwell. They both, in their own fashions, were helping him out, but why? To a certain degree, he could understand Maxwell's motivations. The man knew that Lawlor had the only team on the ground that was hot on the trail of the group responsible for killing his NSA employees, as well as their marine security details. Caldwell's motivations, though, were much less clear.

Lawlor had no choice but to go along for the ride. His only hope was that if any leads were to come of this that they came soon—real soon.

SEVENTY-THREE

Before showing Lawlor and Caldwell into the small third-floor conference room chosen for the interrogation, Director Maxwell led them into another room across the hall. "Like a caged tiger," he remarked as he pointed to a bank of monitors that showed a very agitated Mark Schreiber pacing back and forth. "After Stanton, he had the greatest access to the operation. It wasn't difficult to put two and two together. The failed polygraph sealed it."

Once he felt the men had seen enough, the lieutenant general said, "Go and work your magic."

For some reason, Maxwell just rubbed Lawlor the wrong way. He wanted to tell him what he could do with his "magic," but instead kept his opinions to himself and followed Caldwell out the door and across the hall.

When they walked in, Schreiber stopped pacing. He looked the two strangers over as he tried to figure out who they were. Caldwell wasted no time in enlightening him.

"My name is Agent Stan Caldwell," he said as he held his credentials straight out from his shoulder in perfect form—a bit of Bureau conditioning he'd never really been able to shake. "I am the deputy director of the FBI. And this gentleman," he continued as Lawlor did a casual flip-open, flip-closed of his badge and ID, "is Agent Gary Lawlor from the Department of Homeland Security. We're going to ask you a few questions. Are you okay with that?"

Schreiber nodded his head.

"Good," replied Caldwell as he and Lawlor sat down across the table from him. "Why don't you take a seat?"

The young man did as he was told while Caldwell flipped open the file folder Maxwell's assistant had given him and pretended to read through it. He'd already memorized the salient details as they made their way from the director's office. "I see you've been with the NSA for five years."

"Yes, sir," replied Schreiber.

"Do you like your job?"

"It has good days and bad."

"How would you characterize today?" asked Caldwell, not bothering to look up from the file. Lawlor, though, had his eyes locked on the suspect.

"Today would definitely be a bad day," the young man answered.

At that, Caldwell looked up from the file and responded, "I'd be inclined to agree with you. Do you have any idea why we're here?"

Schreiber hesitated a moment and then stated, "I would imagine it has something to do with the impromptu polygraph I was given earlier."

"And you'd be correct. Listen, Mark, you can save us all a lot of time here. Just tell us why you did it."

"I did it because Stanton wouldn't listen."

"Listen to what?" asked Caldwell.

"To *me*."

With all the computer geeks employed by the NSA, the deputy director of the FBI wasn't surprised that this case was quickly boiling down to attention. While most of these people could be brilliant at manipulating data or analyzing intel, many of them lacked the rudimentary social skills necessary to properly function in the real world. They'd rather hack sites, write code, or play video games in their off time than go out in the world and interact with other human beings. They served a vital role for the nation, especially with how rapidly technology was changing, but then something like this happened.

It had long been Caldwell's belief that a lot of these people were ticking time bombs. It was only a matter of when, not if, they would explode, and then the results were anybody's guess. Based on Stan's experience, it happened in one of two ways. Either the violence would manifest itself in a physical form such as a workplace shooting, or it would be more intellectual. The classic *I'll show them how much smarter I am* betrayal was exactly what they were witnessing right now. Caldwell was sure of it. It was one of the worst ways an employee who handled sensitive information could lash out, and it could prove just as deadly as if Schreiber had managed to smuggle in an automatic weapon and a backpack full of pipe bombs to take out as many of his superiors and coworkers as possible before turning the gun on himself.

"So you decided to make Joseph Stanton listen to you. Is that it?" asked Caldwell.

"In a way."

"I don't blame you. In fact, why stop with Stanton? Why not make all of the NSA listen to you?"

Schreiber looked confused. "Is that what this is all about?"

"What do you think? Did you actually believe the rest of the agency wouldn't find out what you've done?"

"It wasn't that big of a deal and definitely not something that should involve the FBI and DHS."

Caldwell placed his arms on the table, leaned forward, and said, "I've got news for you. Treason is a *very* big deal."

"Treason?" replied Schreiber. "What in the hell are you talking about?"

"I'm talking about leaking the location of four top secret NSA facilities in New York City to enemies of the United States."

"I never leaked anything!"

"Mark, you failed not one but two polygraphs. And you've already admitted that what you did was because Stanton wouldn't listen to you. So let's not play any more games. Too many people have died because of this. If you agree to fully cooperate, I'm prepared to offer you a deal."

Schreiber's chin was pulled back almost to his chest and his eyes were wide. He looked like a frightened horse whose reins were jerked *hard*. "People have died? You mean people at the New York facilities?"

"Yes, Mark. And depending on the depth of your involvement, that means you are also an accessory to the murders of multiple federal employees. I know for a fact that the government will seek the death penalty."

Schreiber was panicked and beginning to sweat now. "The only thing I'm guilty of," he pleaded, "is violating a few server security protocols, not treason, and *definitely* not murder."

"I'm not a computer person," replied Caldwell, "but if what you're telling me is that you knowingly violated security protocols and that those violations led to the exposure of four classified locations, then you are in very big trouble."

"But I didn't expose those sites!" Schreiber insisted. "All I exposed were their servers, and even then, it was only for a couple of minutes. Someone would have had to have been waiting right there to have been able to gain anything by it. They would have had to know that I was going to do it, but I didn't tell anyone. Not even Stanton."

Now it was Caldwell's turn to be confused. "What are you talking about?"

"Part of my job is to monitor the four locations in New York. When two of them started acting funny, I brought it to Stanton's attention, but he brushed me off. He could be that way, especially if he had other things going on he thought were more important. He told me not to worry about it and to try to help out elsewhere. He said that on account of the terrorist attacks, the NSA was going to have everyone working overtime."

"What was *funny* about the two locations?" asked Gary.

"Nobody was responding to my e-mails. It didn't make sense."

"Why not? After the attacks, a lot of the infrastructure was overloaded and went down."

"I know," replied Schreiber. "Like the telephones. But all of our data transfer operates via satellite uplinks and downloads."

"Have you seen the news? There's hell of a lot of smoke and ash in the sky."

"It doesn't matter. Only water molecules can wreak enough havoc to interrupt transmission, and it wasn't raining in New York. Even if it was, we had contingency systems in place."

"So people weren't responding to your e-mails," stated Caldwell. "So what? You don't think people were focused on the attacks?"

The young NSA employee looked right at him. "That's the problem. According to the information we were receiving, our people weren't focused on anything but their computers. Everyone was working. Everyone was processing data just like they should be, but nobody was on the e-mail system."

"So what did you do?" asked Lawlor.

"Nothing. Not until the third location went unresponsive and Stanton blew me off about it again. I had pinged all the servers and everything seemed normal, but it didn't make sense."

"And that's when you violated the security protocols?"

Schreiber nodded his head. "I ran a series of remote diagnostics over an unsecured channel."

"What did you find?"

"I didn't find anything. I wanted to talk to Stanton about it, but he'd left the building. Somebody told me he'd gone somewhere via helicopter and that was the last I heard of him until security came down to my office, asked for my ID, and took me to the polygraphs."

"Did you test the fourth location?"

"Of course I did. It came up the same as the other three—the servers appeared to be working, but I couldn't establish any human contact."

"And that's all you did?" asked Lawlor.

"Yes, that's all I did. I swear to God."

Gary gave Schreiber a long, hard stare and then signaled Caldwell to pick up the file and follow him out of the room.

SEVENTY-FOUR

A few minutes later, Director Maxwell exited the monitoring station across the hall and said, "So what do you think?"

Lawlor handed the polygraph transcripts back to Caldwell and replied, "I think your polygraphs are inconclusive."

"What are you talking about? We asked all the right questions."

"Sure, but you asked them in all the wrong ways. Mark Schreiber is guilty, but not of treason."

"Then who released those locations?" demanded Maxwell. "Stanton?"

"It would explain why he wanted to silence Forrester and then tried to take me down."

"I don't believe it. Stanton's been with the agency a long time."

"Believe it," responded Caldwell. "I think we should have one of our polygraphers out here to retest Schreiber, but if I were you, I'd put my money on him passing. What do you think, Gary?"

Lawlor nodded his head. "I'd have to agree. If he's conning us, then he's one of the best I've ever seen. His story makes sense, and it also better explains Stanton's behavior."

Caldwell looked at the NSA director and said, "I think your leak plugged itself, Dick."

Maxwell didn't know who or what to believe. "Until your people polygraph him, I want to keep Schreiber isolated."

"That's fine by me. I can think of about a hundred provisions under the Patriot Act that'll back you up. You can put some of your own people on him or have him transferred to the base stockade. It's your call."

The director thought about it for a moment and then said, "Until I'm absolutely sure he's not a security risk, I don't want him in the building."

"Then the stockade it is."

"I'm sorry to interrupt," broke in Lawlor as he thought of something. "But I'd like to talk to Schreiber one last time, if I could."

Caldwell shrugged his shoulders and said, "I don't know what good it'll do you, but I've got no problem with it. What about you, Dick?"

"No problem here," replied Maxwell, "as long as Deputy Director Caldwell accompanies you. I want this done by the book, just in case. As long as that works with you, then be my guest. I'm going to go back to my office and get ahold of the base CO to arrange for Schreiber's transfer. If you learn anything new, I want to know about it."

"Of course," said Gary as he thanked the director for his time, reluctantly shook his hand, and watched with relief as he disappeared down the hallway.

Back in the conference room and with Stan Caldwell's permission, Gary shifted from interrogation mode to questioning what might be the only witness they had.

"Mr. Schreiber, I'd like to ask you a few more questions about Joseph Stanton."

"Am I under arrest?" the young man asked.

"No," replied Lawlor. "You're not."

"So I'm free to leave this room and return to my office, then?"

"Not exactly," stated Caldwell. "Listen, as far as we're concerned, your story seems to make sense. Director Maxwell, though, needs to be absolutely certain before he reinstates you. I am sure you can appreciate that."

"I guess so," said Schreiber.

"Good," replied Lawlor as he continued. "The first thing I need to tell you is that Joseph Stanton is dead."

The young man couldn't believe it. *"Dead?* How? What happened?"

"I shot him this afternoon."

Schreiber couldn't believe it.

"Was there anything unusual about him? Anything that someone could use as leverage against him? For instance did he gamble? Did he like women a bit too much? Drinking? Drugs?"

"Wait a second," responded the young man as he put two and two together. "You think it was Joe Stanton who exposed the New York locations?"

"It's a possibility we're considering. Is there anything you saw or heard in the office which might be relevant?"

Schreiber was quiet as he thought about the question.

"Anything at all," said Gary. "Anything that might put us on the trail of who he could have been working with. It doesn't matter how small or inconsequential you think the detail might be."

The young man glanced at his watch.

"Are we keeping you from something?" asked Caldwell.

"No, sir," replied Schreiber. "I'm just trying to get a fix on the date."

"What date?" said Gary.

"A few weeks ago, Stanton gave me a pretty weird assignment. He said it was a loose string the NSA was running down. He dropped it on my desk, told me to get on it right away and not to talk about it with anyone else."

"What was it?"

"He wanted me to track all sales over the last few months of a very high-end dialysis machine."

"Did he tell you why, or what it was in reference to?"

"No, just that it had to do with a case involving national security, and then he reminded me again not to talk about it with anyone."

"What did you find out?"

"I found out that the machine was one of the most expensive of its kind anywhere in the world and that it was the number one choice for the premier hospitals involved with treating very particular forms of advanced kidney disease."

"Why the hell would he want information like that?" asked Caldwell.

"I don't know," responded Schreiber. "He wouldn't say. He wanted me to provide him with a list of individuals or organizations who had taken delivery of the machine in the last three months."

"And what did you find out?" asked Lawlor.

"Nothing at first. The company that makes the machines is called Nova Medical Systems. They're extremely tight-lipped about everything they do."

Lawlor paused. There was something about that company name that he recognized, but couldn't place. Synapses were firing all across his brain as he tried to connect the dots and jump ahead to some sort of conclusion. *Why was the company name so familiar?*

Hoping the young analyst could knock the answer loose, Lawlor beckoned Schreiber to keep going.

"I was finally able to hack their private sales information and discovered that they'd sold only one of these super-high-end machines in the last three months," the young man said.

"Who bought it?" asked Lawlor.

"The Libyans."

The Libyans? It had to be a dead end.

Lawlor was ready to write the entire thing off until Schreiber said, "But that's not the weird part. The weird thing is that the machine wasn't sent to Libya."

"It wasn't? Where was it sent?"

Schreiber leaned forward over the table and replied, "To their United Nations mission in New York."

SEVENTY-FIVE

New York City

"How much time is that going to give us?" asked Harvath when Tracy gave him the update and told him her plan.

"Don't worry," she replied. "All you have to do is jump off the platform and make a run for it. I'm the one who has to get out from underneath."

"How much time?" he repeated.

"Probably not enough."

"That's no good, Tracy. It's unacceptable."

"If that's the way you feel, then I guess it's a good thing I'm in control."

"I'm not going to let you do this."

Hastings eased over and looked up at him through the removed floor panel. "You're going to have to accept the fact that you're not the boss here. Not this time, Mr. Harvath."

"That's Agent Harvath to you lady," he chided, "and this is still my operation."

"But this is *my* bomb."

She was right, and he knew that no matter how hard he tried to dissuade her she wasn't going to change her mind. This was how Tracy had been called to face down her demons. If the bomb did go off and take her with it, at least it would do so on her terms. She wasn't running away, not anymore. She was sick of hiding her scars, sick of people trying to make her feel better about her appearance, and sick of feeling afraid—afraid of what had happened and how things might have been different if she'd just been able to defuse that last IED.

No, there was no changing Tracy Hastings's mind. She was in this game till the end, no matter what its outcome.

For his part, Harvath couldn't let her take all the risk upon herself. She didn't deserve to die. She'd already been through enough in Iraq and with everything else she'd suffered since that failed IED disposal assignment. *But what could he do?* The answer wasn't easy to accept, but it was perfectly clear—*nothing.*

"Your insubordination has been duly noted for the record," said Harvath.

He could hear Hastings stifle a laugh beneath the raised floor.

"Really?" she said as she began quoting him almost word for word, "Well, seeing as how I'm neither a federal employee nor a recognized active-duty EOD tech, *and* my participation in this operation is in an unofficial, unrecognized, and most definitely unsanctioned capacity, I fail to see what the downside of that might be."

Harvath thought about it for a moment and then said, "Insubordination on one of my teams comes at a pretty high price. You're going to have to pay for our dinner now, Lieutenant."

Hastings laughed again, though this time it seemed forced. "If we both get out of this alive, then I'm going to be thrilled to pay for dinner. In fact, we'll go anywhere you want."

"I'm going to hold you to that," he said.

"Good," she replied. "Now, when I tell you, I want you to take one step back off that floor panel and then run like hell."

"What are you going to do?"

"Hopefully, I'll be looking over my shoulder and laughing as you get beaten in a footrace by some girl."

This time it was Harvath's turn to laugh. "You're anything but *some girl,* Tracy."

"I'd tell you flattery would get you everywhere, but somehow encouraging you at such an awkward moment doesn't seem right. Just focus on getting ready to run."

"Yes, ma'am."

Hastings looked up through the hole in the floor and said, "That's Lieutenant to you, Agent Harvath."

Harvath smiled back at her and prayed to God she was going to make it. He didn't know why—maybe it was her vulnerability, or maybe it was her smart-ass attitude, but she had really grown on him and he was one hundred percent serious about taking her out for dinner and dancing.

"Okay, on three," she said, once she'd squirmed back beneath the raised platform to where the secondary bomb was located.

Harvath took a deep breath and waited. Then he heard her.

"One, two, *three*!"

Leaping off the raised floor platform, all Scot could think about was making sure Tracy Hastings made it out alive. Something told him that if she didn't, he'd carry that burden for the rest of his life.

He turned, expecting to see her sliding out from beneath the platform, but she wasn't there. He looked back toward the opening next to where he'd been standing, but she wasn't there either. *Where the hell was she?*

Suddenly, there was a splintering sound near his feet, and he realized she must have crawled beneath the floor to the far side to have a better shot at the door. As the panel broke open she yelled, "Run, you idiot! Run!"

Harvath ignored her and leaning down gripped the panel and tore the rest of it away. He pulled Tracy out from underneath and onto her feet. To her credit, or more than likely her exceptional survival instinct, she didn't bother to stop and thank him. She ran like hell. And true to her prediction, she looked back over her shoulder and saw Harvath losing a footrace to some girl.

It might have actually been funny except for the fact that five seconds later both bombs detonated and sent shards of glass and bulletproof Lexan screaming through the room.

SEVENTY-SIX

Hitting the entry corridor, Tracy spun, grabbed ahold of Harvath's tactical vest, and tried to pull him out of the doorway. The blast wave that came through the passage slapped him so hard, it felt like he'd gone off a high dive and had landed right on his back. Tracy lost her footing and they both stumbled to the ground.

When Harvath looked up, he found Hastings sitting against the wall, while his head, or more appropriately his face, was in a rather ungentlemanly position right between her legs.

"I suppose most guys probably just would have said thank you," he joked.

Hastings eyes were wide. "You don't feel that?" she asked, looking down.

Harvath had no idea what she was talking about. "Feel what?"

"Your back."

"It hurts like hell, but it'll pass."

"Not if I don't do something about it," she replied as she pulled a pair of needle-nose pliers from her pocket.

It wasn't until Harvath glanced over his right shoulder that he saw what Tracy was talking about.

"Do you have something to bite down on?" she asked.

Harvath looked at Hastings's very toned inner thigh beneath her pants and remarked, "Maybe I should just focus my mind in another direction. Make it quick, would you?"

"All right, Mr. Macho SEAL. Here we go. Can I get a *Hooyah*?"

The pain was amazing for such a relatively small hunk of Lexan. Harvath accompanied its extremely nasty extraction with a very long and very loud Navy *Hooyah*.

The minute it was out, Hastings tore open one of the QuickClot pouches Morgan had handed her when they were treating the mounted patrolman in Central Park and shoved it into Harvath's wound. Without any gauze to cover it, she reached for the next best thing—duct tape. She still had several pieces hanging from her shirt from dealing with the IEDs, and after tearing back part of Harvath's shirt, she was able to perfectly cover the wound and flatten out the tape so it adhered to his skin.

"You want to keep it as a souvenir?" she asked as she showed him the piece she'd pulled from his back.

"I've got my eye set on another trophy," he said.

Hastings looked down at him still poised between her legs and raised her eyebrows.

Harvath shook his head and began to get up. "I'm talking about the people who are responsible for all this."

A smile came to Tracy's face, and she was about to say something, when Harvath's radio crackled to life. It was Bob Herrington. "Scot? Scot, do you read me? Over."

"I read you, Bob," said Harvath as he swung the lip mic back into place and push-up–style raised himself off the floor and then backed away from Tracy Hastings.

"We heard an explosion. Are you okay?"

"Roger that," replied Harvath. "Only slightly worse for wear."

Hastings shot a glance at the makeshift bandage across his back and Harvath ignored her. "What have you got, Bob?"

"They gained access via some ductwork off the elevator shaft and went out via the concealed garage exit."

Harvath found that hard to believe. "McGahan and his men are on 49th Street. They never would have made it."

"They didn't go out 49th Street. They found a service entrance and cut back through the hotel."

"Where are you now?"

"Right behind them. They're headed for the Park Avenue exit."

"Do you have a visual?"

"Negative."

"How are you following them?"

"You'd be amazed at the stuff they dragged in on their boots from the garage," replied Herrington.

Gasoline, oil, brake fluid . . . Harvath could only imagine. God bless Bob Herrington. Urban tracking was an absolute bitch and something Harvath had never been that good at.

Realizing that it was safer to go out the 50th Street stairwell than to slowly creep down the 49th Street side and hope that McGahan and his men would recognize them as friendlies and not jump the gun and open fire on them, Harvath relayed his plan to Herrington.

If they could get to the Park Avenue entrance in time, they might be able to finally put an end to the terrorists' killing spree once and for all. What they were learning, though, was that things didn't always go as planned.

SEVENTY-SEVEN

Washington, DC

Gary Lawlor had first boarded the helicopter in DC with no idea what to expect from the NSA interrogation or why Stan Caldwell had invited him along. On a day like today, the deputy director should have been glued to the Strategic Information and Operations Center at FBI headquarters. It made little sense that he would break away to personally conduct an interrogation, even if it was at the behest of the NSA director.

Regardless, Lawlor had kept his mouth shut and had gone along for the ride, hoping that something would come out of it that could help his own investigation and Scot Harvath's efforts on the ground in New York City. But now that the Schreiber interrogation was complete and Lawlor had nothing more to gain, he wanted answers out of Caldwell.

Once the Sikorsky S76C lifted off, Gary turned to the deputy director and said, "I want to talk about why you asked me to come along on this."

Stan had known this was coming, and he'd hoped to avoid it by getting on the phone right away and keeping busy with headquarters until they got back to DC. Realizing he was stuck, he turned toward his mentor and said, "I told you. It was a professional courtesy. I thought it might help with your current investigation."

"Just like the interrogation you threw our way in Manhattan?"

Caldwell nodded his head. "We finally got someone over there, but apparently the guy's not talking. Did your guy do any better?"

"Don't change the subject," said Lawlor. "Why the largess?"

"I told you."

"Right, *professional courtesy*. You know, Stan, you always were a bad liar."

Caldwell smiled. "It still didn't stop me from inheriting the deputy director position after you left, though, did it?"

"Apparently not. Now, do you want to tell me what's really going on? No bullshit, Bureau guy to Bureau guy."

Caldwell would have liked nothing more than to answer that question, but he knew he couldn't.

"Stan, Americans in Manhattan are actively being slaughtered. We're talking about government employees along with a significant number of marines. If you know something, anything that might be able to help me put a stop to it, you need to tell me."

"Let it go, Gary. All four NSA locations have already been hit. Whatever the bad guys came for, they already got."

Lawlor couldn't believe what he was hearing. *"Let it go?* I've got a team hot on their trail. I'm not letting anything go. Who are you trying to protect?"

"I'm not protecting anybody. Whatever information your team has compiled, I want it turned over to me. The Bureau is now the lead agency on this, and we're going to take it from here."

"Like hell you will. Right now, my people are the best and the *only* chance we have."

Caldwell hated to do it, but he looked at his mentor and said, "I'm not asking you, Gary. As deputy director of the lead agency in charge of investigating the New York City attacks, I'm giving you a direct order."

For a moment, Lawlor was at a loss for words. Finally he said, "I must be scraping a very raw nerve."

"Just do it, all right?"

"Stan, you realize that when the initial shock wears off and the dust starts to settle in New York, people are going to start calling for blood."

Caldwell didn't respond.

"And the loudest cry of all is going to be for the blood of the people who let our country get attacked, again. The 9/11 Commission will look like a joke, compared to the investigation that'll follow this. And I'll tell you right now, it'll have teeth too—big, sharp, shiny ones. The American people won't let anything get swept under the rug, not this time. No long blacked-out sections to protect ongoing intelligence operations, no political cronyism making sure the most influential asses are covered. Not even the president will be safe on this one.

"They're going to climb up the Bureau's ass so far it'll be sneezing shoe leather. When they get to you, the deputy director, they're going to look at how you spent every minute up to and after the attacks, including this little joyride out to the NSA. They're going to want to know exactly what we talked about and I guarantee you I'll be there to testify. The only question is, what am I going to tell them? And that's up to you. Either I'm going to say the FBI did everything they could to help apprehend the terrorists, or they let the best chance any of us had slip through their fingers. Can you imagine the repercussions of that? The Bureau would look like the Keystone Kops. It probably would never recover. Congress might even call for shutting it down. Wouldn't that be something?"

Caldwell stared out the helicopter's window. He knew Gary was right. It was a possibility the FBI had been privately discussing for some time. There had been whispers about dismantling the Bureau in the wake of the 9/11 fiasco, but they had managed to cut it off at the knees before it gained too much momentum. After what happened today, though, there was no way they'd be able to stop something like that once the wheels were set in motion. The American people were going to want revenge, even if it meant tying an entire government agency to the stake and watching as it was roasted alive. Caldwell couldn't let that happen.

It seemed ironic that a choice between what was best for one's government and what was best for one's country had to be so diametrically opposed, but the deputy director knew what he had to do. And turning away from the window to face Gary Lawlor, he did it, but with one condition.

SEVENTY-EIGHT

New York City

Harvath and Hastings exited the Waldorf via the 50th Street stairwell and took off at top speed for Park Avenue. As they neared the corner, they heard what sounded like a car crash, followed by spurts of automatic-weapons fire.

"Bob, what the hell is going on up there?" demanded Harvath over his headset.

"We've got 'em. They carjacked a minivan but collided with a cab and it got stuck on the median. They're headed for St. Bartholomew's church on the corner. What's your ETA?"

"We're thirty seconds out."

"They're going through the outdoor café area. Hurry up."

As they ran, Harvath relayed everything to Tracy. When they arrived at the church, Herrington, Morgan, and Cates were waiting for them.

"What do we have?" asked Harvath.

"I count five tangos," said Bob. "All in black Nomex with automatic weapons like the ones we found at the Grail facility. The HRT patches are the only way you can tell them apart from the good guys."

"Do we know where they are inside?"

"Negative. Only that they went in this way."

Harvath switched over to his police radio to raise Colin McGahan, whom he'd already given a report to as they were on their way down the 50th Street stairwell.

"I read you," replied the ESU commander. "We heard shots fired. What's going on? Over."

"They've just entered St. Bartholomew's, but we're going to need help with containment. Can you spare anyone to cover the exits? Over."

"I've already sent a couple of guys your way, but that won't be enough to cover every exit. Over."

"Tell your men to place themselves so that they can cover more than one door at once—even if it means they have to stand in the middle of the block. And make sure they know that we're after five tangos dressed exactly like you guys, except with HRT patches on their vests. Over."

"Roger that," replied McGahan, who then signed off.

The St. Bart's outdoor café had been converted into an open-air aid station, with waiters and waitresses providing bottled water and snacks to anyone who needed them. The sound of gunfire followed by heavily armed men running into the church had everyone terrified.

Approaching someone who looked like a manager, Harvath identified himself as DHS and said, "I need a map of the inside of the church with exits, stairwells, and elevators, and I need it right now."

The manager nodded her head and quickly retrieved a narrow red binder from beneath the hostess stand. She withdrew a piece of paper labeled *Fire Evacuation Plan* and handed it to Harvath.

"Other than your staff, is there anyone inside?"

"No," she replied, "the church is closed. Only the café is open."

Harvath thanked her, and after asking her to get everyone off the terrace and as far away from the building as possible, he and the team went inside.

Knowing that the men they were chasing were very fond of booby traps, they made their way very carefully.

St. Bartholomew's was a Romanesque church based upon the Cathedral of St. Marco in Venice and had been built in a traditional crucifix pattern with the altar at the top, facing east. It was an incredible structure, and on any other day this would have made for a perfect place to while away several hours, but they weren't here to sightsee. They were here to take down a team of highly efficient killers.

Having been one step behind for so long, it was tough for Harvath to now place his mind one step ahead. He knew very little about his enemy, but he did know they were disciplined, well armed, and obviously very well trained. They were Chechen soldiers, some of whom probably had even been Russian Spetsnaz at some point. While they didn't shy from conflict, they did seem to avoid it whenever possible, as they had in the Waldorf. Harvath knew this meant that they would probably be looking for an exit on the north side of the church, away from their pursuers.

Looking at the floor plan he'd been given by the manager of the café, Harvath figured the exits that made the most sense were the emergency ones on the northernmost side of the sanctuary. Falling into their conga line, they raced forward toward the doors that led into the main church structure. No sooner had they opened them than they were greeted with a searing wave of deafening weapons fire.

SEVENTY-NINE

"Jesus Christ," said Morgan as they retreated back into the hallway and he looked up at the pockmarked wall just above their heads. "Flechettes."

The word was French for tiny arrows, and that's exactly how they had gotten their name. They were fin-stabilized steel projectiles that looked just like little arrows, which could be fired from a twelve-gauge shotgun, significantly increasing the weapon's lethality.

Herrington looked at the wall and said, "Even so, watch your language in here."

Cates asked, "Am I the only one who finds it ironic that we're in a Christian church duking it out with Muslim terrorists?"

"So far they're the only ones doing the duking," replied Harvath. "Now here's the plan. Bob, Tracy, and I are going in on my command. Cates and Morgan, you're going to provide cover fire. Everybody ready?"

The team nodded its assent, Harvath readied his weapon and said, *"Now!"*

Rick Cates kicked open what was left of the door leading into the sanctuary, and he and Morgan laid down a vicious curtain of cover fire.

Crouching low and moving as fast as they could, Harvath, Herrington, and Hastings raced for the nearest row of pews. They went as far as they could until the men at the end of the church began returning fire, and then they hit the deck.

Harvath pulled the fire evacuation map from his vest and tried to get a fix on where their opponents were. As best he could tell, they were within spitting distance of an exit at the north end of the transept. *But why weren't they using it?*

Grabbing his police radio, Harvath tried to raise McGahan. With the roar of the gunfire filling the cavernous church, it took a moment before he could hear anything over the radio. Finally, he could make out McGahan's voice. "Are your men in place yet?"

"Affirmative," replied McGahan. "I've got one on Fifty-first who almost got his ass shot off, but he just pushed the targets back inside."

That explained it. And it also gave Harvath an idea.

If he could get McGahan's men on the north and south ends of the transept, they could execute a classic pincer movement. Confident for the first time that they might have the terrorists all but in the bag, he radioed his plans to McGahan and then used his Motorola to radio Cates and fill him in.

Crouching near Herrington and Hastings, Harvath prepped them on the plan. As they nodded their heads, he then radioed McGahan and told him to get ready.

Harvath glanced at his Suunto, counted down thirty seconds, and then over both radios gave the command, *"Go, go, go!"*

Right on cue, Cates and Morgan laid down as much cover fire as they could muster. As they did, the terrorists returned fire and retreated into the back of the nave. Harvath didn't need to look at his evacuation plan to know they had them trapped. There was no way out.

EIGHTY

Reloading, Abdul Ali looked toward Sacha and commanded, "Find us a way out of here. Now!"

It had been the Chechen's idea to flee into the church, where he had legitimately expected little to no resistance. But what the enormous warrior had not planned on was for the men chasing him to be reinforced so quickly—at least not in such a manner as to hinder their escape. They needed to put a lot of distance between themselves and their pursuers as quickly as possible.

While he was incredibly adept at thinking on his feet, the Chechen disliked being put on the defensive and being forced to react. A hasty retreat was hard to turn to one's advantage, especially when you had no idea where the hell you were going. The most deadly mistakes in combat often came from operating too quickly and without enough information. In this case, though, Sacha had little choice.

Near the altar, he found the door to the sacristy and ruptured it from its hinges with a kick from one of his enormous boots. Signaling to the rest of the team, he took up position in the door frame and tried to pin down their opponents as one by one his men ran past him. As the last man came through, he took a grenade from him, pulled the pin, and threw it toward the center of the church.

When the device detonated, showering St. Bartholomew's with its deadly shrapnel, Sacha and his men were already running through the sacristy and into a narrow service corridor. The Chechen knew that, if not already, the church would soon be surrounded and that heading back out could be suicide. They needed another route, and as his eyes fell upon a small steam radiator along one side of the corridor, Allah blessed him with an idea.

Once Sacha located the correct door, he opened it, careful not to leave any signs of entry, and sent Ali and the rest of the team down the stairs. Before he could join them, though, he needed a diversion—something that would send the men chasing them in a completely different direction. Moments later he found it.

Sacha didn't bother opening the glass case. Instead he smashed it with the butt of his weapon and tore the ax from its mounting bracket. With one swing he was through the window, and with two more he had torn away the security wire. He then threw the ax out the window into the narrow, ground-level courtyard and ran back toward the stairwell. With any luck, he and the rest of his team would be long gone before their pursuers had any idea what had really happened.

EIGHTY-ONE

The first thing Harvath heard when the ringing in his ears subsided was Paul Morgan cursing at the top of his lungs. As Bullet Bob had done to Cates earlier, Scot was about to admonish the man for spewing obscenities in a church, until he saw the reason why—Morgan had been hit.

The team ran to where he lay, blood oozing from several wounds to his chest. Along with Cates, he had advanced up the south wall of the sanctuary, but unlike his partner, he had failed to drop fast enough when the huge Chechen pitched his grenade into the center of the church.

In a flash, Harvath had undone Morgan's vest, drawn the Benchmade knife from his pocket, and sliced through the marine's bloody shirt. As Harvath looked at the wounds, he asked, "Can you breathe?"

Coughing, Morgan replied, "It feels like somebody whacked me in the chest with a bat."

"But can you breathe?" repeated Harvath.

Morgan coughed again and said, "Yeah, I can breathe, but it hurts like hell."

"Why didn't you duck, dumb-ass?" demanded Cates.

"I had that fucker in my sights. There was no way I was going to let him go."

"So much for discretion being the better part of valor."

"Discretion is for pussies. When you go back there, you're going to find that clown on the ground."

"Fifty bucks says you missed him," responded Cates.

Morgan coughed out a laugh as he tried to stand up. "You're on. Let's go."

"Whoa, whoa, whoa," said Harvath as the marine winced and fell back down. "You need medical attention. These wounds are pretty bad."

"You want the coppers to get all the credit for collaring these guys?"

Harvath ignored him and quickly fished through the pockets of his vest for some gauze and a QuickClot pouch. Tearing it open, he pressed the rapid coagulation sponges against the worst of the wounds and then had Herrington lean him forward so that they could wrap his chest with gauze. The pain from the piece of Lexan that had been lodged in Harvath's shoulder grew so intense as he did this that he had to back off.

"Are you okay?" asked Bob.

"Fine," replied Harvath as he sucked it up and went back to rapidly dressing Morgan's injury.

Once the gauze had been wrapped tight, Harvath leaned him up against the wall and crossed his arms, encouraging him to continue applying pressure.

"That's it?" asked Hastings. "That's all you're going to do for him?"

"It's all we can do," Harvath responded as he radioed McGahan, told him they had a man down, and gave him Morgan's position.

The marine looked up at him and forcing a smile, coughed, "Let's hope this is the worst thing that happens."

Standing up, Harvath turned to the others and said, "Let's go."

With Harvath at the lead, the team raced toward the nave while McGahan's ESU officers from the north and south ends of the transept were already well ahead of them.

When they exited the sacristy and charged into the service corridor they saw the two cops standing in a pile of glass on either side of a broken window.

Using hand signals, one of the officers indicated for Harvath and his team to hold up, because the terrorists they were chasing had gone out the window.

Harvath didn't like it. It was too dangerous. As they went through that window, the terrorists could pick them off one by one. They needed a better plan.

Harvath hugged the wall and began creeping forward. He wanted to tell the ESU guys to back off, when he heard something pop beneath his boot and Bob Herrington grabbed his arm.

Raising his leg, Harvath looked down at what he'd stepped on—a tiny piece of glass. Herrington didn't need to say a word. Harvath knew what it meant. Whoever had broken that window had come back down the hallway in their direction. Maybe his urban tracking skills weren't as bad as he thought.

And maybe they had just caught a significant break.

EIGHTY-TWO

The floor of St. Bart's service corridor was covered in linoleum tiles. Not the most inspired decorating choice, but as far as Harvath was concerned, they were absolutely beautiful. Whoever had broken the glass fire cabinet and the window had managed to get another small piece of glass wedged in the sole of his boot.

Studying the floor, Herrington and Harvath soon discovered the true route by which the terrorists had exited the corridor.

Once Tracy gave them the thumbs-up indicating that the door wasn't rigged, they slowly made their way down the stairs, keeping their eyes open for booby traps the entire time.

Despite Harvath's discovery, McGahan's two ESU officers opted to tackle the window. They were going with their guts and Harvath couldn't blame them, though his gut told him it was a dead end. The real trail was the one he and his team were following right now down an old metal staircase.

As they descended, the brick walls on either side grew slick with moisture. The air was dank and moldy. A series of bare lightbulbs lit their way down until finally, at the bottom, they encountered a large iron door marked *Utility Tunnel Access. Keep Out. Authorized Personnel Only.*

Cates, who was bringing up the rear, smiled and raising his weapon, said, "I brought my authorization."

"Shut up, Rick," replied Tracy. She didn't like what she was seeing. The fact that the door had been left ajar put her on edge. It was almost too inviting.

Harvath, though, doubted that it was rigged. Whoever had gone through the trouble of breaking the window upstairs hadn't expected to be followed—at least not right away.

Once Tracy finished checking the door over and gave the okay, the team filed though.

Rusting pipes of varying sizes lined the fetid walls, while water dripping from the ceiling created a patchwork of stagnant puddles along the floor. Even their breathing seemed to send echoes bouncing off in all directions, and as they made their way forward, Harvath, Hastings, Cates, and Herrington took great pains not to make any unnecessary noise.

The tunnel curved to the right and then intersected with another. The light wasn't very good; even so, when Harvath looked into the new tunnel, he could see movement way down at the other end.

Holding his hand up in a fist, he froze his team in place. Tunnels were very bad places to get into gunfights. The walls had a very nasty habit of funneling rounds right at you. Turning, he used hand signals to let the others know what he was looking at.

Herrington queried him on range and Harvath relayed what he thought the distance was.

Raising one of the M16 Vipers they'd taken from the Geneva Diamond location, Bob indicated what he wanted to do. Nodding his assent, Harvath peered back around the corner just in time to see the terrorists disappear from view.

EIGHTY-THREE

Abdul Ali had no idea where the access door led. He knew only that this was the one they needed to take. Whether it was precognition, a gut instinct, or divine intervention he had no idea, but an overwhelming sense of urgency had overtaken him and it told him to get out of the tunnels as quickly as possible. He sometimes wondered if it was Allah Himself speaking to him. It made no difference where it came from. When the voice spoke to him, he did what it said, and he knew that was one of the reasons he had lived as long as he had.

Crashing through two more doors the team found a set of stairs and followed them up into a large commercial laundry area. From the uniforms of the startled staff as well as the stenciled letters across the large canvas carts, the team realized that they had stumbled into the bowels of the Doubletree Metropolitan Hotel.

One of the Chechens raised his weapon as if he was going to fire, but Sacha quickly pushed it back down and shook his head no. They hadn't been hired to kill civilians. That was what the Arabs did, not them. It was a pointless waste of ammunition and would draw too much attention.

Ali waved the team forward and they threaded through the carts and stacks of laundry to a small corridor and a bank of elevators at the end. As he pressed the button, Sacha withdrew his map of New York and tried to figure out where they were.

"Lexington and Fifty-first," he said as a set of elevator doors opened and they filed in.

Ali did the calculation in his head and replied, "About five blocks from the final target."

As Sacha was not the leader of this operation, he simply raised his eyebrows in response as if to say *How should we proceed?*

His index finger hovering in front of the elevator buttons, Ali tried to decide the best course of action. They had never planned on losing their vehicles. Their dangerous carjacking attempt in front of the Waldorf had almost cost them their lives, but might be worth trying again. Confident that he would come up with something, he pressed the button for the lobby level and stated, "Allah shall provide."

Little did he know that what Allah chose to provide were four very well armed and extremely dangerous American Special Operations personnel.

EIGHTY-FOUR

Bursting into the laundry area, Harvath and the rest of the team swung their weapons from side to side but saw no trace of the terrorists save for a few barely detectable wet footprints they had tracked in with them.

The team kept their weapons up and at the ready. Harvath identified himself to the nearest employee he saw as a federal agent and quickly asked about the men who had just come through. The woman, who apparently spoke no English, could only stare. Rick Cates then tried in Spanish.

Seconds later, he translated, "Five men. They went down the hall to the elevators, and just my luck, there's a stairway right next to it."

Herrington glanced at Harvath, who could barely hold up his weapon. His shoulder was obviously giving him increasing trouble. "I'm going to take point," he said.

Harvath shook his head no. "Let's catch that elevator."

Herrington had a bad feeling about letting Harvath remain on point in his condition, but he didn't argue. This was Harvath's operation. Kicking it into gear, he and the rest of the team took off for the elevators.

As they approached, they could see one of the elevators was already on its way up to the lobby. With no time to spare, they headed for the stairwell. Everyone, including Cates, took the stairs three at a time—the adrenaline coursing through their bloodstreams.

Hitting the lobby-level landing, Harvath paused for a moment to let the team regroup and slowly cracked the door to see what was happening on the other side.

A line of hotel guests were backed up against a wall near a bank of elevators, staring at something that must have just rushed by. Harvath knew it could only be one thing. Nodding his head, he pulled open the door and the team rushed out in pursuit of the terrorists.

With its swanky sixties retro feel it looked like they had fallen down the rabbit hole and landed in the private lair of Auric Goldfinger. The only thing that kept the scene from being completely surreal were the looks on the faces of the hotel's guests as they closed the distance with the terrorists.

Coming around the corner into the stainless-steel lobby, the team fanned out into a wedge formation, and not a moment too soon. The Chechen bringing up the rear of his group's escape spun just in time to see them. Yelling a warning to the others, he raised his weapon and began to fire.

Immediately, Harvath and company took cover behind anything they could find. They then all began to fire; all, that is, except for Harvath. Suddenly he could no longer lift the heavy Troy CQB assault rifle.

Dropping it to the floor, he transitioned to his pistol and let the rounds fly.

Hotel guests screamed as they ran from the mayhem, several of them cut down by stray rounds in the process.

Realizing the Chechens were wearing body armor, Tracy Hastings yelled for her team to go for head shots and seconds later, Herrington and Cates had one kill apiece.

The remaining terrorists emptied their magazines and reloaded, their assault furious and unrelenting. A thick cloud of cordite hung in the air, and though less than a minute had passed, it seemed like a lifetime.

Down to only three men, Sacha wanted to get the hell out of the hotel and motioned to Ali and his remaining comrade to make for the exit. Ali nodded his head and the trio laid down a swath of fire to cover yet another hasty retreat.

As they did so, Harvath and company continued to reload and pull their triggers, completely shattering the glass doors at the front of the lobby.

Arriving at the exit, Sacha and Ali continued to fire as they slipped out of the hotel toward the street. The remaining Chechen wasn't as fortunate. When his weapon jammed, he fumbled with it just long enough to catch a very well placed bullet through his throat, courtesy of Scot Harvath.

The Chechen fell to the floor gurgling blood as his associates on the sidewalk searched for a way to make their escape. Ali pointed his gun at a shuttle van approaching the hotel on Lexington Avenue and when the van refused to stop, he put two rounds through the windshield, killing the driver, who slumped forward over the steering wheel as the van picked up speed, veered up onto the sidewalk, and slammed into the front of the hotel.

With no regard for the lives of the people inside or for his surviving comrade, Ali began firing in the direction of the gas tank. Sacha barely made it away before the vehicle exploded and sent a roiling fireball deep into the lobby of the Metropolitan.

The mammoth Chechen had a million curses he wanted to hurl at Ali, but he held his tongue. Now was not the time. While the man's rash actions had almost cost Sacha his life, the al-Qaeda operative had just created the distraction they so needed to escape.

Heading south on Lexington Avenue, they made a left on 50th and kept moving until Ali found a spot where he could remove his balaclava and wiggle out of his tactical gear.

"What are you doing?" said Sacha.

Ali responded by raising his weapon and asking a question of his own. "Where's your bag, Sacha?"

"What are you talking about? We need to get away from here, now," he replied.

"The electronics bag you used at all the other locations."

"It's gone. I threw it away."

"Why?"

"Because there's only one location left. We don't have to worry about them alerting anyone else."

"Is that it?" said Ali. "Or is it something else?"

"Something else? Are you mad?" demanded Sacha, as his hand tight-

ened around the grip of his own weapon. "We don't have time for this. We need to go, now."

"You knew all along we wouldn't find Mohammed at those other locations, didn't you?"

A minute change in expression swept briefly across Sacha's face. It was all that Ali needed to see. Pulling the trigger, he shot the Chechen right between the eyes.

The Troll must have known all along that Mohammed bin Mohammed was being held at the fifth location! That was why he had insisted on taking the others down first, and Sacha had been a part of that plan from the outset. What a fool Ali had been. The locations had indeed been secret government facilities, but not for the holding and interrogating of prisoners. They had to do with the Troll's stock-in-trade—information. It explained all the computer workstations and arrays of sophisticated servers. The first four locations were all about collecting information for the man's evil little empire.

Ali now wondered if the Troll had ever intended for him to succeed. Maybe he and Mohammed weren't even supposed to leave the city alive. There was no telling what the Troll had planned for them, but Ali was now more determined than ever before that the man would die an unspeakably painful death. It was a mistake to have trusted the Troll, especially after al-Qaeda had discovered he was the one who had given Mohammed's whereabouts in Somalia to the Americans.

It didn't matter now, though. Ali had been prepared for this eventuality. In fact, he had envisioned several different outcomes the afternoon might bring and he had prepared for all of them.

Moments later, like a snake that had just shed its skin, Ali returned to the street anew. Matching his pace to the other pedestrians, he proceeded east to one of the many strategically placed hotels he had taken rooms in. Looking more Italian than Arab, he had little fear of being stopped or accosted along the way. The passport he carried would identify him as an Italian businessman and though no one should have any reason to examine him any further than that, he had a complete backstory, or *legend* as it was known in the intelligence community, which would explain who he was and what he was doing in New York City.

Even though this was an exceptional masquerade, it wasn't his best. The best was yet to come.

EIGHTY-FIVE

On some subconscious level Harvath had understood what the rounds plinking off the side of the shuttle van meant and had been able to knock his team to the ground moments before the explosion.

Now the lobby was engulfed in flames and survivors stampeded in search of exits at the back of the hotel.

Herrington picked up the Troy CQB, slung it over his shoulder along with his own weapon, and gently shoved Harvath toward the back of the hotel. "Let's get outside and see if we can find these guys."

Harvath knew that wasn't going to happen, but he grabbed onto the suggestion nonetheless as a reason to get moving. As he did, the fog of battle began to lift and his adrenaline was replaced by a budding anger with himself for having lost the two remaining terrorists.

Cutting through the hotel gift shop, the team exited onto 51st Street and pushed their way through the crowd of stunned hotel guests.

Signaling Rick Cates to come with him, Bob Herrington suggested the team split up. Harvath nodded his head and took Hastings around the front of the hotel. The damage was bad, very bad, and several civilians lay dead or dying near the still-burning shuttle van. Even if they'd had medical supplies with them, there was little they could have done.

From what Harvath had seen just before the explosion, the terrorists had looked like they were prepared to head south on Lexington and so that's the direction they decided to go.

He and Hastings crossed the intersection at 50th Street and continued moving south, but to no avail. The remaining two terrorists could be anywhere. They had a decent head start and there was just too much ground to cover on foot. At 49th Street Harvath radioed Bob and asked, "Anything?"

"Nada," replied Herrington.

Harvath instructed him to come up 48th Street and meet them at the corner in front of the Lexington Hotel. Several of the hotel staff were standing in front passing out bottled water to anyone who needed it. New York was an amazing city. Harvath marveled at how the absolute worst of times in a rather rough city could bring out the absolute best in so many people. Instead of hoarding supplies for themselves or even for hotel guests, which would have been understandable, the hotel was helping anyone who walked by.

Seeing Harvath's and Hastings's weapons and realizing they must be plainclothes police, the hotel manager offered each of them extra bottles of water and thanked them for what they were doing. The manager, of course, had no idea what they were doing and, in Harvath's opinion, how poorly they were actually doing it, but he was grateful for the water as well as the opportunity to rest while they waited for Herrington and Cates to catch up with them.

Less than a minute later a man ran up to the front of the Lexington and relayed to the hotel's manager the details of the shootout and the shuttle bus explosion in the Metropolitan's lobby.

Taking their luggage carts from near the front door, the manager and three of his doormen loaded them up with water and ran off toward the other hotel. Harvath watched them leave. When they had disappeared, Harvath realized how utterly exhausted he was. His shoulder was killing him and he probably should have sought further medical attention, but he ignored the pain as best he could and closed his eyes.

EIGHTY-SIX

When Harvath's eyes snapped back open, he had no idea how long he'd been out. Nearby, Hastings sat on the hotel steps talking with Cates and Herrington as she tried to shake pieces of ash and charred soot from her hair. Across the street, a Greek restaurant had taken over handing out bottled water to thirsty passersby. A group of businesspeople standing near the restaurant even managed a smile as one of them apparently said something worth smiling at. New Yorkers were an amazing bunch, and as terrible as it had been, they seemed to know that this day too would pass.

Harvath was about to close his eyes again, when he felt something vibrating between his elbow and his hip and realized it was his BlackBerry. Pulling the device out of its cradle, he saw the icons indiciating that he had new voicemail and e-mail messages, as well as an incoming call from his boss.

Putting the phone in his left hand, he raised it to his ear and said, "Harvath."

"Scot, it's Gary," replied Lawlor. "I've been trying to reach you for the last half hour. What's going on?"

Scot filled him in as best he could and then fell into an exhausted silence.

"Listen, I may have some *good* news for you," said Gary.

"There isn't much I'd consider good at this point, but go ahead, shoot."

"The terrorists may be hitting a fifth location not far from where you are right now."

Hearing that, Harvath sat up straight. "What location? Where? Wait a second. How do you know this?"

"Do you remember all the reports that bin Laden was on dialysis?"

"Of course, it was a rumor based on the Pakistani president claiming al-Qaeda had smuggled two dialysis machines into Afghanistan, right?"

"Exactly. Then one of our Delta Force teams discovered a sterile facility used for dialysis treatments at bin Laden's Tora Bora base near Jalalabad."

"So?"

"So they also found a patient log and discovered it wasn't bin Laden getting treatment, it was Mohammed bin Mohammed, aka Abu Khabab al-Fari."

"Wait a second," said Harvath. "M&M? Al-Qaeda's master bombmaker? He was the head of their entire weapons of mass destruction committee until he disappeared a couple of days before 9/11. Nobody has seen him since."

"The DIA has," said Lawlor.

Harvath was floored, and smoke was nearly coming out of his ears as his mind raced to put all of the pieces together. "What's this have to do with them grabbing Sayed Jamal from us?"

"Apparently, they're related—as in *family.* The DIA wanted to use Jamal as leverage in their interrogation of Mohammed."

"The DIA has Mohammed?" Harvath couldn't believe it. "Who told you this?"

"Stan Caldwell," replied Lawlor.

"How does the deputy director of the FBI have that information?"

"According to Caldwell, it was DIA's chief of staff who coordinated the Joint Terrorism Task Force ruse and then swore the Bureau to secrecy."

"Based on what? What kind of sway does the DIA have over the Bureau?"

"I don't know," said Gary. "That's all he would tell me. In fact I was surprised to get that much from him."

Harvath thought back and replied, "That high-level al-Qaeda operative the U.S. took down—the one with the exploding laptop. Do you think that was Mohammed?"

"The timing on it would be right."

"Then that intercept about the U.S. grabbing a bombmaker and bringing him into America against his will and in violation of international law wasn't about Jamal after all. It was about Mohammed."

"I think so," said Lawlor.

"And you believe he's here, in New York?"

"I'm almost certain of it."

"But what's the connection with the NSA's deep black intelligence sites?" replied Harvath. "I don't get it."

"I don't get it either. The only one who might have been able to explain it to us is Joseph Stanton, and he's dead."

"So how do you know there's a fifth location and that it's here in New York?"

"It all comes back to the dialysis machines. We interrogated one of Stanton's analysts—a young man who worked closely with him on the Athena Program, and he told us that Stanton was very interested in recent sales of high-end units sold by a company called Nova Medical Systems. The name sounded familiar to me, but I couldn't remember why. When I got back to my office, I did some checking."

"And?"

"The machines found in the treatment room at the Tora Bora complex were the exact same kind Stanton had his analyst searching for."

"And did he find any?"

"Yup, and that's where I think the fifth location is."

Though some of the dots still needed to be connected, there were enough of them lining up at this point to make Harvath believe that Lawlor really might be on to something. "We're on it. Where is it?"

"That's the problem. We can't touch it."

"What do you mean, *we can't touch it*?"

"It's recognized as the foreign soil of a sovereign nation. We're not allowed in unless they invite us in."

More bureaucratic bullshit, thought Harvath. All he wanted was an address. He'd let the hacks back in Washington mop up the fallout. "Gary, if that's where these terrorists are headed, trust me, whatever sovereign nation we're talking about, they're going to be begging us to come inside and help them."

"I wouldn't be so sure. The Libyans can be incredibly stubborn when they want to."

EIGHTY-SEVEN

LIBYA HOUSE
309 EAST 48TH STREET

Mike Jaffe bent down in front of his prisoner and whispered, "You are one heartless bastard, aren't you?"

Mohammed bin Mohammed looked over at the bloody, slumped body of his nephew but said nothing.

Jaffe stood up and said, "That's okay, though, because I'm a heartless bastard too. This is a battle of the wills, Mohammed—a clash of the Titans. But I've got to tell you, I don't know if you've got what it takes to go the distance. Lately, you haven't been looking so good."

Mohammed tried to stifle it, but a chuckle escaped his lips.

Jaffe smiled at him. "The man's got a sense of humor. How about that? Tell me, Mohammed. All those little boys you've buggered over the years, how do you think their senses of humor have fared? Do you think they're pretty happy-go-lucky? Think they look back on having your flabby, sweaty body hovering over them, pumping away as a character-building experience?"

The smile vanished from Mohammed's face.

"We found a lot of interesting souvenirs in that house of yours in Somalia," said Jaffe, "and that got me to thinking. I've been going at this the wrong way, haven't I? Like we say in Arabic, I want you to hold me *close* to your heart. But how do I get there?"

Walking over to the table near the door, Jaffe reached into a two-pocket olive-drab pouch and removed a small canister with a long piece of clear, flexible tubing attached to the nozzle. Holding it up so his prisoner could see it, he said, "You've seen one of these before, right? It's pepper spray. It's been around a long time, but it took a very clever man in New Jersey to realize that we'd been limiting ourselves in how we used it."

Mohammed shifted nervously in his chair.

Unraveling the tubing, Jaffe continued, "Suppose you're in your hotel room and somebody—a bad guy, let's say—comes knocking on your door at three in the morning. We know he's a bad guy, because what nice guy pounds on a door at that hour, right?

"Anyway, you've got your pepper spray in this hand, you unravel the hose with the other, slide it under the door, hit the button, and presto! All of a sudden the hallway is uninhabitable. Pretty neat, huh? But wait, there's more.

"I know the guy who makes these things. He's sold tons to our government. One night we're sitting down having a beer and we're talking about all the different tricks his stuff can do and suddenly it dawns on me. Pepper spray is biodegradable. If it enters your body, eventually it'll be flushed out with no trace left behind.

"Now, if I'm close to your heart, I figure you'll tell me what I want to know. The problem is, though, that we're running out of time. So what's the quickest way to a man's heart? Well, in America we say it's through his stomach, but in your case, I think it's just a bit lower."

Mohammed's gaze dropped to his groin.

EIGHTY-EIGHT

"I haven't tried this yet," said Jaffe as he stuck the tube into his mouth to moisten the tip, "but I gotta believe it's going to hurt like hell."

Removing a pair of EMT shears from his pocket, he threw them to Brad Harper and said, "Prep him. I want him as naked as the day Allah made him."

Even if the two Libyan intelligence officers Rashid and Hassan were called back in to do the actual procedure, Harper knew prepping Mohammed for this made him a direct accessory to the man's torture.

Up until this moment, neither he nor Jaffe had actually touched either of the prisoners. In all fairness, they'd danced dangerously close to the line of what was allowed, but they'd always stayed on the proper side of it. Now, though, Jaffe was telling him in no uncertain terms to jump right across it.

"Hello? Marine?" said Jaffe when Harper failed to act. "Anybody home?"

"Shouldn't our two colleagues be handling this?" he asked.

"Who? Frick and Frack? They're on their coffee break. Let's not bug them. Besides, I think I'm going to add this to my repertoire, and I want to know firsthand how it works."

"You're talking about shoving that tube up his . . ." Harper paused, the image incredibly ghastly even for a marine.

Jaffe looked at him and said, "What's wrong? Cat got your tongue? You can say it, son. I'm going to shove that tube right up his piss pipe. His urethra, Franklin, if you want to get clinical. Once it's up as far as it'll go, then I'm gonna gas him with the pepper spray. If he's ever had gonorrhea it'll feel like the world's best blow job, in comparison to this."

Looking at Mohammed, Jaffe then asked, "You ever catch gonorrhea from any of those little boys you buggered?" He wasn't expecting a response, and when none came, he turned to Harper and said, "What are you waiting for?"

The marine's mind was made up. "With all due respect sir, I'm not able to do what you asked."

Jaffe's eyebrows went up and he replied, "What I *asked?* Son, I didn't ask you for anything. I gave you a direct order and I expect it to be carried out. Now *prep* this prisoner."

"Negative, sir."

Jaffe was quickly losing his temper. "You want to piss in the tall grass with the big dogs, but you don't want any to land on you. I'm disappointed, son," he said as he grabbed the shears back from Harper. "I thought you had more backbone."

Walking over to Mohammed, Jaffe plunged the shears into his trouser leg, narrowly missing his thigh, and began cutting. As he did, he said, "The problem all along with this interrogation has been respect. I can see it in our friend's eyes here. He doesn't respect us. Do you, Mohammed? You've got nothing but contempt for us, because when it comes down to the real dirty stuff, the physical stuff, we let our Libyan pals do it for us.

"Well, if I don't have your respect, I just don't think I can take it."

It was obvious from the look on Mohammed's face that Jaffe had hit the nail right on the head. The al-Qaeda man wasn't afraid. He felt nothing but contempt for his captors. But that was all about to change. Now that he was naked from the waist down, he could see the American was serious, very serious.

For a man who took so much pleasure from life via the organ between his legs, the torture Mohammed was about to face was hideously personal. In his most disturbing dreams he doubted he could have ever come up with something so repulsive.

When the American came back with the device, he writhed in his chair and struggled against his restraints—anything to stop the tube from entering his penis. His struggles, though, were entirely in vain. The American grabbed his organ in a death grip and inserted the tubing most violently. Once the tip was in, the man began feeding the rest of the tubing after it.

When Jaffe felt it was in deep enough, he looked at Mohammed and said, "You know the information I want."

"Go to hell!" Mohammed screamed.

Jaffe raised the Guardian Protection Devices canister so that Mohammed could see his thumb slip under the safety mechanism and said, "I can't go to hell today. I still have so many more things to do."

The shrieks of wretched agony were instantaneous. So horrible were they that even the two Libyan intelligence officers burst into the room, certain that the Americans were either filleting or disemboweling their prisoner alive.

As Jaffe sent another shot of pepper spray into the terrorist's penis, Mohammed screamed at the top of his lungs for it to stop, his body absolutely rigid from the pain. Tears streamed down his face, and no matter how hard he tried, he couldn't seem to catch his breath.

Jaffe had no intention of letting up. The pain this piece of human waste was prepared to unleash upon America was nothing compared to what he was being subjected to at this moment. Jaffe had never known hate as strong as he felt it right now. What god could ever support what al-Qaeda did in His name? Jaffe wanted nothing more than to watch this man die, because he knew if anybody was going to hell, it was Mohammed bin Mohammed.

Jaffe let up for a moment only to watch the man's body go slack against his restraints and his chest heave for air.

Then, without warning, he gave the man another blast.

Mohammed's body tried to leap off the chair as if it were a thousand degrees.

Jaffe should have worn earplugs. Mohammed had the lungs of a lion.

He kept the button depressed on the pepper spray, determined to drain every last drop into the monster in front of him until in addition to the screaming he suddenly heard another sound—*gunfire*.

EIGHTY-NINE

With his phony diplomatic Libyan passport, Abdul Ali found the security at the twenty-four-story Libya House easily navigable when he arrived. His Libyan dialect was flawless and he demanded that the man behind the reception counter pick up the phone and dial the ambassador's office straightaway.

When the ambassador's assistant answered, the receptionist spoke several words, waited for a response, and then, satisfied, hung up.

After being offered a seat and told the assistant was on his way down, Ali berated the man by asking how anyone could sit at a time like this. Libyans placed a high value on courtesy, and to berate another in public was considered extremely rude. The receptionist was not stupid. He'd met this man's type before, and he knew that regardless of what his passport said, he was no diplomat. In fact, he'd met enough arrogant intelligence agents to know that's exactly what this man was. The receptionist had long ago developed a theory that there was a farm somewhere back in his homeland where they grew these insufferable assholes by the truckload.

Moments later, the elevator doors opened and out strolled the ambassador's assistant accompanied by a rather large man who Ali assumed was part of Libya House's security detail. The assistant walked over to the reception desk, chatted briefly with the man behind the counter, and then studied the visitor's passport, scanning through it a page at a time. Finally he made his way over to Ali.

After exchanging the customary Libyan greetings, the assistant offered his hand and introduced himself. He did not offer the passport back. "I thought I knew all of the *Haiat amn al Jamahiriya* operatives stationed in New York," he stated. "Why is it we haven't met?"

Ali remained calm, as well as somewhat aloof—the attitude he felt best suited the role he was playing. "Because I am not stationed here," he replied. "I'm based in Washington."

The assistant brushed the explanation aside. "You stated you have business to discuss with the ambassador?"

"Correct."

"I hope you can appreciate that with everything going on today, the ambassador is quite busy. Why don't you share the nature of your business with me and I will pass it along."

Ali feigned a smile. The weapons he had hidden beneath his specially crafted suit weighed heavily on his tired body. "If the business I have been sent to conduct was at the level of an ambassador's assistant, I would happily do so, but my visit is for the ambassador's eyes and ears only."

The assistant was not fond of the visiting intelligence officer's smug attitude. "And why is it that we were not alerted to your arrival?"

Ali was more than prepared for the assistant's questions. "At our diplomatic missions abroad, especially when it concerns matters of state security, it is not uncommon for messengers to arrive unannounced. You and I both know this. Now, please stop wasting my time and direct me to the ambassador."

"Interesting," continued the assistant, determined to scrape some of the arrogance off this man. "But what is uncommon is for a messenger to show up in the midst of such unfortunate circumstances. I would think it more appropriate to have waited before making yourself known here. This is not a time for the U.S. missions of Arab nations to be holding clandestine meetings."

Ali nodded his head. "Waiting, of course, would have been a more prudent course, but the information I bring for the ambassador is extremely time sensitive."

"I'm sorry," replied the assistant, "but without some idea of what this is in regard to, the ambassador cannot be disturbed. We have been placed on our highest security alert."

Ali smiled, and this time it was for real. "Tell the ambassador, Tripoli no longer wishes this facility to be used as a hotel."

"A hotel? What are you talking about?"

Looking at the detail agent, Ali said, "Radio the agent with the ambassador right now and relay my message. Tell him that the Americans and their package are no longer welcome here."

The security agent looked at the stunned assistant, who, though he couldn't believe what he was hearing, nodded his head and gave his assent.

The agent spoke into a microphone in his sleeve, and once a response came back over his earpiece, he turned and whispered it to the assistant.

Looking at Ali, he reluctantly replied, "The ambassador will see you now. Please follow me."

NINETY

Sizing up the two men as they ascended in the elevator, Ali thought about taking them right there but forced himself to wait. His attack was only moments away.

Getting the ambassador's undivided attention turned out to be the easiest part of the entire plan. Once the man had foolishly dismissed both his assistant and his security team from his private office, Ali stopped answering questions and began asking ones of his own.

Once he had everything he needed, he forced the ambassador to call his assistant back into the office. When the smarmy little man appeared, Ali fought the urge to make his death long and painful and instead broke his neck, delighting in the rather delicate pop as it finally snapped. There was no other sound in the world like it, nor was there any greater feeling of power than to take another's life with your bare hands.

A little too high from the kill, Ali took a few deep breaths and relaxed. The next several minutes had to be perfectly smooth and without incident. He had come too far to fail now. Only one floor above where they now stood, the ambassador had confirmed that Mohammed bin Mohammed was being held and interrogated. The thought of how the Troll had betrayed him, had betrayed al-Qaeda once again, entered his mind, but he quickly pushed it away. There would be time to deal with him later. Right now, Ali needed to concentrate on the task at hand. There were still the ambassador's security guards to deal with and then the two Libyan intelligence officers and four Americans guarding Mohammed.

Knowing he was about to be killed, the ambassador made a run for the door and began yelling for his bodyguards.

He had taken less than two strides when Ali felled him with a single silenced round. The damage, though, was already done. The security agents came charging into the room with their weapons drawn and upon seeing the ambassador and his assistant sprawled on the floor, opened fire.

Thankfully, their shots went wide as Ali dove for cover behind the desk.

The security agents managed to get off several more rounds before Ali found his opportunity, rolled from behind the desk, and took out each of them with exceptionally clean head shots.

With the bodyguards down, Ali leapt from behind the desk. He had no idea if the shots had been heard by anyone else, but he didn't want to wait around to find out. This would be his one and only chance to free Mohammed bin Mohammed, and either he would succeed or they would both die trying.

Ali quickly found the items he needed, and once he had retrieved his diplomatic passport, he wheeled his little surprise toward the freight elevator.

One of the few pieces of useful information he'd been able to squeeze out of the ambassador as the man blubbered for his life was that the Americans had welded their stairwell doors shut and that the only way to gain access to their floor was via the freight elevator. Though they were many things, stupid was not one of them. They had gone to considerable lengths to ensure their security. And who could blame them? The last thing they wanted was for someone like Abdul Ali to spoil their party.

After prepping the door upstairs with the remaining plastique he had hidden inside his specially made belt, Ali returned to the ambassador's floor and using the man's keycard, swiped it through the card reader and summoned the elevator.

When the elevator arrived, Ali looked up and saw that the hatch had been welded shut. He smiled. The Americans really had thought of everything. But he doubted they had a contingency plan for what was about to happen next.

Swiping the card again on a reader inside the elevator, Ali punched the button for the next floor, positioned his surprise aboard, and headed for the stairwell. Things were about to get very interesting.

NINETY-ONE

From the streaks of blood on both the floor and along the wall of the elevator, it looked as if the ambassador had stumbled inside after being shot and had managed to swipe his keycard and press the button for their floor before collapsing.

"Don't touch him!" commanded Jaffe as the two Libyan intelligence agents rushed into the elevator. Until he knew what the hell was going on, he wanted everything taken very slowly.

That plan, though, fell to pieces when the agent they called Hassan leaned down close to the ambassador's face and could hear the sound of breathing. "He's alive!" he shouted.

Jaffe gave a rapid series of orders and after sending Harper for the medical kit and telling the two Libyans to back out of the elevator, he stepped inside to have a look for himself.

Shouldering his weapon, Jaffe carefully approached the ambassador to check on his condition. The man was in bad shape, and what Hassan had thought to be the sound of breathing was actually the sound of the ambassador choking on his own blood. If they didn't do something and fast, the man was going to die.

Calling Rashid, Hassan, and his two other marines back into the elevator, Jaffe placed them along both sides of the ambassador and prepared them to carefully turn the man while he supported his head. On three, they began to roll him over, and that's when Jaffe realized he hadn't been cautious enough. The ambassador was indeed choking on his own blood, but he was also desperately trying to warn them not to move him. By the time Jaffe realized what was happening, it was too late.

The improvised device rigged to the ambassador exploded in an enormous fireball, ripping the roof off the car, shearing the cables, and sending it plummeting into the basement.

NINETY-TWO

Upon hearing the explosion, Ali ran back up the stairs and detonated a second device, blowing the welded door right out of its frame.

He stepped into the freight area and saw the blackened elevator doors standing open, but nothing else. It was like an enormous gaping mouth with smoke billowing from its throat.

His weapon up and at the ready, Ali began his search for Mohammed. Moving quickly, he swept into the first three offices along the hall and finding them empty, moved on. In the fourth, he found a television set, a cooking area with a sink as well as a table, chairs, and some couches, but nothing more.

The next door was marked with both the English and Arabic words for *washroom.* He pushed the door open and quietly slipped inside. Having looked inside every stall and confident that they were all empty, he exited and continued his search. There were only about five offices remaining. The next was empty, as was the next after that. As Ali quickly moved toward the last three rooms, he found the next one he approached was locked. A handwritten sign identified its function as a sterile treatment room and listed a set of instructions to follow before entering. Abdul Ali kicked it open and inside found a surgical table, a medical recovery recliner, a wheelchair, various first aid supplies, and right in the center of it all a high-end Nova Medical Systems dialysis machine.

The next room was the nerve center of the interrogation operation. The walls were covered with dry-erase boards, maps of the Middle East and Africa, multiple photographs of the al-Qaeda hierarchy, as well as various organizational and relationship diagrams. Desks were laden with audio and video equipment as well as monitors tuned to cameras that must have been positioned all over the floor. Seeing the image on the largest monitor, Abdul Ali turned and fled.

Bursting into the room across the hall, he was ready to weep with joy. There, bound to a small, wooden chair was Mohammed bin Mohammed. Next to him, unconscious and severely beaten, was a man Ali had never met but most definitely knew of. The last he'd heard, the man had been in Canada. He had no idea Mohammed's nephew, Sayed Jamal, had been taken prisoner.

As he rushed to Mohammed's side, he saw that he was naked from the waist down, his penis red and swollen beyond belief. "What unspeakable acts have they done to you, my brother?" he asked as he removed a knife and begun cutting away the restraints.

At first, Mohammed didn't want to believe his eyes. His body was so racked with pain and his mind was clouded by the horror of his torture. Surely it was some sort of trick. Then he saw Ali holster his weapon and remove a knife to help cut him free. *It was Ali, wasn't it?* At this point, he didn't know what to believe. "Is it you?" he asked, his voice hoarse from his screaming.

"Yes, Mohammed, it is I. I have come to take you home," replied Ali.

Looking in the direction of his nephew, Mohammed asked, "And Sayed?"

Ali reached over and felt the man's pulse. It was weak, too weak. "I'm sorry. There is nothing we can do for him. He is not going to make it."

Mohammed hung his head. "At least his family is already waiting for him in paradise."

"What do you mean?"

"The Americans took each one of his children and killed them. Then they took his wife. They made us both watch it on television, hoping it would force me to tell them what they wanted to know."

"And what did you tell them?" asked Ali, concerned that everything he had been through, everything they had risked might now be for nothing.

Mohammed's face was a block of implacable granite. "I told them nothing. Even while they killed Sayed's family one by one, I told them nothing."

Ali looked at Jamal once again. His trouser legs had been sheared away, and his knees were a mass of bloody pulp. "What did they do to him?"

"They used a drill," he croaked.

Ali had no intention of making his colleague relive any more of the brutality. "Can you stand?" he asked as he helped Mohammed to his feet. "I have a safe place I can take you."

Mohammed shook his head. "My pain is too great. They stopped my dialysis as a part of the torture. You're too late. Soon I will follow Sayed."

Ali shook his head. "I have a hotel room near here with a small dialysis machine. You are not going to die, my brother. Not today. But we must get to safety quickly."

"I fear I won't be able to walk very far. I have grown too weak."

Ali thought about it for a moment and then told Mohammed not to move. Leaving him, Ali went back out into the hallway and made his way to the dialysis room.

After unfolding the wheelchair, he rifled through the cabinets until he found a pair of surgical scrubs big enough to fit Mohammed. He gathered a few additional supplies and was putting them all in a small bag, when he heard a voice from behind him say, "Don't even think about moving."

NINETY-THREE

Though Abdul Ali had been meticulous about clearing the otherwise empty rooms, what he didn't realize was that, as in many consulates and embassies around the world, hidden passageways as well as escape exits were often part of the architecture. It was just such a passageway that had allowed the surviving marine, Brad Harper, to create an advantage and assume the upper hand.

He had already been on his way back with the medical kit when the blast from the first explosion had knocked him to the ground. When the second, smaller explosion detonated, he wisely rushed back to the control room to see what was happening on the closed-circuit monitors.

Now, as Harper held his modified M16 Viper on the man who had just assassinated his entire team, he was very tempted to administer justice himself. All it would take was a simple pull of the trigger, and this entire nightmare would be brought to an end, but Harper knew better. He also knew the man he had in front of him was extremely dangerous and could have any one of a hundred possible tricks up his sleeve. "I've got every reason in the world to kill you right now. Try anything stupid and I will pull this trigger. Do you understand me?"

Ali had no idea how he had missed this man. His eyes darted around the room as his mind scrambled for a way out.

Harper shifted his sights a fraction of an inch to the right and he pulled the trigger, sending a quick burst of fire over the man's shoulder and into the Sheetrock in front of him. *"Do you understand?"* he repeated.

Ali nodded his head.

"I want you to raise your hands, slowly. That's it. Nice and easy. Now interlace your fingers behind your head."

Once Ali had complied, Harper ordered him onto his stomach. With the man fully prone, the young marine cautiously leaned down to cuff him. It was at that moment that Mohammed bin Mohammed snuck up behind him and with the very last reserves of strength, hit the large marine not once but twice across the back of the head with a fire extinguisher, knocking him to the floor unconscious.

NINETY-FOUR

As Harvath and the rest of his team rapidly made their way to Libya House, things were beginning to make sense. In 2003 the United States made headlines when in exchange for agreeing to lift its sentence of rogue-nation status and restart diplomatic ties with Libya, the Libyans agreed to abandon their weapons of mass destruction, discontinue any support of terrorism, and enact sweeping social and democratic reforms.

Such unprecedented cooperation in the war on terror might very well have been just the surface of a much deeper and much quieter deal. It was no wonder that even with his Polo Step clearance Harvath had not been able to learn which top al-Qaeda member the United States had taken into custody. Somewhere at State or the Department of Justice, somebody was walking a very thin legal line. The only way Harvath could figure they had pulled it off was to have brought M&M up to the edge of international waters on a private craft of some sort and flying him the rest of the way by chopper, then dropping him on the roof of Libya House, where the Libyans took over.

Though he was sure the American involvement was supposed to be nothing more than "observer" status, he knew who was really running this show. In fact, he had a pretty good feeling he knew the person by name: Mike Jaffe. What he didn't have a good feeling about was their being able to get access to Libya House. Gary was right. It was sovereign territory and without an invitation, the only way they were going to be able to get inside was by force. But as it turned out, that wasn't necessary.

When they arrived, the few people who were in the lobby were in an absolute panic. Harvath flashed his DHS credentials and was told by a man who identified himself as the mission receptionist that there had been an enormous explosion from somewhere within the building and that they couldn't raise their ambassador, his assistant, or the ambassador's security team.

After Harvath explained that they were there because terrorists had targeted the building and they believed that an attack was eminent, the receptionist assigned them the building's only security guard and sped them into one of the lobby elevators for the ambassador's office on the twenty-third floor.

The moment the doors opened, the guard showed them into the ambassador's office, where they came upon the bodies of the assistant and the two bodyguards.

Borrowing the guard's radio, Harvath called down to the receptionist to ask how long it had been since the man had last had contact with the ambassador, his assistant, or any members of the protective detail.

The man filled Harvath in on everything he knew, including the unannounced visitor with the diplomatic passport. He provided a full description, but when Harvath asked his next question, the receptionist became very quiet.

The entire staff of Libya House had been told that the twenty-fourth floor was absolutely off-limits, and even its existence shouldn't be discussed with anyone. The receptionist had suspected it had something to do with the two stern-faced intelligence agents who had joined the mission from Tripoli. Faced with the very real fact that the building was under siege, the man shared the rest of what he knew.

Before the receptionist was even done speaking, Harvath and company. were rushing for the freight elevator. They were halfway there when the receptionist came back over the radio. Based on what he could see from his security panel, the freight elevator was no longer operational. What's more, even though the rest of the building was supposedly empty, one of the main elevators had unexpectedly risen to the twenty-second floor and was now beginning to descend.

Though he couldn't put his finger on why, Harvath had a very bad feeling about who was inside that elevator.

Shrugging off the pain in his shoulder, he made for the stairway, but Bob Herrington and Tracy Hastings were already in front of him.

Relieving the lumbering security guard of his radio and with Rick Cates and his bad knees bringing up the rear, Harvath hit the stairwell and barreled down as fast as he could go.

The landings, which he normally would have taken by gripping the handrail with his right hand and swinging his body around, were nearly impossible because of his wounds, and so he took the tight turns as best he could, relying only on his feet. More than once, his excessive speed caused him to slam his left side up against the wall before he could regain his path and tackle the next set of stairs. Invariably, he lost sight of Bob and Tracy, who were making much better time than he and considerably better time than Cates, who was sucking up the pain and moving as fast as he could.

Twice, Herrington and Hastings stopped on random floors to depress the elevator's call button in hopes of stopping it. But without a keycard, it was no use. Once they finally realized they couldn't stop it, the pair tore back into the stairwell and continued their mad dash down the stairs.

Within ten floors of the ground level, Harvath radioed Herrington on his Motorola. "Bob, what's your status?" he asked.

It was a moment before Herrington replied, "At the lobby now. We're going to intercept that elevator."

"Negative," said Harvath. "Wait for me."

"What floor are you on?"

"Eight. I'll be right there."

"You're not going to make it. The elevator's already on four."

"Wait, for me, Bob," repeated Harvath.

"Listen, there's a mail room kitty-corner from where you're going to hit the lobby," said Herrington. "That's where we are. You can give us fire support from the stairwell when you get here."

Harvath, who was now touching one, maybe two steps in between each landing as he flew down the stairs, was about to remind Herrington who was in charge of the operation, when Bob's voice came back over his radio. He was counting down the elevator's arrival. "Two. One. Bingo!"

Based upon the scene in the ambassador's office, Harvath knew that if this was their guy, he wasn't going to come easily, and based on Mohammed bin Mohammed's extremely bloody history, neither was he.

Harvath expected to hear gunfire the second the elevator opened, but nothing came. Instead, Herrington's voice crackled over his earpiece, "Shit. It's not stopping. They're going for the garage."

"I'm coming up on the fifth floor," said Harvath, his chest heaving for oxygen. "Wait for me in the stairwell."

"We're going to lose him," replied Herrington.

"You've seen what this guy can do. We're all going in together."

Harvath waited for Bob to reply, and when he didn't, Harvath knew it meant that Bob had decided to go without him. If he could have run any faster, he would have, but as it was, Harvath was tackling the stairs faster than anyone in their right mind should have. He'd be lucky if all he got out of it was a bruised shoulder from bouncing off of each of the landing walls.

Harvath was at the second floor when the ear-splitting thunder of automatic weapons fire started and filled the narrow stairwell. When he hit the lobby level, just one floor from the garage, Tracy Hastings's frantic voice came over the radio yelling, "Man down! Man down!"

NINETY-FIVE

Harvath hopped the railing from one set of stairs to another and landed hard on his right foot, twisting his ankle. Bursting through the garage door, he could immediately see where Bob lay, ribbons of crimson spreading out from beneath his body and flowing downhill toward a metal floor drain several yards away.

Harvath ran to where they had taken cover alongside several dumpsters. Hastings was covered in blood up to her elbows, her hands pressed hard against Bob's chest. Seeing Harvath approach, she looked up and the tears began to roll down her face. He didn't need to ask. He knew. Bob was gone, and at that moment time stood still for Harvath.

It was Tracy pushing at his good shoulder, yelling, "Scot, go! *Go!*" that brought him back to reality.

At the far end of the garage, an engine had roared to life. Pulling an extra magazine as delicately as he could from one of the pockets of Bob's vest, Harvath ignored the pain throbbing throughout his body and half limped, half ran toward the sound. He felt guilty beyond words, and while part of him wanted to bend over, puke his guts out and mourn the loss of a friend who had been like an older brother to him, another part wanted to bathe in the blood of the people who had just killed Bob Herrington. It was from that part of himself that he summoned the strength to keep moving.

The vehicle was accelerating now and the rev of its engine was quickly joined by another unmistakable sound—the heavy metal garage door rumbling open.

Harvath used his other radio to hail the receptionist and tell him to override the door, but the man said his system wouldn't do that. Dropping the radio, Harvath ran faster, trying to close the distance with the unseen vehicle. His adrenaline all but spent, the Troy CQB assault rifle he'd taken back from Bob began once again to feel like a hundred-pound barbell. Harvath's back, his arms, and his shoulders begged for him to drop it, but he refused. Having tapped the last of his reserves, he used his rage to push him forward, but it did little good. He finally closed on the ramp leading out of the garage and up to the street, only to see the taillights of a green Mini Cooper crest the top and pull a hard left, its tires screaming as they bit into the sidewalk, and it disappeared from sight.

Undeterred, Harvath stumbled up the ramp, and as his legs began to fail him, he willed them to keep going. He could not let the terrorists get away.

Out of breath, his chest heaving, Harvath hit the top of the ramp and pivoted to the left, the Cooper halfway down the block. Raising the weapon to his injured right shoulder, Harvath aligned the car in his sights and with no breath to hold, squeezed the trigger.

The rounds flew down 48th Street, and when Harvath saw the vehicle swerve, its brake lights illuminating the night, he knew he'd made contact. The tires squealed as it careened and scraped along several parked cars. Harvath lined up another shot, tried to control the desperate filling and emptying of his lungs, and then pulled the trigger again. He heard the distinct *pop* that indicated that he had fired his last round and without even thinking about it pressed the magazine release, slapped the new mag to make sure the rounds were seated, and slammed it into the weapon.

He ripped back the charging handle and let go of it just as fast. With the car nearing the end of the sidewalk, this was Harvath's very last chance. Firing in short bursts, he kept the Mini Cooper in his sights as its driver swerved back and forth, trying to avoid being hit.

As Harvath began to squeeze the trigger once more, the vehicle hit First Avenue, pulled another tight left turn, and disappeared from sight.

The white-hot anger swelled up inside him once more. Based on the little he had seen, he knew these people were incredibly professional and would have put just as much effort into Mohammed bin Mohammed's evacuation as they had his rescue.

It was a bitter pill to swallow, but Harvath had to accept that they were gone.

NINETY-SIX

It was not Hastings or Cates who found Harvath propped up against a parked car and unable to move outside Libya House, but the receptionist.

Without saying a word, the man bent down and helped Harvath to his feet. When Harvath had trouble balancing on his damaged ankle, the man offered his shoulder. He tried to steer him toward the steps leading to the front of the building, but Scot shook his head and motioned toward the garage. At the bottom of the ramp, he thanked the man and told him to return to his post. What Harvath had to do now, he wanted to do without strangers present.

It took him several minutes to limp back to where he had left Hastings and Herrington, but when he got there he saw Rick Cates covering Bob's body with a tarp. Cates looked up expectantly, and Harvath shook his head. He knew the question, and unfortunately the answer was no. He didn't get the people who had done this to Bob.

Scot and Tracy and Rick stood there, staring down at the tarp, and said nothing. They had lost not only a teammate, but also an exceptional fellow soldier who was an even better friend.

There was no telling how much time had passed when Harvath finally said, "Let's go back upstairs. I want some answers."

The receptionist provided them with a keycard, but it got them only as high as the twenty-third floor. From there they walked up one more floor and realized why the freight elevator wasn't working. Its charred doors stood wide open, and it didn't take much of an imagination to realize what had happened. A severed hand and a lone Quantico boot with part of a leg sticking out of it, suggested at least one person, or probably more had been standing near the elevator when it exploded. What was left of the car was probably in the basement, and Harvath didn't envy the forensic team that would have to go through it later.

As they continued on, each of the rooms they cleared was empty, until they reached the one that must have been used for bin Mohammed's dialysis treatments. There they found another man—a marine, by the looks of him, who had taken a couple of severe blows to the head, but who was still alive. With no choice for the moment, they quickly made him as comfortable as possible and then continued with their sweep.

At the end of the hall, they found one last survivor—Sayed Jamal. He was Flexicuffed to a chair and had been beaten almost beyond recognition. Because this was Jaffe's operation, Harvath didn't need to recognize the prisoner to know who he was. He felt for a pulse and found one. It was weak, and even with immediate medical attention the man was probably not going to make it.

Leaving him alone, they went to clear their last and final room—the interrogation's nerve center. After deeming it to be safe, they stared at the sophisticated electronic equipment as well as the dry-erase boards, the relationship diagrams, and the multiple photographs that had been taped up along the wall. Seeing one that bore a resemblance to the prisoner across the hall, Cates asked, "Is this what the guy in the other room used to look like?"

Harvath looked at the photo and nodded.

"They really did a number on him. Who the hell is he?"

"His name is Sayed Jamal. He's an al-Qaeda bombmaker who—"

Suddenly, Cates spun around and seeing that Hastings was no longer in the room said, "Oh, shit!"

"What the hell's going on?" demanded Harvath as Cates ran for the door.

"Sayed Jamal was the man behind Tracy's last bomb in Iraq."

Harvath was about to echo Cates's *Oh, shit,* when the crack of a single round being discharged in the interrogation room stopped him dead in his tracks. Without even seeing it, he knew that Tracy had killed him.

NINETY-SEVEN

GRACE CHURCH
BROOKLYN HEIGHTS
JULY 10

Search-and-rescue efforts throughout New York City had turned to search and recovery. Because of the overwhelming number of dead needing to be buried, churches were conducting group funeral masses. But in the case of one of their distinguished parishioners, Grace Church had made an exception.

At a special request from the family of Master Sergeant Robert Herrington, traffic around the church had been blocked off by McGahan and several officers from various NYPD Emergency Service Units. The media respectfully kept their distance.

As a dark blue hearse rolled forward and came to a quiet stop in front of the church, a lone bagpiper played. Supported by his teammates, who had all been granted leave from Afghanistan to attend the service, Bob's family watched as his flag-draped casket was removed from the vehicle and carried up the stairs by pallbearers in full military dress.

There were a significant number of soldiers in attendance, many from some of the world's most elite fighting units—men Bob had had the pleasure of either training or fighting with. More than a few of them owed their lives to the brave man who had so tragically lost his life just a week before.

Some of the soldiers Harvath had known previously and some of them he didn't, but he had gotten to know almost everyone the night before at Bob's wake where, despite the sad circumstances and aided by lots of cocktails, everyone seemed to be able to come up with several funny stories about Bob. As a result, most of the tears that were shed were not tears of sadness, but actually bittersweet tears of joy remembering what a wonderful and inspiring person Bob Herrington had been.

For Harvath it was cathartic and something he desperately needed. His entire assignment in New York had been a catastrophic failure. Mohammed bin Mohammed had gotten away, as had the man who had been leading the Chechens, whom Harvath suspected was also the man who had helped spring Mohammed from Libya House, killing Bob Herrington in the process.

The SEALs have a saying that the only easy day was yesterday, but nothing about yesterday was easy, nor were any of the six days before that. For the last week, Harvath had remained alone, convalescing in his hotel room after having been patched up at the VA. He ran the operation through his mind again and again and again, each time trying to figure out a way he could have done things differently. No matter how hard he tried, he couldn't think of anything he could have said or done that might have saved Bob's life. This realization, though, did little to assuage his guilt.

Harvath let that guilt simmer, and it invariably turned to anger, which he focused directly on the bureaucracy back in Washington. Like most people, he wanted answers, but not even Gary Lawlor had them for him. He urged Harvath to be patient, but Harvath had no patience left. He called his pal at Valhalla and began negotiating the terms of his new job.

Inside the church, the guilt, the anger, and the sheer exhaustion with the system still weighed heavily on Harvath as he sat alongside Tracy Hastings, Rick Cates, and Paul Morgan, who had told the VA doctors to go to hell when they refused to discharge him for Bob's funeral. In the end, it was Sam Hardy who finally stepped in and made it happen.

It was good to be there with them, and Harvath tried to let go of everything he was stewing over so he could say a proper good-bye to his friend.

As the reverend introduced both himself and the military chaplain who had come from Fort Bragg to assist in the service, he informed the mourners that the program was going to be short and simple—marked not by saying good-bye, but by saying hello as Bob was welcomed into the kingdom of heaven. With a smile on his face, the man then apologized for not having enough holy "water" or wine on hand to make his service as enjoyable as the Irish wake from the night before. The crowd, many of who were still hung over, chuckled good-naturedly.

The invocation was given and then came the readings, most of which were given by Bob's teammates. The final reading was one Harvath had heard umpteen times, but which had never really hit him as hard as it did today: *There is no greater love than this, that a man lay down his life for his friends.*

As Harvath turned to look at Tracy, Rick, and Paul, he could see they were each fighting a losing battle to hold back their tears.

When the priest finished his sermon, one of Bob's teammates, a man named Jack Kohlmeyer, was invited to share some of his reflections. Kohlmeyer was the perfect speaker and spoke eloquently and with the right degree of humor to help ease the sadness everyone was feeling.

"I only knew Bob for a short time. He and I met about three years ago in a valley beneath the mountains of Afghanistan. There I was at eight thousand feet, packing an eighty-pound rucksack, about to head up into the mountains, and Bob just sat on his cot laughing at me—in front of everyone, 'Nope, you don't need that,' he'd say. 'Or that. Or that. Nope, you don't need that either.' "

Harvath had had the same experience with Bob just days earlier and he couldn't help but laugh.

"But Bob could get away with it," continued Kohlmeyer. "He could get away with laughing at us for looking silly. Bob's trick was that he laughed not at us, but with us. He didn't laugh to make us look foolish, he laughed to win us over and to make us his friends. And in that he was successful.

"It's a testament to his success with people that so many of us have traveled so far to be with him today, for the sum of the miles traveled by all of us reach into the tens of thousands.

"Bob loved people and we loved him back. We sustained him and he sustained us. Especially, when we were down.

"Bob reminded me on more than one occasion that life isn't fair so get over it and keep doing the best that you can do.

"A few weeks before Bob left to come home, the team that I had been assigned to suffered several casualties. The job of packing their bags was given to me. It was one of the hardest things I have ever had to do. Bob, though, sat with me and talked—and he talked, and he talked, and he talked. He knew what he was doing. He was keeping my mind off the job at hand. He was a natural with people and he knew it.

"So, Bob kept my mind occupied and when I was done, he put his arm around my shoulder and reminded me once more, *Life isn't fair. Keep doing what you're doing and make sure you're doing the very best you can.*"

As Harvath sat there, it was almost as if Bob was speaking to him. Hearing those words, Harvath knew he wasn't going to quit his job—he couldn't. As much of a pain in the ass as it often was, Harvath knew why he was doing it. It wasn't for the politicians he had grown progressively more disenchanted with, it was for the people of this country, brave and good people like Bob who along with their honorable way of life were worth fighting for.

Harvath was going to keep doing what he was doing and he was going to continue doing it the very best he could—for himself and also for the memory of Bob Herrington.

When the service had ended, the reverend asked if everyone would follow the procession outside onto the steps of the church.

The street was still devoid of traffic, the ESU officers dutifully at their posts. Chairs had been set up on the sidewalk for family members and those who needed to sit. It was hot and humid, but a faint breeze blew in from across the river. And though the air had gotten much better, it still wasn't one hundred percent. The scent of death and destruction still hung over everything. It was a smell Harvath would never be able to forget. Like everyone else in New York, it had become a part of him.

Bob Herrington was given a twenty-one-gun salute by seven Special Forces soldiers from across the street, and as taps was played, the flag covering his coffin was folded and handed to his parents.

The coffin was then placed inside the hearse and the rear door closed. Everyone stood or sat in silence. A minute, maybe two passed, the birds of Brooklyn Heights the only accompaniment to people's private thoughts and remembrances of Bob Herrington.

There was a faint noise from somewhere off in the distance, and Harvath wrote it off to the ongoing S&R efforts on Manhattan, until it began to grow much louder. Looking up from the hearse, Harvath watched as a UH-60 Black Hawk helicopter came in and hovered directly overhead. A heavy black rope was lowered, and it was then that Harvath realized what he was seeing. Someone, probably one of Bob's teammates, had arranged for a symbolic final extraction.

The helicopter then flared and flew off toward the river as the mourners watched. When it was gone from view, Harvath and everyone else looked down to see that Robert Herrington's hearse had already driven away.

NINETY-EIGHT

"So are we going to the reception, or not?" asked Harvath as the crowd outside the church began to break up.

"We thought we'd do our own private send-off for Bob," replied Cates.

"What? You mean just the three of you?"

"No. The four of us," said Morgan. "After all, we're a team, right?"

Harvath smiled. As he did, Tracy Hastings removed a bottle of Louis XIII from her bag and said, "Bob mentioned he owed you a drink. We all chipped in and bought this in his honor."

Harvath smiled even wider.

As they had all paid their respects to the family at the wake last night and had stayed well into the early morning hours drinking, nobody could fault them for missing the reception. In fact, few would probably even notice their absence. Besides, swapping stories while they consumed a $1300 bottle of cognac was the kind of send-off Bob would have approved of.

They decided they'd take the Fulton Landing Ferry back over to Manhattan and find a quiet place in Battery Park where they could look out over the Hudson and maybe forget, at least for a while, about everything that had happened.

A block from the church a black limousine pulled up next to them, and when the tinted window rolled down, Harvath thought he recognized the voice of the man calling his name. As he turned to look, he saw Robert Hilliman, the U.S. secretary of defense, waving.

"Quite a moving ceremony," he said, beckoning Harvath over to the vehicle. "I need a couple minutes of your time. Would you mind?"

Harvath told the others he'd meet them at the ferry and then climbed inside the limousine.

"How've you been, Scot?" said Hilliman once the door was shut.

"Fine, sir," he replied, not exactly happy to be sitting in a limo in the middle of Brooklyn Heights talking to the secretary of defense.

"Fit for duty? The shoulder's okay? The ankle?"

"The shoulder's about eighty percent, but the ankle's okay now."

"Good, glad to hear it."

"Sir, what are you doing here?" asked Harvath.

Hilliman smiled. "I knew Robert Herrington. Not well, but I knew him. He was a good man. He was part of my protective detail the first time I visited Afghanistan. There was a situation. It never made the news, but suffice it to say that if it wasn't for Bob's efforts in particular, I might not be here right now.

"I paid my respects to his parents earlier this morning and kept a low profile in the back of the church during the service."

"And the Black Hawk? Was that your doing?"

"His team had asked for it and were getting some static. With everything that's happened in Manhattan, there were certain people that felt a funeral flyover was an inappropriate diversion of resources. I disagreed. Bob Herrington was a hell of a guy and one of the finest warriors this country has ever seen."

Hilliman removed a folder from his briefcase and handed it to him. "I read the debriefing they did on you while you were getting patched up at the VA. I thought you deserved to have some of the blanks filled in."

As Harvath looked through the file, the secretary of defense continued, "Scot, you've been in this game long enough to know why certain operations must remain classified. Sometimes it's of vital national security that the right hand not know what the left hand is doing. Sometimes, though, we begin with the absolute best of intentions and clarity of purpose, but the walls we build to protect our operations can actually prevent us from sharing strategic information of paramount importance. It's clear now that's what happened last week and we lost a lot of good people because of it.

"Though I have some incredible resources at my disposal, I can't change the past. I can, though, have a significant impact on the future."

Harvath wasn't listening anymore. When he looked up from the folder the anger was chiseled across his face. "I can't believe what I'm reading. You were actually getting ready to let him walk? After everything we know about Mohammed bin Mohammed? After the incredible amount of manpower and money that went into tracking him down? What about the people who were killed trying to apprehend him? What about what he is planning to unleash on this country?"

"You don't know the full story."

"You know what, Mr. Secretary? I don't see how that could possibly make a difference."

"Listen to me and I'll tell you."

Harvath tossed the file onto the seat next to him and prayed the man had a good answer. If not, he was going to rip his throat out right in the back of that limousine.

Hilliman took a deep breath and replied, "Nobody can withstand torture indefinitely, not even a man like Mohammed bin Mohammed. The problem lies in knowing when you've truly broken them. To know that, you have to verify the intel a subject gives you, and that can take time. Time was not something we had on our side in Mohammed's case. Making matters even more difficult were his extensive dialysis treatments.

"Therefore, it had been agreed that if we couldn't make measurable progress within a certain window, we were going to transport him to another nation that collaborates with us in interrogations, a nation we knew his associates might be likely to subvert to help facilitate his escape."

"I still don't understand why you'd do that."

"So we could track him."

"But it took you guys years to find him in the first place. What makes you so sure you wouldn't lose him?" demanded Harvath.

"That's the thing. We were over ninety percent certain we wouldn't lose him—and in our business, that's a percentage we were willing to bet the house on."

"How were you going to track him?"

"Through a radioisotope we'd been administering as part of his dialysis treatments. It creates a very specific signature which can be tracked via satellite."

"You've got to be kidding me."

The secretary held up both hands and said, "So help me. It's a very new technology, but it works. We'd seen the data, but we went a step further and did a slew of comprehensive tests ourselves. The bottom line is that it works."

"Ninety percent of the time," clarified Harvath.

"Correct."

"So, do you know where Mohammed bin Mohammed is now?"

Hilliman looked at him. "Yes, we do."

"So what are you waiting for? Why don't you grab him?"

"Because we need to know who al-Qaeda is about to get their nuclear material from."

"And once you do? What then?"

Hilliman pulled two more files from his briefcase, handed them across to Harvath, and said, "That's what I want to talk to you about."

NINETY-NINE

Gibraltar
Three Days Later

Of all the places Harvath had ever traveled to, he'd never had a reason or a desire to see Gibraltar. As his plane circled on its approach, he quickly realized that he'd been missing something extraordinary.

The enormous limestone Rock of Gibraltar rose dramatically from the Mediterranean Sea, forming one of the two ancient Pillars of Hercules, which once marked the very edge of the known world.

Staring out the plane's window, Harvath could make out the various grassy glens that were home to the only free-ranging monkey in Europe, the barbary ape. He could almost smell the aloes, capers, cacti, and asparagus that grew wild along the nearly 1400-foot-high rock. And though he barely knew her, he could already tell this was the kind of place Tracy Hastings would like—a lot.

After the secretary of defense had dropped Harvath at the ferry, he had joined her, along with Rick Cates and Paul Morgan, to make the somber trip across the East River to Manhattan. As a way to ignore the search-and-recovery efforts happening up and down the river, they staked out a piece of turf on the aft deck and cracked open the bottle of Louis XIII the minute the ferry set sail. Cates, ever the procurement specialist, had secured small plastic cups and by the time they reached Manhattan, the bottle was half empty.

The balance of it was drained as they made their way up First Avenue and deposited Paul Morgan back at the VA. From there, Harvath, Hastings, and Cates proceeded to Bob's favorite watering hole, the same tavern he and Harvath had been on their way to when all hell had originally broken loose. There, already well lubricated, and fueled by their shared sense of loss, they toasted Bob's memory again, and again, and again.

The next morning when Harvath awoke, he did so as slowly as possible. It was unlike him to tie one on so bad that he couldn't remember where he was or what he had done. Knowing that the moment he opened his eyes the wicked machinery responsible for ushering in his inevitable hangover would kick into gear, he lay there and tried to figure out where he was. The first thing he noticed were the silk sheets, and because he could feel the sheets with *all* of his body, he was relatively confident that he was naked. That fact made his next observation a little more uncomfortable—the smell of perfume.

Reaching out his hand, he had first felt a well-toned calf and then a firm yet feminine thigh. As his hand slid farther up his bedmate's body, he felt a taut midriff leading to a pair of perfectly sculpted shoulders. Slowly opening his eyes, he saw Tracy Hastings lying next to him and instantly decided she had one of the most beautiful bodies he had ever seen.

For all of the jokes she made about her face, Harvath found it just as beautiful. Looking into her eyes, he saw that she was awake, and they both smiled.

After recounting the balance of the evening and telling him that he was indeed a good dancer, but that their conversation had been a bit below sparkling, they laughed and made love again. They spent the next forty-eight hours together and were inseparable right up until Harvath had to leave for his operational rendezvous point in Europe.

For his part, Harvath's only regret about the entire experience was that after being patched up at the VA, he had blown a whole week recuperating in his hotel room—alone. Tracy had offered him the guest room at her parents' house, as they had decided to remain overseas while Manhattan got back on its feet, but Harvath had politely declined. Somehow, somewhere inside himself he had known this was bound to happen. Now that it had, they were both okay with it. Whether there was a future for them was another question. Harvath knew well enough not to get his hopes up, but he also knew that he was looking forward to spending more time with Tracy and getting to know her much better.

As the plane came in for its landing, Harvath saw traffic being halted in both directions, as one of Gibraltar's main thoroughfares actually cut right across the airport's landing strip. A rocky promontory at the southernmost tip of Spain, Gibraltar occupied an area of only 2.5 square miles, but what it lacked in measurable terra firma the minuscule British dependency more than made up for in the size and scope of its international intrigues.

It was one such intrigue that had brought Scot here. A joint CIA/DIA team had been tracking Mohammed bin Mohammed since he had returned to Africa. They had followed him up to Tangiers and onto a ferryboat for the quick jaunt across the straits to Gibraltar. They now had him under surveillance in a sumptuous, yet discreet villa near the harbor—not far from the hotel where Harvath was booked. Once Mohammed's deal for the rogue nuclear material went down, the team had their orders to immediately back off. From that point forward, the al-Qaeda terrorist belonged to Scot Harvath and Scot Harvath only. No bullshit, no bureaucracy, and absolutely nobody but himself to answer to.

For two days, Mohammed played the merry holidaymaker, hitting the beaches by day and then prowling the open-air restaurants and discos for young boys at night. It made Harvath sick. He couldn't wait to put a bullet in this scumbag. The only thing worse than seeing him pick up the boys was joining the CIA/DIA team in its daily sweep of his villa while he basked on the beach and the staff ran errands. The man was quite the budding cinematographer, and watching him actually in the act made Harvath want to vomit.

It was on the third night in Gibraltar that things finally started getting interesting.

Forgoing his usual nightclub trolling, Mohammed picked one of the more upscale restaurants in town, where he put away a considerable amount of food accompanied by an incredibly expensive bottle of Bordeaux. Afterward, he headed down to the marina and a vintage Riva runabout, which, once he climbed aboard, sped off into the open ocean.

With a host of airplanes, watercraft, and helicopters at his disposal, the lead CIA/DIA agent immediately mobilized all of his assets to follow Mohammed out into the Mediterranean. When offered the opportunity to tag along, Harvath declined. He had a strong feeling that if Mohammed didn't plan on coming back, he never would have abandoned his newly minted video library back at the villa.

So while the joint task force pursued their man out into the darkening Mediterranean Sea, Harvath returned to his hotel room and, for the hundredth time since he'd arrived, disassembled and oiled his weapons.

Listening to the radio set in his room, he followed the team's progress as Mohammed's landing craft spirited him out to a large yacht with an innocuous Bahamian registry. The minute the highly sensitive nuclear materials aircraft zeroed in on it, their monitoring equipment started bouncing. Using the advanced microwave devices aboard the various covert pleasure craft that had sailed within listening range, the team was able to monitor almost the entire transaction.

Convinced they had what they were looking for, they informed Harvath that Mohammed bin Mohammed was on his way back to the marina and that the suspect was all his. Leaving his hotel, Harvath threw his gear into his rental car and headed toward the marina. Something told him that Mohammed might just be in the market for one last night of pleasure before leaving Gibraltar.

Little did Harvath know that someone else was banking on the exact same hunch.

ONE HUNDRED

The Troll disliked leaving the comfort and security of Eileanaigas House and had done so only because Mohammed bin Mohammed's escape from American custody had made it absolutely necessary.

Never in a million years would the Troll have believed Abdul Ali able to pull it off, but looking back on the operation, he realized it was his own plan that had been flawed. Once Sacha had helped Ali locate Mohammed bin Mohammed, the Chechen was supposed to kill them both—something that never happened. The Troll had underestimated Ali, but for the moment, none of that mattered. What mattered was that Mohammed be decommissioned once and for all. The fact that the bearded grease tub had forced unspeakable sex acts upon the Troll decades earlier in the Black Sea resort of Sochi made his reasons for killing the man all too personal.

Having searched for him for years and finally locating him, the Troll had hoped that the Americans would do the job for him. The fact that there had been a five-million-dollar bounty on Mohammed's head had only been icing on the cake. Now, though, the man was free once again, and from what the Troll had observed over the last several days among the bars, restaurants, and discotheques of Gibraltar, this leopard had no intention of changing his spots.

Customized by a reclusive gunsmith in southern France, the diminutive weapon the Troll was carrying had been specially designed to accommodate his exceedingly small frame. Chambered for the devastating .338 Lapua round, its optimal range was between 500 and 1200 meters, with anything below that necessary only when very deep penetration was called for. To use it for any other reason at close range was considered overkill, to say the least.

While the Troll prided himself on being a master of subtlety, he had no reservations about taking Mohammed at even point-blank range, if that was what the situation called for.

While the pedophile had frolicked on the beach by day and had cruised the nightclubs for conquests at night, the Troll had familiarized himself with routes both to and from his potential sniping areas, as well as the routes that could be used for egress from Gibraltar. As with everything else in his world, the Troll was ready for any eventuality.

That changed, though, when he noticed Mohammed bin Mohammed was under covert American surveillance. The team tracking him was exceptional, but not so good that the Troll couldn't detect their presence. Even so, he decided to remain in play. There was a slight problem, though. The team had an additional man on board—a hitter. The Troll was sure of it. But who was he charged with taking out? Was it Mohammed? Was it the people he was doing business with? Was it both parties?

While the thought of leaving the job to the American assassin was tempting, the Troll knew that if he wanted this done right, he would have to do it himself. And if the American hitter got in his way, he would have to take him out as well.

Attaching a lightweight silencer to the front of his weapon, the Troll reaffirmed to himself that the only thing that mattered was taking down Mohammed bin Mohammed once and for all. If that meant sawing through one or two Americans who happened to be in the wrong place at the wrong time to do so, then that was just the way it would have to be.

ONE HUNDRED ONE

Though Harvath had been provided with an extremely efficient sniper rifle, he left it in the trunk, deciding instead on several tools designed for up-close work. When he took Mohammed bin Mohammed's life, he wanted to look the man in the eyes and see the expression on his face.

He had watched the CCTV footage the Libyans had given the United States from New York over and over again. From what they could piece together, Mohammed's accomplice—a man the CIA had tentatively identified as Abdul Ali—removed a wheelchair from the medical room, helped Mohammed down two or three floors via the stairwell, and then rode the elevator the rest of the way to the garage. While Ali pushed the wheelchair, bin Mohammed cradled the short-barreled M16Viper of the marine they had overpowered, Brad Harper, and had used it to kill Bob Herrington. That was why Harvath wanted to look into bin Mohammed's face when he killed him. He owed Bob that much. The only challenge was deciding where to make the kill.

While Harvath was confident that Mohammed would return to the villa to retrieve his clothes and cache of X-rated vacation footage, there was a possibility that his exploits might keep him out all night. If that was the case and he was pressed for time the next day, he might abandon the footage. The way Harvath saw it, his best bet was to wait for Mohammed at the harbor and quietly follow him, trusting that the right opportunity would present itself. For someone who liked to have all of the angles completely plotted out beforehand, this marked quite an operational departure for Harvath, but at the same time, this was not his usual kind of assignment. This was extremely personal.

Hearing from the joint CIA/DIA team that Mohammed's boat was on its way back in, Harvath mentally checked the first obstacle off his list. How many were left, though, was anybody's guess.

So as not to be forced to potentially pursue two targets over the water, it was agreed that the team would wait until Mohammed had set foot back on dry land before taking down the yacht.

As the al-Qaeda operative stepped off the dock and headed for Casemates Square, Harvath radioed the CIA/DIA team leader. "Gravedigger, this is Norseman. Mickey Mouse has dry feet. I repeat, Mickey Mouse has dry feet."

"Roger that," came the reply. "Good luck."

Harvath removed his earpiece, turned off his radio, and began to stalk his prey.

ONE HUNDRED TWO

Forgoing Casemates Square altogether, Mohammed bin Mohammed walked up to the main post office, where he turned onto Bell Lane and headed for a long set of stairs known as Castle Street. Partway up on the left was a large sign that read *Charles' Hole-in-the-Wall.* Harvath had only to observe a couple of the customers heading inside to know what kind of a club it was.

On the bright side, he figured a handsome single man with his eyes constantly scanning the room wouldn't be that out of place there.

He gave Mohammed a few minutes to get himself settled and then headed inside.

The dimly lit interior was awash in a fog of cigarette smoke. Eighties dance music blared from the sound system while patrons danced, drank, or made conversation. At a small table on the other side of the room, Mohammed bin Mohammed sipped a cocktail and surveyed the scene.

Harvath would have preferred to have taken him in a dark doorway or between a couple of parked cars somewhere outside, but it was high season in Gibraltar and the streets were just too crowded. That was okay with Harvath, though. He could just as easily do what he needed to do here. The only thing different would be which weapon he used, and he had plenty to choose from.

With his untucked linen shirt hiding the deadly array of tools affixed to his carbon-fiber belt, Harvath leaned back against the bar and tried to decide how best to make his move. Because he wanted to make this as personal as possible, a knife seemed the best choice. Considering how dark the bar was, he could slide up right next to the man, plunge the weapon in, and tear it right across his abdominal cavity with no one near Mohammed bin Mohammed being any the wiser.

Harvath would be able to sit with him and maybe even have a drink as he watched him die. Then, all Harvath would have to do would be to gently lay the man's head on the table and it would look like he'd passed out from too much to drink. It wouldn't take too long for the other patrons to notice something was wrong, but by the time they did, Harvath would be long gone.

As he stood up to make his move, a young man entered the establishment and, after flitting around for a moment or two, made his way over to Mohammed bin Mohammed's table and sat down.

With no choice but to wait it out, Harvath ordered a beer and kept his eyes glued to the table. There was no way he could kill Mohammed when there was a witness present.

After two more rounds of cocktails, Mohammed and the boy stood up to leave. Harvath left some money on the bar, and once the pair had passed him, he counted to twenty and followed them outside.

As the two walked, Mohammed slid his hand down the boy's back and let it linger on his rear end. Harvath hoped that when he dispatched Mohammed to the hereafter, Allah would have a very special cell waiting for him.

When they arrived at the villa, Harvath took up the post he had been using to surveil the house for the past couple of nights. He would wait until the boy left and then he'd sneak inside and take Mohammed out. Though he wasn't crazy about having to wait, there was nothing he could do about it. Harvath had no desire to kill an innocent bystander, and while he could probably take a shot through one of the open windows, he wanted to be as close as possible as he watched the very last drops of Mohammed bin Mohammed's life drain away.

The al-Qaeda operative led the boy out onto the veranda, then stepped back inside to make another cocktail. As he did so, Harvath noticed movement at the other end of the house.

As his eyes swung in that direction, he couldn't believe what he was seeing. Inside were two enormous white wolves that were carefully making their way toward bin Mohammed.

ONE HUNDRED THREE

When Harvath looked closer, he realized that what he was seeing weren't wolves at all, but rather two extremely large dogs. They resembled the type of animal he'd seen the Russian army use. They also appeared to both be wearing harnesses of some sort. And where there were dogs, Harvath knew there was normally a handler, though for the moment he couldn't see one.

He watched as the animals silently crept forward—obviously taking great pains so as not to be detected. Harvath was marveling at their discipline, when he finally saw the handler. It was only a glimpse at first and then, as one of the animals turned, he could make the figure out in its entirely. It was amazing. From Harvath's vantage point the man couldn't have been more than two-and-a-half to three-feet tall, max. The dogs towered over him.

Harvath focused on the bizarre weapon the man was carrying. It looked like it was crafted of plastic-style polymers and some kind of alloy. Obviously, it had been custom-made to accommodate the dwarf's small size. *But who the hell was he and what did he want with Mohammed bin Mohammed? Were the people Mohammed was doing the nuke deal with trying to double-cross him?*

Leaping the small wall at the far end of the veranda, Harvath took cover just as Mohammed bin Mohammed stepped outside with a drink in each hand, oblivious to the threat quickly advancing on him from within the villa.

Handing one of the cocktails to his guest, Mohammed prepared to lie down alongside him on the chaise, when suddenly he heard a terrible growling from behind. Spinning around, he saw a hideous little dwarf flanked by two of the most vicious-looking dogs he'd ever encountered in his life. The sight was such a shock that the man's large glass slipped from his hand and shattered on the flagstone terrace.

"Who are you?" demanded Mohammed. "What do you want?"

The dwarf signaled for the boy to rise from the lounge chair and step away from his host. Mohammed was surprised to see the young man so readily comply. His confusion evaporated as the young man approached the dwarf, stuck out his hand, and was given several large bills before quickly leaving the villa.

At the dwarf's command, the dogs fell silent.

"Who are you?" repeated Mohammed. "What do you want?"

The Troll smiled. "You don't remember me, do you?"

"Of course not. We've never met. I have absolutely no idea who you are."

"You may not remember me, but surely you remember the Black Sea. There was a brothel near the town of Sochi."

What little color remained in the al-Qaeda operative's face now completely drained away. Could this be the same dwarf? If it was, then yes, he did remember him. He remembered the brothel too. Mohammed had wanted a very young boy, not a dwarf, but when the madam and her husband said that the dwarf was the best they were able to do, he had decided it was better than nothing and had had his way with him. Afterward, he had felt so disgusted with himself that he had beaten the little creature almost to death. If it hadn't been for the quick thinking of one of the whores, who was able to give the dwarf the breath of life and compress his chest until his heart restarted, he would never have returned to the realm of the living.

"I paid dearly for that misunderstanding," replied Mohammed. "The proprietors' silence did not come cheap."

"You might have paid them, but you never paid me," answered the Troll. "I spent a good part of my life looking for you. When the Americans took you into custody, I was prepared to let you rot, but then you escaped. So tonight I will recoup what is owed me, with interest."

"How did you know I was held by the Americans?"

"Because he was the one who turned you in," said Abdul Ali as he stepped from the shadow of the villa.

As exceptional as the dogs were, they had never even detected the assassin's approach. Now they began barking at both Mohammed bin Mohammed and Abdul Ali.

"Shut them up," said the assassin as he pointed his silenced Beretta at the Troll. "And drop your weapon."

When the Troll hesitated, Ali turned his weapon on the nearest Caucasian Ovcharka and pulled the trigger.

The Troll felt the round just as surely as if it had pierced his own heart. He wanted to cry out, but he retained his composure and signaled his remaining animal to be still. Then he dropped his weapon.

Even from where he remained hidden, Harvath could see enough of the newest party crasher to recognize him. He was the man from the CCTV footage at Libya House. The man who had not only helped Mohammed bin Mohammed escape, but who was responsible for the deaths of the NSA employees, the marines, and all the other victims of the terrible terrorist attacks on New York. Even more important to Harvath, it was this man, the one the CIA was calling Abdul Ali, who had armed Mohammed bin Mohammed and helped him to kill Bob Herrington.

Harvath had expected a long, hard hunt for Ali, but now the man had been delivered right to him. The promise he had made to Bob the night he was murdered was going to be easier to carry out than he had thought.

With a silencer already affixed to his own weapon, Harvath raised his H&K pistol and took aim at the most logical primary target—the only other man holding a gun. Though it wasn't the long and painfully drawn-out death he would have wished on Ali, it was what the circumstances dictated. Taking a deep breath, he squeezed the trigger and watched as Ali's brains exploded out the other side of his head. And with that shot, pandemonium instantly erupted.

Mohammed bin Mohammed threw his considerable bulk to the ground and began crawling for the villa as fast as he could. To help slow him down, Harvath put a round in the back of each of his legs.

As the al-Qaeda operative screamed in pain, Harvath swept his pistol from left to right, searching for the dwarf, who had suddenly disappeared. At the last minute, he found him.

With the bizarre weapon slung over his shoulder, the tiny man had leapt onto his gargantuan dog and, holding on to the beast's harness, was riding him as if he were a thoroughbred.

The last glimpse Harvath had of them was as the amazingly agile animal leapt the high wall at the other end of the veranda and disappeared once more from sight. While he didn't have any immediate reason to kill the man or his dog, there were a lot of questions he would have liked to have had answered—questions he was sure that Mohammed bin Mohammed wouldn't be willing to answer. On the other hand, Harvath wasn't really in the mood to ask. What he was in the mood for was payback.

ONE HUNDRED FOUR

Grabbing bin Mohammed by the back of the neck, Harvath dragged him inside and threw him against a large white column. As he removed two pairs of Flexicuffs and secured the man's hands behind the pillar, Harvath said, "Ten days ago, you killed a very good friend of mine. I'm here to repay the favor."

The man looked up at Harvath. "I am not afraid to die."

"I was hoping you'd say that," said Scot as he removed two glass vials from a pouch on his belt and showed them to Mohammed. "Each of these little things are known as *Dermestes maculatus.* Museums use them to strip flesh away from carcasses so the skeletons can be studied. Once they start eating, they just can't seem to stop."

Unscrewing the top of the first vial, Harvath grabbed Mohammed in a headlock and inserted the vial into his ear. Instantly, the man began screaming. Harvath removed a lighter from his pocket and heated the vial until the beetle ran, scurrying into Mohammed's ear canal. Once he was sure the creature was in good and deep, he repeated the process on the other ear and stood back.

Like a rabbit trapped by a cave-in, beetles will dig furiously to try to extricate themselves. If they happen to be in someone's ear, the resultant frenzy is enough to drive that person mad. Harvath had read about it in a book a long time ago, and though he wasn't one to stay up late at night devising new means of torture, this had always been one of the things he thought would be exceptionally worth trying.

Stepping back, Harvath watched as the man writhed and shrieked, trying to shake the insects from his head. He was in the grip of sheer terror. Though it delivered a certain degree of satisfaction, it still wasn't enough to make up for everything else the man had done.

Raising his pistol, Harvath pulled the trigger and sent one searing hot round into Mohammed's stomach. It was considered one of the most painful ways a person could die, and victims could languish for many hours in unbearable agony until their bodies finally succumbed. As far as Harvath was concerned, it was still too good for Mohammed bin Mohammed.

He was contemplating kneecapping the al-Qaeda terrorist, when a noise from the veranda caught his attention.

Having affixed a makeshift pressure bandage to the wound in the dog's chest, Harvath gently slung the enormous beast over his shoulders and stepped right over Mohammed's twitching body as he carried it from the villa. Outside, he had the very real feeling that the only thing preventing a bullet from being fired at him from a rather bizarre weapon was that, hidden somewhere out in the dark night, the dying dog's owner understood that Harvath was trying to save his animal.

ONE HUNDRED FIVE

The White House
Washington, DC

"And the dwarf?" asked Harvath as the meeting was drawing to a close. "What was his role in all of this?"

The president looked at his newly appointed director of National Intelligence, Kenneth Wilson, and said, "Do you want to take this?"

Wilson nodded his head and clearing his throat said, "We actually know very little about the man you saw in Gibraltar, but based upon your description of him, and in particular his two dogs, we believe he's a figure known as the Troll."

"The *Troll*?"

"Rumors of his existence have pervaded the intelligence world since before the fall of the Berlin Wall. It's said he deals in the purchase and sale of highly sensitive information. We think he's the one who bought off Joseph Stanton to get the Athena locations in New York City."

"What makes you think that?"

"After the sites were secured, a thorough sweep was conducted to search for any signs that the intelligence being gathered and analyzed there had been compromised."

"And had it?" asked Harvath.

"Significantly. Everything the NSA had on their servers at those locations is gone."

Nothing at this point surprised Harvath.

Removing a small silicon device from his pocket, Wilson held it up and said, "We found remnants of devices like this one here at each of the locations. They can be programmed to covertly transfer a server's data to a remote location while making it look like the servers themselves are still carrying out their normal functions."

"Which is why nobody at NSA suspected anything and the alarm was never raised."

"Exactly. Our best explanation is that the Troll traded al-Qaeda the location of where Mohammed bin Mohammed was being held in exchange for them breaching the Athena Program locations and planting the devices for him. Which, by the way, self-destructed after the data was transferred and which is why we only found remnants.

"We also believe the Troll managed to get to someone inside the Defense Intelligence Agency who revealed where we were keeping Mohammed bin Mohammed. The circle of people in the know is pretty small, so we expect to have something soon."

Director Wilson continued on, but Harvath was no longer listening. After killing Abdul Ali and Mohammed bin Mohammed, he thought he had fulfilled the promise he'd made Bob Herrington, but now there was one more name he was going to have to cross off his list—the Troll's.

Once Wilson had wrapped up, the president asked Scot if he had any other questions. This was a relatively rare event. Because he was not always privy to the entire intelligence picture, there were many instances when he was unaware of the full impact of the success of his assignments. Sometimes, out of sheer gratitude, he was allowed access to information that otherwise never would have been made available to him. On days when this magnanimous flow of intelligence occurred, Harvath was able to forget, if only for a moment, how fed up he was with Washington politics. Today had turned out to be just such a day.

The president didn't have to gather his top people to spend an hour and a half spelling everything out and answering all of Harvath's questions, but he had, and Harvath appreciated it. He did, though, have one final question. "How is Amanda?"

Rutledge smiled and said, "She's doing much better, thank you."

"A collapsed lung is pretty serious."

The president nodded. "I think the death of her friends and so many of the agents on her detail was harder for her to handle than anything else."

"I'm sure it was," replied Harvath.

"I'll tell her you asked about her."

"Thank you, Mr. President."

Always uncomfortable with the president's fulsome praise of his efforts on behalf of his country, Scot thanked him for both his time and his candor and then prepared to stand up.

"If you wouldn't mind, I'd like you to stay for a few more minutes," said Rutledge as he excused the rest of the people in the Oval Office.

Once they had gone, the president removed an envelope from his desk and handed it to Harvath.

"What's this?"

"Scot, you are a tremendous asset to this country."

Harvath tried to interrupt, but the president stopped him. "It often seems to me that we should be doing more in return to thank you."

"I don't do it for the thanks, sir."

"I know you don't, and I also know you don't do it for the money. There certainly are places that would pay you a lot more for what you know."

Harvath couldn't tell for sure, but he had a sneaking suspicion that the president knew he had been looking for another job lately. He made a mental note to get in touch with his contact at Valhalla out in Colorado to let them know that for the time being, he was going to remain in his current position.

"Well?" said Rutledge, snapping Scot back to the here and now.

Looking down, Harvath realized the president was talking about the envelope he was holding.

"In addition to signing the leasehold, we're going to need to amend your file to show you as caretaker," Rutledge added.

Harvath looked up and said, "I'm sorry, caretaker? I don't understand."

"Two days ago, I spoke with the secretary of the Navy. Are you familiar with the Navy's Federal Preservation Office?"

"No, sir. I can't say that I am."

At that moment, the president's chief of staff, Charles Anderson, knocked and poked his head into the Oval Office. After saying a quick hello to Scot, he pointed at his watch and indicated to Rutledge that they needed to get going.

The president pointed at the envelope and said, "All the information's in there. Take a few days and then let me know what you think."

Not really knowing what he was thanking the man for, Harvath shook the president's hand, tucked the envelope inside his breast pocket, and left the Oval Office. Once he got outside, he opened the envelope and read its contents. Halfway through the first page, Harvath couldn't believe his eyes.

Exiting the White House grounds, he made his way down Pennsylvania Avenue to where he'd parked his TrailBlazer and then got on the road and headed toward Fairfax County, Virginia. He had to see this for himself.

ONE HUNDRED SIX

On several acres of land overlooking the Potomac River, just south of George Washington's Mount Vernon estate, was a small eighteenth-century stone church known as Bishop's Gate. During the revolutionary war, the Anglican reverend of Bishop's Gate was an outspoken loyalist who provided sanctuary and aid to British spies, which resulted in the colonial army attacking the church and inflicting great damage.

Bishop's Gate lay in ruins until 1882, when the Office of Naval Intelligence, or ONI, was established to seek out and report on the enormous post–Civil War explosion in the technological capabilities of other world-class navies. Several covert ONI agent training centers were established up and down the eastern seaboard to instruct naval attachés and military affairs officers on the collection of technical information about foreign governments and their naval developments.

Because of its isolated, yet prime location not far from Washington, DC, Bishop's Gate was secretly rebuilt and funded as one of the ONI's first covert officer training schools.

As the oldest continuously operating intelligence service in the nation, the ONI eventually outgrew the Bishop's Gate location. The stubby yet elegant church with its attached stone rectory was relegated to a declassified document storage site. Apparently, the fate of Bishop's Gate was not out of the ordinary. As Harvath read the letter, he learned that the Navy often was forced to mothball assets that served no immediate need, but might at some point in the future. This "laying away" of properties, many of them historic like Bishop's Gate, might be for a short term, an intermediate, or an undetermined period. Regardless of how the properties might once again be used, while still under the jurisdiction of the Navy, the Navy was obligated to protect and preserve their historic significance, as well as maintain their physical integrity.

Most of the Navy properties suitable for use as dwellings were saved for high-level defectors and other political personages the United States government found themselves responsible for. In Harvath's case, the secretary of the Navy, a former ONI officer, was apparently quite pleased to see such a distinguished American entrusted with the property. The fact that Harvath was an ex-SEAL probably didn't hurt his standing with the secretary either.

Bishop's Gate in its entirety—the church building and the rectory that had been converted into a nice-sized house, an outbuilding that had been converted into a garage, and the extensive grounds—were deeded to Harvath in a ninety-nine-year government lease with a token rent of one U.S. dollar due per annum. All that was required of Harvath was that he maintain the property in a manner befitting its historic status and that he vacate the premises within twenty-four hours if ever given notice, with or without cause, by the United States Navy.

It had been over fifty years since the Navy had any use for Bishop's Gate other than as a file graveyard, but Harvath was still stunned to have been offered it. Not including the garage, the unique house formed by the church and the attached rectory came to over four thousand square feet of living space, and all Harvath had to do was make sure the grass was mowed and his one-dollar-a-year rent was in on time. He couldn't help but wonder at what he might do with the real rent payments he wouldn't have to make anymore if he accepted the president's generous offer.

Of course, the practical side of Harvath would plow as much of the windfall into investments as he could, but there was also part of him that had always wanted a sailboat, and now that he had the opportunity to live right on the Potomac, it didn't seem like such an unreasonable goal.

He spent the better part of the day wandering the property and exploring the old church buildings as he tried to make up his mind. Though not a particularly spiritual person, he hoped somewhere along the way he'd be shown a sign. It was in the rectory attic that he found one—literally.

On a beautifully carved piece of wood was the motto of the Anglican missionaries. It seemed strangely fitting for the career Harvath had decided to remain in: TRANSIENS ADIUVA NOS—*I go overseas to give help.*

At that moment, Harvath knew he was home. What's more, he didn't need Emily Post to tell him that turning down a gift, any gift, from the President of the United States was not only impolite, but also a very bad career decision for a federal employee.

Though he still had reservations about accepting such a lavish reward, Bishop's Gate had taken hold of Harvath, and it seemed a shame to allow it to go uninhabited for another day.

With the help of a few buddies, including Kevin McCauliff, Harvath rented a truck and spent that following Saturday moving his belongings from his small apartment in Alexandria over to Bishop's Gate.

While his friends marveled at his luck, they were unanimous in their agreement that Harvath had a lot of work to do on the place. His pal Gordon Avigliano even joked that it looked to him that the Navy had actually gotten the better part of the deal. Not only did they now have a free night watchman in Harvath, but the sap was also paying them for the privilege. It didn't matter that it was only a dollar a year. Nobody believed Harvath anyway.

Once the last of the beer had been consumed and all but the pizza boxes had been eaten, Harvath politely gave his friends five minutes to vacate his new estate before he threatened to release the hounds. It got a good laugh, and as he let them go, he secured promises that they'd be back to help him with the renovation work. There was a lot that needed to be done.

After a quick shower, he pulled on jeans and a Polo shirt, then hopped into his car for the airport. On a lark, he had decided to call Tracy Hastings to see if she wanted to come down and spend some time with him at his *new* place.

Hastings was thrilled and had booked one of the last seats on the shuttle for that night. They picked up takeout from A La Lucia in

Alexandria and had a wonderful dinner picnic-style in front of the rectory's fireplace.

The next morning, Tracy allowed Harvath to sleep in. He was exhausted from his last assignment, as well as the move, and was still recovering from the injuries he had suffered in New York. In all fairness, she hadn't exactly gone easy on him either. Damn, they were good together.

With a smile on her face and a cup of coffee in her hand, Tracy opened the door and stepped outside. It was a gorgeous summer morning, and she took in a deep breath and tried to pinpoint the wonderful smells that seemed to be coming at her from all directions. She was worlds away from Manhattan, and being here with Scot was like nothing she had ever known. If their lives would let them, she could stay here forever and never leave.

As she bent down to pick one of the flowers growing wild alongside the rectory she noticed that someone had dropped off a beautiful wicker hamper. A large satin ribbon was tied to the top and she could hear rustling coming from inside.

Lifting the hamper's lid, Tracy discovered a beautiful white puppy. Along with it was a book on Caucasian Ovcharkas and a note. Picking up the puppy and holding it to her chest, she read the crisp white card. *Thank you for saving Argus. I will forever be in your debt. A friend.*

Tracy had no idea who the note had come from, but she figured Scot might. Either way, he was absolutely going to love this dog. She just knew it. It was time that both of their lives started being filled with things that were good.

Nuzzling the puppy under her chin, Tracy Hastings turned to go back inside, but before she could cross the threshold, a bullet with her name on it came ripping through the trees.

As the weapon was disassembled, the assassin from Scot's past took a perverse pride in knowing that this was only the beginning of the pain and retribution that was coming Harvath's way. Harvath was about to learn that you never buried anyone unless you were absolutely certain they were dead.

AUTHOR'S NOTE

I make no secret about the deep respect I hold for the brave American men and women who selflessly serve our nation in our military, law enforcement, and intelligence communities. As someone who wanted to do more than just write about these extraordinary people, I became involved with several different organizations that strive to serve them and their families. I strongly urge you to visit my Web site for a list of these organizations, but I want to single out one in particular here.

At a fundraiser for the Naval Special Warfare Foundation last summer, it was announced that I would name a character in this novel for whoever made the evening's largest contribution. I am honored to say that the president and CEO of Zodiac North America, J. J. Marie, was that person. When the applause had subsided and Mr. Marie stepped to the podium, he called up Virginia Beach, VA, police chief A. M. "Jake" Jacocks, whom I've had the pleasure of knowing for many years. Once the chief had joined him, Mr. Marie announced that Zodiac North America wanted to honor the memory of the Virginia Beach PD's own Bradley Harper—a twenty-five-year-old United States Marine Reservist who was killed south of Haditha, Iraq, in August 2005—by having the character named after him.

While I did not have the pleasure of knowing Marine Sergeant Bradley J. Harper, I hope in some small part the character I have created in his name lives up to the high standards I know he set for himself as an American, a member of the Virginia Beach Police Department, and as a United States Marine.

ACKNOWLEDGMENTS

First and foremost, I have to thank my beautiful wife, **Trish,** for keeping the world at bay while I wrote this book. The last year has been incredibly busy for us both, and I could not have done any of it without you. You are the love of my life and I know no greater honor than being your husband and the father of our two wonderful children.

The next person I have to thank is my dear friend and lead sharpshooter, **Scott F. Hill, PhD.** The only thing more valuable to me than your advice and guidance is your friendship. Thank you for all of your help and all of the airline miles you logged working with me on this novel. Clear some space in your game room, your reward is coming.

Having relocated overseas in service to his country, my good pal **Chad Norberg** discovered he could be just as big a thorn in my side via e-mail as when we were both living in Utah. Though I miss being able to discuss plot points over a beer at Fiddler's Elbow, his advice via the Internet was no less creative, resourceful, or vital than on projects past. Thanks, buddy.

Rodney Cox is my newest sharpshooter, and I couldn't have met him at a more perfect time. Not only is Rodney a lot of fun to hang out with, his real-life experiences in Iraq and Afghanistan proved invaluable in the writing of this book. Rodney has become a very good friend of mine, and a lot of *Takedown* couldn't have been written without his help. Thanks, RC.

Two other people who are a lot of fun to hang out with are old friends of mine and have been helping with my novels since the beginning.

They are **Chuck Fretwell** and **Steve Hoffa.** They understand my desire to get everything right and always take the time to answer even the smallest of questions. When a Hofbrauhaus opens in South Africa, I'll buy the first round and *then* we'll go on safari, I promise.

Once again, I was expertly led through the wilds of American politics by my two good friends and Washington insiders **Pat Doak** and **David Vennett.** I owe you both dinner and more than a couple of nice bottles of wine the next time I'm in DC.

If the bad guys got shut down right out of the gate, thrillers wouldn't be very thrilling. **Rich Henderson**—one of the good guys—understands this and was very helpful with all things New York. Thanks for answering countless e-mails from me and for all of your great advice.

Both **Gary Penrith** and **Tom Baker** continue to be incredible fonts of knowledge for my novels, and I thank them for their invaluable assistance. These gentlemen have given much to their country and continue to do so daily. This nation is indeed fortunate and better for their service. See you in Sun Valley.

Carl Hospedales, Rudy Guerin, Kevin Dockery and **GySgt Tony Masucci USMC,** each made contributions to the novel for which I am grateful. Gentlemen, thank you not only for what you have done for me, but for the service you have rendered and continue to render to our country (and the UK/Canada in Carl's case) on a daily basis.

Vince Flynn stopped by my house while on tour for his last novel, and in addition to stealing my three-year-old daughter's heart, he also dispensed some sage writing advice, which I very much appreciated. Thanks, Vince.

Chief Steven C. Bronson, U.S. Navy (Ret.), is a patriot whose love for his country and support of fellow warriors—be they in the military or LE arenas—knows no bounds. The Chief has become a very good friend of mine and I thank him not only for the valuable assistance he lent on this book, but also for all of the real-world opportunities he has made available to me. Stay safe in Iraq, Chief. Hooyah!

I also want to thank my intelligence and military sources who asked to remain nameless. Your commitment to the security of our nation is very much appreciated. Thank you for taking the fight to the terrorists so we do not have to face them here at home.

Now I need to thank two of the most important people in my writing career: my incomparable editor, **Emily Bestler,** and my outstanding agent, **Heide Lange.** Thank you for your wit, wisdom, friendship, and guidance. You are two of the most remarkable people I have ever had the pleasure of working with, and I look forward to our doing many more books together.

Judith Curr, my publisher at Atria Books, and **Louise Burke,** my publisher at Pocket Books, are two of the most talented people in the business. Thank you for your overwhelming support of my novels, your creative marketing, and for your friendship.

Jodi Lipper and **Sarah Branham,** the amount of things you have done and continue to do for me at Atria is too long to list. I appreciate all of it. Thank you.

To everyone in the **Atria** and **Pocket sales, art, marketing,** and **production** departments—I know how hard all of you work and I thank you for every minute of it. I couldn't do what I do without you.

David Brown, my friend and my unparalleled publicist. Knowing you as well as I do, I can write this with the knowledge that when it comes out you will have put together the best tour yet. Oprah's thriller club, here we come!

Kent Wilson, thank you for your friendship and the years of expert advice. Trish and I sleep a lot sounder at night knowing you are on our team.

Scott Schwimer, the man who can spot the difference between "show" and "business" from a hundred miles away. Thank you not only for your sage counsel, but also your incredible friendship. Diogenes' lamp rests upon your doorstep.

Finally, I want to thank you, **the readers.** You have my deepest gratitude not only for your support of my novels, but for introducing so many of your friends, family, coworkers, and book clubs to my work. It is because of you that I am able to pursue a career I so enjoy.

Sincerely,
Brad Thor